THE KREUZBERG FILE

THOMAS GRIFFIN

authorHOUSE®

AuthorHouse™
1663 Liberty Drive
Bloomington, IN 47403
www.authorhouse.com
Phone: 833-262-8899

Published by AuthorHouse 08/22/2020

ISBN: 978-1-7283-6911-2 (sc)
ISBN: 978-1-7283-6912-9 (hc)
ISBN: 978-1-7283-7045-3 (e)

Library of Congress Control Number: 2020915309

Print information available on the last page.

This book is printed on acid-free paper.

CHAPTER 1

Bill McDonald, in charge of security at the law firm Taylor, Hinchcroft & Martell, returned late from an extended weekend trip to the Adirondacks. It was already dark when he arrived at his apartment building in lower Manhattan. He had needed an extra hour to get back, since the traffic had been unusually heavy. After almost five hours behind the wheel, he was tired and looked forward to a quiet meal at home. The moment he opened the apartment door and stepped into the small vestibule, he noticed something unusual. There was light in his living room. He was certain that he had turned off all lights before leaving on Thursday. For a few seconds, he stood close to the door without moving. Was there an intruder? But he didn't hear any noises. Cautiously, he moved toward the light, making sure that he could not be seen from the inside of the living room. Suddenly, there was a strange sound: the rustle of paper. Bill peeked into the room. There was a tall older man sitting on his couch reading a newspaper. It took him only a second to recognize the intruder. He was Amos Hinchcroft, one of the senior partners of his law firm.

"Ah Bill, finally you are back," the lawyer said in a calm voice, when he recognized Bill in the doorway. "I have been waiting for more than an hour."

"What are you doing here, Mr. Hinchcroft?" Bill asked. "This is my apartment, a private space and not your office."

"Calm down, Bill, must I remind you that I own this apartment and that I am your landlord?" Hinchcroft replied, putting the newspaper aside and motioning Bill to sit down.

1

"Yes sir, you are, but this doesn't give you the right to show up unannounced," Bill exclaimed, still angry.

"When you failed to return my phone calls and messages on Friday, although I made it very clear that there was urgent business," Hinchcroft said, raising his voice just a little, "I decided that it was time for me to inspect my apartment and wait for my tenant. Please, sit down and listen."

Bill sat down in an armchair without responding. Although still irritated, he did not want to cross the old lawyer, who had offered him a job at his firm five years ago when he, just twenty-two years old, had decided to drop out of law school. He was an old friend of his father and had supported him when Bill really needed help.

"By the way, Bill, your father sends his regards," Hinchcroft continued, "I talked to him yesterday, hoping that you were visiting your family in Chicago. As it turned out, this was not the case. He had no clue about your whereabouts. You should give him a call. So, where have you been?"

"I spent a long weekend in the Adirondacks. I needed time out after three hectic weeks without a break on the Wilcox case. Surveillance work, as you'll remember. Mr. Taylor told me to take a few days off. It was agreed that I would be completely out of touch."

"Sam Taylor never mentioned this," the lawyer responded.

"That's not my fault," Bill replied, shaking his head.

"In any case," Hinchcroft continued, "we have a difficult case that needs our immediate attention."

"Then tell me. What was so urgent that it couldn't wait until Monday?" Bill interjected.

Hinchcroft glanced at him with an expression of surprise. Then he said:

"I guess you are aware of the pharma company Alerta, one of our important clients. They had developed contacts in Berlin, I understand, to a small start-up. From their Frankfurt office, they sent a man to Berlin in order to move the discussion along. A meeting was set up, but it never took place."

"What happened?"

"There was a mishap. The German contact was killed in an accident just before the meeting. I understand that he had critical information in his briefcase, but these papers never reached Alerta."

Bill looked at Hinchcroft: "Do we know the content? Do we know anything about the negotiations?"

The lawyer hesitated for a moment: "No, we don't. Our client has not given us this information."

"That's strange," Bill interjected, "given the nature of the business."

"You have a point," Hinchcroft replied, "It seems they want to keep the whole affair very quiet."

Bill looked at the lawyer, who picked up a folder from the coffee table and handed it over to him: "Here is the file. It contains everything we know. Try to find out what happened. At this point, we can only guess what they were up to. Possibly a buyout. As I said, the whole thing is somewhat mysterious. Obviously, Alerta wants to keep a low profile."

"And now they turn to their lawyers for help," Bill remarked, "we are expected to deal with the mess. They have their own security department that could deal with this."

"Bill, they are one of our important clients. We can't say so no. So, we send you. You know the place, you have been there and know some German. You spend a few days in Berlin to check out the accident. Nothing big really."

Hinchcroft got up from the couch, looking Bill straight in the eyes. Then he shook his hand.

"Bill, I know I can count on you. I'll deal with Alerta, which can be a difficult client."

He turned around and left the room. A few seconds later Bill heard the sound of the apartment door being closed.

Bill was holding the folder in his hand for a moment staring at its cover. He realized that Hinchcroft wanted to get rid of a case he didn't know how to handle. So, he did to Bill what the Alerta people had done to him. He outsourced the problem and made him responsible. Bill briefly opened the folder, then he put it back on the table. He was much too exhausted to get involved in the details. He walked into his kitchen, looking for a beer in his refrigerator. He sat down on a stool and took a sip. That felt good. He also noticed that his hunger returned. He had been without a meal since an early lunch. He took a pizza out of the freezer and put it into his oven. Tomorrow morning, he would go to the office to make travel arrangements and take care of canceling appointments. Right now, he wanted to focus on his meal.

He went to bed early and fell immediately asleep, but three hours later he woke up from a confusing dream. He had been in an unknown dark room, looking for a person. There were other persons as well whom he could hear but not see. Then, there were shots and screams. He fired his gun as well. Someone was hit. Finally, he woke up. This was a recurring dream, a reminder of the final confrontation with the Russian Kartell in Berlin two years ago. He had killed a member of the Russian gang who was about to kill one of the F.B.I agents. In the official report this episode was never mentioned. Without success, he tried to fall asleep again. He got up and walked to the kitchen where he poured himself a glass of water. The memory of his mission two years ago was keeping him awake. He was sent to find a young journalist who had been missing. It had been an exciting but also frustrating task. In the end, freeing the young woman, who had been kidnapped by the Russian Mafia, did not lead to the professional recognition he had hoped for. The reward for the safe return of the journalist went primarily to the F.B.I. and to a lesser extent to the American Consulate in Berlin. I was assigned the role of the help who did some valuable preliminary work, Bill thought. Even my own firm accepted the official version of the events, diminishing the crucial contribution of their man. Possibly, the lawyers didn't want to call attention to my methods. Some of the necessary actions were outside the sphere of lawful procedures, he had to admit. But there was another aspect as well: the presence of Ulrike. He had met the young reporter when he arrived in Berlin, trying to figure out what could have happened to Julia Newman, who had disappeared without a trace six weeks earlier. The chance meeting at a police station changed everything. What began that morning became a very unusual and highly intensive collaboration. Professional and the private side were completely intertwined. Compared with those weeks in Berlin, business in New York appeared less interesting. Now he was expected to go back. Maybe this is the turn I have been waiting for, he thought. He returned to his bed. After a while, he fell asleep.

The next morning, Bill arrived early at the office. When the receptionist saw him, she greeted him with a wave of her hand and exclaimed:

"Bill, Mr. Hinchcroft has been looking for you. He wasn't in a good mood. You may want to get in touch with him right away."

"Thanks, but don't worry. We met last night. A new mission, I have to go back to Berlin. Can you please make the travel arrangements? I have to leave this afternoon."

"Today? That may be difficult, but I'll try."

Bill gave her a brief smile. Then he walked to Sam Taylor's office. On Thursday, he had already submitted his final report for the Wilcox case. All that had to happen now was a brief meeting with the second senior partner. He found him in his large office instructing a new intern.

"Oh Bill, do come in," he said. "Say hello to Helen White, our new intern. By the way, did Amos get in touch with you? He was very eager to talk to you?"

Bill briefly nodded to the intern and said: "Yes sir, he found me. He was waiting for me in my apartment when I came back last night."

Taylor shook his head, muttering: "I kept our agreement and didn't tell him where you were. He was in your apartment? Without an invitation? Really? Only Amos can do that. You know he means well."

"I do sir, still, very unusual," Bill replied in a low voice. "I'm here to say good bye because I have to go back to Berlin. I shall be back in a week. I understand that you have looked at my report."

"Yes, I did. Thanks, good work. All the best for Berlin."

It took Bill a while to cancel all rearranged meetings and appointments. When he returned to the front desk, the receptionist had already booked the flight. When he found out that he had to fly business class because this was the only available seat, his mood improved. A pleasant flight, and then he would be in Berlin again. Suddenly, memories flooded his mind. Among them the time with

Ulrike. These were intense but mixed memories. He would never forget the weeks in Berlin and Riga. Then the time after his return to New York had been more difficult. The visit she had promised had never happened. Twice she had announced that she would come and twice she had canceled at the last minute. Sometimes the contact had been very close and then there had been times when she didn't answer his emails for weeks. Should he send her a message to inform her of his imminent visit? He decided to postpone any action until later. First, he had to get ready for the trip. Most importantly, however, before his arrival in Berlin, he had to familiarize himself with the Alerta file. This he would do during the flight.

When Bill arrived at the airport in the late afternoon, he felt exhausted. He needed a quiet and restful flight. But first he wanted a good dinner. Only after that would he be ready to study the file. He was intrigued. Why was this contact with a small German company so important for Alerta that they would send someone to Berlin, yet not their own man but the detective of their own law firm? The whole thing didn't look right. Maybe the file would tell him more.

For his dinner Bill ordered a glass of red wine and later coffee to prepare himself for the scrutiny of the file. After the meal he leaned back and spread the documents on the small table in front of him. There were two parts. One was the description of the circumstances of the accidents that had happened on the Kurfürstendamm. There were pictures and sketches that documented the accident in front of the hotel where the meeting was supposed to take place. The time had been around 11:00 in the morning. A car making a right turn at the intersection had hit the bicycle of the man who was supposed to meet the representative of Alerta, Bill assumed. The man did not survive the accident. In fact, he was declared dead at the scene of the accident. The other part was a summary of the plan for the meeting. The representative had been waiting in the hotel to meet with the representative of the German company. His name was given as Dr. Herwig Stollberg. The name of the company was KreuzbergChem. Bill looked for more information about this start-up, but there was very little. It was established five years ago, but what exactly it did or produced was unclear. Stollberg, a partner, was supposed to bring his file to the meeting. This file, it turned out, never reached the Alerta contact whose name by the way was also missing.

The more Bill studied the documents in front of him, the more he got the impression that it was primarily the missing file that upset the Alerta people. There must have been something in these papers that was very important to them. Bill focused again on the pictures of the accident, which looked like police shots. It appeared that someone had gotten access to the police file. I have to make a note of this, thought Bill. If the file was the really important part of his mission, then there was a question: Was there a connection between the accident and the missing file? What happened to the file? If the information was crucial, why not get it to the recipient electronically, encoded of course. That should have been more secure than carrying the information in a briefcase. Were they afraid of hackers? Was the dead man in the pictures Stollberg? And how exactly did the accident occur? One of the shots showed a twisted figure on the ground. Another one showed a close-up of the head and the face. There were heavy bruises and traces of blood in the face, the result of a violent crash. In the background one could see the curb and a part of a tree.

The place of the accident was clearly the Kurfürstendamm. As he remembered, a major and very busy street in West Berlin. There must have been witnesses. According to the report, the vehicle had come at high speed and then suddenly made a right turn. The bicyclist must have been hit with great force. However, there was no description or picture of the vehicle. According to the report, the driver of the vehicle did not stop and fled at high speed. The more Bill studied the accident, the more suspicious the whole story looked. He would have to go over the details when he was at the location. Possibly he could revive his old police contacts. Maybe Hauptkommissarin Charlotte Herberg would help him and he might get support from Ulrike, who had her own contacts. After all, crime was her beat. But he was by no means sure. They had not seen each other for two years and the connection had been uneven. Just before he boarded the plane, Bill had sent her a brief message, telling her that he was on the way to Berlin. He had not mentioned the purpose of his trip. Would she meet him at the airport? She might, if she thought that his presence in Berlin would result in a good story. After all, two years ago when they were searching for the young journalist, she got more out of it than he did. The narrative about the kidnapped American journalist in the *Berliner Zeitung* was a big boost for her career.

Bill decided not to follow this line of thought. It made everything only more complicated. The close intertwinement of professional interests and personal feelings had been exciting but also difficult to manage. Bill forced himself to concentrate on his new case. Who was the victim of the accident? And why was he important enough for a major American pharma company to send a detective to Berlin? The photo in the file showed the face of a young man in his thirties, with blue eyes and a pair of rimless glasses. The face of a scientist who is at home in a lab or a library. He was 36 years old, trained as a chemist at Humboldt University. According to the file, he was a partner in a small company that focused on chemical research. One of the many start-ups in Berlin, looking for international capital. A street in Berlin- Kreuzberg was given as the address. The question was: Why was Alerta interested in Stollberg and his little company? Was there something that he and his partners could offer to the big American company? Or was it Stollberg who was interested in Alerta? Was he looking for a new job? But in that case, he would have been asked to come to the US or at least to Frankfurt where Alerta had an office. Instead, Alerta sent a man to Berlin. Nothing made sense. Bill put the documents back into the folder. He had gone as far as he could and he was tired. I will stop here and try to get some sleep before I arrive in Berlin. He closed his eyes and found himself in a strange dream. He was riding on a bicycle along Kurfürstendamm, chased by an Italian sportscar. He was going as fast as he could but the car was getting closer and closer. There would be a crash any moment.

When he opened his eyes, a stewardess stood next to his seat offering him hot coffee in a paper cup. He took the coffee without paying attention to the Danish in front of him. He found the mere thought of eating at this time repulsive. Maybe later at the hotel. But he needed a plan. Much would depend on Ulrike. Would she meet him at the airport? He checked his watch. In half an hour the plane would land at Tegel Airport. What would he do next? After finding a place to stay, he would focus his research on the dead man. He needed more background information to bring light into the case. At this point, he had only pieces that did not fit together. Then he would look more closely at the scene of the accident. He had to be at the actual location and reconstruct the details. There were too many loose ends. Bill collected the documents and put the file back into his briefcase. In the meantime, the plane had lost altitude. Bill looked out of the window staring at the houses that came closer and closer until the plane landed with a thud. Again, Bill was surprised by the size of the airport, which appeared to be much too small for the big city. It took him no more than 20 minutes to get through the passport control and customs. Then he was on his way to the exit. Now came the decisive moment: Would Ulrike be on the other side of the door? When he stepped into the exit hall there was no Ulrike. Bill repressed his disappointment. Why should she meet him at the airport? Would he have come to Newark to pick her up? Of course not, he told himself, although he knew that this was not entirely true. But he had to find a hotel. When he was moving towards the street, he decided to get a room at the very hotel where the accident had happened. That would be a good location for beginning with his research.

Half an hour later he looked out of the window of his room on the third floor of the Brandenburger Hof. It was an older hotel, built in the 1920s with high ceilings and a dark entrance hall. He had asked for a room facing the Kurfürstendamm because he wanted to get a better sense of the traffic patterns. As he remembered, it was a busy street indeed. For a few minutes he stood there and watched the dense stream of pedestrians and the rush of cars. He followed the pattern until he suddenly realized that he was quite hungry. The easiest solution to this problem would be breakfast in the hotel before he would start with the first item on his agenda. He picked up the file from the small desk and moved towards the elevator. In the restaurant he found a nice table close to a window. Most of all he needed coffee.

In addition, he ordered a continental breakfast He was enjoying his first cup of coffee together with a croissant when his phone buzzed. It was a text message: "Sorry, couldn't meet you at the airport. I 'm not in Berlin, will be back tomorrow. Where can I meet you? Liebe Grüsse. Ulrike" Bill stared at the text with great intensity, as if he was afraid that it could disappear any moment. All of a sudden, the day looked very different. He sent a message back with his address. I'm in Berlin again, he thought, and I'm ready to get started with my new case. The first step was a visit to the location of the accident.

Holding the photos in his hand, Bill stood at the intersection of Kurfürstendamm and Fasanenstraße. He needed a few minutes to get his bearings and find the exact space where the accident had occurred. He recognized the street sign and the tree. Now he could find the spot where the victim had been lying on the ground. The position of the bicycle became apparent as well. Indeed, the accident must have occurred when the car made a right turn, while the bicyclist was moving straight forward to cross the intersection. The car rammed the bicycle from the left side, pushing the bicyclist to the ground with great force. Bill looked more closely at the pavement of the intersection. Were there any rubber marks on the pavement? He couldn't detect anything. And what about eye witnesses? There must have been people close by at 11:00 in the morning. The file did not mention witnesses. This could not be a thorough report. Who did this? I must go over the details again, Bill thought. I need access to the police file. Bill decided to break off this line of questioning and returned to the hotel. Crossing the lobby, he noticed that the man at the front desk was not occupied with a guest. He quickly stepped over to the reception and said: "I understand that there was a serious accident here at the intersection a few days ago. Did you see the accident?"

The clerk looked up, facing him: "No, I didn't. I was on the late shift that day. I just heard about it. It must have been terrible. The guy was practically crushed by the car. He was still alive, I understand, when the medics arrived, but he didn't make it."

"What happened to the driver of the car?"

"He fled without ever stopping,"

Bill shook his head and said: "Horrible, what a horrible event. Just like that and no way of identifying the car?"

"That's what it looks like, but remember I wasn't there."

"What about your colleague at the desk during the time of the accident?"

"He didn't see anything either. He knew only what some guests told him. They had been in front of the hotel when it happened."

"And what about these guests? They have probably all checked out?"

"Most likely, but there is still the old lady in 215. She was standing outside and saw everything. The medics had to look after her because she was in shock. The police wanted to have a statement but she was too weak and refused. Which meant that the police had to come back the following day."

Bill immediately made up his mind that he wanted to talk to this lady even if her memory was incomplete and distorted. There would be clues that would help him. Bill thanked the clerk for the information and returned to his room where he took out his laptop and focused on his notes. There was another aspect that he had to pursue. Stollberg had an appointment at the Brandenburger Hof, that was clear, but with whom? He had to identify the visitor, most likely an American who was supposed to receive the file that Stollberg had presumably with him when he was killed. There must have been an observer very close to the accident who removed the file from the body or the bicycle. Was this an accident or part of a coordinated effort? Bill guessed that he could find more information on Stollberg on the internet. This turned out to be the case. Google gave him the professional background and a link to a company with an address in Berlin Kreuzberg. He looked up the company on Google. What he found was somewhat helpful but not specific enough to advance his search. The website of KreuzbergChem mentioned three owners, beside Stollberg there was David Klein and Stefano Brindisi. Brindisi was a university-trained chemist as well. He received his degree from the Free University of Berlin. David Klein came with a degree in Engineering from the Technische Hochschule in Aachen. The three had collaborated on a number of projects in the area of food processing. The website listed cooperations with German and French food companies. There were also links to labs at a number of universities. But the connection with an American pharma company was something else. This was a different field of research and a much bigger company. There was no clue on the website that KreuzbergChem was involved in pharmaceutical research. Bill stared at the screen of his laptop for a couple of minutes to process the information. I need more extensive background information, he muttered to himself. There must be more than meets the eye. He had to get hold of the partners and talk to them. They had to be aware of what was going on. And, on the other side, it would help him to know more about Alerta's recent research efforts. Yet he was pretty sure that this kind of information was kept secret. Here we were talking about products that promised billions in profits. Alerta was not one of the very big companies, but it was well known for its advanced products. All of a sudden, he had an idea. He shifted his search to the stock market and glanced at the recent development of the pharma industry. How was Alerta doing? What he discovered confirmed a hunch. Alerta's stock had been going up recently. Not a huge amount but there were significant gains, while the other companies had remained flat. Something was happening, for instance an announcement about a new medication? Bill checked the business news. But there was no information at all. He stood up and paced up and down in his room. He was excited and eager. There must be some rumor about a potential breakthrough at Alerta, he guessed. If this was true the Berlin contact would have a much bigger relevance than he had been told. His strange mission could be connected with the latest development at Alerta. At the same time, Bill realized that he had no factual information to prove his hunch. Where would this lead him? He strongly felt the need for fresh air. He picked up his jacket from the bed, grabbed the file and left the room. When he had reached the Kurfürstendamm, he turned right and walked slowly in the direction of Gedächtniskirche until he found a café where he could sit outside. He ordered a large latte and focused on the traffic in front of him.

By now it was late morning, a sunny day, hardly any clouds. It was still pleasantly warm and Bill closed his eyes, leaning back in his chair. He felt the warm air touching his skin. For the first time, he was really content and grateful for his new assignment that brought him back to Berlin. It's good to be back, he thought. I have done what I could do today, it was a start and tomorrow will be another day. Later he would send an email to Hinchcroft. That should keep him happy. Maybe I will go to Kreuzberg later to have a look at the location of KreuzbergChem. Right now, he enjoyed his latte, while he was observing the crowds of people in front of him, most of them tourists, it seemed, looking for an exciting experience, which in most instances failed to materialize. Then his thoughts returned to his task and from there to Ulrike. They would see each other tomorrow. What would it be like? Just professional? In his head there were feelings that had little to do with his job. What were her expectations? The promise of another story for the *Berliner Zeitung*? Her ambition would be the same. And that might shape their reunion. Would it be all business focused on his new case and her latest story? Or would their close personal friendship be the dominant side? At this moment he was uncertain. Of course, he mustn't assume that she had not been together with other men, as he had met other women during the last two years. He recalled the reporter in Hamburg, who worked for the *Hamburger Abendblatt*, whose interest in Ulrike was obviously not just professional. The guy had kind of irritated him, although he had been friendly and quite helpful. These feelings were real, although he hated to admit them.

Bill gave himself ample time to finish his coffee. Then he walked to the next underground station and took the number 9 train and later the number 7 to get to Kreuzberg. Once in Kreuzberg, he drifted with the crowd until he found himself in the correct street, now looking for the building in which KreuzbergChem had its office. It turned out to be an older building, more an apartment than an office building. He saw the sign next to the door and stepped into the dark hallway, trying to find the office, which wasn't too difficult. Realizing that the house opened up to an inner court and a second building, he walked to the end of the hallway and peeked into the court. There was a door and a number of windows, which could possibly indicate the location of a lab. Bill decided to postpone a closer search of this part of the building. Right now, more than anything he wanted a meeting with

Klein and Brindisi. For them the death of Stollberg must have been a shock and likely a terrible loss. Possibly, the existence of the small firm was threatened. What had looked like a fairly simple task when he discussed the case with Hinchcroft in New York, turned out to be much more complex. Bill turned around and walked back to the front door. When he came to the door of KreuzbergChem, he stopped for a brief moment. A young woman who was busy emptying a letter box, saw him and said: "There is nobody home. The office is closed, because there was a death." Bill nodded and walked to the exit without saying anything.

When he stood on the street again, he checked his watch. It was almost 1:00pm, He realized that he was hungry and began looking for a restaurant. This was not too difficult, since the area was filled with small places. He chose a tiny pizza place with a number of tables outside where he could sit in the fresh air. After he has placed his order, he took out his notebook and started making a list. Slowly a plan began to materialize. There were a number of searches where he would need help, for instance getting access to the police report of the accident. He might need help as well getting information about KreuzbergChem. He needed to know much more about the research projects of the company. Especially Stollberg's recent project would be of interest for his case. It was likely that there was a connection between Stollberg's project and the information that he was trying to deliver. Unfortunately, Bill did not have a good grasp of the material. Chemistry had never been a strong suit of his education. He had been a political science major and taken geography and geology classes to take care of his science requirements. He knew that he couldn't follow a chemistry research article.

While Bill was eating his pizza, he had an idea. He decided to call the police woman with whom had worked two years ago. He had played a small but significant role in solving an important case. She had succeeded in destroying a notorious gang that sold young women from Eastern Europe into prostitution in Germany. He looked for her phone number. Would she answer his call? It's not likely, he thought, but I have nothing to lose. To his great surprise she accepted his call.

Charlotte Herberg, Hauptkommissarin, even remembered his name. When he told her about his new case she invited him to meet her the following day at Headquarters. Bill mentioned Stollberg's name and the day of the accident.

"I'll see what I can do", she said. "There must be a file. The question is whether I can locate it by tomorrow. In any case, stop by."

This was much more than he had reason to expect. He remembered her as a stern police officer, who had been somewhat reluctant to work with him on the case of he kidnapped American journalist. He had never been quite certain why she was so cautious. Was it his status as a private detective or the fact that he was an American? She struck him always as very German in her approach to things. At the same time, he remembered that Ulrike thought very highly of her.

Bill returned to the hotel with the feeling to have accomplished more than he had expected when he arrived in the early morning. He had no solutions but a much better grasp of the task. Tomorrow, he would begin with his systematic scrutiny. The first thing he did when he was in his room was to send an email to Hinchcroft. He wanted the lawyer to know that there was progress, since he was aware that he was nervous and eager to have news. Bill was supposed to deliver, but it was not entirely clear what he was expected to deliver, the cause of the accident or the recovery of the lost file? He would have preferred that the security guys of Alerta would have arranged a face-to-face meeting with him to have a frank discussion about the stakes of this case. Clearly, this had not been a desirable option for the company. They wanted to keep a very low profile that would allow them to deny any accountability if something went wrong. I have to keep this in mind, he thought. Caution was needed. Why had his law firm at all accepted this case? But they had agreed, which meant that he had to accept the rules of the game. To overcome his irritation, he turned on the radio and searched for a station with classical music. When he found it, he stretched out on the bed and closed his eyes. His body felt tired. The lack of good sleep last night overwhelmed him now when the effect of the coffee he had taken in the early morning and after lunch decreased. When he opened his eyes again, his room was almost dark. He must have slept several hours and felt fresh energy running through his body. He decided to go to the restaurant. Before he left the room, he glanced at his computer; there he found a message from Hinchcroft, who thanked him for his report and urged him again to provide details. He wanted information as soon as possible. There must be considerable pressure from Alerta, Bill thought. Why? There must be a deadline of which I am kept in the dark.

The restaurant was almost empty. Which allowed him to find a table close to the entrance. He needed a drink. A whisky would be good, but then he changed his mind and decided to order a glass of red wine that would be more suitable for a dinner. It took a while until a waitress approached him with a menu. What he found on the menu was less than exciting. He hesitated and looked up to the waitress, "How about the steak? he said, "Not much can go wrong with that.?"

"That' s true", the waitress replied, "Still, I would recommend the liver tonight. It's really fresh and delicious."

"Really, I'm not sure, but If you say so, I'll give it a chance."

The waitress smiled and recommended a glass of Bordeaux. Bill nodded and gave her the menu back: "I read in the papers that there was a fatal accident in front of the hotel a few days ago. Did you see anything?"

It turned out that the waitress had not witnessed the accident herself. What she knew she had learned from an old lady in this restaurant when she served her last night.

Bill wanted to know: "Did she talk about the details?"

"No, not really. Not a complete story. From her remarks it became clear that she was overwhelmed by the event. There was sense of terror."

Bill was somewhat disappointed, yet he was not ready to give up: "Did she say something about the car that hit the bicyclist?"

The waitress looked at him hesitating a moment: "I think she mentioned a truck, but I'm not sure. Everything happened so very fast. That's what she remembers most of all. It must have been like a flash. The truck came and was gone within seconds. It seems that the driver didn't try to slow down. I hope they find this bastard. He should be punished for what he did."

Bill nodded: "Yes, the driver has to be found."

So, it might be a truck Bill mused. A heavier vehicle and more likely a professional driver. Maybe this is more than a fatal accident Yet he had to be cautious. What he had listened to was the copy of a copy. He needed something much more reliable.

When the young waitress came back later with a glass of red wine Bill saw another chance. and mentioned casually: "Do you by any chance recall an American businessman as a guest in this hotel? We were supposed to meet here a couple of days ago but I was delayed because I became ill."

The young woman put the glass down in front of him: "We have American guests all the time They like this part of town, the old West, but not recently. At least I don't recall an American businessman."

The answer surprised Bill, since he had assumed that the contact person for Alerta would stay at the hotel for a night. Something must have gone wrong. Bill was still trying to figure out what had happened when the waitress came with his meal. Her recommendation turned out to be on the mark. He really enjoyed the dish and the wine. He would get back to his case tomorrow morning.

CHAPTER 2

There was a strange noise from behind the wall. Bill couldn't figure out what it was, it annoyed him a great deal and it didn't go away, even when he turned around. I have to do something about it, he thought and moved his head. Now it stopped, but then it started again. It was a knock at the door. Then Bill heard a voice, a voice that sounded familiar. "Bill open up, it's me, Ulrike. I am standing in front of your door. Get up and open the door. It's 8:30." His first reaction was surprise, his thoughts were confused. I'm not ready. I must get dressed before I can open the door.

"Please, wait a moment until I'm dressed," he called, "I'm not decent."

"Don't be ridiculous, Bill", he heard Ulrike's voice, "Just open the damned door. I'm coming with our breakfast."

Bill stumbled out of his bed and walked to the door. When he opened it, Ulrike stood right in front of him with a big smile and a large paper bag filled with croissants. All he could say was "Hallo". He stepped back, inviting Ulrike to enter the room. She rushed to a small table where she dropped the bag and turned around moving toward Bill, who just looked at her, still surprised by her actual physical presence.

"Welcome back," she said with a cheerful voice, "how are you?"

Finally, Bill moved toward her: "Great to see you, Ulrike. Yes, I'm fine. When I was told yesterday that I had another case in Berlin, to be honest, I wasn't excited to go. But now, seeing you next to me, I'm very glad to be in here."

"I need a hug right now," Ulrike said and came closer. He embraced her and held her closely in his arms. That was all he could do. As far was he was concerned, they could stay like that forever. It appeared that Ulrike felt the same, she was leaning into him pressing her head against his shoulder. The two years of separation instantly disappeared. They were totally in the presence, drawn to each other without the need for words. Finally, Ulrike stepped back.

"I can't believe it that you are actually here in Berlin. I so much wanted to meet you at the airport, but I was in Hamburg where I spent a couple of days doing research for a book. What a huge surprise. You have to tell me all about it. But first, let's have breakfast. I brought croissants and other stuff. There must be a coffee machine in your room. While I am working on the coffee, you can get dressed."

Only now Bill noticed that he was standing in front of her in his pajamas and felt slightly embarrassed.

"I'll get dressed," he said and retired with his clothes to the bathroom. While he took a quick shower, Ulrike was busy with the coffee machine and the croissants. When he reappeared a few minutes later, he saw two cups filled with black coffee and a plate with croissants and Danish rolls. Ulrike did not notice that he was back, because she was busy with her smart phone. He looked at her. Had she changed during the two years that he had not seen her? Bill was not sure. The same small energetic figure, the same dark red hair and the light skin with a few freckles here and there. In short, the same lively Ulrike he met two years ago. Still, there were changes. The most obvious one was the dress, gone were the jeans and the heavy sweater. Instead, she was wearing elegant pants and a silk shirt. There was also something about her face that was different. He couldn't say what it was. He wished that he could look at her like this for a long time without words coming in between them. She must have felt his gaze and looked up giving him a smile that touched him deeply.

"I hope you are hungry," Ulrike said, "I brought more pieces that we can possibly finish."

"Don't worry," he replied, while he was sitting down next to her,

"I always seem to have a bigger appetite in Berlin than in New York. I don't know why."

He picked up the cup in front of him, holding it with both hands, sipping the very hot strong coffee.

"I made it extra-strong," Ulrike said, while she picked up a croissant, "we will need to be awake when we talk about your new case. Bill just nodded and helped himself to a Danish. He did not want to talk about his case, at least not now. He wanted to talk about Ulrike and himself. He asked: "How have you been? Your emails never said that much."

Ulrike turned her head away, looking toward the window. "Fine, quite busy as you can imagine. I moved from the *BZ* to the *Morgenspiegel* where I do local stuff, including crime."

This is not what he wanted to talk about, but she stayed away from the personal side. So, he replied: "Was that a move up?"

Now Ulrike looked at him: "Yes, no doubt about it."

Bill wanted to find out more: "And do you like it there? Sometimes the better place is not the happier place."

The way she looked at him told him that she didn't want to talk about the private side of his question. Her own question emphasized this resistance. She wanted to know why he had come to Berlin. She wanted to hear about his new case. Of course, he wanted to tell her more about his new assignment, but only after finding out how her private life was shaping up. Bill took another croissant, still hoping that she might shift to the personal and intimate side of their first case two years ago. But she didn't. Instead, she stood up and began clearing away the remnants of the breakfast. So, he changed the topic and told her about the accident in front of his hotel. She had heard of it and even remembered a short article in the *Morgenspiegel*.

Once Bill explained the suspicious circumstances, Ulrike became eager to hear more about the details. Bill got the folder and spread the sheets and pictures out on the small table. Ulrike nurtured her second cup of coffee, while she studied the various documents.

Then she asked: "And why do they send you to investigate this accident?"

He hesitated for a moment, thinking about the confidentiality of the client.

"There was supposed to be a meeting in the Brandenburger Hof between the victim and a representative of Alerta, a major American pharma company, a meeting that never happened. The Americans want to find out why."

Ulrike looked at the picture of Herwig Stollberg and asked: "What was the purpose of the meeting?"

"Good question. I don't know. What I do know is that Stollberg was carrying information, a file or something that he was supposed to give to the contact person, but the file disappeared. The purpose of my assignment is to investigate the circumstances of the accident and to find out what happened to the file."

Now Ulrike got up and paced up and down. She was clearly engaged. Bill knew he had her full attention. She had shifted gears from friend to journalist. He had to explain the minute details of the case. Then, all of a sudden she asked him: "Do you believe this was an accident? I mean do you believe that Stollberg's death was accidental?"

"Ulrike, I have my doubts. It looks suspicious, but I don't have any evidence to prove intention."

"Something doesn't look right. I smell a rat."

"Let's assume for a moment," Bill interjected, "that it was not an accident where the driver left the scene, then we have to assume as well that the driver knew when Stollberg would be at the specific location at the exact time when the unknown driver made a right turn at the intersection. He must have known in advance about the meeting and its purpose. That's a lot of assumptions."

"Yes, there would be a lot of unproven assumptions," Ulrike replied. "On the other hand, an important file is now missing, important enough for a major American company to begin an investigation. Bill, I smell a rat. Remember, I'm a journalist, if I were asked to look at this case, I would definitely include the possibility of foul play."

"Yes, you would," Bill replied with a chuckle, "It makes a much better story. Just imagine the headline: *Murder on the Kurfürstendamm*, but I am not writing stories, I deliver information."

"Yes, you do, at least most of the times," Ulrike said, "but the information has to be complete and in-depth. That's what we journalists do."

Bill laughed: "At least sometimes. Ulrike, let's not quarrel again, not here and now. You know this town much better than I do. I would appreciate your help with some of the deep background information. I have an appointment with Lotte Herberg this afternoon. I want to see the full police report. The file I received in New York is strangely incomplete, either because facts are actually unknown or because they are deliberately suppressed. Lotte Herberg said that she will help me. But there is Stollberg and his little company. I need to know much more about him and his projects. He and a pharma company – what is the meaning of that? Is KreuzbergChem involved in pharma research?"

Ulrike glanced at some of the documents on the table: "That would be news. All I know is that these guys were involved with food companies. Yes, that would be critical. By the way, I'm surprised that Charlotte invited you."

"Why? Do you think that she thinks of me as a dangerous person?"

"No, that's not the point. Charlotte is very correct, and collaboration with a foreign private detective is not quite proper for a police officer."

"Then, she must have changed her mind. She invited me after we had a nice chat on the phone."

"Good for you, Bill, but to come back to KreuzbergChem, we definitely need more information. There should be more on the internet than you found."

Bill was delighted that she used the word "we", that was a promising development. She must have decided that this case had the potential for a good story. That was fine with him, as long as she provided the research that would help him solve the case. He was ready to propose a plan when she all of a sudden looked at her watch.

"My god," she exclaimed, "I have to run. I'll be late for a meeting. I will be busy at the office for the rest of the day. How about dinner? Come to my place at six. We take it from there."

Ulrike jumped up, grabbed her things and moved to the exit: "Say hallo to Lotte. I have not talked to her for a while. Take care."

At 2:00 sharp Bill stood in front of Charlotte Herberg's office at Police Headquarters. He knew he had to be punctual if he wanted to get the information he was looking for. He knocked expecting a female voice to answer. But it was a male voice. He entered finding himself in front of a tall young police officer in uniform who invited him to take a seat.

"I am Werner Kraft, Hauptkommissarin Herberg's assistant. She has been called away and has asked me to help you with your search."

Bill smiled politely, trying to hide the fact that he was disappointed because Charlotte Herberg was absent. The young officer must have noticed his reaction and turned to him with a smile:

"She sends her regards. She wanted to discuss the matter with you in person, but she had to attend an unexpected meeting. She has asked me to look for the file that was opened on the Stollberg accident and make it available to you."

"That's really very kind of you," Bill replied, trying to make the best of this unexpected turn. After all, looking at the file was the purpose of his visit. The officer explained to him that Bill could examine the file in his presence and make notes, but he would not be allowed to take it out of the room or copy documents. Bill nodded his consent and followed the officer to a smaller office next door where he saw the file on a desk. When he opened it, he immediately realized that there was more material than he had received. There were more pictures of the accident. In addition, there was the report of the doctor and statements of eye witnesses. Bill turned to the young officer: "The police assumes that is was an accident, right?"

"That's correct," Kraft replied, giving Bill a strange look. "We haven't been able to find the driver, but the case is treated as an accident. Do you have doubts? Is that the reason that you have been asked to investigate?"

"Well," Bill replied, "The whole thing looks odd."

"How so?"

"Because a file is missing, the file that Stollberg meant to bring to the meeting at the Brandenburger Hof."

"How do you know that? There is nothing about a missing file in our report," said the officer.

"That piece of information comes from my file."

Kraft hesitated a moment before he said: "Okay, and where is that file coming from?"

Bill replied: "It was given to my employer with the request to examine the facts of the accident."

The young officer nodded: "Foul play, I'm beginning to understand the interest of your client. It's less about the accident than the missing file."

"It seems that way," Bill asserted.

"If it's more than a hit-and-run, we have to look at the facts in a rather different light," asserted the officer.

"Yes, that's why I'm here. Is there any information about the vehicle that caused the death? And what about the driver? A description? Or the missing briefcase? Was it attached to the bicycle?"

The young officer shook his head. He returned to the file, putting the documents on the desk.

Then he said softly: "I examined the documents before we met. I don't believe that there is an answer to your question in this file. But let's go through all the pieces one more time."

Bill and Werner Kraft sat next to each other sifting slowly through the documents. There was no mention of a briefcase or a description of the driver. More frustrating was the fact that there was not even a description of the vehicle. The eye witnesses did not agree on the type. Some thought it was a small truck, other believed it was a SUV. No agreement on the color either. Most of them believed that the plate was not issued in Berlin. Yet nobody could remember the letters or numbers of the plate. Bill was frustrated. He had hoped to find reliable information that would help him to unravel the larger issues. This was like hitting a brick wall.

"There must be a search for the vehicle and the driver, I assume?" asked Bill.

"Of course, there is," replied the officer, "however, no results, not surprising, given the lack of solid information."

Bill realized that this search had reached a dead end. He had to look at his case from a different angle. Who really was Herwig Stollberg and why was he planning to contact Alerta in person? He took his leave not without thanking the police officer for his time and special efforts. He really liked him.

Werner Kraft was still busy in Charlotte Herberg's office when she returned from her meeting. It had been one of these administrative meetings in which there is a lot of talk but little gets done. Charlotte hated them. It took Kraft no more than a second to see that she was suffering from a migraine again. The episodes had become more frequent in recent months. He suspected that the episodes were in part connected with the upheavals in her personal life, but of course, he was not in a position to ask her. Although they worked closely together, private stuff remained outside their relationship. Without saying anything, he got a glass of water and some aspirin and put them on her desk. She thanked him with a nod of her head, looking at the pile of files on her desk. It seemed to be a hopeless battle, the more she tried to take care of these files, the faster the pile grew back. This was the price for her promotion: she had to spend more and more of her time at her desk. She missed the early days when she was on the move. She had enjoyed the action on the streets, the confrontations with the bad guys. Now she spent her time going to administrative meetings. She realized that this was the inevitable result of her success, a success that she had wanted and had worked for. At the same time, the result had changed her professional life in ways that she did not care for. I have become an administrator, she thought looking at the files in front of her. She took the pills together with the water that her assistant had placed in front of her.

"Did Bill McDonald show up?" she asked.

"Yes, he did, Kraft replied, "you missed him by twenty minutes."

"How was he? Still the young man in a hurry?"

"Certainly energetic and focused, but I had the impression that he has slowed down a bit."

"And his new case, could we help him?"

Kraft hesitated a bit before he said: "I'm not so sure. We looked at the file together. Yet there seemed to be no obvious answer to his question."

"How come," asked Charlotte, taking another sip of water from the glass. Then she pressed her hands against her temples.

"He's looking for the driver, as we do. But there is more. He's also looking for a file that the victim was supposed to deliver at a meeting at the Brandenburger Hof. A file containing important information. The file is missing."

Charlotte turned around: "A missing file, connected to this accident. This is new information, I guess."

"Yes, it is, and it may well change the nature of the case. McDonald is working for his law firm, which got the case from an American company. It's my impression that they are primarily interested in the recovery of the missing file."

Charlotte looked at her assistant: "Did McDonald say anything about the content of this missing file or about the person who was supposed to receive the file?"

"Actually, he remained pretty vague. My impression was that he didn't know. The recipient was, if I got the story right, an American company that approached Bill's law firm."

Charlotte shook her head: "This is a strange story. Frankly, it doesn't sound quite right."

"No, it doesn't," replied Werner Kraft, "but we don't have any reason to doubt McDonald's words. It means that the case is more complicated than we had assumed. It could be more than a hit-and-run car accident."

Charlotte stood up: "Our guys should take another look at this case. If the accident was not really an accident but was planned in order to get access to the file, then we are talking about premeditated murder."

Werner Kraft nodded and promised to return the file to the proper department, however with the request to doublecheck all of the pieces in light of the new information. After he had left her office Charlotte Herberg was just sitting in her chair without moving. Her headache was beginning to recede a bit. The more Charlotte thought about the accident on Kurfürstendamm, the more she felt that they had to be prepared for a murder investigation, whether they liked it or not. Which also meant that she had to be prepared to work together with Bill McDonald. Her first reaction was ambivalent. As she remembered, he could be difficult, since he felt no obligation to follow proper police procedures. On the other hand, he was energetic, focused and got things done, qualities which she respected. She knew that freeing the young American journalist was largely due to his efforts, although the official report had hardly mentioned him. What would he do next? He might well be in touch with Ulrike who had been his sidekick in the missing person case. If this is the case, there will be a call from Ulrike within the next twenty-four hours, she mused. I have to be ready, Ulrike will be relentless once she is following a lead. How was she doing these days? They had not been in touch for several months. She had been preoccupied with her own problems. Then she forced herself to focus on the pile of files on her desk that she had to study and take care of before the end of the day.

Bill McDonald sat in a small coffee shop from where he could observe the entrance of Ulrike's apartment building. It was almost 7:00 pm and there was no sign of her. He had tried to call her several times, but she didn't answer. His mood was low, since the afternoon, after he left the police headquarters, had not been very fruitful. He had gone back to Kreuzberg to check on the office of KreuzbergChem, only to find out that nobody answered the door. He decided to go to Ulrike's place in Neukölln, hoping that she might be at home. When he found out that she was not at home, he moved with his laptop to the coffee shop across the street. There he ordered his second latte and tried to find out more about Stollberg on the internet, but he didn't get very far beyond what he knew already. He realized that he needed access to Stollberg's recent projects. What he found on the internet was at least two years old. They were focused on food processing in connection with a Swiss and a French company. He didn't understand the details, but he got the central idea. It was obvious that Alerta would not have been interested in these projects. His search was interrupted by an email from Hinchcroft asking him for an update. This was an obvious reminder that his boss was eager to have results. Bill decided to send a positive but vague answer. At the same time, he knew that he had to present more concrete results in the near future. He requested more information about the content of the missing file without seriously expecting an answer. If Alerta wanted him to know the details, it would have been part of the file. He was supposed to retrieve something that he would not understand. He had to start from the other end. Somebody beside Alerta was interested in the file because it contained valuable information. Alerta was a pharma company, specializing in advanced drugs. If he followed that logic, the interested person or group must be a drug company, a competitor. That was a highly chilling thought. Murder had become part of the business competition. This was an interesting line of analysis. But there was no evidence at all, Bill reminded himself, that KreuzbergChem was involved in the development of drugs. Of course, there was also no hard evidence that the accident was planned. If he knew more about the driver, Bill thought, he had a better chance to figure this out. Here he had to rely on Werner Kraft and the police apparatus. Focused on his computer screen, Bill almost overlooked a young woman crossing the street and moving to the entrance of the house across. When she reached the door and briefly turned around he clearly recognized Ulrike. His mood improved instantly. He closed his laptop, paid for the coffee and followed her to the apartment on the third floor.

When Ulrike opened the door, Bill immediately realized it had been a difficult day for her, she looked exhausted.

"Bad day at the office?" he asked.

"You don't want to know," she replied with a shrug.

"Let's go out for dinner, he suggested.

"I have seen enough of the public for a day. How about raiding the fridge for something edible?"

"Fine with me," Bill responded, "shall I focus on a salad? One of my stronger points."

As it turned out, there was not much left in the refrigerator that could be turned into a salad. Instead, they agreed on spaghetti with meatballs and tomato sauce. Somewhere Bill even discovered half a bottle of red wine. Half an hour later, they were happily sitting at the kitchen table, digging into a big plate of spaghetti with meatballs. Ulrike's mood had clearly improved. She wanted to know what Bill had found out about the accident at the police headquarters. Bill gave her a detailed report of the meeting with Werner Kraft.

"That is less than you wanted to find out, right?"

"You may say that. I 'm not much further than this morning. So far, no information on the driver, and no trace of the file. The victim was not carrying a briefcase or knapsack. Of course, the team at the location of the accident was not looking for a briefcase."

"Do you think that somebody could have removed the briefcase or some other container? I mean when the attention was totally focused on Stollberg."

"That strikes me as unlikely, but we can't rule it out, as long as we assume that the accident was carefully planned.", said Bill.

Ulrike raised her glass: "Well, that would be my working hypothesis. But then I am a reporter, not a detective."

Bill laughed, raising his glass as well. "Cheers, your input is certainly appreciated."

"Okay, but before we go there, let's have coffee. I really need a strong cup to get some energy back."

While Ulrike got busy with the coffee machine, Bill took the glasses and the wine bottle together with his laptop to the living room. Something interesting had happened. Almost effortlessly, without a discussion, they had found back their former mode of being together, eating together, talking together. Her curiosity had been stronger than the exhaustion caused by her own work. All he had to do now was to wait for her questions. A few minutes later Ulrike entered the living room with two large mugs with strong black coffee. No cream, but some sugar. They were sitting next to each other on the couch looking at the file and the notes on his laptop.

"Where do you mean to go from here?" Ulrike asked, holding her mug with both hands.

"I 'm not sure," he replied, "I definitely need more information about Stollberg and his colleagues. And what is the link between Stollberg and Alerta, the pharma company? I have searched on the internet. There is a website for the company and also a separate one for Stollberg and the other partners. We get a basic story about their education and the goals of the whole enterprise, but not the details I need, for instance Stollberg's latest publications."

Ulrike started to work with her own laptop, using different browsers to access journals in the field of organic chemistry. After a while she said: "I don't find a link that opens up his recent publications, but tomorrow I will go to the office of *Morgenspiegel* and get some help from their technical staff. They are really good and very helpful. But before I forget. There is an important bit of information I found this morning in *Morgenspiegel*."

She went back to the kitchen and returned with a page of the newspaper. She pointed to an obituary for Dr. Hedwig Stollberg. Bill glanced at the notification and then at Ulrike. He seemed not to comprehend the relevance of this information.

"The funeral is tomorrow at 10am at the Waldfriedhof." Ulrike told him, "I mean to be there, and I hope you will be there as well."

Bill nodded: "Yes, of course, this is our chance to observe the partners and the family."

Ulrike pointed to the names: "Here are the parents, followed by a brother and a sister. No wife and children. Was he not married? There is another obituary put out by Klein and Brindisi, stating the loss of a valuable and cherished partner.

"Let me try something else," said Ulrike, beginning a new search. She gave in the name Stollberg. There were several Stollberg's in Berlin, among them two women. In the case of Dorothea Stollberg, the private address was identical with that of Herwig Stollberg.

"Look at this," she exclaimed, "this looks very much like a wife, but she is not mentioned in the notification. Do you understand what this means?

Bill looked at her: "I'm sure you will tell me."

"Indeed," she replied," I will, we have found a wife who is not acknowledged by the family."

Bill turned to her: "Right. Great, Ulrike. They split up recently, still the same address on the web. But his family does not acknowledge her."

Ulrike turned to Bill, touching his arm: "Bill, we are getting somewhere, at least a small window. I mean to talk to this Dorothea Stollberg. If not tomorrow, in the near future. She may have interesting things to say."

Bill nodded. He was at the same time excited and tired. His body had not yet fully adjusted to Berlin time. He wanted to continue the search, although he realized that his energy was dropping fast. Ulrike was still busy searching on her laptop. All of a sudden, she exclaimed: "Brindisi, why did I not notice this before. This is the name of a well-known restaurant in Berlin-Mitte. One of the best Italian restaurants."

Do you think there is a connection between our chemist and the restaurant?"

"I have no idea, but I'm interested in finding out. How common is the name Brindisi? The Brindisis have been around in Berlin for two generations. He could be a son. If this is the case, the interest in food and food processing makes sense."

Bill leaned back before he said" "Hey, I think we are beginning to speculate without solid foundations. Let's stop here."

"Yes, we do, but what else can we do today? And it's fun. By the way, you look dead tired. You need sleep. You can stay here and sleep on the couch. Tomorrow we'll be up early to be ready."

Bill realized that Ulrike was right. He needed sleep. Both of them needed sleep. Ulrike was already on her feet looking for a blanket. She found him a towel and a toothbrush as well before she retired to her bedroom. I am back in Berlin, Bill thought, and in her apartment before he fell asleep. This had been a good day after all.

CHAPTER 3

The next morning the weather had changed. When he looked out of the window Bill stared at dark clouds. Ulrike was already busy in the kitchen. When he checked his watch, he realized that he had overslept. It was 8:30, high time to get dressed and have a bite to eat before they would attend the funeral.

He heard Ulrike's voice: "coffee?"

His reply was still hesitant: "Yes, please. I'll join you in the kitchen in a second."

His brain was barely functioning. In the kitchen he found Ulrike sitting on a high stool, holding her coffee mug in her hands and smiling at him. She looked terrific, that was all he could think while he was grabbing the mug she offered him.

"We have to make plans" she said brightly, "this is our chance to get some of the information we need, if we are prepared."

Bill was sipping his coffee, remaining silent for a while. What could be the justification for them to show up at this funeral? He was meaning to stay in the background and keep a low profile. Then he asked: "Do you mean to approach the family in our role as a reporter, asking questions about the accident?"

"I have to play it by ear," she said, "I 'm certainly meaning to show up as a reporter for my newspaper. This is an unusual case where the public has a right to find out why and how the victim died."

"Do you really believe," said Bill, "that the family is ready to answer questions at the funeral?"

"Not likely," Ulrike conceded, "maybe the brother will talk to me. At least, I will try. How about you?"

"I must stay invisible, just observing."

Suddenly, Ulrike stood up and moved to the hallway, coming back with a camera: "How about this old piece? You could present yourself as a colleague of mine."

Bill's first reaction was negative, because he couldn't see himself in the role, but then he changed his mind. This would be a good cover for getting pictures.

When Bill and Ulrike arrived at the church of the cemetery, there was already a large crowd of people in front of the building waiting to enter the hall. There were at least fifty persons, possibly more, most of them young. Bill was looking for the parents and the siblings, but he couldn't discover them.

"Where's the family?" he whispered to Ulrike.

"They are just arriving," she replied, pointing to a large black Mercedes that pulled up in front of the church. After they proceeded to the building, the crowd followed. Bill and Ulrike were looking for a bench near the exit. All of a sudden, Bill touched Ulrike's arm, whispering: "Look over there and you'll see a familiar face."

"Who?" she asked, trying in vain to discover the familiar face.

Bill said: "Werner Kraft, Charlotte Herberg's assistant. Of course, not in uniform. This means that the police show more interest in the case. He isn't alone, he's got a young woman sitting next to him."

The service took longer than Bill had expected, since after the priest several people addressed the congregation, among them the brother and Stefano Brindisi, the business partner. Bill didn't pay that much attention to these speeches, all of them in German. Ulrike could fill him in later. He focused his attention on the faces around him. There was a sense of shock and disbelief. How could this have happened? Unfortunately, he couldn't see the faces of the family members who were sitting in the first row. What he did notice was the subdued response of the brother when he addressed the mourners. He had expected stronger words, maybe anger about this senseless, premature death. Instead, what he heard sounded more like acceptance of the intervention of a higher power. He would have to talk to Ulrike about this later.

After the service, the coffin was being moved to the gravesite, followed by the large crowd of mourners. At the gravesite the priest spoke once more. Then the coffin was lowered into the ground. The family stood close to the grave accepting the condolences of the long line of mourners. Bill had chosen to stay in the background, looking for a spot from where he could observe the crowd. He noticed that Werner Kraft and the woman had done the same. They took pictures as well. When he turned around, he made an unexpected discovery. There were two men in the far background who were clearly observing the funeral. Who were they? More police? Not likely, thought Bill. Alerta's men? He decided that he wanted to get closer at a later time and try to talk to them. Now he took a picture. Then he turned his gaze back to the group around the grave. Here he got a better view of the family members. Especially the parents appeared to be shaken. The father looked almost absent-minded when he shook the hands of the people lining up at the grave. The brother supported the mother, who was hardly strong enough to stand.

After the service, which had taken almost two hours, Bill returned to Ulrike's little Fiat. He had to wait a while until she met him at the car.

"Any success getting an interview?" he asked.

"The father refused to answer questions, but the brother was willing to answer a few. He made it clear that the family was not only distraught but also angry. There was no resolution to the accident. The driver has not been identified, and it seemed that the police have not made much of an effort to solve the case. By the way, I agree with him. This looks like a sloppy job. And I'm glad that Charlotte sent her people to have a look. What did you discover?"

Bill got into the car before he responded: "I took plenty of pictures of the crowd. This may help us later. By the way, Kraft did the same, which means that they consider Stollberg's death now as suspicious. There was something else. I saw two men in the far background when I turned around. They were observing the funeral but not as mourners. I wanted to approach them later, but when I was looking for them again, they were gone.

"Did you get a picture?"

"Yes, I did, but not a good one, because I didn't want to alert them to become suspicious."

"Still, that's great. Maybe we can identify them when we look at the archive."

For a while they were driving back to town without talking. The sky was still gray, only here and there the sun brightened the day. Ulrike appeared to be absorbed in her own thoughts, while Bill was trying to come up with a summary of this morning. He wished that he could tell himself that there had been a major change, however, this was clearly not the case. What he remembered most was the strange speech of the brother and the two guys next to the Oak tree, clearly observing the funeral. Both of them possibly relevant, but how? Not yet enough material for a second message to Hinchcroft. Maybe, he would have to twist things a bit in order to come up with interesting news.

Suddenly, Ulrike's phone rang. She pressed the speaker button to accept the call. It was a voice that Bill immediately recognized: Charlotte Herberg's. "Hello Ulrike. How are you? Am I interrupting important business? I can call back later."

Ulrike glanced at Bill before the answered: "No, go ahead, I 'm on the way back to my office after attending the funeral of Herwig Stollberg."

"That's why I am calling. I sent two of my officers to the same funeral. Did you come up with interesting observations? I just got a preliminary report from my people and would like to compare notes with you. I understand that Bill McDonald is with you?"

Ulrike laughed: "Yes he is, right next to me. You can say hallo to him. Comparing notes?! Sounds good, but when? Not today. I 'm already late for a staff meeting. Maybe you want to talk to Bill? He might be available."

Ulrike glanced at Bill, who gave her a nod. Charlotte Herberg expressed interest and asked for the number of his cellphone. She would be in touch later to arrange a meeting.

"I can't believe it," Bill chuckled, "Hauptkommissarin Herberg seeking a meeting to consult with me. Collaboration with the private sector! That could be constructed as treason."

"Okay, Bill, enjoy your moment, but you better play along, because you need her as much as she needs us," Ulrike responded. Bill just shrugged his shoulders without replying. After a while he asked: "Can you drop me off at my hotel. I really need a fresh shirt, etc."

She shook her head: "I wish I could, but I 'm really in a hurry. I have a boss, who doesn't like me that much, she is the methodical type, which I am not, as you well know. I drop you off at the next train station, unless you want to take a cab."

He only asked: "When will you be free?"

"Late afternoon, after a reception I have to attend. I will come to your place but I don't know exactly when."

Then she stopped the car at an intersection where Bill recognized the sign of the underground. He quickly got out of the car and moved toward the train station. After walking for a minute, he changed his mind. He didn't know the underground system well enough to get to his hotel efficiently. So, he went back to the intersection and hailed a taxi. Within minutes he found himself in a cab on his way to the Brandenburger Hof. Before I meet anybody, I need a shower and a shave, he told himself. This was certainly more comfortable than a train ride. Only minutes later his peaceful ride was interrupted by a phone call. It was Werner Kraft who wanted to set up a meeting.

"Sure, I want to meet with you and Charlotte Herberg, but first I have to go home and get a shower," Bill said, "how about this afternoon?" There was a pause on the other end, then he heard Kraft's voice:

"Frau Herberg suggests that we can meet you at the hotel and have lunch together. That beats the atmosphere of the police station."

"Sounds great, Bill replied, What time?"

They agreed on 1:00pm at the Brandenburger Hof. This would give Bill plenty of time to get ready. He wasn't sure what the police officers would like to find out, but he needed their help with some of his own questions. This promised to be a better collaboration than two years ago when there were some basic trust issues.

When Bill came to his room, he first checked his email. As he expected, Hinchcroft had sent another message, asking for an update. What was he supposed to write? All he had to offer was a bunch of loose ends without a coherent narrative, not to mention no answer to the main question, i.e. where was the missing file? While Bill enjoyed the hot water of the shower running over his body, he gave more thought to his impending response. He would mention his police contacts, suggesting that there might be answer in the near future, although he had serious doubts that this would be true. This case had not become clearer. Whenever there was a new fact or additional observation, the more blurred the whole picture became. The atmosphere at the funeral had been strange as well, although he couldn't clearly explain in what way. Of course, the oratories had been in German, which made it difficult for him to get all the details, but the emphasis of the brother's remarks struck him as odd, almost inappropriate for the sudden death of a younger man. And the speech of Brindisi was difficult to follow, in many places incoherent, a lament that took back what it said. He would have to discuss this with Ulrike. Maybe she could make sense of the event at the church. After the shower he had enough time to have another look at his notes. Then he grabbed his laptop and the file. But before Bill went downstairs to meet the police officers, he composed a brief message for Hinchcroft, assuring him that there was progress, although not yet a solution to the case. He promised to be in touch. There must be pressure from Alerta, Bill thought, otherwise the lawyer would leave him alone.

He was early and settled in a chair from where he could observe the entrance. He noticed the clerk at the reception desk to whom he had talked on the first day. As soon as the clerk recognized Bill, he made a gesture indicating that he wanted to talk to him. Bill walked over, still keeping an eye on the entrance.

"I have a piece of information that might interest you," the clerk said, "you remember the old lady who saw the accident?"

"Yes, of course," Bill replied, "what about her?"

"She believes that she can't remember the license plate."

Bill focused his full attention on the young man: "What do you mean?"

The clerk said: "She believes that there was no license plate"

Bill nodded, then he asked: "Do you think that she really remembered this fact?"

The clerk shrugged his shoulders: "It's unusual, but what do I know. I have the information from the night clerk who talked to her last night."

At this moment, Charlotte Herberg and Werner Kraft entered the hotel. Bill thanked the clerk and walked toward the police officers. Charlotte smiled at him and shook his hand, the way one greets an old acquaintance. Bill wasn't quite sure about the protocol in this situation. He realized that he couldn't address her by her first name but did not want to use her formal title. Werner Kraft noticed his hesitation and motioned him in the direction of the restaurant where they settled at a quiet table at the far end of the room. Charlotte seemed genuinely interested in his life in Manhattan, asking specific questions about the nature of his job. After they had placed their orders, Werner Kraft pulled out the police file on the accident, while Bill opened his laptop and kept his own file close.

Charlotte wanted to know more about the funeral. She tried to speak slowly, remembering that Bill had difficulties following a fast conversation in German. As it turned out, Bill had no problems grasping the meaning of her questions, answering them in English, now himself cautious to articulate clearly because he was not certain how fluent her English was. Bill tried as best as he could to describe the atmosphere of the funeral service, mentioning the incoherence of Brindisi's speech and the strangely subdued nature of the brother's remarks.

"I had the feeling," Bill said looking at Charlotte Herberg, "that

Brindisi did not want to be there, that he was under pressure to perform in a situation with which he was deeply uncomfortable."

"Did you have the same impression, Werner?" asked Charlotte Herberg.

Kraft hesitated a second before he replied: "Of course, I noticed that his remarks were not very coherent, but that is to be expected, the shock of a sudden and violent death."

"True, of course the shock," said Bill, "but I sensed also something different, because I paid more attention to the tone of his voice than the content of his speech."

Charlotte nodded: "We should keep this in mind, although at this point it's no more than an impressionistic observation. The same with the brother's speech."

They discussed the details of the funeral for a while until Charlotte Herberg turned to Bill, wanting to know whether there were any concrete facts that came to light.

"Yes, there is," said Bill, getting his smart phone out of his pocket, "I got a picture of two men in the far background, obviously not part of the funeral party but keenly observing the procedures."

Both Charlotte and Werner Kraft looked at the picture. Because of the distance the faces were fairly small. They were unable to identify the men in the picture.

"We have to run the picture through our archive," said Kraft, "there can be no doubt that these guys were not there as mourners. And they are not our people. I would recognize those. Could the Americans have sent them?"

Bill shook his head: "Not likely, I 'm their eyes and ears in Berlin."

"Are you sure about this?" asked Werner Kraft, "because we got a picture of a man also on the periphery, keeping his eyes on Brindisi and Klein."

Both Bill and Charlotte Herberg looked carefully at the figure in the picture. "Not exactly an American face," Bill suggested. Charlotte agreed. "If you want my opinion, he could be a German private detective, possibly former police. We want to compare the image with our records. I am pretty sure something will come up."

Bill suggested to have another look at the accident and reported what he just learned: "One of the hotel clerks just told me that an eye witness thinks there was no license plate on the front of the vehicle."

Werner Kraft wanted to know: "Who is this witness? If this is true, it suggests intention."

"An old lady who saw the entire accident because she stood in front to the hotel when it happened."

"Did you talk to her? And why is this not in our report?" Kraft wanted to know.

Bill shrugged his shoulders: "Don't ask me, Werner, for me this is second-hand. But you may want to talk to her."

Charlotte agreed, turning to Bill again, wanting to find out more about his own interest in the case: "Your firm wants you to find out how and why Stollberg was killed and what happened to the file he supposedly carried with him. Is that correct?"

Bill had expected this question. From her perspective the answer was crucial. For his firm confidentiality was critical. How far should he go? If he told her nothing or very little, she would not be inclined to help him, if he told too much, there might be problems at home.

"Yes, I have been sent to learn more about the circumstances of Stollberg's death and find out what happened to the missing file," he replied.

"He was on the way to a meeting with this file?"

"Yes, this was the case, I was informed."

"Do you know anything about the content of the file?" Charlotte asked.

"Unfortunately, I don't. This makes my job more difficult."

"I can imagine that. This is actually not an easy position. If we knew more about the content, it would be easier to figure out who had a motive to interfere with the meeting and look for the file."

"Any guess?" Bill asked.

"No, none so far" Charlotte replied. "But if we can identify the visitors at the funeral, we might get a clue."

"Good point," Bill interjected.

"Once we are finished with lunch and had another look at the location of the accident," Charlotte continued, "we should go back to my office and run the pictures through the system."

An hour later they were sitting in Charlotte Herberg's office, waiting for the results of the search. Within a short time, they had an answer for the single man. He turned out to be a private detective from Frankfurt, the owner of a small but very respected company that served mostly business corporations.

"Why would he be at the funeral?" Charlotte Herberg asked, looking at Bill and Werner Kraft. They looked at each other. Finally, Bill said: "I understand that Alerta has an office in Frankfurt. Maybe someone wanted to find out more about Stollberg?"

"This connection seems to be really important for this company, almost like overkill" Kraft added. Charlotte Herberg nodded: "In this case, however, we can follow up. I will ask our colleagues in Frankfurt to approach him to find out what he was doing at the funeral."

"Have you looked into Stollberg's background, for instance his small company? Any reason why there should be a link to Alerta?" Bill wanted to know.

"In general terms, it makes sense," Charlotte replied, he was a chemist and Alerta is a pharma company."

"In more specific terms, we had hoped that you would know more," said Werner Kraft. Bill shrugged his shoulders and replied: "Sorry, I wish I knew more."

It took another half hour until they heard from the technical service. They had a preliminary result for the two men. Given the relatively poor quality of the picture, there was no absolutely certain identification, but most likely the men were connected to the Mafia, though not in Berlin. One of them had an address in Duisburg, the other one came from Munich.

"The Mafia," said Herberg, "this fact radically changes our case. It is now highly likely that the accident was not accidental. This calls for a formal criminal investigation. I will have to inform my superior to discuss strategy."

Bill needed a minute to take this in. Why was the Mafia observing Stollberg's funeral? His file had not mentioned the Mafia at all, also

Hinchcroft had not referred to them. He had never heard of the presence of Mafiosi in Berlin. His first impression was that there must be a mistake. But, as he noticed, Herberg and Kraft appeared not to be totally surprised about the identification of the men in his picture.

"The Mafia in Berlin, that is news for me," Bill said in a low voice.

Werner Kraft chuckled: "Well, these days they are much more prominent in West Germany, but they have a presence in Berlin as well. Where ever there are Italian restaurants you have to figure that they are potentially in the background: forced co-ownership or protection money, not to mention drugs."

"But what is the connection between the Mafia and a young German chemist?" Bill asked.

"Drugs?!" Charlotte Herberg suggested: "We will have to examine this avenue as well. The start-up would actually be a good cover."

Werner Kraft nodded: "In fact, a great cover."

Bill was not convinced, but he remained silent because he didn't have a good argument against the hypothesis of the police officers. He felt that he needed time to reassess his case. When Charlotte was called to a meeting, he used the opportunity to take his leave, promising to stay in touch. He got the same promise from Werner Kraft, who walked him to the elevator.

Bill decided to go back to his hotel. He needed time to look at the different pieces of his case and set new priorities. When he arrived at the Brandenburger Hof, it was late afternoon. He checked his email, expecting another message from Hinchcroft, however, he was lucky, the lawyer had not tried to reach him. Bill would have to write another mail either later today or tomorrow morning. But what was the story? He had to figure out the relevance of the men who showed up at the funeral. Were they also looking for the missing file? But who sent them? How did the Mafia get into this case? The fact that the German detective came from Frankfurt suggested a possible link to Alerta. Maybe he was the contact who was supposed to receive the file. Bill had assumed the contact would be an American, but there had been no American in the hotel at the time of the accident. If this hypothesis was correct, he had returned to Berlin with the plan to reconnect with

KreuzbergChem to get the information from another partner of the company.

Bill paced up and down in his room. There were still too many unknown elements to put together a clear picture. He had the name and the picture of the Frankfurt detective. A man in his fifties, it seemed, very much a middle-class owner of a small company, nothing shady there. This was the type of man Alerta would pick, he thought. He would show the picture to the hotel staff. Maybe someone remembered him. Also, Bill had a name and an address. Tomorrow he would try to get in touch with him. The Mafia link, on the other hand, worried Bill. Drugs? Drugs didn't make sense when he thought of Alerta. A prominent American pharma company is not involved in drug trafficking. Still, Bill realized that he could not afford to neglect this fact. Either Herberg and Kraft were mistaken about the background of the men or there must be a different explanation for the link.

Bill went back to the table and had another look at his notes. If he knew more about the content of the missing file, he would be in a better position to assess the relevance of the men. I am moving in a circle, Bill thought, I need to find out what Stollberg was working on. This should be possible from accessible records. From there I can guess what the file was about and who was potentially interested in the file and decided to eliminate Stollberg. At this moment there was a knock on the door and he heard Ulrike's voice.

"Open the door, it's me."

Bill moved to the door, letting her in. She walked into the room, then turning around and facing Bill. She had changed her outfit. Instead of pants, she wore a sleeve-less light green summer dress. In her right hand she held something that looked like an article.

"We are in luck," she cried, "my research guys at *Morgenspiegel* found a more recent journal article by Stollberg and Brindisi."

"Where?" Bill wanted to know.

"One of the lesser known Dutch chemistry journals," Ulrike replied.

"And? Have you read it? What does it say?" Bill asked.

"I have just glanced at the article, but don't ask me to summarize the content. I got lost after a few sentences," Ulrike admitted, "we can study it later. But first I get my reward: You will take me out for dinner."

Bill laughed: "Since you have worked as my consultant, dinner is on my expense account." He moved toward her and embraced her. She put her arms around his neck, bending his head down until his face was very close to hers. His lips began to touch her face lightly until she responded and their lips locked. He was holding her, while she was moving very tight to his body. Bill realized that this was not the path to dinner, but it was much better, much sweeter. He lifted her, while she was clinging to him, and carried her to the bed. They were side by side, touching each other. Now Ulrike was on top of him unbuttoning his shirt, while he helped her getting out of her dress. Their lips were still seeking the other with growing excitement.

"Bill, bad boy," he heard her voice close to his ear, "why did you leave me. I wanted to have you here in Berlin. I missed you."

"And I was waiting for you in New York," he whispered, "you promised, but you never came, bad girl."

"It was never the right time, but now I 'm at your place, right!?" she exclaimed, covering his head and chest with kisses. "Did you miss me?"

Yes, he had missed her, more than he realized. And he had to say it. She wanted to hear it. He had forgotten how much fun it was to make love to her. Dinner could wait.

It was Ulrike who first freed herself from his embrace: "Bill, I am really hungry, I didn't get much of a lunch, because I had a pressing deadline,"

Bill just grunted, he could have stayed like this much longer. He checked his watch. It was just past 7:00pm. He looked at the ceiling, still in his thoughts, while she was dressing. Then he said: "There is a pretty good restaurant in this hotel, if you are starving, I tried it out when I arrived."

Ulrike made a face, indicating that she was not excited.

"I know of a really nice small place off Kurfürstendamm in the neighborhood. Let's go there."

"Fine with me," Bill replied, while getting up and getting dressed himself, "I can fill you in about my meeting with Charlotte Herberg and her assistant, whom I really like, by the way. Not stuffy at all."

"Was Charlotte stuffy?" Ulrike asked.

"No, not at all," Bill assured, "quite the contrary. We got along famously."

"I 'm glad to hear this because she is really not stuffy. And I don't want you to badmouth her," Ulrike said, while she was looking for her bag. "Let's go, I am hungry."

Fifteen minutes later Bill and Ulrike were sitting at a small table in a crowded restaurant looking at the menu. Ulrike recommended a fish dish that she had tried before, but Bill resisted any deviation from red meat, ending with a filet minion, while Ulrike ordered sea bass.

"You so much lack imagination when it comes to food, Bill," Ulrike said, "clearly no improvement during the last two years."

"That's not fair," Bill replied, "two years ago it would have been a hamburger."

Ulrike shook her head in disbelief. There was clearly room for education. But right now, she wanted to hear more about the meeting with Herberg. Bill gave her a summary, emphasizing the result of searching for the men at the funeral. He also told her that he was not yet convinced of the involvement of the Mafia. But he was pretty sure that the private detective was the contact at the hotel.

"I will check this out later," Bill said with emphasis.

"The Mafia, you say," Ulrike responded, "I think we should not exclude this option, although it seems far-fetched at this moment."

"Of course not," replied Bill with a gesture that underlined his skepticism. Then he wanted to know Ulrike's reaction to the speeches of the brother and Brindisi.

"What do you mean?" she asked.

"Brindisi was almost incoherent," Bill replied, "and the brother's remark sounded strange, not what I expected."

Ulrike looked at him: "Now, that you mention it, I think you have a point. Brindisi was definitely weird. Also, the family dynamics was certainly strange. I'm meaning to talk to Stollberg's ex. That's high on my list."

Once the food arrived, they dropped the case entirely. Ulrike talked about her new job at the *Morgenspiegel*. It was not too difficult for Bill to notice that the move had some aspects that were less than great. Ulrike looked into his eyes and realized that Bill got it. There was something in his face that told her that he really understood what she was talking about. The last two years they realized, had been a mixed experience. Advances as well as setbacks.

Only when they had coffee after the meal, they came back to the case. They had to look at Stollberg's article. Ulrike took the article out of her bag and shared it with Bill, who tried to figure out its meaning. After a few minutes he gave up.

"Sorry, this is too difficult for me, although it's in English," he exclaimed.

Ulrike sighed: "I 'm not getting much out of it either. Clearly, we need an expert to tell us more about the content. But maybe we can figure out at least the direction of Stollberg's research."

"Do you think there is a change?" Bill asked, looking at Ulrike.

"That is the really important question. Isn't it," she replied, "It appears to be about human processing of food under different conditions. That seems to be close enough to the work KreuzbergChem did in its early years. But in this article the term insulin comes up several times. Do you think that this is meaningful?"

Bill seemed to be lost in thought, then he said: "Yes, I think it could be relevant for our case. Remember, Alerta is a pharma company. Maybe they are getting involved in the development of a new insulin."

Ulrike looked surprised: "Could that mean that KreuzbergChem was shifting its research to pharma projects?"

Bill took a sip of his coffee before he answered: "If our guess is correct, we have an explanation of Alerta's interest in KreuzbergChem and specifically in Stollberg. His research was for some reason of interest to our American friends. It's an interesting hypothesis, however at this point no more than that. We need more facts before we can follow this lead."

Ulrike had become very excited: "Of course, we need a better reading of this article, but I have the feeling that we are moving in the right direction. I will try tomorrow to find an expert at the newspaper."

"Great, Ulrike, I'm grateful for your support. Let's call it a day," Bill said, taking Ulrike's hand, "this was a wonderful meal. I wouldn't have found this place in a million years."

Ulrike laughed: "True, this place is not in the tourist guides, at least not yet."

Ulrike dropped Bill off at the Brandenburger Hof where he briefly checked for mail at the front desk. It was a different clerk who answered his question. He was relieved to learn that there was nothing for him. He meant to ask the clerk about the private detective from Frankfurt, then he decided to postpone this question until tomorrow morning when there was a familiar face. He would write a brief email to Hinchcroft and then retire. It had been a long day.

CHAPTER 4

The following morning Hauptkommissarin Charlotte Herberg made a critical decision. When she arrived in her office at 8:30, she made an appointment with Kriminalrat Hartmut Sieverts, her supervisor. Because she claimed that the matter was urgent, she received fifteen minutes on his calendar later the same morning. It had not been an easy decision, since what she had to report would interfere with the business of another department. She had learned in her fifteen-year career that such interference should be avoided if possible at all, especially when it would throw an unfavorable light on the work of colleagues. When she had talked to her friend and old mentor Bernd Moeller the night before, the Stollberg case had come up and she had asked for his advice. He was a generation older and was now retired after forty-five years with the Hamburg police. Charlotte had always thought very highly of him, initially as an experienced older colleague and teacher whose seminars she had attended as a young police officer in Kiel, more recently as a close friend. She appreciated his prudent judgment. He was rational and circumspect without being distant and cold. She always thought that he had been the best teacher she ever had. Now he was retired, a widower with two grown daughters, one of them in Australia. It was obvious that after his retirement he was a bit lonely, looking for things to keep him busy. Because of his keen interest in opera, he came to Berlin occasionally for outstanding production at the Staatsoper or the Deutsche Oper. He made a point of looking Charlotte up, which she, to her own surprise, had encouraged. She felt very comfortable in his presence. There was no pressure, like being with a father, an experience that she had not known in her childhood. She had even accompanied him several times to the opera after the separation from Ernst. She felt respected in her work, which was really important to her, and accepted as a person. It was obvious that he liked her. How much? She was not certain and was not eager to push anything. During the last year they had become closer without emphasizing the shift. He had come to her apartment for dinner, and it had hardly been a step when he had stayed overnight. She still thought of him as a close friend, and it was clear to her that he did the same. He never made claims or expressed expectations. Charlotte was comfortable with this situation, closeness but no formal commitment. She was actually happier now than in her relationship with Ernst that was supposed to lead to marriage and family. Neither she nor he had ever felt quite comfortable with this expectation expressed by relatives and friends. And she had resented the hope of Ernst's mother that one day she would give up her career in favor of motherhood and family. Sometimes she had mocked Herbert's mother as a full-time wife, assuming her husband's title as "Landgerichtsdirektorin", a move that Ernst had deeply resented, although he admitted that it was apt and funny.

When Charlotte had mentioned the Stollberg case in their last phone conversation, Bernd Moeller had sensed quickly that there was more than a case with unusual circumstances. He had asked Charlotte to explain the details before he responded to her request for advice. He had spoken in a low voice without claiming any authority in the matter. He had simply pointed out that, given the additional information coming from Bill McDonald, the circumstances of the death were suspicious, the possibility of foul play likely, if the American detective could be trusted, which Charlotte had strongly confirmed. Under these circumstances, a police investigation was called for--whatever the colleagues believed. "If I were you," Moeller had calmly said, "I would report this case to my superior officer." Then he had moved to a different topic, telling her about the new production of "The Marriage of Figaro" at the Komische Oper that he was planning to see. She had been very pleased because it meant that they would see each other in

Berlin in the near future. This conversation had been crucial for her decision the next morning.

At 11:00 sharp Charlotte entered Sievert's office. The secretary hardly gave her a nod, asking her to take a seat without announcing her presence to the boss. It was obvious that she did not like Charlotte and would try to make her appointment as difficult and unpleasant as possible. Charlotte was familiar with this treatment, but decided to keep quiet, since she wanted Sievert's full attention for the Stollberg case rather than the manners of his secretary who had worked for him for a long time and whose loyalty he appreciated. A few minutes later Sievert opened the door to his inner office and asked Charlotte to come in.

"Good to see you, Ms. Herberg, how have you been?" he said, pointing to a chair next to his desk, "it will be a brief meeting because I have a court appointment at 11:30. Please tell me what needs my attention."

Charlotte knew that in this situation she had to be as focused and rational as possible. He was a good listener with a good grasp for details. She gave him a summary of the events that led to the death of Herwig Stollberg and briefly developed the context, which suggested that the death was not just an accident. Sievert had looked at her while listening. Then he asked a number of pointed questions, which told Charlotte that he had immediately grasped the complicated nature of the case.

Finally, he said: "This looks indeed like a suspicious death. There are however too many uncertain or unknown elements to state that this is a murder case, but I agree with you that we can't simply wait until the driver is accidentally found. We need an investigation. Please follow the leads and report back tomorrow or the day after."

After giving her a nod that concluded the meeting, he ordered his secretary to get his car ready, leaving the room through a backdoor.

As short as the meeting had been, it had been a complete success. Charlotte had what she wanted: green light for the first phase of an investigation. She knew that she had to bring more facts before Sievert would approve a full investigation or a special team, a SOKO. When she returned to her office, she called Werner Kraft in to brief him. His face told her that he was very pleased with the outcome of the meeting.

"Great," he said, "now we can do something to get to the bottom of this case. I will contact Bill McDonald. This is good news for him, as well."

Bill was on the way to the dining car of the express train to Frankfurt when he received Werner Kraft's call. The latter was completely surprised to learn that Bill was on the way to Frankfurt.

"What's going on?" he asked.

"This morning I found out that the man in the picture was indeed a guest at the Brandenburger Hof on the day of the accident. He had checked in the night before and left the same day in the early afternoon."

"How did you find out?" Kraft wanted to know.

"I asked the waitress this morning at breakfast. I had talked to her before and she confirmed his presence at the hotel. I decided spontaneously to follow up by talking to him in person. He can tell me more about the Alerta side. What did they want from Stollberg?"

For a moment there was silence, then Bill heard Kraft's voice again: "Do you really believe that. He will just tell you want you want to know?"

"No, not immediately and directly," Bill admitted, "but my hope is that some of his remarks will give me a better understanding of the whole affair. After all, we are working for the same side."

"Sometime I wonder, Bill, if this is really the case." Kraft replied. "You are, it seems, ultimately reporting to Alerta but not working together or even expected to know of each other."

"Werner, this is what I want to change. We should be working together."

Bill heard Kraft's voice: "Good luck, keep me posted. By the way, and this is the reason for my call, as of now we are investigating Stollberg's accident as a suspicious death. Which means, we will see more of each other."

"This is definitely good news."

"This feeling is shared," Kraft responded, "keep us posted from Frankfurt."

While he was talking, Bill had reached the dining car. He even found an empty table and asked for the menu when a waiter approached. Bill loved German high-speed trains. Whenever there was a chance he used them instead of flying. Since this train was almost booked out, he decided to travel first class, which definitely increased the pleasure of the ride: the smoothness of the train's movement, the elegance and neatness of the cars, not to mention the comfort of the seats and the service in the dining car. Even the firm click of the automatic doors when they closed at the station was special, a noise that promised a controlled adventure.

When Bill had learned that the man in the picture had been a guest at the hotel, his first idea was a phone call. However, he soon changed his mind, when he thought about the nature of the conversation. He is not going to tell me much on the phone, Bill mused. I have to encounter him in person, see his face when I mention names and ask pointed questions. I have to look him up in Frankfurt. With a bit of luck, I can be back late tonight. Now it was early afternoon, which gave him enough time to get to Walter Kellner's office before 3:00pm. Bill had barely finished his omelet when the loudspeaker announced that the train was approaching Frankfurt. He quickly moved back to his car to collect his things. Minutes later the train moved swiftly into the station. It took Bill a while to orient himself, since this was the first time for him to arrive in Frankfurt. He rushed as quickly as possible to the exit, looking for a sign that would lead him to a taxi stand. The dense passenger traffic inside the large hall slowed him down more than he had expected. It took him a good ten minutes until he sat in a taxi on his way to Kellner's office. All he knew from Werner Kraft was that the office was located in the Westend, part of a tall building in which an international bank was located. The driver had promised Bill to choose the fastest route when he had told him that he was in a hurry. Fifteen minutes later he stood in front of the tall glass tower, looking for the detective's office. He walked around the building until he found the entrance, which was modest without giving the impression of being second class. To the contrary, everything about the firm suggested wealthy clients, mostly corporations.

When Bill opened the heavy metal door, he found himself in a large, elegantly furnished room. At the reception desk he was greeted by a young man in a suit and a tie who was eager to assist him. Bill pulled out his business card and introduced himself, asking to speak to the boss. Bill was disappointed to hear that Herr Kellner was not available, but he could speak to his associate. Although he doubted that the associate would be able to help him, he accepted the offer and was shown into a smaller office at the end of the room. Here he was greeted by a man in his thirties, also elegantly dressed, who looked at him with a gaze that expressed surprise and skepticism. Bill didn't show his irritation, he only mentioned his firm and explained in somewhat vague terms why he wanted to see Herr Kellner. It was obvious that the associate did not get the connection. When Bill casually mentioned Alerta the man did not recognize the link, at least this was Bill's impression.

"The senior lawyer of my firm, Mr. Amos Hinchcroft, has asked me to speak to Herr Kellner in person," Bill said in German, knowing that he was on thin ice, both in linguistic and personal terms. His opposite immediately grasped Bill's problem and switched to English, which for Bill was both a relief and an embarrassment. He had to work on his German, if he wanted to operate successfully in this country. But, of course, a visit every two years would not be enough.

"I am sorry, Mr. McDonald," said the young man, "Herr Kellner decided to take the afternoon off. Private matters, I understand. Of course, I would be more than happy to assist you in any way I can."

Bill realized that he would not get the answers he needed in this office. He promised to be back tomorrow when the boss would be available and took his leave. When he left the office the skeptical gaze of the associate followed him. It seemed that he had not quite looked the part of the security chief of a respectable New York law firm. German dress code! Were I to stay in this country, I would have to adjust, Bill thought. However, the real question for him at this moment was the next step. He had also Kellner's private address. Should he attempt to force a meeting at the private home or come back tomorrow morning? He checked his watch and realized that there was still time to get to the residence before dark. Kellner lived in Bad Homburg, a place he was not familiar with. With the help of his smart phone he found out that a visit to Bad Homburg would be a substantial trip, either by train or by car. He was not in the mood for wasting precious time by using the public transportation system. Instead, he used his Uber app. Minutes later he was on his way to Bad Homburg. As it turned out, the driver lived in Bad Homburg as well and was more than happy to tell Bill more about the history and the present situation of the small town. To own a place in Bad Homburg meant, he was told, that you were well-to-do. This information confirmed Bill's impression at the office. Herr Kellner was not a man of small means. His house, obviously built rather recently, was located outside the old center, surrounded by other houses that looked rather similar, brick buildings with large windows, surrounded by a lawn and single mature trees. After paying the driver, Bill walked to the front door and rang the bell. There was no response. After a few minutes he tried again. The result was the same. Was the entire, fairly expensive trip in vain? Bill was not ready to give up. He wanted to make sure that Kellner was actually not at home. He walked around the house, looking through the windows. When he reached the backside of the house, he made an unsettling discovery. The glass door to the living room was not locked. It yielded to the pressure of his hand when he tried to knock.

Bill stepped back and announced his presence to the invisible owner. There was no answer. He repeated the call several times, waiting for a response. Then he slowly and cautiously stepped into the large living room. This was not good, Bill thought, it could well mean trouble. But he continued his search for the owner, calling his name. The living room was elegantly furnished, mostly modern Scandinavian pieces and expensive oriental rugs. It would be wiser to withdraw, instead, Bill moved forward, slowly and cautiously. The house seemed to be empty. Nobody in the hallway. The door of the adjacent room stood partly open. Using his right hand, Bill pushed the door wide open. It was then that he caught a glimpse of something on the floor, a shoe, it seemed. Bill moved into the study, every muscle tense, his eyes focused on the desk. He got closer, then he saw the body on the floor, the back partly leaning against the large desk. Bill needed a few seconds to adjust his position. He looked around. There was only the body and he himself. He kneeled to get a better look. The drawers of the desk were partly open, papers covered the floor. There was a strong box that had been forced open. There could be no doubt: the man was dead, hit by several bullets. And there could be no doubt that the man on the floor was the private detective who was seen at the funeral. He had come too late.

I have to call the police, Bill told himself. This is not going to be pretty. He would have to explain what he was doing in the house. He might even be treated as a suspicious person who had to be questioned. This would definitely happen in New York City. He would have to reveal his mission in Berlin, which had brought him to Frankfurt. Amos Hinchcroft would disapprove of such confessions. He was about to call 911 when he realized that he was not at home. What was the proper number here? He searched his memory. Ulrike had told him. What was it again? It came back to him: 110. He pressed the numbers. Then he heard a male voice asking for his name and address. He gave his name and the address, speaking in English, reporting what he had found. The police officer responded in English, asking him to stay at the scene.

"Stay were you are, sir, do not touch anything. Police officers will be there shortly."

A few minutes later Bill heard the siren of the approaching police car, the noise increased until the car stopped in front of the house. Then Bill heard the steps of the approaching police officers. He waited for them in the living room, two uniformed officers. He had his passport and his identification as a licensed private detective ready for them.

One of them asked: "Where is the body?"

Bill pointed to the study. One of them moved into the room while the other one stayed in his vicinity, obviously keeping an eye on him. Bill grabbed a chair and sat down. He knew what the next steps would be. The uniformed officers would call the police station to ask for the detectives and the forensic team. He realized that this process could take hours, the detectives would have plenty of questions. He would be lucky if they let him go. More likely, they would ask him to come with them to the police station. At this moment he noticed the vibration of his phone. It was a message from Ulrike, asking him where he was, mentioning that she had briefly talked to Dorothea Stollberg. There would be an interview later. Ulrike's text only said: "Very interesting news, will talk to you later."

The forensic team showed up half an hour later. They immediately started their work, asking Bill to leave the living room after he had told them how he had entered the house and where he had been. He and one of the uniformed officers moved to the kitchen, while the other one stood guard in front of the house. When Bill made an effort to answer Ulrike's message the officer told him not to use his phone until the detectives had spoken to him. Bill decided to comply, since he knew that resistance would only complicate his already complicated situation. He had to persuade the detectives that his presence in the house did not mean that he was involved in the murder.

When the detectives finally arrived, it was late afternoon. Once more, Bill answered their questions: Who he was and why he had entered the house. He explained his assignment without going into much detail. He wanted the officers to understand that he had a legitimate reason to come to Bad Homburg in order to speak with Kellner. From the point of his investigation, it was the Frankfurt private detective at the funeral who was suspicious. The older one of the two, a man in his fifties, remained skeptical. He was not persuaded by Bill's narrative. Bill encouraged him to contact his law firm to verify his story, but the officer, who conducted the conversation in German, was not interested in calling New York. The younger officer, a woman in her thirties, switched to English when she realized that Bill's command of German was limited. She was quite fluent in English, although with a strong German accent. She wanted to know more about his contact with the police in Berlin and suggested to her colleague to call the colleagues in Berlin. However, the older detective didn't follow this suggestion, asking Bill instead to accompany him to the police station once they were done with the local scene. Bill got increasingly irritated, since he realized that the senior detective did what he did, because he didn't like him. He had to control himself. Any strong response would just make his situation worse. They might even keep him overnight. When the leader of the forensic team told the detectives that the man had died approximately between 2pm and 3pm, Bill felt relieved. He could prove without much difficulty that he had not been in the house at that time. Both the guy at the office in Frankfurt and the driver of the Uber car could testify. Still, just to find the driver would take time.

As Bill had suspected, the detectives asked him to come with them to the police station. When Bill showed his frustration, the woman tried to calm him down by suggesting that the request was more a formality than anything else. They would do a proper report, she used the word "Protokoll," and then he would be free to go. But at the police station he saw himself confronted with more police officers who had questions about his stay in Germany and his background. Bill tried to be as patient as possible, answering these questions, demonstrating his willingness to cooperate. But he realized that these questions had little to do with the murder in Bad Homburg, they related to something much bigger that he could not fully grasp. Several times he heard the word LKA. He remembered that this was the abbreviation for criminal investigations at the state level, in short, the big stuff. By now it was 7:00pm and still no sign that he would be released. Still, the tone had changed. He was treated with more respect, like a witness rather than as suspect. He was even offered coffee, which he gladly accepted because his energy was running low. Also, he needed to get some food. When he requested something to eat, the younger female detective brought him a ham and cheese sandwich.

"It's not very fresh, she said with a shrug, "it's the best we can do right now. They want you to look at pictures before you can go."

Another half hour passed. Then two officers entered the room with a folder holding shots of men. They placed them in front of Bill.

"Have you seen any of these men in the vicinity of the house?" one of them asked.

Bill pushed the plate aside focusing on the photographs. Initially they looked just strange. Then, he recognized the man in one of the shots. He had seen him at the funeral in Berlin. He was not absolutely sure, but a similarity was certainly there. When Bill informed the officers of his opinion, they seemed not to be surprised. But they didn't tell Bill how his statement was fitting into their investigation. They just wanted to know whether he knew Charlotte Herberg.

"Yes, I do," Bill replied without elaborating what the connection might be.

"We have been in touch with her," the older of the two said, "she called us this morning to find out who Walter Kellner was and what his business in Berlin might have been. This was of course before he was killed. By the way, she also mentioned you and your investigation."

Bill decided just to acknowledge the statement by a nod.

"So, you came to Frankfurt to talk to Kellner?" One of the officers asked him.

"That's correct," Bill replied.

"Can you elaborate," the other one said in a low voice.

"Gladly, Kellner was the contact for Stollberg at the Brandenburger Hof meeting that didn't happen because of the accident. Then he showed up at the Stollberg funeral. I wanted to know what the purpose of the meeting was and why he made an appearance at the funeral."

The first officer nodded before he asked: "Do you have any idea what the purpose of the meeting was?"

"Actually, I don't. I have no factual knowledge."

"Isn't that strange that you have been sent to Berlin to investigate the accident without any information about the purpose of the meeting?"

"Yes," Bill agreed, "when I arrived in Berlin I didn't even know that Kellner was the contact."

"It must have been unpleasant to be sent on a mission with no background info."

Bill just shrugged his shoulders. Not knowing much about the purpose of this conversation, he decided to give as little information as possible. They are trying to find out how much I know. Maybe I will get some information from them if I play along, he thought.

"Why do you think Kellner showed up at the funeral?" the second officer wanted to know.

"I meant to ask him this very question. Maybe he wanted to talk to a family member or a partner? I don't know. I have no idea if he succeeded."

"What do you know about the company, KreuzbergChem?"

"What I could find on a website, but not enough to help me with my search. Do you believe that the company is part of this case?" Bill asked.

"Yes, we do," replied the first officer, "definitely, but at present we don't know how. Is it a product or a service that has become valuable and who might be interested enough to eliminate one of the partners?"

Bill added: "And who is ready to eliminate a contact man who must have important information?"

"Good question," the other officer replied, "you know what bothers me about this case is that the pieces don't fit properly. The players don't do what they are supposed to do. Take this murder. Someone comes to his house looking for information and then kills him. But he probably didn't have the crucial information in the first place because the contact between Stollberg and Kellner failed."

"Maybe the killer didn't know this?" Bill suggested, "or he believed that Stollberg had left the information at another place where Kellner found it when he returned to Berlin."

"This looks like a dead end," said the first officer, looking at Bill, "you mean to go back to Frankfurt?"

"Can you give me a ride?" Bill asked.

"Sorry, no, we are on the way to Wiesbaden. But we can drop you off at the train station."

Half an hour later, Bill found himself in an S-Bahn on the way to Frankfurt. There were numerous messages from Ulrike on his phone. They became increasingly more concerned. When he called her, she picked up right away.

"Bill, where are you? Why didn't you answer my messages this afternoon?"

"I'm on the way from Bad Homburg to Frankfurt."

"Bad Homburg? What on earth are you doing in Bad Homburg?"

"That's a long and complicated story."

"OK, tell me. Still no reason not to answer messages,"

"When you are questioned at a police station you don't get to answer messages. I was trying to persuade the local police that I didn't kill Walter Kellner."

"Kellner was killed? When did this happen?"

"It happened this afternoon, but I don't know why"

"And why did the police think that you were the killer?"

"Because I found him dead in his house and called the cops. It was the right thing to do, but it still looked suspicious to the detectives who investigated the case."

"O Bill, you poor man, but now you are a free man again?"

"Yes, I am. On the way to Frankfurt where I mean to stay tonight and then take an early train tomorrow morning."

Ulrike gave him the name of a decent hotel in the neighborhood of the central station.

"It's clean and the rates are reasonable," Ulrike said, "See you tomorrow, give me a ring when you are back. By the way, there have been changes in Berlin as well. Charlotte has been asked to put together a special team and I have an appointment with Dorothea Stollberg. She wants to talk about her ex. Sweet dreams."

Then Ulrike's voice was gone. But there was a message from Werner Kraft, confirming what Ulrike just told him: Charlotte Herberg had been asked to form a special team, a SOKO, and she invited him to attend the preliminary meeting tomorrow at 9:00. This was good news. Bill sent him a message explaining why he would be unable to be at the meeting. "I will be in touch as soon as I am back in Berlin," he wrote. All of a sudden, things are moving, Bill thought. And the case is getting bigger. What started out as a suspicious accident has become the investigation of two murders, involving Berlin, Bad Homburg, and the LKA of the state of Hesse. Not all of that would find its way into his report to Hinchcroft that he would have to compose later. He decided to mention the extension of his search to Frankfurt and the untimely death of the German detective without going into the stay at the police station and the conversation with the LKA men. Too many unknown elements for a concise and positive report. Was he closer to a solution? He could not possibly say that. For a brief moment, he was considering to take a late train to Berlin in order to be at the meeting with Charlotte Herberg, but he decided against this move. He needed rest and time to reflect. As much as he might gain from the police investigation, his own search had a different goal. It was the missing file that he was expected to find.

When his train arrived at the central station Bill looked for a restaurant to get something to eat. What he found in the main hall turned out to be pretty decent, fairly noisy but clean. He ordered a large bowl of lentil soup with sausages and a beer. He got out his computer to have a look at his notes. How did the events at Kellner's house fit into the big picture? The body had been in front of the desk. The right door of the desk was open. The strong box had been broken open. Did the intruder expect to find the file in the box and was surprised by Kellner? Or had Kellner opened the box and got surprised by the intruder? Only the forensic team could decide that question. In any case, it appeared that the forces that were trying to take possession of Stollberg's file, whoever they were, had not succeeded in Berlin. They must have assumed that Kellner got the file after all and therefore searched his house. Two persons were killed in order to obtain the file. The stakes were extremely high. He had to get closer to the surviving partners of KreuzbergChem, as soon as he got back to Berlin. He had to find out what exactly the company was working on. And why did Brindisi act so strangely at the funeral? He had to find an indirect way, since it was not likely that they would just tell him. Could he pretend to be a journalist who was interested in the project of this start-up? The problem was that he didn't have the science background to play this role. But maybe a journalist interested in the financial aspect? How are German start-ups doing in their search for international capital? That could possibly work. Maybe together with Ulrike. Of course, there was also the official police investigation under the care of Charlotte Herberg. It would begin tomorrow. The more Bill thought about this side of the case the more he worried about the meeting tomorrow morning. I really have to be there, he thought, I cannot afford to miss the first meeting. He changed his mind and after taking care of the check, he walked back in the direction of the tracks. There he checked a schedule, which told him that the next high-speed train would leave in half an hour. Using that train, he would be back in Berlin by 12:30. Six hours of sleep, that would be enough. He boarded the train, which was fairly empty, and settled down in a compartment where it would be quiet.

CHAPTER 5

Checking her watch, Ulrike Pfanner realized that she was late, when she left her office to meet with Dorothea Stollberg. They had agreed on a small café close to the train station Friedenau where they could talk quietly. Dorothea Stollberg had suggested this place because it was close to her school and also very close to the S-Bahn, which would allow Ulrike to leave her car at home. But it had not worked out that way. Ulrike wanted to reach Charlotte Herberg early in the morning, before the first meeting of the new group would get together. As it turned out, Charlotte was already busy preparing the meeting and didn't have much time when she finally returned the call. At least, Ulrike had a few minutes to reconnect and explain that she was involved in the Stollberg case and might well be able to provide useful information, with the understanding that the police would keep Ulrike informed of the progress of the investigation. She wanted Charlotte to know that she was planning an interview with Klein and Brindisi to explore the background of the case, especially the financial aspect of the start-up company. Ulrike hadn't mentioned the interview with Dorothea Stollberg in this conversation. She wanted to have more specific information before she was ready to share. When she first met Dorothea Stollberg in front of the school building where she had been waiting to approach her, she had not expected to get much out of her and she was surprised about her first reaction. It had been anger, almost rage. Dorothea Stollberg was clearly very upset, not only about Herwig Stollberg but also about his family. And she was willing to talk about it. Ulrike had proposed a meeting, which

Dorothea Stollberg had spontaneously accepted. Because of the phone call with Charlotte, Ulrike had arrived late at her office, trying to catch up the rest of the morning. Now it was too late for using public transportation. She rushed to her small Fiat, hoping that the traffic would not be too bad. Initially, she was lucky. It took her no more than fifteen minutes to reach Friedenau, but then she lost more time than she had expected to find a parking place. When she finally entered the café, she saw Stollberg at a small table checking her watch. I have to be extra-friendly, Ulrike told herself, to keep her motivated to talk. If she is in a bad mood already, this is going to fall apart.

"I am so very pleased to meet with you," Ulrike exclaimed, giving the waiting woman a big smile, "finding a parking space is really a major task in this area."

"I had warned you," Dorothea Stollberg replied, "the S-Bahn is much more efficient."

Her voice was cool and somewhat distant. Ulrike grabbed a chair, while focusing her eyes on Dorothea Stollberg. It was obvious that this meeting needed an immediate turn or it would have a negative outcome.

"You may be interested to hear," said Ulrike in a low voice, moving closer to Dorothea Stollberg, "that there will be a full-scale police investigation of your husband's death."

"Ex," replied Dorothea in a low voice as well, "definitely ex; we were separated and I was in the process of divorcing him when he died."

"As I found out this morning, the car accident was probably not an accident. The police assume now that there was a successful plot to kill Herwig Stollberg. Do you think the police got it right? Why would anyone kill your ex? I mean he was a chemist and the co-owner of a successful small company."

Dorothea Stollberg took a sip of her coffee before she answered: "I don't know the facts and you are right. Typically, chemists don't lead a very dangerous lives, but in the case of Herwig Stollberg it strikes me as possible."

"Why?" Ulrike wanted to know. The conversation had taken the right turn. Now Ulrike had to make sure that Frau Stollberg would continue to talk.

"His life was so screwed up, you know, so totally screwed up that such an outcome seems fitting."

"What do you mean by screwed up?" Ulrike asked lowering her voice.

Dorothea Stollberg put her cup down and looked at Ulrike. For some time, she remained silent. Finally, she said: "I have to be sure that you will not print this. His family would be after me. They might even sue me. Once I decided to divorce Herwig, they broke off all contact. In their eyes, I was the guilty party."

"Yes, you can be sure. This is off the record. Deep background."

Dorothea Stollberg nodded: "OK, under these conditions I am willing to explain the situation. At this moment, I am responsible for a debt of 900,000 Euro, money that my ex owes, partly to our bank, in part to individuals."

"How did this happen? Did you know this when he was still alive?"

"I knew that there were serious problems. We had exhausted our line of credit at the bank. Herwig told me that it was for our business, but I didn't believe it because these things would be handled by David Klein and when I asked David he was quite surprised. Then there were strange phone calls that he wanted to hide from me. Our life became quite weird. Sometimes he didn't come home or came home very late, without a good explanation where he had been. Once I was accosted by a man in the street who told me that we had to pay or we would be in big trouble."

"This sounds horrible," interjected Ulrike.

"Believe me, it was. I couldn't believe what had happened to our marriage in a short time. Finally, I confronted him. It turned out that he had been gambling and owed a lot of money. Of course, I got very angry and accused him of recklessness. We were fighting most of the time. It became unbearable and I moved out."

Ulrike was stunned, then she took Dorothea Stollberg's hands: "My god, I am so sorry."

"It took me a while to regain my balance. Fortunately, I had friends who were there for me, because the Stollberg family became quite hostile when I moved out."

"Really, why?"

"They expected me to stay with him, to be the supportive wife., etc. Instead, I started divorce procedures, once I realized that I shared his debt. I wanted to get out."

"What is your financial situation right now?" Ulrike wanted to know.

Dorothea Stollberg replied: "He died before the divorce became final, which means that I'm still part of the mess. I don't have the money to pay the creditors. As you know, I'm a high school teacher, biology and math."

"Are you aware that your ex was ever threatened by his creditors and made efforts to pay back the money he owed?" Ulrike asked.

"Frankly, I don't know," Dorothea Stollberg replied, "as long as we lived together, he seemed to be mostly depressed and passive. Maybe he tried to do something later. Some of his creditors were certainly aggressive and threatening. Do you think one of them finally killed him?"

"That was the point of my question," said Ulrike.

"What a horrible thought," Dorothea Stollberg whispered, "he was weak and addicted to gambling, but he didn't deserve that."

"How long have you known each other?"

"We met at the Free University here in Berlin. He studied chemistry with a minor in biology. I was a biology major with a minor in chemistry. I always wanted to be a teacher, while he planned to look for a research position."

"So, there was quite a bit of overlap in interest," Ulrike mused, while she finally had a chance to waive to the waitress, "that must have been a strong tie, I guess?"

Dorothea remained silent for a while, then she said: "Yes, in the beginning, but later not so much. School, you know is so different from a lab."

Ulrike wanted to shift the focus of the conversation to Stollberg's research in order to get more information about the purpose of the meeting at the Brandenburger Hof. Thus, she tried again: "If he wanted to pay back the money he owed, how could he possibly raise such a large amount? As you mentioned, his line of credit at the bank was overdrawn. Could he possibly sell his research results? Do you have an idea what he was working on?"

For a moment, Dorothea Stollberg stared at Ulrike, then she said: "I used to know, at least in broad terms. Sometimes he and Stefano Brindisi would discuss critical issues at our apartment. They were friends. More recently, this didn't happen. I had the feeling their relationship had changed, but I don't know how and why. When they started out, their focus was food and food processing, but about two years ago there was a shift. I believe it was primarily my ex who wanted to change the field. He wanted to do medical research."

"Was this about money?"

"Since you mention it. I think money was at least part of the reason. But at that point I didn't realize that he needed money for his gambling habit. I was completely blind..."

There were tears in her eyes. I have to be cautious, Ulrike thought, I must not push her too hard or she will break down and close up. She took her hand. "Sorry, I didn't mean to open old wounds."

"It's okay," Dorothea replied drying her tears.

Ulrike gave her a friendly nod before she resumed the conversation: "There is a rumor that your ex was on the way to a meeting when he was killed, a meeting that might be linked to his research. Do you believe that this rumor could be true? Do you think that there were results of a research project that he meant to offer to someone?"

Dorothea Stollberg looked at Ulrike for a moment: "What kind of rumors? Of course, in principle. The company does applied research. Results would be offered to industry for money. But this aspect has been the job of David Klein. Herwig was, I think, a very good chemist but not good at making deals. I think the rumors got it wrong."

Ulrike decided not to pursue this line of questioning, since it was obvious that Dorothea Stollberg was unwilling to follow this lead. At the same time, Ulrike was aware that the information she just received could be interpreted very differently. Stollberg needed money desperately, he had found something the Americans wanted and he was planning to sell it to them – behind the back of his partners. Did they realize that he did not share all his work with them? Maybe someone found out and was determined that the deal should not go through. But who? Was that the reason why Brindisi acted so strangely at the funeral? But if this argument made sense, the murder of the private detective in Frankfurt did not fit well, Ulrike thought. She would have to discuss this with Bill later this afternoon. While listening to Dorothea Stollberg, it became very clear to her that she needed to know more about KreuzbergChem and its partners.

"Have you recently talked to Klein or Brindisi?" Ulrike asked.

"Maybe I should have, but I was so fed up with the whole situation, with their projects and their anxieties about getting money for their research that I withdrew, completely withdrew, I tried to rebuild my own life," Dorothea Stollberg said, "do you know what that means after investing years of your life in a common project. We have known each other for fifteen years. When our marriage fell apart, these guys did nothing, they became invisible. Why should I see them now?"

Ulrike leaned forward: "Sorry Dorothea, I didn't mean to upset you. I'm just trying to figure out what led to Stollberg's death."

"Brindisi and my ex were close friends, when I first met him they had known each other for years. Later they developed the idea of building up a small research company. David Klein came later. He joined the company when they realized that they needed an engineer and someone who was good at finding capital."

Ulrike knew that she was on thin ice but she wanted to ask this question:

"Do you believe there was a falling out between your ex and Brindisi?"

"I have no idea. Herwig never mentioned anything and I haven't seen Brindisi for a while. All I know is that they started a new project a year ago, maybe eighteen months. Listen, I have to go. I told you what I know and I don't want to relive this stuff. It hurts."

She stood abruptly up and moved over to the waitress getting out her wallet to pay for the coffee. Ulrike needed a moment to grasp the sudden turn then she followed Dorothea Stollberg to thank her for the interview. She felt sorry for this woman whose life had been messed up by a succession of events that she still didn't really understand.

In a low voice she said: "What we talked about is off the record, you can be sure, and, by the way, if the creditors harass you again, you should contact the police."

Dorothea Stollberg just nodded turning around and left the room. Ulrike returned to the table and sat down. She needed time to process what she had heard. She got her laptop out and ordered another latte. Then she tried to call Charlotte Herberg, but there was no answer. Her attempt to reach Bill McDonald was no more successful. They must be in the meeting, she thought.

It was almost noon when Charlotte Herberg left her office and walked to the cafeteria to grab a bite. The first meeting of the new SOKO had been a disappointment, she felt. It began with Werner Kraft's call that he woke up with a bad cold and had to stay home. This was irritating, since she was used to his presence at meetings where he took care of the organizational stuff, making sure that the various parties were properly instructed and followed up on their assignments. Then came the news that a colleague on whose presence she had counted was replaced by someone whom she didn't trust. Still, as expected, she had outlined the task and set up the components. The first thing was the accident. The location had to be reinvestigated, all eye witnesses had to be questioned again, the medical report had to be examined once more, and the victim and his background had to be thoroughly investigated, which would include KreuzbergChem and his partners. One of the positive aspects of the meeting, she had felt, was the presence of the young American detective as an informant who talked about the American side of the story, especially the missing file and the failed meeting at the Brandenburger Hof. And of course, he had talked about the murder of the private detective in Bad Homburg. The fact that he had seen the scene of the crime had turned out to be quite useful. They all felt that this case was linked to the Stollberg case, although the exact nature of the link remained unclear. Bill had made a good impression on the group, which was important for future cooperation. And Charlotte had the feeling that this would be likely.

Once in the cafeteria, she deliberately avoided the crowd of her colleagues and, after getting her food at the counter, chose a small table at the end of the large room. She meant to return Ulrike's call, who would not have tried to contact her without offering information. She knew Ulrike: she wanted to trade. Charlotte looked at the things on her plate: meatloaf, potatoes and beans. Why did I choose this, she asked herself? Was this what she really wanted to eat? She tried the meatloaf first and was pleasantly surprised. It was better than usual. Maybe a new cook, but the potatoes were overcooked as usual and the beans tasted as if they came from a can. After trying to get excited over the meal without success, she put the plate aside and got her phone out. First, she tried Ulrike, who didn't answer. Next, she tried Bernd Moeller who had sent her a message, telling her that he would be in Berlin for the weekend. This information had kept her going during the morning when the meeting began to get lost in details. He picked up right away, greeting her with his warm voice, which instantly improved her mood.

"Where are you?" he wanted to know.

"In the cafeteria, looking at a plate filled with meatloaf, beans and potatoes that I couldn't finish."

That bad?"

"Not really, but I didn't have much of an appetite after the SOKO meeting this morning."

"What went wrong?"

"Nothing, but it wasn't a good start. Low energy."

She heard his calming voice: "Don't worry, it will change as soon as you get deeper into the investigation."

He told her that he was planning to arrive Saturday and stay until Monday. He had tickets for *The Marriage of Figaro* for Sunday night. She was glad that he proposed to go to a restaurant on Saturday night. She would enjoy good food for a change. She had found out that cooking for herself wasn't a great deal of fun. When Charlotte tried Ulrike again, she was successful. Ulrike was eager to learn more about the first meeting of the SOKO and she was particularly pleased to learn that Bill had made a good impression.

"I am really glad to hear this," said Ulrike, "I told you he would be useful for your investigation. By the way, I have not been idle myself and dug up very interesting information,"

"What?" Charlotte asked.

"Not on the phone, I promised to be discreet. Let's set up a meeting later today or tomorrow. It changes the case."

Charlotte smiled. This was not about discretion, Ulrike wanted to trade. And Charlotte was not certain that she had anything that was worth trading, since all the hot news had come from Bill McDonald. She needed time to think about the case before they met.

"Not today, Ulrike, "How about tomorrow? Lunch or coffee later in the afternoon?"

"Let's do lunch," Ulrike replied, "then I don't have to worry about conflicts. 12:15 the usual place?"

They always met at a small pizzeria close to the police headquarters, a convenient place for both of them, although the food was mediocre. Charlotte was certain that Ulrike would have valuable pieces of information, but it would take her group more time to come up with significant results. Police work takes time. Where would she invest her own energy? She had to decide. There were two pressing issues, she thought, on the one hand there was the background of the victim. Why was he killed? And then the strange connection with the murder of the private detective in Bad Homburg. What Bill had mentioned was not very clear and obviously only a fragment. One thing, however, was clear. This was more than a local case, otherwise the state police of Hesse would not be involved. This was a lead she had to follow as soon as possible. It would not be easy, since it was by no means certain that they would talk to her.

Bill stood in front of the window of his room at the Brandenburger Hof observing the dense traffic on the Kurfürstendamm. It was a gray day, light clouds but no rain. While his eyes were focused on the cars and the pedestrians, his mind was engaged with the meeting at the police headquarters. He had been surprised about the friendly reception, which differed so much from the contact two years ago when Charlotte Herberg and the officers had been rather distant. He didn't find out anything new about the case, but he learned quite a bit about German police procedures and strategies. No doubt, he had to admit, Charlotte Herberg was forceful and experienced. Still, it was not quite clear to him how they would cooperate, since he was not a good fit for her machine. I will continue my own search, he thought, and then decide when and where we will share results. He needed to plan the next move, but he was too exhausted to get serious about it. His stomach was very empty and he didn't get enough sleep between coming home very late and getting up early to get to the meeting. There had not even been enough time for a decent breakfast. During the meeting he had stayed awake by drinking a lot of coffee. Now he was just very tired. He moved over to the bed and lay down. Just for a few minutes, he thought. Within a minute he fell asleep.

It was the harsh ringtone of his phone that woke him up. It took him a few seconds before he found his phone and pressed the button.

"Are you napping again, Bill," he heard Ulrike's voice, "what 's the matter with you?"

"Come on, Ulrike, the last couple of days have been rough, not much sleep and very irregular meals. God, I'm starving. Never got lunch."

"Poor thing, shall I cook you a meal?!"

Bill resented the sarcasm: "Never mind, I'll find something to eat here. What's up?"

"We have to meet to rethink the case, Bill. I have news that changes everything."

"Really? What is the news?"

"Are you free to come to my place later?"

Bill agreed to be at her apartment by 5:00pm. Before that he had to make an important phone call. It would be difficult and possibly unpleasant but he couldn't postpone it. It couldn't be done by email. He had to call Amos Hinchcroft to inform him of the death of Walter Kellner. He had no idea whether the news of his death had already reached Alerta and from there Hinchcroft as well. If he called at

3:00pm, it would be 9:00am for the lawyer. There was time enough for a snack before that, Bill went down to the restaurant and ordered a hamburger. Good that Ulrike can't see me. She would be on my case again. What's wrong with a good Hamburger? Bill asked himself. He couldn't figure out why Ulrike disliked his taste for hamburgers.

When he was back in his room and checked his watch, it was still too early for the call. To pass the time, he took his laptop out and went over his notes once more. The Bad Homburg part was still sketchy. He would have loved to get access to the forensic report, but that was highly unlikely. Maybe Charlotte would have a way. He made a note to that effect. Where was the file? He had assumed that it never reached Kellner. That was the reason why he came back to Berlin and showed up at the funeral. But his killer must have assumed that he was in possession of the file. In that case there would have been another channel. Kellner must have found the file in Berlin and took it to his home to make it available to Alerta. The other explanation would be that the killer got it wrong. Kellner never got his hands on the file. But where was the file? Was he the only person who knew about the meeting with Kellner? Maybe Brindisi as well? I have to talk to the partners Bill thought. This is urgent, if possible before Charlotte's officers schedule a meeting.

At 3:00pm Bill called New York. He got Hinchcroft's secretary, who was very surprised to hear his voice. "Bill, how are you? Still in Berlin? You want to talk to Mr. Hinchcroft. I'll try to find him."

It took several minutes before Bill heard the lawyer's voice.

"Bill, it's you?"

"Yes, sir, I have to share important news that throws different light on our case. Maybe you have already heard from Alerta?"

"No, there is no new information from Alerta, Bill," Hinchcroft replied slightly irritated, "what is the news?"

Bill hesitated for a few seconds: "You remember the contact man at the Brandenburger Hof. He is dead. He was murdered."

Bill waited for the response. There was silence. Then Bill heard only one word: "Damned."

"His name was Walter Kellner, a private detective from Frankfurt.

The company apparently decided not to send one of their own men. Extreme caution. By now they must know, sir."

Hinchcroft sighed: "Of course, they must know by now. But they haven't informed me. We are being kept in the dark. I don't like this, Bill."

"I don't like it either, Sir," Bill replied, "right now the situation is unclear. The file is still missing. Unless you tell me otherwise, I will continue my search."

There was another pause. Then the lawyer said in a low voice: "Yes, do continue and keep me posted. I will talk with the partners about the changed situation."

That was the end of the conversation. Bill realized that Hinchcroft had been both surprised and irritated by the information. The law firm had been kept in the dark. Why was the client doing this? The whole affair was shrouded in mystery.

Bill was looking forward to the meeting with Ulrike. Just being close to her would get him out of the gloomy mood of this case. There was nothing straight forward about it, and what he needed right now was a simple task, a problem that could be solved by way of action. On the way to her apartment he made a stop at a liquor store in her neighborhood and bought a bottle of red wine. He remembered that she liked Spanish wines and chose a brand that was recommended by the store. He was better at this now than two years ago, but he knew that his knowledge of wines still left room for improvement. When he stood in front of her building and rang the bell it took a while until she responded and buzzed to open the front door. And her voice sounded strange, as if she wasn't sure whether she wanted to see him. He found the front door of her apartment open, but she was not there to greet him. He stepped inside calling her name. He heard her voice from the kitchen. She spoke in German, which was unusual, since she was aware of the limits of his knowledge of German. This didn't sound like the Ulrike he was used to. She sounded very upset. He moved to the kitchen, calling her name and holding the bottle of wine in front of him as a sign of friendly intentions. When he entered the kitchen, Ulrike was sitting at the kitchen table looking at him absent-minded.

Then she made a gesture that could be interpreted as an invitation to come in.

"How are you?" she said in German, "how was your day?"

"To be frank, it was a mixed day, some good parts and others not so good. I got a bottle of wine to enjoy the rest of the day and do some smart planning. What about you? You don't look so happy. Did something bad happen?" Bill inquired while sitting down next to her. He was still not certain that she fully realized his presence in the room. She continued to use German when she addressed him:

"Everything was fine until an hour ago. Even my boss was nice to me, which is rare. Then I got a surprise visit from Volker, which changed everything."

"Who is Volker?" Bill wanted to know.

"My baby brother. He needed money as usual. He was in some kind of trouble again. He is always in trouble. I don't know what to do."

Bill took he hands: "I'm very sorry to hear this. This is the first time you mention this younger brother. Do you think he's doing drugs and owes money?"

"I don't know," she replied in German, "he never tells me what the money is for. Usually smaller amounts, 20 or 50 Euros."

"That doesn't look like drugs, more like food."

Ulrike continued without looking at Bill: "I was so happy when he told me that he signed up with the army, a regular job with benefits. I believed that it was a promising turn. Accepting responsibility, growing up. Now this."

"What did he do?" Bill asked in a low voice, still holding Ulrike's hands.

"He just quit, he decided not to renew his contract. They wanted him to stay. He had a very good record, but he was bored with the job. The idea of moving up slowly through the ranks didn't appeal to him."

Bill nodded, waiting for Ulrike to continue. What he heard sounded strangely familiar as if she was talking about him. In his family he had been the difficult baby brother. The idea of finding reliable employment in the army with the prospect of moving up through the ranks sounded very unattractive to him as well.

"Ulrike," he said after a while, "I would have done the same. Who needs the regular structure of the army at 20 or 21?! How old is he, by the way?"

"He turned 22 three months ago."

"That's when I quit law school, which made my parents very unhappy," Bill replied with a chuckle, "I survived and now I'm gainfully employed, wondering sometimes whether it's a good job."

For the first time she looked at him pressing his hands.

Then she asked: "Can you talk to him? Maybe he listens to you?"

Bill promised that he would talk to Volker with the understanding, however, that he couldn't promise results. Bill stood up, still holding her hands tightly between his own, inviting her to stand up as well. Then he embraced her without saying anything.

Finally, she said: "Let's get something to eat. It's nice that you brought wine. How about pizza? There is a good store close by. We can just order and have it delivered in twenty minutes."

Ulrike had switched to English, which Bill interpreted as a sign that the immediate crisis was over. He opened the bottle of wine and poured her a glass, while she was on the phone to order the pizza.

The rest of the evening worked out better than expected. They finished the pizza with another glass of wine. Bill volunteered to use the new coffee machine to brew a cup of strong coffee and Ulrike discovered some chocolate cookies, which transitioned them to the Stollberg case.

"What is the big news you mentioned?" Bill wanted to know.

"It's Stollberg's financial situation. He owed a lot of money," Ulrike said.

"How do you know this?" Bill asked.

"I interviewed Dorothea Stollberg, his ex. She was in the process of divorcing him because of his heavy gambling debts. This guy needed money fast to keep his creditors calm. And, according to Dorothea, he didn't have a big savings account. This throws new light on the meeting at the Brandenburger Hof. My guess is that he was planning to sell part of his recent research to Alerta and somebody didn't like that idea."

"Wow," said Bill, looking at Ulrike, who was sitting next to him on the couch, "this could mean that the missing file is about the research results that Stollberg offered to Alerta. The question is: Did the partners know about this move? My guess is that they didn't."

"I agree," interjected Ulrike grabbing another cookie, maybe they found out and decided to stop the transaction. Bill, this means there is another group of suspicious men. Klein and Brindisi could have lost a lot of money if the deal had gone through."

"But what about the Mafia guys and the murder of the detective in Frankfurt?" Bill asked. "How do these events fit into the larger picture?"

"No idea," she muttered, "tell me more about the murder in Bad Homburg."

Bill gave her a more detailed report about his trip to Frankfurt and Bad Homburg. Now it was Ulrike who was holding his hand, asking questions about details. Especially, she wanted to know more about the officers who were connected with the LKA, explaining the relevance of their presence to Bill:

"Their involvement means organized crime," Ulrike exclaimed. "They probably suspect that the Kellner murder was somehow related to a larger investigation, most likely organized crime. That's why the shots of the Mafia guys were important to them."

Bill got up pacing up and down in the room. "But that link would not point to Klein and Brindisi", he exclaimed raising his hands. Or do you suspect that their company is a front for the Mafia?"

Ulrike chuckled: "That would be an incredible story. Berlin start-up is Mafia front! No, I don't think so."

Bill stopped pacing looking at Ulrike: "Okay, not likely, but not totally out of the question. What is Brindisi's background?"

"Bill, come on, we are not in New York City. This is Berlin!"

"Still, the way I see it," Bill said with emphasis, "we have to know more about the financial side of KreuzbergChem? Do you have sources?"

Ulrike thought for a while before she replied: "I will talk to my colleagues who cover economic news. But we should talk to them as soon as possible. I'll request an interview tomorrow morning."

"Can you somehow include me?" Bill asked. "An American freelance journalist who is interested in German start-ups. How does that sound?"

"Not bad, I could try that."

Ulrike got up as well, picking up plates and glasses. Bill turned around and helped her. In the kitchen he started putting the dirty dishes into the dishwasher. He was almost finished when he heard Ulrike's voice calling him from the bedroom. He closed the dishwasher firmly and followed her voice.

CHAPTER 6

Charlotte Herberg sat in silence next to Werner Kraft in an unmarked police car, an older Mercedes model, on their way to Herwig Stollberg's family. Kraft knew when to start a conversation, and this was not one of those moments. Obviously, she was lost in her own thoughts, hardly noticing the streets and the dense traffic surrounding them. They had an appointment at 10am and Kraft was getting concerned that they would be late for the interview. Charlotte seemed not to care. The entire investigation was not progressing the way she had hoped. The reexamination of the accident had not resulted in much useful information. And there was still no definitive information about the driver. The only positive piece was the general identification of the vehicle. A camera installed at a store on the opposite side of the street had the image of a small grey van making a right turn at the time of the accident. Unfortunately, the image was not sharp enough to identify the license plate. But it narrowed down the search and they had a clue what kind of driver they were looking for. The process of interviewing the eye witnesses again turned out more time-consuming than expected. The more time passed the less the witnesses would remember. She needed the details that might help them figure out whether it was an accident or a deliberate hit. They worked with the assumption that it was a hit, but there was no proof that would satisfy a prosecutor. Our case remains murky and frustrating, Charlotte thought, while her eyes took in the changing images of the road in front of her. She wanted to speak to the family members of the victim to find out how much they knew about his gambling habits and his heavy debt, information that she had received from Ulrike. They must have known that something was wrong, when they found out that Dorothea Stollberg had moved out and filed for divorce. This reminded her of her own decision to move out after living almost ten years together with Ernst, a painful reminder even now, almost two years after it happened. It also reminded her of a wonderful weekend with Bernd Moeller, who had become part of her life when she thought that there was nothing left outside of police work. With him she was at ease in a way that she had never reached with Ernst, although she was really in love with him. They had been this extraordinary couple that all their friends admired. The model of a successful professional couple. What went wrong? Why was there a growing rift? Charlotte found it still difficult to get a clear picture of their relationship. It had to do something with their professional careers. She felt that he didn't take much of an interest in her work as a police officer and her rise through the ranks. If she was honest she had to admit that she never really understood his interest in architecture and his rise to prominence. She had been unable to relate to his work. With Bernd Moller these problems never came up. He had been a detective himself, one of her mentors. It was so easy to explain to him what she was doing. He had calmed her down when she had casually mentioned her frustration with the new case. It was so good to have him around. He didn't expect her to worry about his family, the problems of his grown daughters, one of whom had moved to Australia. When he was in Berlin, he was there to enjoy life together with her. Even going to the opera, which wasn't her greatest interest, was fun. He had a way of explaining the music to her that felt good.

All of a sudden, Charlotte heard Kraft's curses, who had to step on the brakes because another car had tried to pass them and was forced to move in front of them, when a third car approached from the opposite side. "Damn it," he exclaimed, "that was a close call. If we weren't in such a hurry, I would have loved to stop him." Charlotte just nodded. Driving in Berlin had become a real hazard. Then her thoughts went back to the weekend. She had consulted Bernd on the LKA Hesse connection and he had warned her that she might run into resistance if she wanted information about their interest in the

Bad Homburg murder. As it turned out, he had been right. When she called them on Monday, she experienced a surprisingly complete lack of support. She had the distinct impression that her argument that the Stollberg and the Kellner case were connected was not taken seriously at all. The colleague in Wiesbaden admitted that the private detective had been in Berlin twice and seemed to be connected to Stollberg, but didn't follow her argument that there might be a significant link. In fact, he questioned her assumption that Stollberg had been murdered and insisted on getting proof before he was willing to share files. His arrogance was hard to bear. She had wondered if this guy would have been as negative if she had been a man. She might be forced to ask her boss to establish some form of fruitful collaboration, since in her mind there was little doubt that the death of Kellner right after his second visit to Berlin was connected to her case. Kellner was the link to the Americans and the missing file. But she had not mentioned the file. Too early, she thought. They have to show their readiness to cooperate before they get this kind of information. She was about to ask Werner Kraft if there had been any new development in the search for the driver, when he turned to her informing her that they would arrive just in time.

A few minutes later, they stood in front of the Stollberg residence, a house from the 1920s, square with two floors and large windows, built on a fairly small lot. There were many houses of this style in Dahlem, the land must have been too expensive to have a comfortable lot even in those days, Charlotte thought. Kraft took the lead when they approached the house. It was Stollberg's older brother who opened the door and asked them to come in. He guided them to a large living room where the parents had been waiting. For a moment there was an uncomfortable silence, which Charlotte broke by introducing herself:

"I am Hauptkommissarin Charlotte Herberg and with me is Obermeister Werner Kraft. We want to meet with you because there are a number of unanswered questions concerning your son's death."

The father welcomed the officers and asked them to sit down. The son offered to serve coffee, an offer that was politely declined. Charlotte simply began her interview:

"I was asked to look at the accident again to make sure that we haven't overlooked anything. As you know, it was a hit-and-run, and the sad news is that we haven't been able to identify the driver."

It was the brother who interrupted her at this point to articulate his deep frustration with the police. The father just nodded to express his agreement. Charlotte had expected this criticism and told them that it was only a matter of time until they would identify the driver who had killed their son. Then she quickly moved to the critical point:

"We assumed that we were dealing with an accident. But there is another possible explanation."

The mother for the first time showed any interest in the interview, she wanted to know what other explanation there could be.

Charlotte looked at her, lowering her voice: "Did your son have enemies who could have planned this accident? Can you think of a person or persons who had a grudge and might have wanted him dead?"

There was no answer. The members of the family looked at each other, clearly uncertain how to respond. I have to hit them harder, Charlotte thought.

"I assume you are aware that your son owed a lot of money. Around 900,000 Euro to be more precise. Could one of his creditors have become impatient, when your son didn't make any payments, and took action?"

The effect of this question was immediate. The brother responded with a terse question: "How do you know this? This has nothing to do with the accident."

Then the mother said: "Yes, he had told me that the company had financial problems, but he assured me that David Klein was looking for additional capital."

"We have a statement from Dorothea Stollberg to this effect," Charlotte replied.

"Instead of making statements, my daughter-in-law should have been with my son when he needed her most," exclaimed the mother, "Instead, she chose to divorce him."

"Please calm down," said the elder Stollberg turning to his wife, "this business doesn't interest the police, mother. My answer to your question is that I didn't know. My son never told me about money problems. I found out only when Dorothea moved out and started divorce procedures."

"Do you feel the same way," Charlotte asked turning toward the brother.

"I'm not so sure," the brother replied, "I wouldn't rule out the possibility that one of his creditors got impatient and meant to threaten him. It seems that some of the money came from sources that you would not mention to your bank."

"How do you know this?" Werner Kraft wanted to know.

"When I pressed my brother, he admitted that he owed more than his line of credit at the bank. But he didn't want to talk about details. The story was that David Klein was looking for fresh capital that the company needed urgently. They had to use their private resources to bridge the gap."

Charlotte was stunned. Stollberg had kept his family completely in the dark about his gambling habits. And his wife had apparently been unable to communicate the truth. For the parents she had been just a bad wife. But she decided not to follow this lead at this time. She needed objective proof before she could discuss this question with the family. I have to talk to David Klein as soon as possible, she thought. Maybe there is another side to this story that could be relevant for the case. One thing was clear: Something went terribly wrong. But it had also become apparent in the conversation that the family didn't know much about Stollberg's private life. Charlotte promised them to find the driver who had caused the accident and bring him to justice, which the family wanted to hear. She encouraged them to contact her immediately if there was any information that might help to solve the case.

When Charlotte and Werner Kraft had returned to their car and were on the way back to the headquarters, they decided to look for a quiet place to assess the information they had received this morning. It was too early for lunch, still, a cup of good coffee would be the right thing. Charlotte knew that Kraft didn't drink coffee, which she approved without changing her own habit. A mid-morning coffee did wonders to her brain. Kraft suggested to get closer to the city for a good coffee shop. She just nodded and let him look for the right spot. It took him no more than ten minutes when he parked the car and pointed to a bakery with a few tables in front of the store.

"Is their coffee any good?" Charlotte asked him, while they were still in the car.

"I haven't tried it, but it's supposed to be strong", Werner Kraft replied, "I know that their sandwiches are really good, and I need something. I had no real breakfast this morning."

"All right, let's go," Charlotte said and got out of the car.

They tried a table outside. It turned out to be too windy and noisy. So, they retreated to the inside, which was narrow and rather dark. They settled at a table near a light and ordered a dark coffee for Charlotte and juice and a cheese sandwich for Kraft. When Kraft had finished his sandwich, Charlotte invited him to share his impressions of the family. Did he observe something unusual? Did the family members tell them everything they knew? What about the turn that Stollberg needed the money for the company?

"I think he kept his parents pretty much in the dark about the real cause of the debt," Kraft said. "As far as the brother is concerned, I'm less certain. I suspect that he knew more or was at least suspicious of his brother's story. But how much did he really want to know? The truth was very unpleasant."

"So, you believe that the tale about the needs of the company was no more than a cover?" Charlotte asked.

"I think so. Of course, we need to talk to the partners to get the truth."

"Exactly," Charlotte exclaimed, "we can't rule it out."

"And we should talk to Dorothea Stollberg," Kraft insisted, "not to mention Klein and his partner."

"Good point. Make arrangements as soon as we are back at the office, also, we need access to Stollberg's bank accounts."

"What about the brother?" Kraft asked, "is he of interest?"

"Maybe later, right now he seems to be less relevant for our case."

Charlotte had finished the coffee, which had been surprisingly good, and was ready to leave. She wanted to push the team that was looking for the driver and the van and, as she just remembered, she owed Ulrike a message with an update.

Ulrike was waiting impatiently for a message from Charlotte Herberg. Before she met with David Klein she wanted to know how much Charlotte had found out. They had agreed on a meeting at 2:00pm at the Kreuzberg office, which would include Bill, whom she had introduced as an American freelance colleague from New York who was working on a piece on start-ups in Berlin. David Klein had been surprisingly easy going about adding the American journalist. Because Bill had asked her, she had suggested to include Brindisi. Klein's response was predictable. He would invite him but couldn't guarantee that he would have time. Ulrike had decided to leave it at that. If he showed up, good; if not they would find other ways to talk to him. Finally, her phone rang, but it was Bill, not Charlotte. He informed her that he was at the lab of KreuzbergChem, which was located in an old factory from the early twentieth century in Friedenau. He was there together with Werner Kraft, observing the staff that was coming and going. Nothing unusual was happening there, the message told her. Ulrike immediately replied asking for the presence of Brindisi. The answer came back within seconds: "No, he has not shown his face here this morning." She was just reminding him of the 2:00pm meeting in Kreuzberg, when Charlotte's text message came in: "Family tells us that S. needed the money for financing the company. Mother very upset about Dorothea Stollberg. I will ask for access to his bank account. See you soon." There was no assessment of these facts. Did Charlotte take them seriously? Ulrike remained convinced that the debt was caused by uncontrolled gambling. She was meaning to bring this up. Did Klein know about Stollberg's problem? Was there a motive for him and Brindisi to eliminate Stollberg, because he might secretly sell the results of their common research?

It took Ulrike longer than expected to find the building. It was old and somewhat run-down, she didn't believe that a future-oriented start-up would rent an office here. Bill, who had been waiting outside, laughed when she explained to him that she had expected a shiny front. "Why put money into an expensive office. When you need every penny for research?!," he said dryly."

Ulrike just shrugged her shoulders as she entered the building looking for the office. She rang the bell. It took a while until the door was opened by a man in his mid-thirties. He was tall with dark hair and rimless glasses. He gave them a broad smile and invited them in. Ulrike mentioned her name and introduced Bill as Sam Taylor, a freelance journalist from New York. To play the part, Bill was wearing large dark glasses, which changed his face more than Ulrike expected. He really looked like a journalist who does off-the-beaten-track stuff. Klein showed them to a larger room that might have been the living room of the apartment before it became an office.

"Sorry about the mess," he said with a gesture of his right arm, "we have gone through a difficult week. As you know, we lost one of our partners. What can I offer you? Coffee? Tea? Water or juice?"

Bill opted for water, while Ulrike asked for coffee. Klein disappeared for a moment. They heard his voice telling another person what the visitors liked to have. He ordered tea for himself before returning to the room where Bill and Ulrike had settled in armchairs that had seen better days. Ulrike glanced at the curtains, which clearly needed cleaning when Klein grasped a chair for himself and greeted them again in the name of the company. He proposed that they would do the entire interview in English. This would make it easier for Mr. Taylor to follow the conversation. Bill was pleasantly surprised by this offer, which he eagerly accepted. They agreed that there would be two parts, first, Ulrike would ask questions about the company in general and its recent development; this would be followed by a discussion of the financial side of the operation. Ulrike wanted to know why Herr Brindisi was absent. She got the impression that Klein was not very concerned about this question, expressing his hope that he would show up later.

"Before I ask you to tell me more about the history of KreuzbergChem," Ulrike opened the interview, "I want to express my sincere condolences for the loss of Herwig Stollberg. You have lost a partner, possibly at a critical juncture of your development."

"Thank you," Klein replied with a brief movement of his head, "I appreciate your concern. Yes, Herwig Stollberg's death was a terrible blow to us, to his partners and friends. We are still in the process of assessing the problems we are facing without him. As you can imagine, he was critical for our research. I was out of the country when it happened and learned about the accident only when my plane landed in Berlin."

Ulrike invited him to talk about the early phase of the company and its subsequent development. Klein responded by explaining that he was not a part of this early phase, that he had joined the company only three years ago, when it became clear that they needed an engineer who could develop and build the machines that they needed for their products. Bill noticed that Klein's English was completely fluent, he had the ease of a native speaker, although he didn't sound British or American.

He asked him: "Where did you get your fluency in English? I can't place your accent?"

Klein looked at him with a smile: "I got part of my education in the US, BS in Engineering at Cornell."

"Really, so you know Ithaca?" Bill exclaimed,

"Why?" Klein replied.

"I spent a year at Cornell's Law School, until I decided that the law wasn't for me."

"I had a great time there, learned a lot and enjoyed myself" Klein said, "I wish I could go back for a visit."

"So, do I, "Bill replied, surprised about his own response.

At this moment a middle-aged woman entered the room with coffee, tea, a glass of water, and cookies. She placed the tray on the small table in front of the armchairs and left without saying a word. Ulrike was especially grateful for the coffee, since she had left her apartment in a hurry without time for making coffee. After taking a few sips, she resumed the interview. Because she was getting concerned that the conversation got off the track, she encouraged Klein to talk about the more recent turn of the company. She asked whether there was a new project that he could explain to them. Klein gave her a smile indicating his willingness to continue his presentation:

"Yes, you are right, we shifted gears about two years ago. I was already part of the team. We had been mostly working on food projects, the chemistry of industrial food processing, its safety and quality. It was Herwig Stollberg who suggested the turn. He saw better opportunities in the pharma field."

"you mean more money, Ulrike interrupted,

"Yes, better profits but also more interesting research," Klein replied, "we are a start-up, necessarily looking for profits."

Klein resumed his narrative, emphasizing the advantages of pharma research, especially from the point of view of finding capital, which had been his task. Ulrike wanted to know to what extent he had been part of the new turn and was told that he played only a marginal role in the first phase, which was mostly chemistry. Stollberg took the lead. However, when Ulrike asked him what specifically they were working on, Klein's answers became vague. Obviously, he was not ready to disclose the concrete results of their work. Only when Ulrike made it clear to him that she couldn't really publish a story without writing about the content of the research, he changed his mind.

"There have been important developments recently in the field of diabetes research, not only monitors but also new medications for better control," he explained, "in the latter arena, Herwig has been looking for new and better solutions."

"Then you must be familiar with the recent research at Alerta?" Bill asked.

Klein looked at him with a puzzled face: "Should I be familiar with this company?" he asked.

"You tell me," Bill replied, "the company's stock has gone up significantly lately because there are rumors on Wall Street that they are working on a new pill."

"That's news to me, I'll ask Brindisi later if he is aware of this company. You think of them as our competitors?" Klein asked.

Bill looked at him: "Hard to say without more information. I know next to nothing about the research of Alerta and not enough about your work. I was just curious."

Ulrike used this answer to ask more questions about the recent research of Stollberg and Brindisi. It became obvious that he could describe the project in general terms but didn't have the insight into the details of the procedures and the ultimate goal, if such a specific goal had already been defined at all. Ulrike and Bill got the impression that KreuzbergChem was still far away from concrete results. Klein confirmed this impression when he said:

"The way I see it, we may need another two years or so to achieve results that we can market. Among other things, we will have to hire more people, which means that we have to raise more capital."

This turn of the conversation gave Bill the opportunity to ask more questions about the financial side of the enterprise. Klein nodded and looked at his hands before he replied:

"Good question, Mr. Taylor, we are still underfinanced, very much underfinanced, which by the way, is true for many German start-ups. Germany is not a very good environment for start-ups because there are not enough venture capitalists. The very notion seems to be still alien to German capitalism, one of the reasons for the difficulties Stollberg and Brindisi faced when they started out. Their capital was too small to tackle large problems."

"And how do you mean to fix this problem?" Bill wanted to know.

"I'm just back from Israel where I have useful family connections, some of them extend to the US. Given our new product, I'm pretty confident that I can raise additional capital."

"How much do you have in mind?" Bill asked.

"We need at least 10 million in the near future and another 10 million later."

"And you are sure that you can raise that much?" Ulrike interjected, her voice expressing doubt.

Klein looked at her with an expression of irritation: "Yes, I do. I wouldn't have joined this company three years ago and put my own money into it if I had not been confident about its future."

The conversation continued for a while, until David Klein looked at his watch and informed his visitors of another meeting. They had to come to an end. Ulrike smiled at him before she asked her last question: "Herr Klein, where do you see your company in five years?"

Klein leaned back in his chair returning the smile:

"You know, we just experienced a serious setback by losing Herwig Stollberg, who was a brilliant chemist. We will have to replace him as soon as possible. As I said earlier, we will have to hire more staff. In five years, the company will have tripled in size and capital."

Bill got up from his chair and shook Klein's hand: "Good luck, I'm impressed. Hope it works out."

At this moment, the secretary knocked at the door to remind Klein of his next appointment. Ulrike had just a minute to thank him for the interview. Then Klein left the room in a hurry, asking the secretary to see them out. On the way to the front door Ulrike turned to her: "This must have been rough, I mean Herwig Stollberg's death."

"Yes, we are still trying to cope with the loss. I can't believe that he will never open the door asking for his tea in the morning. It was always tea. By the way, during your interview with Herr Klein Herr Brindisi called. He meant to come to the meeting but didn't feel well. He sends his regards."

Once Ulrike and Bill were back on the street, they had to split up. Ulrike had to cover a conference on migration and assimilation at Humboldt University and Bill had promised Werner Kraft to show up at his office to go over the results of several new statements of eye witnesses of the accident. They agreed to rendezvous later. There was much to discuss.

When Bill arrived at Police Headquarters, he found Werner Kraft on the phone. He just gave Bill a nod and gestured him to find a chair. Bill took his laptop out of his bag and started checking his email. Was there another message from Hinchcroft? The lawyer had not been in touch for a couple of days. Either he tried to contact Alerta and was unsuccessful or he considered the news from the company as too confidential. In either case, it left Bill without any information about the strategy of the company. Were they pretending that they had never been in contact with Stollberg? Or were they waiting for Bill to come up with the lost file? Bill realized that despite the interview this afternoon he was not much closer to the goal of his assignment. Unless Klein was a really accomplished actor, there was no indication that he knew anything about the contacts between Alerta and Stollberg. According to Klein, there was no product that could be sold. Their research was far away from completion. Clearly, Klein was misinformed. Stollberg had kept the progress of his work to himself, because he meant to sell the results behind the back of his partners. Or he was pressured to do so by his creditors. It must have been something that Alerta either needed or at least found useful Bill thought. Where was the missing file? Sometimes he wondered if this file existed. But Kellner had believed it existed and his murderer must have been convinced that he had taken possession of it. He decided to discuss this question with Kraft who was still on the phone.

It took another ten minutes until Kraft got off the phone and turned to Bill.

"Sorry," he said coming over to the table where Bill had put his laptop, "I had a long conversation with Bad Homburg. Finally, they are ready to consider a possible link between the Kellner murder and the Stollberg accident. It took them a few days to examine Kellner's visits to Berlin. They don't share information with me, but I think they will do so with Herberg."

"Did you speak to the younger female detective?" Bill asked.

"No, it was a male officer, Kraft replied, "I'm not even sure whether he was the investigator. I was just trying to develop some form of cooperation. No fun at all."

"The next time you call them try to talk to the female detective. She struck me as much more reasonable and open-minded than her colleague when they grilled me. I was the suspicious stranger."

Kraft laughed when he imagined the Bad Homburg police questioning Bill. Then he pointed to the material on the table:

"Let's have a look at the results of the second rounds of interviews. Unfortunately, no break-through but at least smaller pieces of helpful information. We found two eyewitnesses who confirmed that the vehicle was a van. They saw it coming down the small street at a dangerously high speed. According to these witnesses, there were two men in the van, one of them bearded."

"Anything about the plate?" Bill wanted to know.

"We got a better picture but not good enough to identify the number with certainty. Here, take a look," Kraft replied pointing at a photograph on the table.

Bill picked up the shot and scrutinized the image.

"It's not a Berlin license plate," Kraft said, "look at the first letter, which is O, standing for Osnabrück. We have already contacted the colleagues in Osnabrück."

Any confirmation?"

"No, they can't identify the vehicle."

Bill looked at the hazy image again. The first letter could be an O, but it could also be a D, he felt.

"Have you considered that the first letter could also be a D?"

"No, we all agreed on O," Kraft said taking the photograph out of Bill's hands and staring at the image.

"Yes, you are right, it could be a D."

"Would that change the meaning?"

"Yes, quite a bit. It would mean that the van was registered in Düsseldorf. We will have to contact the colleagues in Düsseldorf to check this out," Kraft said, "in any case, if this was premeditated, the plan was not developed in Berlin."

"Or at least not organized locally," Bill interjected.

Kraft looked puzzled: "Why would someone in Düsseldorf want to eliminate a young chemist and entrepreneur in Berlin?"

"It could be even more complicated," Bill said, "someone in Berlin was determined to eliminate Stollberg with a van registered in Düsseldorf rather than Berlin. If we were in the US my guess would be: organized crime."

Kraft's face expressed disbelief: "Organized crime? We are not even absolutely sure that it was a crime,"

"I'm sure," Bill replied, "after the Kellner murder I was sure.

What I don't exactly understand is the purpose. Who gains by killing Stollberg?"

Kraft just shrugged his shoulders while he was going back to the table picking up additional reports. He showed Bill what they had found out about Kellner's visits. The first time he had booked his room a day in advance, indicating that the meeting had been planned carefully. The second time he had come without advance booking and booked a room only in the late afternoon at another hotel. And then he hadn't even used the room but had taken a late train back to Frankfurt.

"He wanted to keep a low profile, I guess," suggested Bill looking at the report. "I'm still trying to figure out how the missing file is connected to this "accident." The attack eliminated Stollberg, but there was no chance for the driver to get to the file, if Stollberg was carrying it,"

"Either this was not part of the plan or a third person was supposed to grab the file after Stollberg had been thrown to the ground," Kraft said. "That would mean that this person was waiting at the intersection for the accident to happen," he continued, "and he or she had to know how Stollberg was carrying the file. Not a likely scenario, if you ask me."

"Agreed, if you were planning to deliver a secret file at a secret meeting, how would you do it?" Bill asked.

Kraft hesitated for a moment, then he said: "Small electronic device, in code, for instance a phone."

"How about a stick?"

"That would work well."

"Have you checked Stollberg's possessions?"

"Yes, we have. There was a smart phone, but nothing unusual on it. No stick or laptop."

Bill was showing signs of frustration. He had hoped to get one or two decisive clues that would get him closer to a solution. Instead, there were only many small pieces in a picture that remained opaque. Kraft who noticed his changing mood tried to cheer him up.

"Look, we are just beginning. Police work is slow. There is always another day and another team effort. I have to go to the shooting range later this afternoon to practice. Maybe you want to come along. Maybe the master will admit you."

Bill looked at his watch. It was clearly too early to meet with Ulrike. Getting out of the office was a good idea. He needed fresh air.

"Let's go," he said.

Minutes later they left the office together.

CHAPTER 7

When Bill arrived at Ulrike's apartment and rang the bell, it was a young man of about twenty-two who opened the door. He was tall and slim with dark hair and light blue eyes. They looked at each other in surprise, unable to figure out who the other person was and why he would be at Ulrike's place. It was Bill who realized first that the young man who stared at him with a hostile gaze must be Ulrike's kid brother, who had left the army and was looking for a job. There was a certain family similarity. He put on a broad smile, introducing himself as Ulrike's friend from New York. He did this in German, choosing his words carefully. The reply was in English:

"O yes, my sister mentioned you. You are the private detective with whom she worked two years ago, the story about the abducted young American journalist and the Pension Birkenhain, where they kept the young women as prostitutes. Big stuff, turned her life around."

Bill was surprised by the fluency, while the accent was unmistakably German.

"Ja, that's me. Can I come in? I'm looking for your sister."

"Ulrike is not yet back, but please come in. I have no idea where she is, I just arrived myself half an hour ago."

The young man stepped aside with a gesture that invited Bill to come in.

"By the way, my name is Volker," he continued while he was walking towards the kitchen, "I was trying to find something edible in the fridge. No luck there, it's pretty empty."

Bill, who had not eaten since lunch, was hungry himself, he was looking forward to have dinner with Ulrike. This was not a promising situation, he thought. He was not interested in spending the evening with her younger brother who had dropped in because he had run out of food it seemed. Then he remembered: He was supposed to have a talk with Volker. This was not an accident. Ulrike might not show up for a while to give him time to talk sense into her kid-brother, who had quit the army without clear plans. Not on an empty stomach, he thought. Both of them would be irritated and the result would be more confusion and just create more problems. Maybe I should just leave and come back later, Bill thought. But he changed his mind almost immediately. If he did do that, there would be trouble with Ulrike later. He had to follow up on this assignment, although he was not sure at all, whether his advice would be welcome.

"Well, this doesn't look promising," Bill said with a gesture to the refrigerator, "we can either wait until your sister arrives or order something to eat."

Volker looked at Bill with a shrug: "Let's order something now. Who knows when Ulrike will show up."

He made a gesture that clearly invited Bill to act.

"Pizza? Bill asked, "there is a pretty good place around the corner."

"I know," Volker replied, pointing to the phone on the kitchen table. Bill smiled, amused by the Volker's obvious attempt to shift the responsibility to him. He picked up the phone checked the list of contacts and dialed the number. Within minutes he had ordered a large pizza with mushrooms, peppers, ham, and cheese, which would be delivered within twenty minutes. Volker looked very pleased and began to set the table, including a third plate in case his sister would come home in time. Bill watched him, while he sat on a stool near the table. Volker's mood seemed to have changed for the better. With eagerness he placed the plates, looked for knives and forks and even found paper napkins, which he folded neatly before he placed them next to the plates. This might be a good time to open a conversation about Volker's future, Bill mused.

"I understand that you just left the army, Volker", Bill said in a casual tone without even looking at Volker.

"Yes, I did," Volker replied, still busy with setting the table. "When I first signed up after I finished school, it looked very exciting: opportunities to get around, not the usual nine to five job. After basic training I signed up for special training, but in the long run, the whole thing turned out to be rather disappointing. Not much action, if you see what I mean."

Actually, Bill wasn't sure at all that he understood what Volker meant, since he knew very little about the German army.

"What were you doing? I meant what branch of the service did you choose?" he asked casually, trying to keep the conversation at a low key.

"I got my special training joining a Panzer Brigade. Sounds exciting, doesn't it? But the daily routine isn't. For one thing, we always had problems with our equipment."

"What do you mean," Bill interjected.

"We couldn't use our tanks because they needed repairs and we couldn't get the parts when we needed them."

"Really," Bill said, "frankly, this sounds unbelievable. And nobody did anything about it?"

Volker shrugged his shoulders: "Not really, it was considered kind of normal. My feeling was that nobody cared about the Bundeswehr. It had the reputation of being the place for dummies."

"Is that the reason you decided to quit," Bill wanted to know.

"Sort of, I was just tired of doing the same thing over and over again. Routine, repetition."

Bill said nothing.

"Look at you," Volker continued, "private detective, out on a mission in Berlin. Searching for something, hunting down the bad guys. That's really exciting."

Bill just nodded. It does look exciting, he thought, but he doesn't see the details in New York, my routine. What shall I tell this kid, Bill thought. No decent job without patterns and repetition. Listening to Volker's story, Bill realized suddenly, that it touched on his own situation more than he had expected. I have come to understand the limits of my position in New York. How long can I keep doing this?

When I started out five years ago everything looked fresh and new. What a change after a year studying law at Cornell. Still, what could he tell this kid? What kind of advice did he have to offer?

"So, what's the next step," Bill asked in a low voice.

"What do you mean?"

"What are your plans now that you have quit the army?" Bill answered with a question.

"You tell me. At this point, I have no plans, at least no plans that my sister would approve of. She wants me to attend university and pick up a profession, but I'm an outdoor person. Books and scholarship are not my thing. By the way, she isn't that different. She never finished her degree in sociology. Instead, she started working as a freelance for the BT."

At this moment the doorbell rang, it was the delivery man for the pizza. Volker made no attempt to answer the door. Finally, Bill got up from his stool moved to the door and took care of the delivery, carrying the large box to the kitchen. The smell was delicious, it reminded him of his hunger. He decided to drop the difficult conversation and focus on the meal. Once they had eaten, things might be smoother.

His strategy seemed to work, when they had finished eating the pizza, except for a good piece that Bill reserved for Ulrike, Volker opened up a bit. He was willing to talk about options, possibilities without committing himself to anything specific, though. He reminds me of myself at 23, Bill thought. He exactly knows what he doesn't want without much of a clue about his future. He needs time and a job for the transition. But this would not be an answer that Ulrike would like to hear. It was obvious that she wanted to have an immediate solution to the problem of an unemployed younger brother who used up family resources. His own father had called up his old friend in New York, who had invited Bill to do some temporary work for the law firm. This had morphed into his present position. As it turned out, Volker was very curious about Bill's work. He wanted to know whether Bill was carrying a gun as part of his regular assignments.

"Do you have to protect the physical safety of your firm's clients?" Volker asked.

Bill chuckled: "Most of our clients don't need that kind of protection. The firm focuses on corporate and tax law. Usually, the issue is money, big money,"

"Is that why you are in Berlin?"

Bill thought for a while before he replied: "I guess so, although in this case I'm not even sure. I'm looking for a missing file."

"Here in Berlin?" Volker wanted to know.

"Yes, it was supposed to be sent to our client, an American company, but it never arrived."

"Any luck with the search?"

"So far not much," Bill mumbled while he got up and moved to the refrigerator. He was looking for something to drink. All he could find was a half empty bottle of white wine. He showed it to Volker who shrugged his shoulders: "I would rather have a beer, but if this is all there is, I take it."

Bill got two glasses out of the cupboard and poured the wine.

"Cheers," he said.

"Prost," Volker replied, "what happened to the file? It got lost?"

"Well, it probably got stolen, but the details are still uncertain."

"That sounds intriguing, I'm sure Ulrike is part of the search. It would be another big scoop for her."

Bill laughed: "Yes, it could well be, right now, the case looks rather murky."

"You want me to help?" Volker asked eagerly, "I have lots of time on my hands. Remember I'm a trained soldier. That could be useful, if you have to deal with criminals."

"Good point, I'll keep that in mind," Bill replied.

Bill wanted to come back to Volker's situation, but Volker was not eager to go back to that conversation. All of a sudden, he looked straight into Bill's eyes and said: "Just fuck the whole thing." Bill was startled, not knowing how to read this verbal outbreak. "Sorry," Volker said when he saw Bill's reaction. "It's not you. It has nothing to do with you. It's my family or the lack of a proper family. You have to know that my father left us when Ulrike and I were little. He lost his position in Rostock after the German unification and took a job at an oil rick someplace far away. The money was very good and he supported his family generously until he died."

What happened," Bill asked.

"Accident, a stupid accident. After that my mother had to work full-time and the kids were on their own. Ulrike had to look after me. I suspect she hated it."

At this moment, Bill heard a key turning in the front door and a moment later Ulrike stood in the kitchen door, smiling and pretending to be very surprised to find both of the here.

"What a surprise," she exclaimed, "having a good time at my place?! Anything left to eat? I'm starving."

Bill pointed to the slice of pizza and invited her to grab a chair.

"Another long day at the office?" He asked.

From the tone of his voice Ulrike guessed that he had seen through her ruse by now to bring him and Volker together for the one-on-one talk that would set her brother straight. She smiled and pretended that she didn't understand the true meaning of his question.

"Uli, are you involved in the search for the missing file?" Volker wanted to know.

Ulrike glanced at Bill before she replied, but she couldn't read him.

"Not really," she said, "of course, I am interested in the story, after all I'm a reporter. But so far there is little to report."

Bill nodded approvingly: "As I said, we are just beginning to put the pieces together."

"Sounds very exciting," Volker interjected, "I hope they pay your expenses."

"They do," Bill replied looking at Ulrike for a clue. What was supposed to happen next?

When it became clear that Volker showed no sign of leaving Bill got up, declaring that it was time for him to get back to his hotel. He shook hands with Volker, wishing him good luck with his search for a position.

"Thanks," Volker replied, "really good to meet you. I hope we'll meet again."

"I'll see you out," Ulrike said getting up herself. She followed Bill to the front door, while Volker poured himself another glass of white wine.

"Call me later," Bill said in a low voice.

"I will as soon as my brother has left. I don't want to kick him out."

Bill just nodded and left.

The following morning began with a surprise. When Charlotte Herberg arrived at her office around 8:30, she saw a thin folder on her desk. Before she had time to open it, however, there was a phone call from her boss asking her to join an urgent meeting. It was Werner Kraft who discovered the folder an hour later when he was searching for Charlotte Herberg who was supposed to lead a meeting of the SOKO put together to solve the Stollberg case. He glanced at the folder and decided to take it along to the meeting room down the hall. On the way, he took a peek. It was a report about Herwig Stollberg's bank accounts. His account at the Berliner Bank was overdrawn by 170,000 Euros. But there was another account. The day before his death there had been a transfer of $100,000 to this account at Münchmeyer & Co., a private bank in Hamburg. Kraft looked for the source. The money came from a bank in Dubai, but no names given. He realized immediately that this information was of great importance for the case. When he reached the meeting room, he saw that Charlotte Herberg had already arrived and was involved in a conversation with one of the officers who had gone over the scene of the accident again. Kraft tried to get her attention. She has to read this report before the meeting, he thought. This is a turning point for our investigation. He waved the folder to get her attention until she noticed him and gestured him to approach her.

"Charlotte, you have to read this file before the meeting. I think it changes the background assumptions of our investigation," Kraft exclaimed.

Charlotte opened the folder and glanced at the report. For a brief moment she was speechless. A transfer of $100,000. There it was in black and white. A private bank in Hamburg. This was clearly not a regular business account with a link to KreuzbergChem.

She turned to Kraft: "We have to find out who sent the money.

There is only a number and the text 'as per agreement.' Charlotte was very excited, because the new information strongly suggested a connection between the incoming money and his death the following day. But she had to prove it.

At 10:00 am Charlotte Herberg called the meeting to order and informed the group of the latest information she had received from the finance and banking department.

"The likelihood that the death of Herwig Stollberg was more than a hit-and-run has increased. We have just received the information that the victim received $100,000 the day before his death from an unknown source, presumably as payment or partial payment for the file that he carried while on his way to the meeting at the Brandenburger Hof," Charlotte said.

"I will go back to our colleagues to find out who sent the money," she continued, "there is no sender on the statement, just a reference number."

"Do we assume that the victim was killed because of the transfer?" one of the officers wanted to know.

"No," Charlotte replied, "we suspect that there was a deal between Herwig Stollberg and a third party, but the deal was disrupted. The information sold never reached the third party. He was killed so that he could not deliver the file. A representative of the third party was waiting at the Brandenburger Hof. Once he realized that Stollberg was dead, he left the hotel and returned to Frankfurt."

"What do we know about the third party and the representative?" another officer asked.

"We have no firm knowledge about the third party, but we do know the representative. He was a private detective from Frankfurt by the name of Walter Kellner."

"What do you mean by *was*?" the officer asked.

"He is dead. He was killed in his home in Bad Homburg after his return from a second visit to Berlin. Werner Kraft will fill you in."

There was another question: "Do you assume that there is a connection between these two killings?"

"Yes, I do," Charlotte said with emphasis, "in my mind they are connected, but it took a while until the police in Bad Homburg and the LKA in Wiesbaden came to the same conclusion."

She stood up and pointed to a board with a sketch of the place where the accident occurred. "Let's hear what the accident team found out by reviewing the evidence."

An older male officer moved to the board, facing the group.

"After looking carefully at the evidence once more, we concluded that it is very likely that the accident was planned. We have eye witnesses who reported that the van had stopped at the intersection, then accelerated and made a right turn, without slowing down, hit the victim and left the scene of the accident picking up speed. We also found out that the vehicle used for the murder was not registered in Berlin. We have a picture of the plate, which is unfortunately not clear enough to make an absolutely certain identification. Please look at the picture on the board. The first letter is either an O or a D, which means that the van was registered either in Osnabrück or in Düsseldorf."

"Thank you," Charlotte said, "that is very helpful."

Then she asked Werner Kraft to report on the funeral. He stood up but remained at the meeting table: "I was assigned to observe the funeral. There were indeed two suspicious moments, one was the presence of a man who took pictures of the funeral party, especially of the family and the close friends of the deceased. This person turned out to be the private detective from Frankfurt. It seems that he came back to figure out why Stollberg was killed and who might be involved. Since we never had a chance to speak to him before his untimely death, we can only speculate why he thought that members of the family or his friends and partners might be involved. The second moment was the appearance of two men at the periphery of the event. They were observing the scene without getting involved."

"Could they be identified?" another member of the team asked.

"Yes, we identified them as members of a Frankfurt gang, but no connection to organized crime in Berlin," Kraft said

There was another question: "Did these men notice the private detective?"

"I believe they did, Kraft replied, "although he was discreet, it was noticeable that he was taking pictures."

"Is there a connection between this observation and the murder in Bad Homburg?" the same officer wanted to know.

"Good question," Charlotte interjected, "we don't know. As I said, I suspect that there is. I 'm trying to persuade our colleagues in Bad Homberg of this, but they are not eager to make this assumption. Let me summarize what we assume at this point and how it hangs together: Herwig Stollberg was involved in a deal with a third party that was interested in important information. It is highly valuable information for which they were willing to pay at least $100,000. More than likely, the $100,000 were meant to show their serious intent. A meeting was arranged at the Brandenburger Hof to which a representative of the buyer was sent. The representative, who is supposed to receive the file, was our private detective from Frankfurt. But the transfer never happened. Herwig Stollberg was killed in what seemed to be an accident in front of the hotel. The file he presumably carried to this meeting is missing. To this I can add that an American law firm has been asked to find the missing file. They have sent a young detective to Berlin. I have met with him and we are collaborating with him in the search for the file. But our primary concern is the murder case. You follow me so far?"

Charlotte looked around. She saw only nods.

"Ok then, there is another piece of information from a reliable source. According to this source, Stollberg was a gambler and owed a lot of money. This would explain why he was looking for a deal. What exactly he had to offer we don't know at this point. It appears that he was under pressure to repay the debt. The second victim is the private detective, who was supposed to receive the file. He was shot to death in his home. The murder happened in the early afternoon of the day after his return. At this point, we don't have details about the circumstances. But we know that his house was searched. The killer was looking for something that Kellner kept in his desk or in a safe, my guess is that it was the missing file."

"But you said a minute ago that the file was missing, the private detective never got it."

"Correct," Charlotte replied, "it seems that the murderer did not know this. He was probably told that Kellner had received the file in Berlin."

There was another question: "So you assume that the killer was acting on behalf of a third party?"

Charlotte nodded: "Yes, I do. The killer was a professional who was probably contracted,"

"And how do we know this?"

"I talked to someone who saw the crime scene, the American detective I mentioned a minute ago. He was looking for the missing file and followed a lead that got him to Frankfurt and then to Bad Homburg. In fact, he was treated as a suspect by the Homburg police for a number of hours."

"You have to admit," said Werner Kraft looking at Charlotte, "this is rather confusing. A file with important information is missing. Two people have been killed because of this file. A third party sends out a detective to find the file. There is something missing in this picture."

"I agree," said Charlotte returning to her seat, "there must be another party that is extremely interested in disrupting the deal. I see two possible reasons for doing this. Either they want to destroy the information because it is dangerous to their interests or they want to use the information for their own interests. In my mind, this is an open question at this point."

The discussion continued for a while, shifting back to the accident and then to the circumstances of Herwig Stollberg, especially his financial situation. Charlotte agreed that the investigation had to dig deeper in this area.

"There are a number of things that we have deal with, first of all, Stollberg's financial problems and how they are related to his death. I'm meaning to talk to his family again and his partners at KreuzbergChem. There is also the matter of the source of the money that he used for gambling. He owed, it seems, much more money than the credit line at his bank in Berlin. There was another lender. Who is he or she? Also, I hope to work more closely with our colleagues at Bad Homburg and the LKA of the state of Hesse. The LKA, I understand, looks at this case as part of a much larger investigation into organized crime in the Frankfurt area."

After the meeting Charlotte Herberg asked Kraft to accompany her to her office to set up the details of the next phase of the investigation. She wanted to schedule meetings with both partners.

"This may be more difficult than you think, said Kraft, "Brindisi has not been seen since the funeral."

"Do you believe that he is in some way involved in the crime?" Charlotte wanted to know.

"I'm not sure," Kraft replied, "but my feeling is that he somehow is part of the mess. His behavior at the funeral was very strange. It was as if he didn't want to be there. He avoided contact with the family."

"Werner, you should look into this. Try to be in touch with his family," Herberg said.

"It's on my list for tomorrow. How do you feel about my taking Bill McDonald along? He's good at this sort of thing."

Charlotte hesitated for a moment, then she said: "Yes, that's a good idea." For the first time, she realized that she actually liked this young American. She was surprised by this discovery.

Bill McDonald was enjoying his breakfast at the Brandenburger Hof, when a ring of his phone told him that there was a new message. It was a brief note from Ulrike thanking him again for his talk with Volker, which to his great surprise seemed to have been a great success. At least this was what she told him when she called him late last night. Volker had decided to stay overnight, pleading that the trip back to his friend's apartment in Potsdam would be too difficult. But he had told Ulrike that he really liked this American detective who had a cool job that Volker could only dream of. Bill had just listened to Ulrike's report, completely surprised by the outcome of a meeting, which he felt was at best a beginning. Of course, there was no concrete prospect of a new job and there was also no intention of following Ulrike's advice to attend university, but there was excitement on Volker's part, for which Ulrike was grateful. At the end of their long conversation there was a remark that Bill did not fully understand. Ulrike mentioned her need to use the archive of the *Spiegel*, the famous weekly magazine, for an essay she was working on. She would have to go to Hamburg. Only now when he looked at the message he grasped the full meaning of her remark. Ulrike would be in Hamburg for several days, maybe even a week. Obviously, Ulrike did not want a discussion over this trip. The message just mentioned her trip as an upcoming event. This hit Bill unprepared. What had been a pleasant German breakfast, turned instantly into a tedious task. Why am I so upset, Bill asked himself? After all, she promised to be back within a few days. But would he still be in Berlin at that time? The pressure from New York had increased. There had been another urgent message from Amos Hinchcroft, asking for a more detailed progress report. Why was he not providing a plausible explanation what exactly had happened? After all, Germany was not some third world country where people and things could simply disappear without a trace. Bill had mentioned in one of his messages that Herwig Stollberg's death was now treated as a possible homicide and asked whether he should try to collaborate with the German police. To Bill's surprise, the answer had been negative. No, he was supposed to follow his own agenda, focusing exclusively on the missing file. The client, he was told, had no interest in getting mixed up with a German murder case. Bill sensed that the law firm was becoming increasingly nervous about the whole matter and might call him back any time. If this case would be picked up by the international media, they certainly did not want to be mentioned as a possible American link. Of course, Bill knew that he could solve this case only by disregarding instructions from New York, since there was clearly a connection between the violent death of Herwig Stollberg and the missing file.

Bill was lost in his thoughts when he heard the voice of the young waitress who had served him the first day: "More coffee?" He looked up and saw her smiling face. For a moment he was confused to be approached in German. Then he smiled back and said: "Yes please" in German. She poured him another cup, showing no signs of being in a hurry. It was obvious that she was looking for a light conversation.

"How is the weather outside?" Bill asked, forcing himself to focus on his immediate environment.

"It looks like turning into a nice sunny day," she replied, "not too hot and humid."

"Great," he said with a grin, "I'm not a friend of rain."

But she sensed that he was not in the mood of carrying on a conversation and moved on with a friendly nod. Bill realized that he had missed his chance to find out more about the hotel guests but it was too late now. He had this unexplained feeling that there was more information about his case here at the Brandenburger Hof, but he couldn't figure out what it could be, since he had explored all obvious and even not so obvious links. His thoughts returned to Ulrike's sudden departure for Hamburg. There was another aspect he didn't like to dwell on. It was her acquaintance at the newspaper, the *Hamburger Abendblatt*. This guy had been really helpful two years ago, when he was looking for Julia Newman. He couldn't fault him. At the same time, Bill didn't like the way he talked about Ulrike. There was more than a professional connection. Now Ulrike was on her way to Hamburg to do research at an archive. It made him uneasy. It's none of my business, he told himself, I have to concentrate on my own affairs, while she is following up on her own plans. He decided to turn his attention to his omelet and a piece of toast. After finishing his second cup of coffee he moved back to his room where he checked his email for messages. He knew that there would have been a meeting of the partners yesterday in the late afternoon where important decisions about his case could have been made. No message from Hinchcroft, Bill was relieved. He had nothing new to tell. The meeting with Klein had been interesting but had not helped with the missing file. It seemed that Klein had no clear understanding of Stollberg's recent research or his connection with Alerta. Stollberg must have been able to keep the details from his partner, who had, it seems, completely trusted him. What about the other partner? Brindisi was a rather different case. For one thing, he didn't come to the meeting with a rather lame excuse. He and Stollberg had been old friends, both of them chemists. They had launched the start-up together. He must have had a much better idea what Stollberg was working on, beyond the broad description of diabetes research.

Bill was pacing up and down in his room. The more he thought about the situation of KreuzbergChem, the more he felt that the small company had been in the middle of a crisis even before Stollberg's death. They needed more capital, this was the task of David Klein with his American connections, but they had a partner with a bad gambling habit and serious money problems, as Ulrike had told him. Stollberg had needed money, much more than he could borrow from a bank. Of course, there was the Alerta connection. Alerta, a pharma company was also doing diabetes research. Yes, this was it: Stollberg was selling his research, it seems, secretly, without informing his partners. At least Klein did not know of this. The meeting at Brandenburger Hof was set up for finalizing the transaction. Research results contained in a file in exchange for money. Possibly cash. Did Kellner bring cash? If so, there was no clear indication. The money was not found at his home. Maybe the killer took it. Maybe the killer knew about the money and the murder was about the money!?

Bill decided that he had to get in touch with the Bad Homburg police. Maybe they had a clearer picture by now why the private detective had been killed. If I can speak to the young female detective, maybe I have a chance to find out. But I need a reason for my call. He looked at the contacts of his I-phone. No luck there. I have to call Werner Kraft, he must have the number. When he reached Kraft's office, he was told that Kraft was in a meeting. He asked the person to tell Kraft to call him back as soon as possible. But instead of waiting for the return call, Bill went on the internet and looked for the police department of Bad Homburg. It took him no more than five minutes to find the website and a general phone number. He asked for the homicide department, hoping to get connected with the young detective who had interrogated him. This time he was lucky. It was her voice. Should he talk German or in English? After deliberating for a second, he decided to try English, she might even enjoy a conversation in another language.

He reintroduced himself: "Hi, this Bill McDonald. Remember me?

You arrested and interrogated me a few days ago in the case of the killed private detective, the Kellner case."

There was a moment of hesitation on the other end, then she replied: "Oh yes, I do remember you, the PI from New York who was looking for a missing file. Have you found it?"

She was clearly teasing him. So, he kept his answer light: "Not yet, but there is progress here in Berlin. How about your end? Have you been able to figure out why Walter Kellner was killed and who did it?"

"You know that I shouldn't tell a stranger the results of our investigation, don't you?"

"Come on," he said in a low voice, "we're working on the same side"

"Let's hope so," she replied with a chuckle, "We don't have the identity of the killer, by the way, we assume there were two, professionals, they posed as gardeners. The reason could either be information or money. Possibly there was a large stack of cash in his strong box, which they opened."

"OK, this would make sense. It's possible that Kellner was supposed to deliver a large amount of cash in Berlin. As we know, the transaction didn't work out, so Kellner took the money back to Frankfurt and kept it in his house. The killer may have known this," Bill explained.

"Do you know this for a fact?" the detective asked.

"Not exactly," Bill admitted, "but it's a likely scenario. This was the kind of deal where you don't want to have traces."

"What kind of a deal are you talking about?" she wanted to know. Bill realized that he was getting in deeper than he had wanted. He had to retreat softly:

"Well, for details you may want to get in touch with the special police team in Berlin."

"This is the job of my senior colleague," she answered with a sigh, "I 'm in charge of the local scene, talking to the neighbors, etc."

"Good luck, great talking to you," Bill replied.

"What was the reason you called in the first place? I expected you to be back in New York."

Bill had to come up with a reason fast: "Oh yes, I'm missing a small notebook, black leather. Did I leave it at your office by any chance?"

"No, we haven't found a notebook, but if we do, I'll contact you."

"Thanks, and good bye."

The moment he finished the call there was another ring. It was Kraft who called back.

"Bill, what's up?"

"I just had a chat with the young detective in Bad Homburg, the one who arrested me."

"Any interesting news?"

"They don't know who killed him, but they assume that it was done by two professionals. There is also speculation that a large stack of cash was taken from Kellner's strong box, which would fit my theory."

"Let's postpone discussing your theory. We just finished a meeting of the special team. I have been asked to find the missing partner, Stefano Brindisi. How about coming along?"

"Yes, I'm game. We have to talk to Brindisi. I think he is more involved than we can see."

They agreed to meet at the hotel an hour later.

CHAPTER 8

Werner Kraft had picked a dark blue unmarked VW Golf for the excursion. He was looking for Bill at the Brandenburger Hof. He had told him that he would show up around 1:30 pm. Bill was already waiting in front of the hotel when he saw the car approaching and slipped into the right front seat as soon as it stopped. He greeted Kraft with a nod and fastened his seat belt, while Kraft moved the small car back into the dense traffic on the Kurfürstendamm.

"Where are we going?" Bill asked.

"The idea is to pay Brindisi an unexpected visit. Before I left my office, I called both the firm's office in Kreuzberg and his lab in Friedenau. The answer was the same. Stefano Brindisi had not been seen for days.

"So, he is hiding, but where?"

"I thought we pay his family a visit to find out," Kraft replied.

"Why his family? Is that a likely place to hide? He's a man in his thirties," Bill wondered.

"Good question," Kraft laughed, while he was making a left turn at an intersection.

"The Brindisis own a well-known restaurant in the center of town, in fact one of the best Italian restaurants in Berlin. You have to make a reservation at least a week in advance if you want to get a table. I checked his official address. It's identical with that of his parents."

"Unusual, isn't it?" Bill mumbled.

"Maybe for you and me, but not so much for a very successful Italian family that came to Berlin in the 1950s. It must have been the grandfather who opened a small place in the old West, in the vicinity of the university. The place became very popular and grew. After the fall of the Wall they moved to Gendarmen Markt, looking for a different kind of customer.

"What kind?" Bill wanted to know.

"More affluent, interested in refined Italian cuisine. By then, it was the son who was running the show. He figured correctly that Gendarmen Markt would be the right neighborhood for his ideas."

"What's so special about Gendarmen Markt?"

"It became one of the most sought-after neighborhoods in the nineties, there was a lot of rebuilding and restauration going on. Within a few years, a run-down area of East Berlin became one the most desirable parts of town."

"And the Brindisi family was part of this change?" Bill asked.

"Exactly, their timing was perfect. When they opened the new place, they could count on the kind of customers who don't mind to spend more money on a really good meal."

"Have you ever eaten there?" Bill wanted to know.

Werner Kraft chuckled: "No, that's out of my range. I would have been more comfortable at the old place where they had served basic Italian dishes."

"Maybe I'll try it out with Ulrike before I return to New York."

Kraft just nodded, paying more attention to the heavy traffic. He navigated the small car with great skill at high speed. They were now in a part of the town that Bill recognized from an earlier visit. The buildings had obviously received a lot of attention, not only fresh paint, but also new doors and windows. Elegant shops invited international customers.

"I could see myself living here," said Bill.

"Sure, but very pricey. How much is a chief of security making in New York City?" Werner Kraft asked.

"Barely enough to rent a small apartment in Manhattan," Bill replied, "I was told that Berlin is affordable."

"Maybe ten years ago. Those days are gone."

The VW Golf stopped in front of a large building with a ground floor that was occupied by a restaurant. No one could overlook the name of the owners in big letters above the windows. Kraft and Bill moved to the entrance to the apartments, looking for Stefano Brindisis' name. It was not listed on the board.

"Let's go to the restaurant and find out who is in," Kraft suggested. At this time of the day, the place was almost empty. There were only a few customers finishing a late lunch. A waiter approached them and wanted to show them a table, but Kraft took out his police ID, asking to speak to the boss. The look of the waiter became instantly stone-faced, asking them to wait at the bar. It took a few minutes until a middle-aged man with greying hair came from the kitchen.

"I am Bruno Brindisi," he said in flawless German, "what can I do for you.?"

Although the man was very composed, Bill noticed that he seemed to be slightly nervous, as if he had expected the police to show up and was prepared to deal with the intrusion.

"We are looking for Stefano Brindisi."

"That's my son. Why do you want to speak to him?" the older Brindisi wanted to know. His voice was polite but distant.

Werner Kraft assured him that they had come because of Herwig Stollberg's death. They needed to talk to his partners at KreuzbergChem.

"We tried his office in Kreuzberg as well as his lab in Friedenau. He wasn't there. Maybe you can help us."

"What is there to discuss? His death was a tragic accident, a hit-and-run, I understand. But that does not involve my son."

"Of course not, Herr Brindisi, this is not the point of our visit. We have questions about the purpose of Stollberg's trip that morning. Where was he going? Did he have an appointment? Maybe your son has information. After all, they were partners and old friends."

Bruno Brindisi remained silent, yet he appeared to be calmer now. Finally, he replied in a low voice:

"I saw my son at the funeral and briefly talked with him later that day, but since then I have not seen him. Of course, he has his own apartment in this house, top floor, and can have come and gone without my knowledge."

"What about other members of your family, for instance your other son?" Kraft asked.

"No, he has been out of town for several weeks. He is in Düsseldorf where we open another restaurant in the near future," Brindisi replied.

Werner Kraft realized that they would not get any helpful information from Bruno Brindisi and ended the conversation by getting his card out handing it over to the restaurateur, who put it into his pocket without even looking at it.

"Well, this conversation didn't get us very far," Bill said when they were back in their car. "Actually, I'm not surprised about this outcome," Kraft replied, while starting the engine, "I didn't expect to find him at his home. He is hiding someplace, and I have an idea where this could be."

"Wait," Bill exclaimed, "don't accelerate, look to the other side of the street. Do you see the parked tan SUV? The two men in it are watching the entrance of the Brindisi house."

Kraft stalled the engine and took a pair of binoculars out of the car's side pocket.

"Yes, you are right, these guys are observing this building."

For several minutes Werner Kraft and Bill remained motionless in their seats with their eyes turned to the other car.

"Who are these guys? Can you read the license plate?"

"No, it's too dirty, but. Doesn't look like a Berlin number."

All of a sudden, the SUV moved away fast. They decided that they couldn't do anything about this strange incident right now. Kraft started the engine again and cautiously joined the traffic.

"So, where is Brindisi hiding?" Bill asked.

Kraft briefly checked the mirror before he replied: "The Brindisis own a cottage at the Wannsee. That would be an ideal hiding place."

On the way to the lake Kraft filled Bill in, telling him about the most important results of the last meeting of the SOKO team. He mentioned the new evidence showing that the accident was planned and therefore a homicide case. He also mentioned the bank statements that showed Stollberg's financial problems and the likelihood of some deal with a third party.

Bill nodded: "This confirms our hypothesis that Stollberg was on the way to a meeting with Kellner at the Brandenburger Hof where they would conclude the transaction. Stollberg would have delivered the file and received the money, either in cash or in some other form."

"I guess so," Kraft replied.

"By the way," Bill continued, "I bet it was a cash deal, because there was supposedly a lot of cash in Kellner's strong box, which was broken open and cleaned out by his killers."

"How do you know?" asked Kraft.

"I talked to the detective in Bad Homburg this morning, they came either for the file or the money."

"Do they know who did it?"

"No, but they are sure it was a professional job," Bill said, "two guys who posed as gardeners in the neighborhood."

Meanwhile, they were driving through a suburban district, here and there still apartment buildings, but in between single brick houses and duplexes with front yards. They followed a wide street lined with old trees that gave ample shade. After a twenty-minute ride Bill all of a sudden saw the water of the lake to his right, still part of a suburban scene. He had expected a much more rural scenery. When he looked to the left, he noticed the sign of the city train and people coming out of the station, moving to the bus station on the other side of the road. Werner Kraft now followed a local bus that entered a smaller road close to the lake. On both sides of the street there were villas, most of them from the early twentieth century. After another ten minutes, they had to park their car and followed a footpath leading closer to the water. The large houses had given way to smaller cottages with access to the lake. Here it was surprisingly quiet. Bill felt a pleasant breeze coming from the water. Most of the cottages they passed seemed to be empty. Far out on the water, Bill recognized boats with colorful sails. A peaceful scene, Bill thought.

It was Kraft who first recognized the number of the Brindisi cottage and slowly opened the gate. They followed the path to the dark-green house with white-trimmed windows. Bill was about to knock on the door when Werner Kraft motioned him to step back.

"Let me go around the building, if he is here, we want to surprise him," Kraft said in a low voice.

Bill remained at the door, while the policeman followed a small path to the right leading to the backyard and the water. For several minutes it was completely quiet. Bill was wondering what Werner Kraft had discovered, but then there were several gun shots, clearly from a hand gun. Bill instinctively moved away from the door and ducked. Then he moved to the left of the house, trying to get a glimpse of the backyard. He couldn't see anybody. Was it Kraft who had used his gun or had he been the target of an attack? I should have brought a gun, he thought. I would feel much better with my gun right now. Then there were more shots, obviously from a different gun. Bill took cover behind an old birch tree, waiting for a person to move to the front of the house. He had a view of the path leading up to the cottage. Nobody was leaving the front entrance. He crouched and cautiously moved toward the back of the building. All of a sudden, the air was filled with the noise of a speedboat engine. It roared and then seemed to get more distant. He waited for a moment, just listening. Then he heard Kraft's voice:

"Bill, you can come around the house, they are gone."

When he came to the backyard, he saw Kraft close to the water, looking at a speedboat that was by now far away from the shore.

"Are you OK?" Bill asked.

"Yea, I'm fine. I was lucky that the first shot didn't hit me. After that it was an even match," Kraft said, "when I came around the corner I caught sight of a guy coming out of the backdoor. It seems he saw me first and had his gun ready. He fired a couple of shots but missed. Then he ran towards the water where a speedboat was waiting with another guy. I may have hit him with my second shot, because he was limping, but I'm not sure. When he reached the boat, they left in a hurry."

"So, we are not the only party trying to find out where our friend Brindisi is spending his time.," Bill exclaimed.

"Clearly not," Kraft replied, "he is obviously much deeper involved in the action than we thought, but I still don't really understand the entire plot, do you?"

Bill hesitated a second then he said: "This morning I thought I did, but now I'm not so certain. Let's check the cottage, maybe Brindisi is in there."

Kraft had his gun ready when they searched the cottage, but there was no sign of Brindisi. The door had been forced open, but otherwise the only traces they could find were a few used dishes in the sink. Maybe he had occupied the cottage.

"I have to call Herberg right away because of the use of my gun," Kraft informed Bill, stepping outside and moving away. A few minutes later he came back, searching for Bill who had gone back into the cottage searching for possible clues. Nothing had been touched. It appeared that the intruders were only interested in finding Stefano Brindisi.

"We are expected to meet with Herberg at Headquarters in an hour to discuss our next move. She has decided to send a forensic team to find traces that will tell us more about the identity of the intruders. She wants us to wait until the team arrives, OK!?"

Bill gave him a nod: "Fine, there is a bench close to the water. Let's go there and try to figure out how this whole thing hangs together."

They sat down looking at the lake and enjoying the fresh breeze without saying anything for a while. Finally, Bill said without turning to Kraft:

"Werner, I'm glad you didn't get hurt. This encounter could have ended very differently."

"I know," Kraft replied in a low voice, while he was kicking a small stone with his left foot, "I know, but this is part of my job."

They looked at the water for a while in silence. Finally, Kraft turned to Bill:

"Who are these guys and why would they go after Brindisi?"

"I don't know, Bill said, "can we be sure that they were going after him? Maybe they had come to protect him. But one thing is clear, they are not on the side of the law. Possibly they are part of the party that wants to block the deal between Stollberg and the third party in the US. In that case, they would be allied with the guys who killed the private detective in Bad Homburg. But then we would have to assume that Brindisi was somehow part of this deal, that he and Stollberg were working together, yet there is no evidence to support this hypothesis. Stollberg's motivation was unique: He wanted to take care of heavy gambling debts with one stroke. The American partner, it seems from what we have found out, offered him this kind of deal, good for him, but potentially bad for his little company."

"OK, I get that," Kraft interrupted, "but then Brindisi, if he suspected the deal, should also have been interested in blocking it. Therefore, the guys should have been friendly allies"

Bill thought for a moment: "Maybe, but not likely. Brindisi may have wanted to interrupt the deal for the sake of his company, but he was not interested in Stollberg's death. Stollberg was a close friend and a brilliant chemist. For me there is no immediate reason to assume that he wanted to hurt Stollberg."

Kraft remained skeptical: "There is still the question of Brindisi's disappearance after the funeral and the strange behavior of his father when we talked to him this afternoon. My guess is that the old man knew more than he told us."

"Agreed," said Bill, "he may know where his son is hiding. So, he wants to protect him, but who is the enemy? I suspect that the enemy showed up at the cottage this afternoon, looking for young Brindisi, who was smart enough not to be caught. Maybe his father warned him after we showed up. Remember the car in front of the house. In my opinion this is part of a larger plot."

"But what is the meaning of the larger plot?" Werner Kraft asked.

"I wish I could tell you" Bill replied. "At this point, there are still too many gaps."

At this moment, his phone beeped, informing him that a message was waiting. He didn't have a good feeling. This could be New York again with more questions and additional instructions. He glanced at his phone. It was indeed his law firm, demanding another detailed report and reiterating warnings not to get close to the German police. There was the line: "Do not get in touch with the police in Berlin or other German cities. Our client insists that you focus solely on the retrieval of the lost file. Neither our client nor this firm means to be involved with a murder investigation of the German police. This is strictly a matter of missing property." He was given only a few extra days to solve the case, otherwise he would be called back and replaced by a different detective. The tone of the message left no doubt that the firm was prepared to drop him. Of course, he realized that the case of the missing file could not be solved without solving the murder case. My only hope is the meeting with Charlotte Herberg later today. Maybe she has the missing pieces. The more he thought about this message and the behavior of his firm the more irritated he got. He stood up and walked away from the bench. He couldn't discuss this with Werner Kraft

"Are you OK?" Bill heard Kraft's voice from the bench.

"Yes, I'm fine," he replied, "just an unpleasant message from my boss. What he wants doesn't make sense and he knows it, but he still insists on having it his way. There must be pressure from the client that wants to keep a very low profile."

"Why?"

"What they are doing is legal but not good for public relations, if it gets into the media" Bill said.

Bill returned to the bench where Werner Kraft was trying to get in touch with the forensic team that was on its way to the cottage. He was told that they would arrive any minute now, which seemed not to improve his mood. Finally, they heard the footsteps of three men with their gear coming down the path from the gate to the house. Kraft gave them a brief report of the encounter before he and Bill left on their way to the meeting with Charlotte Herberg.

It was a few minutes past 4:00 when Werner Kraft and Bill entered the HauptKommissarin's office. She was on the phone, inviting them with a gesture to sit down. When she was done. she ordered coffee and asked Kraft to give a more detailed report of the encounter at the cottage. Meanwhile, Bill kept quiet, waiting for the coffee that would give him a much-needed boost. He had decided to minimize his input, unless she had explicit questions. Kraft had just completed his report when the secretary with the coffee arrived. It was a dark strong roast that revived Bill's spirits. It appeared to have the same effect on Charlotte Herberg who had looked tired.

"Well now," she said, looking at both of them, "how do we make sense of what happened at the cottage? Brindisi not there, but two men presumably looking for him, becoming instantly hostile when you show up.?"

"We have discussed this question at the cottage, while we were waiting," said Kraft, "but there seems to be no clear answer."

Bill remained silent. Noticing this, Charlotte turned to him asking for his opinion.

"Well, there are different ways of putting the known facts together," he replied in a low voice, suggesting that he wanted to keep his opinions to himself, "one can either assume that the men had come to help him or they had hostile intents. I am inclined to believe the latter. I think they are somehow connected to the men who killed Walter Kellner in Bad Homburg. They are part of a force that wants to stop the deal at all cost." He spoke in German, rather slowly, choosing his words carefully. "But frankly, I don't know why and to what ultimate purpose this party is doing this. There are still too many gaps. For instance, why are they after Brindisi who, we thought, was not part of the deal between Stollberg and the unknown group that Kellner represented.

"I agree with you," said Charlotte Herberg after a brief pause, "I also believe that the two men at the cottage meant harm to Brindisi, who was lucky not to be there. Maybe he was warned or he was never hiding there. I just talked with our colleagues at Bad Homburg. They have become much more willing to communicate lately, presumably after our brass talked to theirs. Their focus is the murder of Walter Kellner, who was supposed to meet Stollberg at the Brandenburger Hof. They hope to arrest the killers in the near future after getting good descriptions from local witnesses who saw them approach the house. They are local criminals from the Frankfurt milieu, professionals who do contract work. They may have been lured by the promise of a large amount of cash in the strong box."

Bill just nodded, this was old news to him but then she said something that changed his understanding of the case:

"The case has also broader ramifications, which are in the hands of the LKA in Wiesbaden. For them, the murder is related to a much bigger problem: foreign organized crime moving into Germany, trying to find suitable investment places for their money."

Werner Kraft stared at her: "What do you mean? These guys are actually looking for solid German companies where they can invest their money?"

"Sort of," Herberg replied, "I understand that they behave more like venture capitalists, who are looking for small companies that need capital."

"Like KreuzbergChem," Bill interjected.

Charlotte nodded: "Right, they could be the target."

"In that case, Stollberg's deal was a serious threat to their plans and had to be stopped by all means, murder included, "said Kraft, shaking his head, "but who are they? Who is organizing this?"

"I don't know," said Charlotte Herberg, turning to Bill McDonald, "do you?"

Bill just shook his head. For a moment he remained silent, then he said quietly:

"I still can't figure out Brindisi's role in all of this. Here is what we know. The start-up needed fresh capital for its new research. At the same time, Stollberg was in trouble, needing a large amount of money to cover debts. He planned to sell all or parts of the latest research and found an interested party in the US. Somehow, another party that is possibly interested in this company found out and decided that the deal had to be stopped. So, they eliminated Stollberg. How does Brindisi fit in? Maybe he somehow found out that his partner was about to sell out and is allied with the new group. But in that case, he has no reason to fear them and hide. Why is he hiding?"

"And where? Werner Kraft added, "we have no idea where he is, correct?"

"I'm afraid so," Bill admitted.

"But we need to talk to him, this is really urgent" Charlotte Herberg exclaimed. "We'll keep the Brindisi family under observation, around the clock. Also, if you can think of another hiding place, let me know immediately."

Kraft nodded.

"By the way," Charlotte continued, "I will join a meeting in Frankfurt the day after tomorrow to discuss the flow of dirty money into Germany, it will be our LKA men and the LKA of the state of Hesse. I have been invited as an observer because of the Stollberg case. Let's hope that I'll come back with more information."

She rose from her chair, indicating that the meeting was closed. Bill and Werner Kraft got up as well and walked to the door. At this moment, Charlotte said: "Bill, can you spare me another minute of your time?"

Bill turned around and approached the desk: "Yes?"

"I'm wondering, if you could tell me a bit more about the client of your firm. The reason why you are in Berlin, looking for a missing file. We have shared important information with you and hope that you will do the same for us."

There was even a smile on her face when she asked the question. Bill looked at her, returning her smile. Yes, he thought, he had expected this question, sooner or later, she would insist on finding out about the client. At this moment, he had to make an important decision. If he refused, as he was expected to do, she would cut him off, greatly diminishing his chances of solving his case. If, on the other hand, he gave her the name of the client, he betrayed his firm and might be liable, possibly losing his job. His answer was tentative:

"I have been ordered not to reveal the name of the client, not only once but repeatedly, but I fully understand your interest in this information. Maybe a generic answer will be helpful as well. The client is an important pharma company that is, I guess, interested in the results of recent research at KreuzbergChem. They have switched from food research to medical research. This is what Ulrike and I found out when we interviewed David Klein. Ulrike may have mentioned that to you. There must be some piece of the work at KreuzbergChem that is really important for our client. But they want to keep this deal out of sight. Does that help?"

"Well, Charlotte Herberg answered, "it's a good first step, and I will not push you further, there may be a time, however, when you have to reveal the name. Thank you."

Bill gave her a smile and left the room.

Charlotte remained in her chair, trying to decide what the next move should be. The search for Brindisi had not gone well. She was convinced that his father knew more about his present location than he had told Kraft. But what was Stefano Brindisi's role in this case? Either he had been in this together with Stollberg from the beginning. In that case the people who were looking for him at the cottage where presumably the same who had arranged the accident that killed Stollberg. Or he was allied with the group that tried to stop the deal. In that case the men who were searching for him might be part of a different group. The information she had received from Bad Homburg suggested that the men who had killed Kellner were professionals. It had been an execution. They were supposedly also looking for the mysterious missing file. There was nothing about this case she liked. And there was clearly no end in sight. Maybe she would get more background information at the meeting in Frankfurt. Until then there was not much she could do. There was another point that was going through her mind. The van that killed Stollberg was registered in Düsseldorf, at least most likely. Was that an accident or was the location a significant element of the puzzle? We need more information about this van and the driver, she thought. I have to push my men to follow up. She made a small note on her computer to bring this up tomorrow. Fortunately, the weekend was getting closer, which meant that Bernd Moeller would visit her. As much as she was looking forward to his visit, even here there were dark shadows. He had been talking about visiting his younger daughter in Australia, always postponing the trip, hoping that she might come to Hamburg instead. But that had not happened. Bernd had asked her opinion and she had encouraged him to go. It would be good for him to see his daughter again and it would also be an interesting trip to a part of the world he had never seen.

But now, after he had decided that he should go, she was not excited at the prospect of not being with him for at least a month or even two. He had suggested that she should come along, an idea that she had immediately rejected. This would be awkward. Father coming to see his daughter, bringing his new girlfriend along. She felt no desire to meet his daughter. In Berlin their relationship worked really well. They had a common professional base and it was clear that he respected her. Also, it allowed her to put the mixed memories of her years with Ernst behind her. Even when she accidentally saw him with his friends at the opera, the initial pain had become weaker and more tolerable. Once he must have noticed her. His facial expression was difficult to read – surprise to see her at this place, maybe also pain. It had become very difficult, she realized, to imagine them together again. They had been drifting more apart with no common ground to stand on. He couldn't relate to her job and she found it difficult to understand his work as an architect. Where is this going? she thought. Then she abruptly decided to end this train of thought. She needed to focus on the present. She stood up looking for her coat and left the room.

Bill made a brief stop at Kraft's office, telling him that he would go back to his hotel for dinner.

"I will keep you posted," Kraft said, "we have to find Brindisi, it's obvious that he is very much involved. I'll trying to set up some form of surveillance right now. We'll start with the house of the family and the lab in Friedenau."

"Yes, those are obvious places, but I'm not sure at all that he is in Berlin," Bill said.

"How do you know?"

"Gut feeling, no more," Bill replied.

Kraft laughed: "That may be good for a PI but not for the police."

"There you have a point," Bill admitted on his way to the door, "if I have more evidence, you will be the first to get the information. I mean to talk to Ulrike later this evening. Maybe she has an idea."

Subway or taxi? Bill thought when he left the building. The more he thought about Taylor, Hinchcroft & Martell, the more irritated he got. Their obvious attempt to put rigid limits on his search made no sense. He couldn't possibly ignore the murder case closely connected to the missing file. It was very likely that Stollberg was killed because of the file. Now they threatened to call him back unless he produced the file within days. Was Amos Hinchcroft serious or is this just a ruse to get out of a case that could become embarrassing for the firm? In any case, they don't deserve that I save money by using the subway. So, he hailed a cab and was back at the Brandenburger Hof within twenty minutes. He briefly checked for mail at the reception and exchanged a few pleasant words with the clerk, the same young man who had told him about the old lady.

"Did you meet with the private detective from Frankfurt?" he asked while handing a key to another guest.

"No," Bill replied, "He was dead before I had a chance."

The young man stared at him in disbelief: "You are kidding me."

"Nope," Bill said in a low voice, "he was really killed."

"Who did this and why?"

"There is no certain answer." Bill said casually, "the Bad Homburg police told me. Anything at this place that looked out of the ordinary?"

"Let me think," the clerk said, "only something rather small. There was someone here at the desk asking whether there had been a package for Herr Kellner that he had missed. Of course, there was no package."

"When was this," Bill wanted to know, "and who asked?"

"About two days ago. I wasn't on duty. I will have to ask the clerk on duty."

"Please do and also find out how the person looked."

Back in his room Bill stood at the window for a while looking down at the busy street. This had been a long and sometime confusing day. He couldn't deny that things were moving, but there was no clear direction. Supposedly, there was a missing file, yet it was as elusive as ever. Stollberg's role had become much clearer, while the other elements of the puzzle seemed to not to fit together. The fact that Ulrike had decided to go to Hamburg to do research didn't improve his mood. And then there was the threat from his firm. One thing, however, had become quite obvious. He had become involved in a dangerous game, as the shootout at the lake cottage had shown again.

Kraft could have been killed. I need my gun back, Bill thought, later tonight when I call her I will ask Ulrike where I can find it. Probably she is keeping it someplace in her apartment.

He decided to have dinner at the hotel, where the food was pretty good, and make plans later. In the restaurant he looked for the young waitress he had met the first day, but she was not on duty. Instead, a middle-aged woman asked for his wishes. He placed his order without much enthusiasm. Then he took his phone out, checking for messages and news from the States. There was a brief message from Ulrike, telling him that she was making good progress in the archive. "Hope to be back in a few days", he read, "how about your case? Any progress?" "Will call you later," he typed, "things are still murky."

After the meal he took a stroll on the Kurfürstendamm before he returned to his room. When he sat down at his small desk he had arrived at a conclusion: He had to go back to Frankfurt. His initial assumption had been that the key to his case was in Berlin, but that assumption was possibly wrong. The seller was in Berlin, but the buyer was in Frankfurt. He had to get in touch with the Alerta office in Frankfurt. They had hired Walter Kellner, who was now dead. They must have a better understanding of the content of the file he was expected to find. This would also give him the opportunity to talk to the detectives in charge of the Kellner murder. Maybe there was more information about the background.

CHAPTER 9

Bill reached the early express train to Frankfurt barely in time. He was still looking for his seat when the train was leaving the station, gliding like a silvery snake between the houses, picking up speed fast. His car was even more crowded than the last time, mostly by young men in dark formal suits, carrying black briefcases. They seemed to have no interest in the outside, focusing their attention instead on the laptop in front of them. Once he had found his seat, Bill closed his eyes for a moment, trying to form some sort of plan for his stay in Frankfurt. The first stop would be the Alerta office, which was located close to the Main river in the neighborhood of the old townhall. Depending on the information he would get there, the second stop would be either Kellner's detective agency or the police station in Bad Homburg. What could he expect to find out in a conversation with the Alerta people, who had been extremely successful in remaining almost invisible? It may not be easy to have a fruitful conversation with them. After all, things had not gone well for them. They must be under great pressure as well to explain to Headquarters why the meeting with Stollberg had not worked out and why the crucial file was missing. Had they been asked to start an investigation or were they just told to keep a very low profile, leaving the search to an outsider? Bill realized that it would have been proper procedure to inform his firm of the planned trip, asking for their endorsement. Fearing that Hinchcroft would have blocked the trip, Bill had decided to postpone the contact until he had information that would justify the contact with Alerta in Frankfurt. His hope was that they would pool information and thereby get somehow closer to the missing file. At the same time, he had to admit that he had no concrete ideas how this might become possible. They were in a similar situation: Kellner, their contact, had failed to receive the file and was killed after his second trip to Berlin. In fact, they are worse off than I, Bill thought, because they had been ordered to make the arrangements and acquire the valuable information. In the eyes of the CEO, they had screwed up. There must be tremendous pressure to correct the failure.

Bill kept his eyes closed, waiting now for the coffee service to come through the car. He badly needed a cup of coffee, since there had been no time for breakfast at the Brandenburger Hof. I will go to the dining car later, he thought, right now all I want is a cup of very strong coffee. When he found out a few minutes later that the young woman who pushed the cart with the coffee service also offered croissants, he changed his mind and added two croissants to his order. The young man next to him did the same, acknowledging Bill with a brief but friendly nod.

"On the way to Frankfurt as well?" he asked, taking a sip from his coffee.

"Yes, I am," Bill said, without looking at the man, who was in his late twenties, "yes, just a short trip to get some crucial information."

"Clearly, Frankfurt is the right place for that, isn't it," replied the young man, while putting the coffee and the croissants on the small table in front of him. "Of course, we can find plenty of information on the internet, but the really hot stuff you get only when you mingle with people on the floor of the stock exchange," he continued.

"Are you a trader?" Bill wanted to know.

"Oh, no, I am working for an investment company in Berlin, smaller outfit but really sharp."

"But you follow the stock market, don't you?" Bill asked.

"Goes without saying, I would be fired within a week, if I weren't."

This answer gave Bill a sudden idea, a question that might help him later in Frankfurt: "Do you also follow the pharma industry?" he asked.

"It's not my special field," was the answer, "but of course, I have to follow the general trend, after all, they are truly important."

"Maybe you can help me," said Bill without much emphasis, "some time ago I bought a few shares of a company called Alerta. How are they doing these days?"

For the first time, the young man really looked at him before he replied: "Well, that's not an easy question. It depends when you bought, before the stock went up or while it was high. There had been a rumor that Alerta was very close to a significant breakthrough in diabetes research. But then it turned out that the rumor was no more than a rumor. As a result, Alerta dropped sharply. More than justified, if you ask me."

He got his laptop out and searched for the information until he found it and showed it to Bill.

"It seems, Alerta took a beating," Bill said with a sigh. "I bought the shares because of the rumor."

"Sorry to hear this, man," the young man said, "I hope you didn't venture too much."

"Fortunately, I didn't get in too deep. I can wait until the stock recovers," Bill said in a casual voice, while he opened his own laptop, looking for new email. But no message from the firm, which was good news. He had to stay ahead of the curve.

"You know, it's by all means possible," said the young man in a low voice, turning to Bill, "that the rumor was never more than a clever move to boost the stock and then sell off quickly to make a quick profit. Happens all the time. You really have to watch out."

Bill just gave him a friendly nod before focusing on his own laptop, not paying much attention to this suggestion.

It was a few minutes past 11:00 when the train arrived at Frankfurt Central Station, spitting out a large crowd, most of them in a rush to get to their offices. Bill was among them, moving along the platform and then looking for a cab when he came to the main entrance. This time, he was not so lucky; there was a long line of people ahead of him. He immediately realized that the wait could easily take as much as twenty minutes. If he wanted to see someone at Alerta before lunch, he had to hurry. Briefly, he considered to walk, but his sense of the Frankfurt map was too weak to take that risk. Bill looked at the grey sky, which was not encouraging. Clearly, rain was in the air and he wasn't prepared for rain. I just have to wait, he thought. In the end, it worked out better than he had anticipated. It was barely 11:35 when he stood in front of the office of Alerta on the fourth floor of a rather faceless modern building. Clearly, the company made no effort to impress potential visitors. Now his task was to impress the person in charge of the German operation enough to share vital information. He realized that he came uninvited and with rather weak credentials. First, he had to win the receptionist and take it from there.

He gave her a big smile, introducing himself as a representative of the law firm Taylor, Hinchcroft & Martell, who needed to talk Adam Evans, the person in charge of this office.

"Do you have an appointment?" she wanted to know.

"There was no time for an appointment. This is a very urgent matter," he replied.

"What does this urgent matter refer to?" she asked, not quite convinced that the visitor had a legitimate claim.

"My firm represents Alerta in critical legal matters, there are questions that I have to discuss with Mr. Evans," Bill asserted, looking at her.

"Still, I need a reference, otherwise I can't help you at all," the receptionist answered.

"I understand," Bill exclaimed, "of course. Please tell Mr. Evans that my visit concerns Herwig Stollberg."

The receptionist looked at him with a doubtful face. "Herwig Stollberg?" she repeated.

Bill nodded: "Yes, Herwig Stollberg. It is urgent."

The young woman left the desk and disappeared in an adjacent room. It took more than five minutes until she returned, inviting Bill to follow her. He followed her to the end of a hallway where she knocked on a door. Bill heard the "come in" and stepped into the large bright office where he expected to meet Adam Evans. But behind the desk he saw a woman in her mid- thirties, a slender brunette, well dressed and clearly poised to talk to him.

She realized Bill's surprise and introduced herself with a smile: "I am Heather Morgan, the deputy director. Mr. Evans is unfortunately not available. Maybe I can help you instead."

She offered him a chair, clearly giving him her full attention.

"Do you know Mr. Stollberg?" she asked.

"No, I never had the pleasure of meeting him. When I first heard of him, he was already dead. But, it seems that he was an important client of your company. There was a deal in which Alerta would buy critical research information from Herwig Stollberg. But according to the information that was given to my firm by your company, the deal was not completed. Stollberg died before he had a chance to meet with your representative in Berlin. And the file with the critical information is missing. I have been sent to recover this file."

Heather Morgan had followed Bill's words. What he saw on her face was a confused look, as if he had said something that didn't make sense.

"I hear what you are saying, Mr. McDonald, and understand your background as a security officer, but I don't understand the part about our representative. There was no representative. Yes, this office was negotiating a deal with Mr. Stollberg, who had approached us with an interesting offer. It was Mr. Evans who met with Stollberg and then negotiated the details, but we never sent a representative to Berlin."

"No representative?" Bill asked, staring at Heather Morgan, "you have no knowledge of Walter Kellner, who came from Frankfurt to Berlin in order to receive the file and pay Herwig Stollberg?"

"I have never heard of Herr Kellner. Who is he?"

"Walter Kellner was a private detective with an office in Frankfurt, who tried to meet Herwig Stollberg in Berlin, but the meeting did not happen, because Stollberg was killed before he reached the meeting place."

"Why did you say 'was'?"

Bill looked straight at the woman when he answered: "Because he is also dead. He was killed after his return from Berlin in his private home in Bad Homburg."

The puzzled look on Heather Morgan's face told him that they were not on the same page. Something did not add up. Had he come with wrong information and therefore false expectations?

"But you had a deal with Stollberg?" he asked.

"Yes, we did, at least we thought we had a deal and were ready to pay him the agreed sum. But then, unexpectedly, Stollberg broke off contact. Evans tried again and again to reach him."

"But he was still alive when this happened," Bill wanted to know.

"Yes, his office in Berlin promised that he would return the call, but he didn't and he didn't respond to emails either. Complete silence. Two weeks later we found out about the accident."

"This must have been a huge disappointment for Alerta and especially for Mr. Evans?" Bill suggested.

Heather Morgan remained silent for a moment before she replied: "Yes, it was. A major setback for us, especially for Evans, who had been the lead for this deal. The expectations were very high, because the information Stollberg had to offer was of great value to the company. I'm not a scientist and neither is Evans. The response from our scientists in Boston was that it would save the company close to two years of research for a fraction of the cost. It was an incredibly good deal."

"Do you know what Alerta offered?"

"I was never given the exact figure. No need to know. My guess is around a million,"

"And how much is it worth?"

"A lot more. Between 20 and 40 million, was Evans' estimate."

"So Stollberg realized this and found a better deal," Bill interjected.

"Yes, that's our guess, but we don't know who the buyer was," Morgan told Bill.

Bill needed a minute to reorganize his thoughts. This was a radical turn for his search. He had been given information leading him to assume that Stollberg had a firm and final deal with Alerta and died in an accident shortly before he met the contact at the hotel. So, he had been looking for a missing file that was supposedly Alerta's property. But there had been no final deal. Stollberg must have been in touch with another buyer, who made a better offer. They sent me to Berlin to find out what really happened. They want to know who the competition is and if there has been a transaction before Stollberg's death. I have been played, Bill thought. The only open question is whether Hinchcroft and the firm were part of this setup. He decided to play it cautiously. He would reveal only what was necessary to get closer to the actual facts of the case.

"It appears there was in fact another buyer with a better offer," Bill said, "we believe that Stollberg was on his way to a meeting with a representative of the new buyer when he was killed. The police are almost certain that the accident was arranged to eliminate Stollberg."

"Why?" Heather Morgan asked with an expression of disbelief and horror.

"I don't know. There seems to be yet another party that wanted to stop the deal at any cost," Bill replied, "and I'm trying to figure out who this party is and what their reasons are. Do you have any ideas?"

"Frankly, I'm not the right person to ask this question. You should ask Evans, but he was called back a week ago."

"When will he be back?"

"He won't. I was notified a few days ago that he will be replaced," Heather Morgan said in a low voice.

"Why? What happened?

"He resigned,"

"In other words, he was fired."

"I'm afraid so," she whispered. There was a long pause. They looked at each other. There had been an executive decision in Boston. An underling had failed and was kicked out.

"OK, Ms. Morgan," Bill said, facing her, "we are dealing with a mess and it's a question of professional survival for you, and possibly for me as well. Can you tell me anything about the nature of the research, the interest of your company and the nature of the deal that would help me solve my case?"

"And what precisely is your case? I'm not sure about your side at all," she exclaimed.

"Understood," Bill said with a shrug, "I don't blame you. I'm expected to retrieve a file with valuable information that got lost when Stollberg died. It vanished. And I want to solve the murders of Stollberg and Kellner. Who killed them and why?"

"This is the first time that I hear about a missing file. For us there was no file. What I can tell you is how the transmission of the information was planned."

"How?" Bill asked with excitement in his voice.

"They, Stollberg and Evans, ruled out any electronic transmission as too dangerous because of hackers. So, it was either paper or another form of storage, such as a disk or a stick. The seller would leave the information in a locker at a railway station and our contact would pick it up.

"Was it supposed to be a cash deal?"

"That I believe was an open question. I was given to understand that Stollberg needed a larger amount of cash, but we hadn't figured out a safe way to deliver the money. Why is this important for you?"

"Because there would be similar problems with the new buyer."

"There was a new buyer?"

"Oh yes, I am pretty sure. Kellner was the contact to pick up the file and possibly deliver the payment."

"And he was killed after he received the information?"

"No, it's more complicated. He could not have received the file because Stollberg was killed before the planned meeting, but maybe the killer didn't know this or killed him for different reasons."

"This is horrible," she whispered close to tears, "I was supposed to be the contact for Alerta."

Bill looked at her with a sense of deja vue: "You were lucky that the Alerta deal fell through. By the way, the hired killers of Kellner have not yet been apprehended, but the police assumes they were local.

What exactly, did Stollberg have to sell?"

Heather Morgan looked at her hands when she replied: "I cannot really answer this question. As I said before, I'm not a scientist. It had to do with diabetes research, a small but vital piece that Stollberg had worked out. It would get Alerta about two years closer to a marketable product. Of course, there are also competing companies. The company that comes out first wins the race and will make a lot of money."

"And who are the competitors?" Bill wanted to know.

"I understand there is a company in India that has shown interest and possibly the Chinese," she replied. "Evans was especially concerned about the Indians, a company that had made money with generic drugs after the patents expired. They recently hired two very bright young scientists with top credentials. One of them had worked for us for a number of years."

Bill nodded without responding to her answer. I need time to rethink this case, Bill thought while he was getting up. I have to get to Kellner's agency. Maybe I can find out who hired him to go to Berlin. That would be the new buyer. And if the Bad Homburg detectives have in the meantime caught and interrogated the killers, there may be more information about the third party.

"I'm sorry that my visit turned out to be so disturbing for you, Ms. Morgan," he said with a smile, "I will check out Kellner's office and the Bad Homburg connection. Then I will be in touch with you again, possibly later this afternoon. Please contact me immediately if you can think of any information that throws more light on the puzzle"

He took out his card and placed it on the desk. She had gotten up as well and reached her hand out to him. "It appears that I have been played as well. Many of the facts you mentioned I didn't know. I was kept in the dark, deliberately, it seems. This is not a good feeling, is it?"

"No, it isn't," Bill said leaving the room.

As Bill was leaving the building, he noticed that the sky had become very dark. It could start raining any minute. He looked around for a café or small restaurant to grab a bite to eat and organize his thoughts. What he had just learned left a bad taste in his mouth. Alerta had turned out to be an unreliable client. Did Amos Hinchcroft know this or had he been kept in the dark as well? Bill rushed along the street close to the buildings, feeling the first drops of rain in his face. To the right he discovered a small Chinese restaurant and decided to take refuge there. He didn't care that much for Chinese food, but at this moment it didn't matter. First of all, he needed a dry place. The small interior turned out to be crowded, mostly tourists, he guessed, smaller and larger noisy groups. Bill was close to giving up in his search for a free table, when one of the waiters directed him to an adjacent windowless room with a small number of tables. Here is was rather dark but quiet. After ordering from the luncheon menu, Bill got his laptop out to check his notes. Had he simply misunderstood his mission or had he been misled from the very beginning? And what was he really expected to accomplish? When he arrived in Berlin he had assumed that there had been a deal between Stollberg and Alerta. There had been a file, prepared by Stollberg for Alerta, which got lost, and he was supposed to retrieve this file. Looking at his notes again, it turned out that the instructions had been less precise. There was supposed to be a file, but it did not state explicitly that this file was meant for Alerta. There was no precise definition of the content either. But was there a file? Stollberg had broken off the negotiations with Alerta, as Bill had just learned. Presumably because Stollbeg had found another customer who offered more for the information. Evans must have informed his superiors in Boston of this fact. So, what are they really looking for, Bill asked himself. The other possibility was that there was a file, prepared for the new customer, which vanished when Stollberg was killed on the way to the meeting at the Brandenburger Hof. There had been a contact person waiting at the hotel, namely Kellner. But who was his client? I will have to go back to Kellner's office to find out.

When the waiter brought his food, Bill just nodded without paying much attention to what he had served. He began eating his wonton soup, while focusing on his notes. I have to look at the case from the perspective of Alerta's top management in Boston, he thought, Then I can figure out my role in the setup. Alerta was interested in Stollberg's offer, because it would save them two years of research, according to Heather Morgan. Then they find out that Stollberg, who had agreed to a deal, broke off contact. They must have suspected that he had received a better offer. The next thing was Stollberg's untimely death. For Boston, there were two questions now: first, had there been a deal with another client before Stollberg died? and, second, who was this client? With whom were they competing? This is where the lawyers and I come in. The search was outsourced to an outfit that looks both legitimate and harmless. The hope is that in my search I stumble on the real link, that is, a new client and a real file with the valuable information. Bill's irritation grew. He had learned during his time at the law firm that the corporate world was not always as clean as it presented itself in the media, but this case gave him pause. Is Hinchcroft, his mentor at the firm and his father's friend, part of this? At one point, I have to find out, he thought, but not now. Now I have to pay Kellner's people another visit and be in touch with the Bad Homburg detectives. Maybe they have arrested the killers.

Although he realized that the appropriate beverage at a Chinese restaurant would be tea, he ordered coffee after he had finished his main dish, which had been surprisingly tasty. The waiter just smiled when he placed the large cup of clack coffee in front of him.

"Is it still raining?" Bill asked.

"It's pouring, you would be completely wet in minutes," the waiter replied.

Bill just nodded, taking out his phone and searching for the number of the police station. This room was not an ideal place for his conversation, but right now there was no other choice. He was lucky again. The receptionist connected him with the young female detective.

"Hello, it's me again," Bill said in a low voice, "anything new that I should be aware of?"

There was no immediate answer. After a long pause, he heard her voice again:

"Yes, there is, but I cannot discuss this on the phone. Where are you?"

"In Frankfurt, close to the old town hall," Bill replied.

"In that case you should come out to Bad Homburg."

"I will, later this afternoon. First, I have to contact Kellner's office. Do they know?"

"Not yet, but it will be public tomorrow. There will be a press conference later this afternoon. Try to be here for that, if you can."

Bill promised to be there before he turned the phone off.

When he was finally on his way to Bad Homburg in the later afternoon, he had regained the confidence that he could solve the case after all. The visit to Kellner's agency in the glass tower had provided small but significant pieces of information. When he talked to the well-dressed young man once more, he learned more about Kellner's recent contacts. It was obvious that the man and the rest of the staff were still coping with the unexpected death of their boss, who had founded the detective agency after leaving the police force of Frankfurt. It also became clear that the trips to Berlin had not been routine business with records and notes to which the staff had access. The well-dressed man had looked puzzled when Bill told him about these excursions for which he had no records and no explanation. This was highly unusual, the young man asserted. Herr Kellner had kept the habits of his many years in the police force. He had insisted on written records for everything. Except in this case. The young man, who was obviously managing the agency now, had been confused but had tried to be helpful. They looked for an electronic file. There was nothing under Alerta or Stollberg. There was nothing under Berlin either. If there was a file at all, Kellner must have used a different code. Bill had asked for Kellner's private notebook, but there was no notebook in the desk. Had there been unexpected appointment and strange visitors, Bill had asked the manager. The man had looked at him with an empty stare until he said "Aber ja" in German without explaining what he meant. Bill had waited patiently for a fuller statement. Yes, there had been an unusual visitor about three to four weeks ago. He had briefly talked to him because Herr Kellner had been in a meeting. He had returned an hour later and left with Kellner. The manager did not recall the name, just the first letter. It was something with a J. Bill insisted and learned that this man was probably from India, fluent English but with a peculiar accent. He had returned only once for a private meeting with Kellner. But there was no record of these meetings. Kellner had treated them as private. When Bill pressed the young man about the background of the visitor by suggesting that he could possibly be from Saudi Arabia or Syria, he emphatically rejected this possibility. He had insisted that the visitor had been from India or Pakistan. As much as

Bill had coaxed the young man, there was not a great deal of details that he remembered. The visitor had been middle-aged, around fifty, well-dressed, greying hair, wearing glasses, somebody who had an air of authority, a person who is in charge. Kellner had never mentioned him again. There had been no point in pressing further. It seemed to be a dead end.

When Bill arrived at the police station in Bad Homburg, the public meeting for the press was almost over. Bill just caught the summarizing statement of the leading officer who told the small crowd of reporters that they were confident to apprehend the second suspect within days. At this point, the police had enough hard evidence to prove that the apprehended man had been at the scene of the crime, as much as he denied to be involved. It was an ongoing investigation, the spokesman asserted, promising that the press would be kept informed. There were additional questions, but the police officer refused to respond. Fortunately, Bill discovered the young female detective among the police officers in the background and tried to get her attention. She signaled him to stay behind and later asked him to follow her to the offices in the back.

"So, you almost missed the great event: We got one of the killers," she said, while she offered him a chair and a cup of coffee."

"Sorry, I took a taxi and miscalculated the rush hour traffic from Frankfurt," he responded.

"At this time of the day, you should have taken the train," she said with a smile.

Bill just shrugged his shoulder, hoping that she would give him a more detailed report about the investigation.

"Are you sure that the man in custody killed Kellner?" he asked her when she made no effort to tell him more.

"We are certain that he was involved. We matched fingerprints and found items that belonged to Kellner when we apprehended him in his apartment," she said looking at a file in front of her, "but we suspect that he was not the man in charge, more the help and potential fall guy, if things went wrong."

"What do you know about the purpose of the crime at this point?" Bill wanted to know.

"At this point, the official version is that the criminals were looking for cash, which they hoped to find in Kellner's strong box."

"But that was not really the reason Kellner was killed.?"

"Probably not, they were looking for something very specific, but the guy we caught doesn't know what it was, he tells us, and I believe him. As I said, he was just the help. The whole thing was supposed to happen during Kellner's absence. But Kellner came home early and surprised them. There was an argument and then Kellner supposedly pulled a gun, but the missing man shot first. Our guy claims that he wasn't even in the room when it happened."

Bill was sipping his coffee, looking at the detective, who was still busy with her file. I have to find out who ordered the search, Bill thought. Who was the client who sent Kellner to Berlin?

"Have you been able to find out who paid these men to search Kellner's home?" Bill asked without looking at her.

Now she looked at him, telling him with her smile that she fully understood the importance of this question. "No, we don't," she replied, "the man we apprehended pleaded that he had no idea. He talked about phone calls of his buddy, etc. I think he wasn't supposed to know. But it is almost certain that there was a contract. He is a gardener, by the way. They used the equipment of his company to stage the break-in. Talking about the client: I thought you had a firm idea about the client."

"I did," he replied in a low voice, "but it turned out to be wrong. I found out earlier today that Kellner did not work for our client. The negotiations failed. They never sent a contact person to Berlin. Which means that Kellner worked for somebody else."

"You know, for us here, trying to solve the Kellner case, this may not be all that important. We just want to nail the two guys at his house, but for the LKA officers this may well be relevant," she said, looking at him while closing the folder. "By the way, they are in the building, but keeping a very low profile."

This conversation has taken a turn that I don't necessarily like, Bill thought. The idea of another interrogation by the LKA of Hesse did not fill him with enthusiasm. On the other hand, however, they might know stuff that would help him with his case.

"Do you expect to get more information out of the man you apprehended?" Bill asked casually.

"I doubt it," she replied, "he seems to be very afraid of his partner and even more of the organization behind him. We suspect organized crime, that's why the LKA officers are here as well. But there is no hard evidence at all."

At this moment, the door opened and two officers entered the room. Bill recognized them immediately, they were the LKA agents. They greeted him with a cheerful smile, suggesting that they were really glad to meet him again. A brief nod to the young detective made it clear that she was expected to leave the scene.

"Still working on your case?" the older of the two asked while grabbing a chair next to Bill. The other one took the chair the young detective had left. It was clear that they were ready to have a serious conversation with Bill.

"I guess our young colleague has filled you in," the younger officer said, opening the dialog.

Bill decided to hold back to find out where this conversation was going. Were they interested in exchange or did they just want to push him. So, he just nodded.

"Since we last met," the second officer added, "there have been quite a few developments. You may be aware of some of them, others will be new to you."

That sounded like an invitation to swap information, Bill felt, giving the officers a cautious smile.

"indeed, there have been," he suggested, "but things are even less transparent than a week ago"

"I'm not so sure about this," the older officer replied, focusing his attention on Bill, "we can tell you for instance that possibly the client of your law firm didn't nail the deal with Stollberg they wanted so much."

"How do you know this?" Bill asked looking back at the officer.

"It wasn't too difficult to figure out that you are working for Alerta.

Your firm has done legal work for Alerta for many years. They have focused on diabetes research and they are vitally interested in the research of KreuzbergChem, but it seems, another company made a better offer."

"And who was that?" Bill, who could not hide his surprise, wanted to know.

"We are getting close," the officer told him, "we assume that Kellner worked for them and went to Berlin to close the deal. We believe, there were a number of players, all of them foreign."

"What's your interest in this murder?" Bill asked. "Why don't you just leave it to the police of Bad Homburg? They appear to get results."

"Good question," the older officer responded. "We are not just interested in the Kellner murder or the Stollberg murder in Berlin for that matter. They are just part of a larger pattern that we are trying to figure out. Wir folgen dem Geld. Do you understand?"

"Frankly, I don't," Bill replied.

The officer leaned back before he responded: "Lately, smaller German companies have attracted foreign capital, legitimate capital as well as illegitimate money. Both the Italian and the Russian Mafia are trying to buy up smaller German companies as a way of laundering their dirty money. This method has a long history in the restaurant and hotels business, but more recently the field has broadened. Now, promising start-ups are on their list."

"Like KreuzbergChem?" Bill suggested.

"Exactly," was the answer. "However, in this case, we have a complication, because one of the partners was ready to sell vital information behind the back of his partners."

"And the client of your law firm was ready to buy," said the other officer, "but there was a higher bid represented by Walter Kellner."

"Do you think that the bidder was a legitimate company?" Bill asked, looking from one of the officers to the other.

"Most likely this was the case," the younger one said, "Kellner was a highly respected former police officer, he would not have worked for the Mafia."

"But why was he killed?"

"You tell us," the older one replied, chuckling. "This is where things become complicated, because the competition becomes lethal, here in Frankfurt and before that in Berlin."

"Tell us more about Brindisi," the other officer interjected.

"I think he's hiding because he's afraid of somebody. We were looking for him, but couldn't find him either at his home or at a cottage his parents own at the Wannsee. His behavior at the funeral was very strange. Do you believe that he's involved?"

"Certainly involved, but how? On Stollberg's side? Or on the opposite side? Trying to stop the deal? We are keeping an eye on the Brindisi family. Where is their money coming from? Just restaurants or are there other sources as well?"

Bill began to realize that these men had a broader scope and a different angle. Maybe the piece of information he got this afternoon would fit in. It was a gamble.

"This afternoon I talked to the manager of Kellner's agency. He mentioned a foreign visitor a few weeks ago. From India or Pakistan. But no records, no official business. Just two private meetings with Kellner."

The older officer nodded: "There you go. This may be relevant, a potential buyer who wants to keep a low profile because what Stollberg offered was not quite regular?"

Bill shook his head: "No, he tried to sell valuable information behind the back of his partners."

"And why would he do that?" the older officer exclaimed.

"He was a gambler and needed money to pay off debts."

"That's a new angle. We didn't know that. This kind of situation attracts dark clients. Have you thought of that?"

"Yes, I have," Bill replied. "I suspect that he got into the hole very deep, but I can't figure out the pattern. According to his ex-wife, there were threats to him and her."

"How do you know?"

"A reliable source, a reporter who interviewed the wife."

"Ah, the young reporter who worked for the BZ?"

"The very same, how do you know?"

Bill realized that these guys were surprisingly well informed. They must have checked him out as well.

Then there was an unforeseen question: "Do you have a theory?"

Bill hesitated for a moment before he replied: "This morning I had a theory, right now I'm uncertain about the connections. This morning I thought that Alerta had a deal with Stollberg. This deal went bad, when a third party killed him before he had a chance to conclude the deal at the Brandenburger Hof. I assumed that Kellner was the contact man for Alerta. I was not sure about the third party, either a competitor or organized crime. The Kellner murder was not a good fit because the killers should have been aware that the deal went bad and that Kellner didn't receive the file. Then I found out today that Stollberg broke off negotiations with Alerta. Kellner didn't work for Alerta. But for whom did he work? And why was he killed when we know that he didn't receive the file from Stollberg. The whole thing doesn't make sense," Bill said with a sigh.

The older officer got up, pacing up and down. "We have to rethink the facts in the context of the larger pattern. The movement of capital into Germany. KreuzbergChem would be a good target Why? It's a successful start-up that has produced very good results during the last two years. The company is worth around 20 million right now. There must have been interest. Stollberg and Brindisi were first-rate chemists. The Alerta management must have known that or they should have."

"OK, but that's not what they did," said Bill, "they tried to get just one piece from Stollberg, because he needed cash."

"Right, that wasn't a smart move," the younger officer interjected, "Stollberg must have realized that and changed course. Maybe his partner Brindisi found out and tried to stop the cheap sell-out."

"Yes, that would make sense, but he would not cooperate with the killers in the van, would he?" Bill asked. "He is hiding and, as we found out, the folks who are looking for him are not friendly. They shot at the police officer with whom I was looking for Brindisi. So, what's your theory?"

The two LKA officers looked at each other with a faint smile.

"Well," said the older one, "we have a basic theory with many open questions. We work on the assumption that KreuzbergChem was targeted for a buy-out by more than one party, some of them legitimate, other not. One of the partners was ready to sell or at least ready to sell parts of the research, the other two we assume were not interested. They may not have known about the secret negotiations or they may have resisted."

"And the murders?" Bill asked.

"They occurred when the parties clashed. The most likely version is that illegitimate organizations used violence to get the outcome they prefer. So, Stollberg was eliminated when he was about to conclude a secret deal with an unknown party, and Kellner was eliminated when he became the contact between Stollberg and an unknown company. The basic feature is the transfer of ownership from a German company to foreign capital. Stollberg and Kellner became victim of this process. We have two competing legitimate companies, one of them your firm's client and in addition one, possibly even more than one criminal party involved."

"And what happened to the missing file?"

"Sure, that's a burning question for Alerta and therefore for you, but not for us."

"And the murders?"

"Not our focus either. We leave that to the detectives of Bad Homburg and Berlin. By the way, your chances of retrieving the missing file are not good, and should you find it, you have to be aware that the content is most likely still the property of KreuzbergChem."

"Are you sure?" Bill exclaimed.

"Ultimately, the courts would have to decide that question, again, not our primary concern."

Which means, that Alerta is still a legitimate player, Bill thought. This conversation had taken another unexpected turn. He saw his entire mission in a different light. He had to rethink his approach and his role. He needed to be alone, but the officers seem to enjoy his company. In fact, one of them suggested to order some food or to go to a nearby restaurant he knew. Bill found himself agreeing, realizing that he needed the good will of these men.

"Let's go to the Greek place," the younger one said, "it's very reasonable and at this time of the day not too crowded."

On the way to the door the older officer turned to Bill: "I meant to ask you a question: What happened to the young American journalist you rescued two years ago?"

Bill looked at him with an air of surprise. "I believe she is fine. I haven't seen her for a while. As you can imagine, she needed time to recover."

"That operation got you quite a reputation on the inside," the other officer added.

"Really? I was not aware of this at all, Bill said, "in the official report I was barely mentioned."

The officers chuckled: "Ja, we know that. It was all the F.B.I. and the 'brave' American Consul. But the facts are known among the people familiar with the story. You did an excellent job. The young journalist was lucky that they sent you to look for her."

CHAPTER 10

Charlotte woke up with a light headache. The next half hour would decide whether the pain would go away or settle behind her eyes and extend from there to her forehead. In that case the day was lost. Right now, she needed a hot shower and a cup of coffee. Maybe the glass of white wine she had during the intermission at the opera was to blame. She knew that she had to be very careful with alcohol, but there were occasions when she did not want to miss a good glass of wine. And last night was one of these occasions. She was very moved by an excellent performance of *The Marriage of Figaro*, especially with Bernd next to her. This time she did not mind the artificiality of the opera as an artform. It had been a great weekend. Even the news that Bernd had finally booked the flight to Sydney had not depressed her mood. For two days the pressure of her police work had disappeared. But now the pressure was back. Bernd would be on his way to Hamburg and she would face a case that seemed to go nowhere. She put her feet on the floor and moved slowly to the bathroom where she stepped into the shower and turned the water on. She allowed the gentle stream of the hot water to cover her entire body, hoping that the headache would disappear. It seemed to work, at least the pain was not getting worse. She would be able to focus on a number of important meetings, among them a conversation with David Klein, who had resisted a meeting at his office and had to be summoned to the police station as a material witness in a murder investigation. Finding the van that was involved in the killing of Stollberg was another item on her list. Both Osnabrück and Düsseldorf had been slow in their responses. It was obvious that the colleagues gave this task a very low priority. They don't care a bit because it's not their case, Charlotte thought, while she was stepping out of the shower and drying her hair. But for me this information could be critical. Once I have identified the owner of the van, I am much closer to the killer. The worst case would be a stolen vehicle, but even in that case fingerprints or other traces could help. The advances in technology had really changed the game. From the kitchen she heard noises, telling her that Bernd was already busy preparing breakfast. They would have breakfast together before he would be on his way to the central station and she would be picked up by her assistant. It looked like a reasonably good day after all. By the time she was dressed, she realized that the pain was almost gone. She needed time to think more about the meeting with the LKA Hesse people, but that could wait a day or two. More pressing was the meeting with Klein. He must know more than he has shared so far, she thought. After all, KreuzbergChem was a small company. One of the partners was dead, the second one was missing, and the third one had not been available for an interview.

When Charlotte stepped into the kitchen, she saw Bernd standing at the table setting up the plates. He looked at her with an air of concern: "Headache?"

She shook her head: "Yes, but I think it's not serious. The pain is almost gone."

"I'm so glad to hear that," he responded, while turning to the coffee machine, "how about a cup of fresh coffee?"

She just gave him a smile and nodded. She took her seat at the table, keeping her eyes closed for a moment. This was the last quiet moment before she entered the pressure that was waiting for her. The Stollberg case, which had begun as an accident and then turned into a homicide, had morphed again. It seemed to be part of a larger problem caused by international organized crime, as she had found out at the Frankfurt meeting. She realized that she and her team had to rethink the case in light of the new information, which confirmed some of Bill McDonald's hunches. When she opened her eyes again she noticed Bernd's gaze.

"Are you all right?" he asked in a low voice, offering her a mug filled with steaming coffee.

"Don't worry, Bernd, just work, a case that has become larger and larger without getting easier."

"Want to talk about it?" he replied pouring himself a cup.

"Let's not do that, not now, I want to keep the weekend mood just a bit longer. I may not see you for a long time."

He did not insist. He realized that this was the danger of their relationship: police work. It had the tendency to intrude. He stood close to her chair putting his hands gently around her shoulders. How things had changed. Just a few years ago she had been just a younger colleague of whom he thought highly. Now four years after the sudden death of his wife she had become the new center of his life. He had even thought about moving from Hamburg to Berlin but then rejected the idea because he was not sure whether she wanted him to be that close.

Thirty minutes later Charlotte stepped out of the front door of her apartment building, looking for the old Mercedes. Kraft had parked the car right in front of the building, the engine already running. When he saw her, he stepped out of the car, came around and opened the door for her. Charlotte knew that he was not expected to do this, but she appreciated the gesture.

"How was your weekend?" she asked when she had fastened her seatbelt and the car was already moving.

"Not bad at all," he replied. "partly catching up on reading, partly spending time on the Wannsee, sailing with friends who own a boat. And you? How was Frankfurt?"

"Actually, better than I expected," Charlotte replied. "You know how much I hate these long administrative meetings. But this one turned out to be important for us. Our case appears to be linked to a pattern where organized gangs try to buy smaller German companies in order to launder money and invest capital. The Mafia is part of it, but there are other groups as well."

"Is there an attempt to buy up KreuzbergChem?" Kraft wanted to know.

"That's what we have to figure out. The Frankfurt discussion never got that detailed. It was more about the larger European pattern. It's not only the LKA Hesse and Berlin that are concerned, but also the federal police, the BKA."

"Well, there will be a chance for us to find out when we talk to David Klein this morning," Kraft said.

Charlotte just nodded.

"He has promised to be at Headquarters at 10 am," Kraft added.

Much will depend on the success of the interview, Charlotte thought. He must know more about the background of Stollberg's death than he has shared so far. Possibly he even knew where Brindisi was hiding. The rest of the trip they were riding together in silence.

David Klein looked pale and tired when he entered Charlotte's office two hours later. He tried to offer a smile, while accepting Charlotte's offer to use the chair in front of her desk, but it was more a grimace than a smile.

"I am glad you finally found the time for a meeting, Herr Klein," Charlotte opened the conversation. "I tried to arrange a meeting with you at your office, but we were told that your calendar was too busy. Do you realize that we are dealing with a murder investigation?!"

Klein looked at her with an air of hostility before he replied: "No, actually, when I came back from Israel, I was told that Herwig Stollberg's death was an accident. You will have to explain to me why you think that he was murdered and what I have to do with this turn of events."

This is not a promising beginning, Charlotte thought. She decided to calm him down.

"Stollberg was your partner and close business associate. Even when we still believed that his death was accidental, we wanted to talk to you. After all, the circumstances of his death were rather peculiar. We found out that he was on his way to a meeting where he planned to sell part of his research to a foreign company. You must have known that!"

Klein looked at her with an air of puzzlement: "No, I did not. This is the first time that somebody suggests to me that Herwig Stollberg was planning to sell part of the company's intellectual property without discussing this with his partners."

"It seems that Stefano Brindisis was aware of this deal," Charlotte interjected, hoping to provoke him.

"Again, I cannot relate to your statement. I talked to Stefano Brindisi briefly after the funeral. Obviously, he was stressed and upset, but he did not mention any deal with a foreign company. Such a deal would have been premature and would have hurt the company."

"But you had financial problems, right? You needed new capital."

Klein looked briefly at his fingers before he said: "Yes, that's correct. We need capital. That was the reason for my trip to Israel. But how is this fact connected to Herwig Stollberg's death?"

"You tell me," Charlotte said in a low voice, "you are the financial officer, I understand. Maybe you found out that Stollberg was ready to sell out and took measures to prevent this?"

This was a shot in the dark, Charlotte realized. It could backfire, but it might push him enough to tell her more about the background.

Werner Kraft, who had followed the interview in silence, got his clue and asked suddenly: "Herr Klein, where were you on the day of Stollberg's death?"

"You must be completely out of your mind," Klein replied. It was obvious that he was angry.

"I was in Jerusalem, meeting with potential venture capitalists, one of them an American from the Westcoast who expressed interest in putting up the money we need. Do you understand anything about financing a start-up?"

"Please, calm down," Charlotte interjected. "We are no financial experts, but we have a murder case to solve. Your partner, Herwig Stollberg, was murdered, run down by a van when he was crossing an intersection. Why did this happen? And who is responsible? Please help us to find out."

Klein remained silent, just staring at her and Kraft. Finally, he exclaimed:

"Why do you harass me? Do you have any idea what it means to be responsible for our company after the death of its leading chemist and the disappearance of his close associate? What am I supposed to tell the staff? I can cover the engineering aspect of the new project, but the real stuff was exclusively in the hands of Stollberg and Brindisi. They were very close, became friends when they were students. Later they founded the company together, which I joined three years ago when it became clear that they needed someone with a background in engineering. Right now, I'm not even sure whether we will survive. If Stefano doesn't come back, it looks grim."

"I am sorry to hear this," Charlotte replied, "we certainly don't mean to harass you, and I can imagine what Stollberg's loss means for the company. Still, I have to ask questions, since we are dealing with a homicide case."

"How can you be so sure that Herwig was murdered?" Klein replied, "he didn't have enemies!"

"I'm afraid he did," Kraft interjected, "you are in denial."

Charlotte gave Kraft a sign not to upset Klein before she said: "There is strong evidence that the hit-and-run was planned. The statements of eyewitnesses and the pictures of a video camera make it clear that the driver of the van meant to kill Herwig Stollberg, who was on the way to a meeting with a person at the hotel Brandenburger Hof. Were you aware that he planned this meeting?"

"No, this is the first time I hear about a meeting," Klein answered, "What was the purpose?"

"Stollberg was ready to close a deal with an unknown company. The object were the results of his recent diabetes research."

"I can't believe this," Klein exclaimed, "Herwig would not do this. He wouldn't sell any results behind our back."

"I'm afraid he planned to," Charlotte replied, "I'm sorry to tell you this. This must hurt."

Klein's gaze moved back and forth between Charlotte and Kraft. It was obvious that he was not ready to accept this information. His pained facial expression signaled disbelief. Charlotte decided to give him time to adjust to the new reality. She offered a cup of coffee, which Klein declined. But he accepted glass of water.

After several minutes of silence Klein said: "Is this a trick? What are you trying to accomplish? I cannot believe that Herwig was meaning to betray us. We were partners and friends. Yes, there were offers to buy us out, but we decided not to accept any of these offers for two reasons. First and foremost, we liked our independence and, second, the offers were too low. They wanted to buy the company before it had produced the decisive results."

"But you needed money?" Charlotte said casually.

"Yes, that's right. We needed and still need capital to expand and conclude our project. That was the reason for my trip to Israel where I have local connections and also a number of useful American contacts. I was very close to a deal."

"How well did you know Stollberg's private life?" Kraft wanted to know.

"We were good friends. Not as close as Brindisi and Stollberg. I knew his wife, but not well. Recently, they broke up."

"Do you know why?" Charlotte asked.

"I understand there had been problems for a while. She was a teacher and used to a stable financial situation. In the case of a start-up that is never possible."

Charlotte gave him a reassuring nod. I have to keep him talking, she thought. We need his help.

Then she said: "Were you aware that Stollberg was a gambler and owed a large amount of money?"

There was another tense moment of silence.

"Are you sure? How do you know this?"

"We had access to his accounts. He owed around 900,000 Euros."

"The lenders were getting impatient," Kraft added. "According to his ex-wife, there were threats"

"This does not sound like the Herwig Stollberg I knew," Klein said in a low voice.

"Now you understand better," Charlotte interjected, "by selling his research he could wipe out his debts, which had become a threat to his life."

Klein looked at the police officers with an air of skepticism before he said: "Let's assume for a moment that he was planning to sell out because he was threatened, why would the lenders kill him when he was on the way to close the deal and then pay them back?"

"Because the killer was not identical with the lenders. The killer wanted to make sure that the deal would not be closed," Charlotte said.

"I'm still confused,' Klein whispered. "You tell me that there was a company that was ready to buy the results, but there was also someone else who wanted to block that move, and then there were more people to whom he owed money?"

"Correct"

"Who wanted to buy the results?"

'Does the name Alerta ring a bell?"

"Yes, of course, a major American pharma company. In fact, we were competing with them."

"There is solid information that they wanted to buy when Stollberg approached them."

"Clearly a bad deal from our point of view. They wanted to get the pieces that they lacked for a fraction of the cost. That makes no sense."

"Correct, but remember that Stollberg was under extreme pressure. He feared for his life," Charlotte explained. After exchanging a brief eye contact with Kraft, she decided to change the topic: "We are trying to talk to Stefano Brindisi as well. Can you tell us anything about his present location? We went to his home and talked to his father, who claims not to know where his son is. We even went to the family's cottage on the Wannsee. But there is no trace of him. He's hiding. But where and why?"

"I wish I could help you. I have been looking for him as well. For obvious reasons. He is now the crucial researcher. Without him there is no future for the company. I talked to his parents as well. They seem not to know where he is."

"Do you really believe this?" Kraft asked. "Maybe he tried to stop the deal when he found out what his friend was planning."

"How should I know?" Klein replied. "I can imagine that he wanted to stop Herwig from doing something stupid, but I don't know. I haven't talked to him since the funeral. This has been very upsetting for me as well."

"I fully understand where you are coming from," said Charlotte, picking up the conversation, "we have to figure this out together. There is some reason to believe that your partner is in danger and may be hiding for that reason. Where would he go if he felt threatened?"

"Again, I don't really know," Klein replied with a shrug. "My guess would be that he would rely on family connections."

"Italy?" Kraft interjected.

"Not necessarily so, maybe cousins in other German towns. But frankly, I don't know much about the Brindisi family," Klein said.

Charlotte looked at David Klein, who looked even more exhausted than at the beginning of the interview. She decided to end the conversation and thanked him for his help. Klein just nodded and left the room with a gesture that expressed his strong irritation.

"We should have pressed him harder about the companies that wanted to buy KreuzbergChem," Kraft said, turning to Charlotte.

"We will have to come back to that at a later time," Charlotte replied. "Today we had reached the limit. Do you think that he was lying?"

Kraft paused for a moment. Then he said: "No, I don't think so. It appears that he was kept in the dark. Frankly, I don't envy him."

"I agree," Charlotte added, "he's in a really difficult spot. But we still need him to figure out the business angle of the murder. He knew Alerta. But who were the other companies interested in his start-up?"

"By the way, how did you find out the name of the American company?" Kraft asked. "McDonald never mentioned it."

Charlotte said with a grin: "At the meeting in Frankfurt. The LKA of Hesse had figured it out."

At this moment, there was a knock at the door. It turned out to be another member of the special team, handing Charlotte a slim folder before she disappeared again. Charlotte glanced at the single page inside and held Kraft back, who had walked to the door.

"Wait a moment, this may be important. News about the van."

Kraft returned to her desk with an air of excitement. Together they looked at the printout of an email. It reported that a grey van had been found in a public parking garage close to the central train station of Bielefeld. It had been sitting there for a longer period and was discovered by a routine police check-up. Bielefeld was asking for instructions. According to the report, there was a good chance that is was the van used in the Stollberg case.

"I think we should get our hands on the vehicle as soon as possible," Kraft cried, "before they mess up the evidence."

"Agreed," Charlotte said. "Are you willing to go to Bielefeld right now to pick it up?"

"Of course, I am, but I need a special truck to load the van. I don't think that Bielefeld will make their special trucks available. I need an urgent order from you and will be on my way."

Charlotte noticed that he looked very excited. Ten years ago, she might have been as eager as he was. She realized that those days were gone. All she wanted were the results of a thorough check that determined that it was in fact the vehicle used for the murder. She hoped that there would be fingerprints of the driver and the other person. Why was the van left in Bielefeld? She thought. She had expected to hear from Düsseldorf or Osnabrück. There must be a reason. But she could not think of one right now. She sent an urgent message to the car pool to release a special truck for Kraft.

After lunch Charlotte decided to pay the Brindisi family another visit. The more she had reflected on the conversation with Klein, the more the felt that somehow Stefano Brindisi was a key figure in Stollberg's untimely death, although she had no clear idea what his actual role had been. Was he part of the forces that tried to stop the transfer of information? That would certainly make sense, given his position as a partner of KreuzbergChem, the company that would be financially hurt by Stollberg's plan. He was in the same situation as David Klein, who had been very upset when he learned that Stollberg had been ready to sell out behind his back. On the other hand, Stollberg and Brindisi had been close friends for a long time. Was it likely that he would kill Stollberg to prevent the transfer? And then there was the uncertainty of his situation vis-à-vis Stollberg. She could not assume as a given that he knew about Stollberg's plan. But if he had no knowledge and there was no involvement, then why would he hide? Why was

Brindisi hiding? Kraft's encounter at the Wannsee cottage of the family had been violent. This meant that not only the police were looking for him. Possibly, Brindisi was on the run, but who was hunting him? So far, the surveillance of the Brindisi's house between 8:00 am and 6:00 pm had not resulted in any useful information. There were no unusual movements. Both the father and the mother had followed their routines, and there was no report that the older brother had been sighted at all. The only remarkable occurrence was the frequent reappearance of the car that Kraft and McDonald had observed when they visited the house. There seemed to be a third party interested in finding Brindisi, Charlotte thought. Maybe this would be a useful tool to put pressure on Brindisi senior. Maybe he would talk.

She was on her way to the car when she received a message from Kraft, telling her that Bill McDonald was back from Frankfurt and had contacted him. It looked like important news. Bill had proposed a meeting. Of course, he had to decline, but maybe someone else could meet with him. Charlotte was smiling. What Kraft really meant was that she should contact the American detective. Charlotte, after reflecting for a moment, decided to change her plans. She sent Bill a message inviting him to meet with her at his hotel. Within minutes she received his answer: "Yes, good idea. You find me at the Brandenburger Hof." When she came to the car pool, she asked for a driver in uniform. Within minutes she was on her way to the Brandenburger Hof where she found Bill waiting in the lobby. She was glad to see him and observed with pleasure that he was much less cautious in his attitude. It seems that he is getting used to the German police, she thought.

"I 'm on the way to the to the Brindisi family to follow up on your earlier visit. Would you care to come along?" she said with a smile, inviting him to share the ride. She chose the back seats where there would be an opportunity for a conversation.

"How was your trip to Frankfurt? Any results concerning the missing file?" she asked in a low voice.

There was no immediate answer. When she turned to Bill, he finally responded: "I'm afraid there is no progress. In fact, what I found out in Frankfurt has made my case only more complicated. It turns out that there was no deal between Stollberg and our American client."

"What? No deal?" Charlotte could not hide her surprise. "But in that case, there was no point in sending you to retrieve the missing file. Why are you in Berlin?"

"I have asked myself the same question," Bill replied with a shrug, "and I don't have a good answer. When I called my firm to inform them of the altered situation, they seemed to be as surprised as I was. It was a rather awkward conversation."

"I'm sorry to hear this," said Charlotte, turning towards Bill and touching his arm lightly. "Have they called you back?"

"No, everything is hanging in the air. My official mission is still the same: Find the missing file."

When Charlotte looked at him in disbelief, he gave her a brief report of the events in Frankfurt.

"So, there was another company seeking to buy the research results," Charlotte exclaimed. "And it was for this company that Kellner arranged a meeting with Stollberg at the Brandenburger Hof."

Bill just nodded. For a few minutes both of them were lost in thought. Bill recalled with some bitterness his strange conversation with Hinchcroft, who initially didn't even believe him and insisted that there must have been a contract between Alerta and Stollberg. He was unwilling to accept the fact that he and his firm had been played, that Bill's entire mission was based on false information. Finally, he had promised to discuss the situation with the other partners and get back to him. This had not yet happened. Meanwhile, Charlotte realized that the information she just received from Bill could also change her case. It had become more complicated. There had been another buyer. And it was for this buyer that the private detective from Frankfurt had come to Berlin. Suddenly, a thought crossed her mind, a strange thought that she couldn't control. What if the American company that had lost the deal, decided to get the information they wanted so badly by other means? What if they had hired an assassin, who arranged the accident. But then something went wrong. He failed to get his hands on the file. So, they contacted their law firm, asking them to send their man to retrieve the file.

"Has it occurred to you, Bill, that it may have been your pharma company that arranged the accident in a desperate attempt to get their hands on the valuable information?"

Bill looked at her with a bewildered face. She could clearly see that this possibility had so far escaped him.

"No, I cannot go there. The law firm for which I have worked for 5 years involved in a murder plot?" But while he was saying this, he realized that Charlotte had touched on something that had been there on his mind, a dark and sinister possibility. But then he recalled Hinchcroft's voice on the phone. There had been painful surprise. Amos Hinchcroft had insisted that Bill must be wrong. Their client would not do such a thing. There must be an error, which he would clarify. But on the other hand, why send him when there was no deal? Charlotte Herberg was right: This made no sense. He recalled the advice of the LKA officer: Follow the money. It was clear that for Alerta the stakes were very high. They would save two years of research by getting their hands on the file. But they were not the only interested party. Still, so far there was no evidence that Alerta was behind the murder. I have to remain rational about this, he thought.

"Yes, I don't deny that this could be the case," he said, "but there is no evidence, is there?"

"No, there is none, but I will include this possibility in my investigation," Charlotte replied.

When they arrived at the Brindisi restaurant a few minutes later, they made a stunning discovery. One of the large windows had been broken and was hurriedly repaired. This looked like a war zone. Cautiously they stepped inside and Charlotte asked a waiter to speak to the owner. She was told that he was not available because he was ill. But Charlotte was not inclined to give up and asked to see his wife or son. After a few minutes a small woman in her sixties, wearing a dark drees, entered the restaurant from the backside. She looked distraught and was clearly displeased to see the police in her restaurant.

"My God, what has happened, Signora Brindisi," Charlotte exclaimed. "Who did this? This was not an accident."

"We don't know that," the woman replied, "it must have been an accident during the night."

"Are you sure?" Charlotte insisted. "To me it looks more like an act of vandalism, something deliberate to create fear, Signora Brindisi. You should have called the police."

"No, no police, there is no need for the police at all. We will have the window repaired by tomorrow. There is no need for an investigation. An accident, nothing more."

Charlotte shook her head. "This was not an accident. Somebody is clearly trying to scare you and seems to be very successful. Please, tell me who did this?"

"I don't know," the woman whispered, close to tears, "I don't know."

"I'm worried about the safety of your family, Signora Brindisi, "Charlotte said. "We are still looking for your son Stefano, who has been missing since the funeral, now I hear that your husband is ill and cannot see me. I'm concerned and not prepared to let it go. Please, tell me: What do you know about your son? Where is he hiding?"

Now the woman was in tears, lifting her arms. "I don't know," she repeated. "I don't know, please, don't ask me."

Fear was written all over her face. What followed was a rapid flow of sentences in Italian that neither Charlotte nor Bill could understand.

While Charlotte took her cellphone out of her pocket to contact her office, Bill looked around. The room had been cleaned up and plastic sheets had been applied to close the large hole in the window. Then he found a brick in the corner close to the window. It looked like the tool that had been used to smash the window. We should take this brick along to check for fingerprints, he though, while moving back to Charlotte who was busy talking to her colleagues. Meanwhile, the woman had calmed down. She was sitting on a chair holding her face in her hands without saying anything.

After completing her call, Charlotte turned to her and said: "I have ordered special protection for you and your family. We will make sure that there will be no second attack. I 'm really worried, mostly about your son Stefano. He should contact us as soon as possible."

"Yes, I'm so worried about him," his mother replied in a very low voice. "I have no idea where is."

"How about his brother?"

"He's still in Düsseldorf. He hasn't mentioned Stefano."

"I will be back, Signora Brindisi" Charlotte said with a smile and turned to Bill, who showed her the brick.

"Yes, let's take it along, maybe there are prints." Charlotte suggested, while she was walking to the exit. Bill asked one of the waiters for a container to move the brick.

It had been a frustrating meeting, but there was clear evidence of a hidden threatening presence.

"The Mafia?" Bill asked.

"Most likely", Charlotte answered. "They are clearly scared, but don't want to admit that they are in trouble. In their mind, asking for police protection just makes it worse."

"They may have a point," Bill interjected, "it's almost impossible for the police to offer full protection. This has been my experience in New York City. They don't trust you."

"I think they are close to a breakdown," Charlotte replied. "I suspect that this attack has to do with Stefano Brindisi."

"How about paying them a visit," Bill suggested.

"Nice idea, but where do we find them? I doubt that this is local. We would need assistance from the BKA."

"The what?"

"The Bundeskriminalamt, the federal police," Charlotte replied.

"Will they help you?" Bill wanted to know.

"I doubt it, from their perspective this isn't important enough," Charlotte exclaimed.

They got back to the car where the driver had been waiting. When they had taken their seats in the back, he turned around: "It seems that the restaurant is under surveillance. The moment we showed up, a grey sedan with two guys, which was parked across the street, suddenly left. Are we keeping an eye on the family?"

"Yes, we are, and I have just added protection around the clock," Charlotte said. "These guys have a very different employer. Too bad that we didn't have a chance to have a chat with them. The next time they are showing up, I want them to be shadowed."

Back at her office, Charlotte tried to arrange a meeting with the head of another special unit that focused on organized crime in Berlin, but it was already too late. The colleague had left. Suddenly her phone rang. It was Kraft, calling from Bielefeld:

"Good news, I'm standing in front of the van in the parking garage near the central station in Bielefeld. Most likely it is the van that was used to kill Stollberg. They washed and cleaned it before leaving it here, but there is a small dent at the right front side of the vehicle. Also, small pieces of paint came off."

"Great. Any fingerprints on the inside?" Charlotte wanted to know.

"Too early to say," Kraft replied. "Obviously, the inside was wiped off, but that doesn't mean that we cannot find prints once we go over the van with a fine comb. By the way, the plates were exchanged. Fake plates from Cologne. There is no vehicle registered to these plates."

"Which means that this operation was carefully planned and executed," Charlotte interjected.

"No doubt, we are dealing with professionals," Kraft said. "I hope to load the van in an hour and should be back in Berlin by 10pm."

"Please, make sure that a special forensic team will get started tomorrow morning," Charlotte emphasized.

"Understood, but you have to push from your end, otherwise it won't happen."

Charlotte promised to contact the head of the forensic team before she ended the call. This was exciting news at the end of a difficult day. The visit to the Brindisi restaurant had only confirmed what she had already suspected, the presence of organized crime. But no sign of Stefano Brindisi. On the way back, Bill McDonald had received a text message from Ulrike, telling him that she was on the way back to Berlin, which greatly changed his mood. He had asked Charlotte to be dropped at the next U-Bahn stop, eager to meet Ulrike at her apartment. He had promised to be in touch before he got out of the car. The interview with David Klein had not gone as well as she had hoped, she realized. It had become clear that she needed to know more about the financial aspect of their company. Who gave them the initial capital?

Unanswered questions, but she decided it was time to go home, where she would call Bernd to find out how his return trip worked out.

CHAPTER 11

It seemed to Bill that Ulrike was in a very positive frame of mind after her return to Berlin. He got a big hug when she opened the door of her apartment for him. It lasted longer than usual and told him that she was glad to see him back.

"Missed me?" she asked.

"I was much too busy to notice," he answered.

"Lier", she exclaimed, taking his hand and pulling him into the apartment. For a while they just stood in the hallway, looking at each other. Then Ulrike walked into the kitchen where she opened the refrigerator. Bill looked over her shoulders, noticing that it was almost empty.

"What are we doing to do about dinner?" Ulrike asked, "Pizza?"

"Nah, we can do better than that," Bill replied. "How about cooking together?"

Ulrike turned around, her face expressing a mixture of surprise and doubt.

Do you really think so?" she said. "We would have to go shopping."

"Why not, that sounds like fun. I can do steaks or Swedish meatballs, which are by the way delicious."

"If I have an American cook in the house, it should be steaks," Ulrike exclaimed.

"Excellent," Bill replied, "with a baked potato and green beans. Let me get the steaks from the supermarket. I'll be back in ten minutes."

"Oh no," Ulrike said, "we'll do the shopping together. There are other things I have to get as well."

At this moment the phone rang. Ulrike looked frustrated, but then decided to accept the call. Bill tried to figure out who the caller might be, but he couldn't recognize the voice, except that it was a male voice. Ulrike listened for a while without saying much. Then she said, while giving Bill a smile: "Volker, this is not a good time, I know it's urgent, but right now is impossible. Have to go. Call you back, ok?"

"Something urgent Volker wanted to discuss," Ulrike said, shrugging her shoulders.

"Was it really urgent?" Bill wanted to know.

"Not really, he just wanted to invite himself for dinner."

Bill laughed. "How does he know that there will be dinner at your place tonight?"

"He assumed that I was back and you would be here."

"Smart freeloader!"

"Not tonight."

"Ok, not tonight, Bill confirmed and his own mood got instantly better. "Then, let's go shopping," he added.

"Just a moment," Ulrike said in a low voice, while she was moving in the direction of her bedroom. "I need a jacket."

Bill was already walking slowly to the front door when he heard Ulrike's voice, asking him to come to her room. When he entered the room, he saw her standing in front of her dresser looking at him with a wide smile. There is going to be a change of plans, Bill thought, taking her outstretched hand. She pulled him closer.

"No shopping?" he asked in a low voice.

"No shopping right now," she replied leaning forward, "but you can carry me if you want to"

Bill lifted her up and carried her to the wide bed and embraced her, while she started to unbutton his shirt.

"I missed you when I was in Hamburg. Silly, how much I missed you."

"And there was no one there to entertain you?" Bill asked touching her lips, gently first and then more intensely.

"Of course, there were colleagues at *Spiegel,* intelligent guys."

What about the guy at the *Abendblatt* whom I met two years ago? Is he still there?"

"He is, and he urged me again to move to his beautiful city, which in his mind is much superior to Berlin."

"Just for professional reasons?"

"Did I say that?"

"For his sake I must assume it."

"Or what?"

"I would be forced to do something about his interest."

"What would that be?"

"I have to think about it. Right now, I am otherwise occupied."

It was getting dark outside when they left the bedroom.

"Let's go," Ulrike exclaimed. "I am hungry."

"So am I," Bill said. "Steaks or Pizza?"

"Steaks," Ulrike replied.

They spent more time at the supermarket than they had expected, since Ulrike realized that she needed many more things than the meat, which Bill selected under her watchful eyes. When they returned, Bill focused on the meat, while Ulrike prepared the beans and the potato. Bill noticed that Ulrike really liked the shared preparation. She even volunteered to make a green salad. We should do this more often, he mused. Her excitement lifted his spirits. He had already opened a bottle of red Spanish wine, filling two glasses.

"I'm glad, Volker didn't come," Ulrike said, holding her glass and taking a sip.

"I share the sentiment, but he wasn't given a choice, was he." Bill chuckled.

Ulrike just smiled, while she got the beans out of the pot.

It had been a delicious meal, they decided after they finished all the food. Bill received a compliment for the steaks and was told that American cuisine was not as bad as everyone had told her.

"And we forgot the sour cream," Bill replied, "With sour cream it would have been even better."

They moved to the living room where they settled on the couch. Ulrike, a glass of wine in her hand, wanted to know how Bill's search was moving along. Bill had expected this moment when his reality would return. He was somehow not eager to talk about the latest complicated turn of his search and encouraged Ulrike to talk about her days in Hamburg. It turned out that she had been very successful. She had found much more material for her book in the *Spiegel* archives than she had expected. It was an old court case from the 1960s that she had discovered and planned to develop into a book. An unsolved homicide and a social scandal in which a number of prominent politicians and businessmen had been involved. The way Ulrike told the story, there had been no interest in finding the killer of the young woman.

"And you believe that you will finally find the murderer?" Bill asked.

"That would be a sensation and a huge coup," Ulrike replied. "But even if this is not the case, it will be an interesting book, a social study of the early Republic. And how is your case developing?"

Bill told her about the second visit to the Brindisi restaurant and the broken window, the scared Signora Brindisi, and the car with two guys in front of the house.

"Mafia", Ulrike muttered. "The lady is scared and probably with good reason. Look, I have followed the crime scene in Berlin for years. This is big. The Brindisis are not just any Italian family. Their restaurant is top. What did Charlotte say about this? She has reason to be concerned."

Bill told her about Charlotte's response and gave her a full report of last few days, including the unexpected turn in New York.

"They set me up," Bill said in a low voice, "they played us. There was no contract, which means that the private detective from Frankfurt was not employed by Alerta."

"They found the killer of the detective," Ulrike interjected, "as colleagues mentioned in Hamburg."

"Yes, they did, the Bad Homburg detectives questioned him, but it turned out he was only the help who doesn't know much about the background."

"A team of hired assassins?" Ulrike asked.

"Yes, mostly likely, but the Homburg police can't figure out who hired them. For that they have to find the other man." Bill replied, while he stood up and began pacing up and down in the living room. Ulrike notice his frustration and growing anger. For several minutes he was just pacing without saying anything. Then he exclaimed: "I'm not even sure anymore what my job is in Berlin. Officially, I'm still expected to look for the missing file, at least, I have not received new instructions from my firm, but if there is a missing file, Alerta has no rights. There was no contract, as I learned in Frankfurt."

"OK, I hear you," Ulrike interjected, "But there is still a homicide that has to be solved. For me that is actually more important than the search for the missing file and the rivalry between two pharma companies for a piece of research."

Bill turned around and looked at her: "You have a point, maybe we have to shift our focus. Who killed Herwig Stollberg?"

"Someone who was aware that he planned to sell a critical part of his research and who was determined to stop that by all means," Ulrike said, getting up from the couch and looking for the wine bottle. "My list would include his partners, especially Brindisi. And I wouldn't exclude Alerta after they realized that Stollberg had found another buyer. Maybe, they arranged the hit and then sent you out to look for the file. Really sinister, if you ask me. And finally, what is the role of the Mafia in this case? Why are they threatening the Brindisis family?"

Bill had poured himself another glass of wine, lost in thought.

Resuming his pacing, he said: "I simply cannot get myself to assume that Alerta was involved in the crime. Dirty deals to get the research advantage, yes, but not murder. Not with the help of my law firm. I have known these guys for five years, one of them is a close friend of my dad."

"Look, you don't have to at this moment. The most obvious lead is the Brindisi angle. How about looking into this connection more thoroughly?!"

Bill nodded: "This is what I suggested to Charlotte, but she was not very interested because it's not her assignment."

"That's not a reason for you and me to close our eyes to this line of investigation. Let's get serious and find out more about their recent moves in Berlin. Do you have any idea where Brindisi could be?" Ulrike wanted to know.

"Not really, I have to admit. Maybe family members at another town?" Bill replied.

At this moment Bill's phone rang. It was a text message from Werner Kraft, asking him to call him as soon as possible. He showed the message to Ulrike.

She nodded and said: "Call him right now. This must be important, otherwise he wouldn't urge you this late.

Kraft's voice sounded very excited: "I'm glad you could call back right away. There is news, good news. We have probably recovered the van that was used to kill Stollberg.

"Where?" Bill asked.

"In Bielefeld, in a parking garage near the central train station."

"Are you sure? Any evidence?"

"Pretty sure, but our people will have to go over the vehicle tomorrow morning. The van had been washed and cleaned on the inside as well. Still, I 'm confident that there will be something that will help us to identify the driver. The van is now in Berlin, I used a special truck to move it."

"Great, I'll join you tomorrow, if you don't mind"

After confirming the invitation, Kraft ended the call.

"What happened?" Ulrike wanted to know. Bill filled her in.

"Wow," she exclaimed, "that's possibly a breakthrough. In the meantime, I'll do some research about the activities of our Italian friends. Maybe I can locate other members of the Brindisi family in Germany."

"What about the brother, who plans to open a restaurant in Düsseldorf?" Bill added.

"I'll keep that in mind."

They worked for another hour, finding interesting pieces of information, but nothing that would throw much light on their case. At 11pm they called it a day.

The first thing Bill noticed when he woke up the following morning was the urgent noise of the coffee machine. It took him a few seconds to realize where he was. He checked his watch before he pushed the blanket away and got up. Then he heard Ulrike's voice from the kitchen, reminding him that she would be leaving in twenty minutes for an early meeting at her office. He realized that there was barely time to get a shower and get dressed. When he entered the kitchen fifteen minutes later, Ulrike just put the used dishes away.

"I have to leave in five minutes. Do you want to want to get a lift or do you prefer to eat before you leave?" Ulrike asked.

"I promised Kraft to meet him at his office," Bill replied. "But before that I have to get back to the hotel to get my laptop. No breakfast, maybe coffee if there is a cup left."

He checked the coffee machine and poured himself a cup. Minutes later he sat next to Ulrike in her little red Fiat. Her driving style always amazed him. Speed limits seemed not to exist for her. Sometimes he kept his eyes closed when she approached an intersection.

"How many tickets you get per year?" he asked in a low voice.

"Don't worry, this is my town and I know how to deal with the cops. After all, I 'm on their side, telling their stories. I am just as important as an ambulance."

"Do you really believe that?"

"Yes, I do," Ulrike explained as she was reaching the Kurfürstendamm and stopping in front of the Brandenburger Hof a few minutes later.

"Keep me posted about the van," she said before Bill got out of the car. "If there is any time after the meeting with my boss, I'll start searching for the Brindisi family."

Bill decided to go to his room first and have breakfast later. He took his laptop out and checked for messages. There was no news from the lawyer, but there was a message from Melissa, one of the paralegals with whom he was friendly. He read: <Look at the business news today. There will be an important announcement at Alerta. The vice president for research will step down immediately. Internal discussion here very intensive.> Bill looked at the message again. He needed time to take this in. What is the meaning of this, he thought. Is the company trying to correct its mistakes or are they just casting someone off who has become a liability like the director in Frankfurt? And it also confirmed that the partners of the law firm could not make up their mind. I'm on my own, he thought. I can't any longer pretend that things are fine. But as long as I don't receive new instructions, I can stay in Berlin. He could help solve two murders.

He was ready to leave his room when his phone told him that a message had come in. It was Werner Kraft who informed him that the special team had begun to go over the van. He figured that it would take at least two hours before any results would be available. Bill sent him a brief text, telling him that he would be would be there soon enough to look at the results. Time enough for a good breakfast at the restaurant. He took his laptop along and moved to the restaurant where he was looking for the young waitress of the first night. She was not in evidence. Instead a young man took his order. His darker skin told Bill that he was most likely an immigrant. It turned out that he was from Libya and came to Germany as a teenager. His English was remarkably good, which encouraged Bill to carry on a conversation. Bill told him that he was looking for a friend from India who had promised to be in touch when he was in Berlin. But somehow, he never did. The young water, eager to keep the conversation going, wanted to know more about this friend. When Bill described him as middle-aged, the waiter smiled and told him that there had been a guest from India some weeks ago: a gentleman from Mumbai on whom he had the pleasure of waiting.

"Glasses?" Bill wanted to know.

"Yes, sir, heavy glasses."

"That could be my friend," Bill exclaimed. "Was he a tourist or on a business trip."

"Definitely a business trip," the waiter replied.

"How do you know?"

"He met twice with a younger man and they talked business in English. It seemed that your Indian friend wanted to buy something from the German guy."

"That's good news," Bill said casually. "So, there is hope then that he will be back."

The waiter just smiled, promising to bring the coffee and encouraging his guest to help himself at the buffet. Bill just nodded, realizing all of a sudden that he was really hungry. He loaded his plate at the buffet, including yogurt and a fruit salad. This would keep him going through most of the day. Before he left the restaurant, he checked the news on his laptop, but it was too early for the news from the US.

An hour later he entered Werner Kraft's office. Kraft was talking to a man in a white coat, who showed him something. When Kraft noticed him, he motioned him to join the conversation.

"Bill, this is Hans Trommler, our forensic specialist. He and his team are going over the van with a tooth brush," Kraft said. He then introduced Bill as a security specialist from New York who assisted the Berlin police with the Stollberg investigation.

"Any results?" Bill asked after he shook hands with the police officer.

"Yes, actually more than we expected. Most of the vehicle was carefully cleaned, but they overlooked some spots. We got good fingerprints from the left door and a smudge from the lower part of the dashboard on the right side. There was another good fingerprint at the backdoor, high up. Right now, we are running the results through our data system."

Kraft looked very excited: "I believe that we will be able to identify the driver, if he or she is in our system."

"I'm less certain about the second person. The print is not very clear," said Trommler.

Bill nodded and asked: "When will we know?"

"In an hour we'll have at least some feedback," Kraft interjected. "I promised Charlotte Herberg a report as soon as there were some results. I'll check back with you later, Hans."

Kraft and Bill walked down the hall where they found Charlotte at her desk studying the summary of the Frankfurt meeting provided by the LKA Hesse. When she looked up, she immediately noticed the excitement in Kraft's eyes.

"There are usable prints," Kraft exclaimed. "There is a good chance that we will be able to identify the driver of the van."

"That's great news," she replied "It comes at a moment when we really need good news. I just learned an hour ago that our colleagues in Bad Homburg have not been so lucky. Very early this morning the Frankfurt police pulled a male body out of the Main. It turned out to be the body of the man they had been looking for in connection with the Kellner case. Investigations are still ongoing. Still, it seems that he was shot twice from a short distance, in other words an execution. My guess is that he was eliminated before he could talk to the police."

Bill and Kraft sat down in front of Charlotte's desk without saying anything for a while. The good mode of the early morning was gone.

"Do we know who ordered the hit?" Kraft asked.

"No, we are not so lucky," Charlotte replied. "But Homburg promised to keep me posted. They have become much more cooperative since the Frankfurt meeting."

"In any case, organized crime," Bill suggested. "Then our question is whether we are dealing with the same organization that killed Stollberg or are we actually looking at different groups."

"What is your take on this?" Charlotte asked, focusing her attention on Bill.

"Statistically more likely, it's one and the same organization that seeks control," Bill replied. "But my gut feelings tell me that the case is more complicated."

"Same here," Charlotte responded. "The lack of hard evidence is very frustrating. But let's review what we know and how the pieces hang together. Stollberg needs money because of personal debts. He approached Alerta with the offer to sell his research. They get close to a deal, but then Stollberg breaks off negotiations because he found another party. Who is that?"

"Possibly an Indian company with offices in New Delhi and London," Bill interjected. I learned at Kellner's detective agency that an Indian gentleman visited Kellner some weeks ago. Details are not known. My guess is that this man hired Kellner to be the middle man in Berlin. Kellner was not working for Alerta."

"OK, so far we have a straight line.," Charlotte interrupted. "Kellner comes to Berlin to meet with Stollberg, but the meeting doesn't take place because Stollberg is killed in an arranged accident before the meeting. At the funeral Brindisi behaves very strangely and two suspicious men are observed. Also, Kellner comes back and shows up at the funeral. The following day he is killed in his home in Bad Homburg. It looks like another hit. But who ordered it? The local police arrested a man who was clearly involved but possibly not the assassin. Now it seems that the assassin was taken out."

"I don't believe we have to account for more than one criminal organization," Werner Kraft suggested, "To me it looks like the Mafia in Berlin and in Bad Homburg. They mean to stop the sale of the research by all possible means, including murder."

"But why?" Charlotte wanted to know. "The Mafia is not known for its involvement in medical research."

At this moment, there was a knock at the door. It was Hans Trommler who entered the room with a file in his hand. His expression made clear that he had important news. Charlotte invited him to join the group.

"Thank you, but I can't stay for more than a minute," Trommler responded: "I just want to share the first results. We have identified the driver."

"Somebody with a history?" Kraft wanted to know.

"Yes, indeed, a long history of brushes with the law," Trommler replied. "His name is Bruno Esposito, registered in Cologne, 43 years old."

"Any known ties to the Mafia?" Charlotte asked.

"Probably, but our guys are still checking this connection. If it the case, he has a low status. Useful to take orders and carry them out, like driving a van."

"What about the second person?" Bill asked.

"Nothing in the federal system. We are looking at different records as well. And don't forget the print is weak. I'll be back," Trommler said, while he was getting up and moving to the exit.

"So, it's the Mafia, as we suspected all along," Kraft exclaimed, looking at Bill with an air of triumphant certainty. Bill just shrugged his shoulders.

"It certainly confirms what we found at the house of the Brindisi's," Charlotte added. "Somehow the Mafia is involved, but how and why?"

"Let's go back to the inquiry of the Hesse LKA," Bill suggested, looking at Charlotte. "They are mostly interested in the flow of money. And there is clearly a lot of money involved in medical research. Alerta expected to save millions by buying a piece of research from Stollberg. Maybe we are looking at investment. Laundering dirty money."

"Assuming for a moment, your theory is correct, the Mafia means to invest its profits in medical research, what's the role of the Brindisi family?" Charlotte asked.

"I don't have a good answer for your question, at least not right now. My guess is that they got involved because of Stefano, who is after all a partner in KreuzbergChem. He was involved in developing the research that his friend was selling behind his back."

"But why was Kellner killed two days later. If the Mafia had interrupted the deal, there was no reason to eliminate Kellner. Kellner did not have the file!" Charlotte interjected. "Our theory seems to be too simple."

"You have a point," Bill replied. "The murder of Kellner makes no sense. We need more details about the execution of the hit man. Maybe that would throw more light on our problem. Let me call my source in Bad Homburg. Maybe, my connection shares relevant details. Give me ten minutes", Bill said getting up and leaving the office. He found a quiet corner close to the elevator where he got his phone out and made the call. This time he seemed to be out of luck. The receptionist told him that the young detective was not available. He was on the way back to Charlotte's office when his phone rang. The caller was the young detective.

"I just tried to reach you," Bill said in a low voice. "I was told that you were not available."

"That's correct, I'm not in my office. I'm at the local morgue where we keep the body of the second hit man. It seems his employer silenced him. My boss informed Berlin this morning. I wanted to check on the hit in Berlin. Have you by any change identified the driver of the van?"

"Curious that you are asking," Bill answered. "It looks like a Mafia job."

There was a moment of silence, then Bill heard her voice again: "That's what we expected in our case as well. Making sure that he couldn't talk. But there is a detail that doesn't fit. I checked the bullets that were removed from the body."

"And?" Bill said in a low voice.

"Not at all a typical Mafia caliber. The weapon used was a Russian gun," the detective replied.

Meaning?" Bill asked.

"More likely that it was a Russian hit," the detective answered.

"Would that change the investigation?" Bill asked. There was a moment of silence again. Then Bill heard her voice: "Yes, it would change the nature of the case. No longer just local. We would have to talk to the LKA. They might take over. Is there any sign that the Russians were involved in the Stollberg case?"

"I don't think so."

"Good, that's all I needed to know. Thank you."

Bill stared at his phone without moving. What was this? Not the Mafia in Bad Homburg! That undercuts our theory, he thought. Bill walked back to the office where Charlotte and Kraft studied the results of the forensic team.

"Complications," Bill exclaimed. "I just got word from my source in Bad Homburg that the Kellner murder looks like a Russian hit, at least not the Mafia. That's not good news for our theory."

Kraft looked perplexed, while Charlotte seemed to be prepared for this sudden turn. Bill felt the same way. In his mind the two cases were connected but in a way that he hadn't yet figured out. He heard Charlotte's voice as he stared at the file of the forensic team: "We need a break. Let's have lunch and then get back."

The cafeteria turned out to be very crowded. Charlotte suggested therefore to go to a small Greek place in the neighborhood. Kraft, who disliked the Cafeteria food in general, emphatically supported the idea and immediately got his phone out to reserve a table. When they arrived five minutes later, the chef was already waiting for them and arranged a quiet table where they could continue their conversation. But it became obvious that Charlotte was not in the mood to discuss the Stollberg case. Instead, to Kraft's surprise, she turned to Bill, asking him to tell her more about his work in New York City. When the food arrived, the discussion had already drifted to the Jazz scene. As it turned out, both Bill and Charlotte shared a longtime interest in contemporary jazz. Bill was surprised to find out that she was well informed about local bands and clubs.

"Have you been in NYC?" he asked.

"No, never had the time or the opportunity," she replied, while she worked on her big Greek salad.

"Too bad, you should give it a try," Bill responded, "there is enough good stuff for a week."

Charlotte just nodded. This would be an exciting trip with Bernd, she thought. But he is on the way to Australia. Werner Kraft picked up on the change of her mood and started a story about his latest sailing adventure. Neither Bill nor Charlotte picked it up. For a while they were just focused on eating their lunch

All of a sudden, Charlotte said: "Any news from your law firm?"

This was a turn of the conversation that Bill did not greet with enthusiasm. For a moment, he just looked at his plate. Then he said: "No change. There appears to be an internal discussion among the partners after my report, but no response."

"Very strange," Charlotte replied without going into the reasons for her remark.

She noticed that Bill was not very happy about this turn of the conversation. Again, it was Kraft who restored the flow by finding a neutral topic, Berlin's incomplete new airport. There had been so many delays that the idea of actually ever using it had become a joke. Kraft was busy telling the latest problems when his phone rang. It was Hans Trommler, urging them to come back because there were new results. Kraft asked for detail but was told that Hauptkommissarin Herberg would have to be there in person.

"It was Trommler. They want us back in a hurry. There is a new development. Shall we go?"

"No, let's finish our lunch first," Charlotte replied. "We'll find out in due time."

After they had finished their coffee, they walked back to the police building. Trommler was already waiting in Charlotte's office.

"We extended our search for the second fingerprint, the one on the right side of the van. What we found is not conclusive, since the print is not clear. Please keep this in mind, but the result points to a person you know rather well."

"Who?"

"Stefano Brindisi!"

"Brindisi? Are you sure?" Kraft asked.

Trommler shook his head: "As I said, we are not absolutely certain, but there it is."

There was a moment of complete silence. Charlotte moved to her desk and sat down. Bill and Werner Kraft just looked at Trommler.

"OK, let's figure out what this information means for the case," Charlotte finally said. "I'll call a meeting of the entire group later, right now we need just a preliminary assessment."

She invited Bill to speak. Bill looked at her, trying to read her face before he replied: "It appears that Brindisi was actually involved in the murder, he was sitting next to the driver when it happened. Maybe it was he who gave the order."

Kraft came to the same conclusion. They had to rethink the case again. The search for Brindisi had become much more urgent than an hour ago.

"It would explain his strange behavior at the funeral," Kraft interjected. "He had to face the family of the friend he killed."

Charlotte closed her eyes for a brief moment, trying to assess the link between the known facts and the fresh information. Looking once more at the piece of paper Trommler had given her, she said: "This would mean that there was some kind of understanding between Brindisi and the Mafia. Maybe he called them in. But what was the motif?"

"if you follow this line of thought," Bill responded, "it means that he had discovered Stollberg's plan and was determined to stop it. Stop it by all means."

"Yes, that would be the logical conclusion," Charlotte said. "But what do we make of the incident at the Wannsee cottage of the Brindisis family? We thought that Brindisi was hiding because the Mafia was after him."

Both Bill and Kraft nodded.

"Maybe it wasn't the Mafia," Kraft suggested.

Bill shook his head, then he said: "I still believe it was the Italians, but possibly they were not looking for Brindisi."

There was another moment of silence. Then Charlotte said: "I will ask for a warrant for Brindisi's arrest." She took out her phone and dialed the number of the prosecutor's office.

CHAPTER 12

It was already past 10am when Ulrike settled down in her small office and found time to work on her own research. As usual, for the most part the early meeting had been a waste of time, listening to a boss who loved to lecture the younger staff about the importance of careful research and journalistic integrity. The woman was a bore, but Ulrike had to be careful not to show her own feelings because the she was known to make the life of younger colleagues difficult. Ulrike was all smiles when she suggested she spend more time on the rise of organized crime in Berlin and Brandenburg. To her own surprise, the boss had consented, although with the understanding that Ulrike would cover the legal courts as usual. Once she was on line, she realized that she had to widen the parameters of her search. For the Mafia, national borders had become almost meaningless. It also meant that she needed more than one language to follow the press coverage. There were numerous articles in Italian that she would have to go through. And her Italian was very weak. Fortunately, some of the Italian books on the subject were available in German translation. It will take me weeks to build up a sufficiently strong background before I can figure out the link to the Stollberg case, she thought. Ulrike decided to change her approach and began searching for members of the Brindisi family. She found a woman by the name of Anna Brindisi in Düsseldorf who owned a boutique. There was a Carlo Brindisi in Frankfurt, owner of a Café, and a Matteo Brindisi in Cologne, who advertised as a wine merchant. There was also a cross reference to a Brindisi family in Naples. Obviously, the Brindisis in Germany had been quite successful, if they were closely related. There was a picture of Anna Brindisi on the internet, a woman in her thirties, Ulrike concluded after looking intensively at the image. A cousin of Stefano? There was no picture of the wine dealer, but the name of the company Brindisis & Son indicated an older man with a grown-up son in the business. Then Ulrike cross-referenced these names with the articles on the activities of the Mafia in Northern Europe. There was no hit. There is no apparent link Ulrike thought. I have to dig deeper. Then she recalled that her old friend and colleague at the *Hamburger Abendblatt* had written an article about the spread of the Mafia in Hamburg. He might be able to help her. She was about to call him when she noticed that there was a new message on her phone. It was Bill asking for an urgent meeting.

"Can it wait until tonight?" She replied.

"No, I have to see you as soon as possible, important news." He wrote back.

"Connected to the van?"

"Exactly, shall I come to your office?"

"No, not a good idea. Will meet you at the coffee shop next door. You can't miss it,"

"Will be there at 12 noon."

Bill was already waiting in the coffee shop nursing a latte when Ulrike entered the small place. She ordered a regular black coffee before she joined Bill at the small table next to the window. Bill looked very serious.

"What's the matter? What's so serious that it can't wait until tonight?"

"Stefano Brindisi is involved in the death of Herwig Stollberg."

"What do you mean by involved?" Ulrike asked, staring at Bill.

"Herberg has asked the prosecution for a warrant for his arrest,"

"I can't believe it. What happened?"

"His fingerprint was found on the inside of the van. You realize what that means?"

"You think he planned the murder?"

"That's now a distinct possibility. It would make sense. He

discovered his friend's plans and decided to stop him to protect the company."

"What a story" Ulrike exclaimed. "Murder in a start-up!"

"If you want to write it, we have to catch Brindisi first," Bill said. "I'm planning to start a serious search."

"When?"

"Right now."

"Impossible"

"Why?"

"I need time to prepare such a trip."

"Who said that you have to come along?"

"I do. There will be no argument."

"OK, when will you be ready?"

"Give me the afternoon to take care of things."

Bill just nodded, nursing his latte: "Pick me up at 6:00pm at my hotel."

It was almost 7:00pm when Ulrike parked her small car in front of the Brandenburger Hof. She found Bill in the lobby with his laptop on his knees checking his messages. There was no response to his last message to the paralegal. Somehow this must be connected to the events at Alerta. The business news on his phone had confirmed that the vice president for research had stepped down. No reason had been given for this decision. Bill had immediately checked the digital edition of the Wall Street Journal and found a brief commentary with the suggestion that there had been irregularities in the development of the new diabetes drug. The reader is expected to figure out what that meant, Bill thought. He had called the Alerta office in Frankfurt to get the details, but was told that the deputy director was not available. She had been recalled to Boston. A new director was expected next week. The voice of the receptionist had been completely neutral. Thorough housecleaning, Bill thought. All traces of the failed deal with Stollberg were removed. In the end there was only the word "irregularities" in the media. Bill felt sorry for the woman. Would she survive the shake-up? Will I survive the internal struggle at my firm? This was

Bill's next thought. To his own surprise, he noticed that he didn't care that much. Maybe it was time to move on.

When Ulrike made a weak effort to explain the delay, Bill just muttered "geschenkt" an expression he had picked up and liked to use.

"Where do we go?" Ulrike wanted to know.

"Düsseldorf, I think. Let's pay a visit to his older brother," Bill replied.

"We would arrive very late," Ulrike said while she briskly walked to her car. "Let's find a hotel on the way and then have a full day for the Brindisis in Düsseldorf. There is also Anna Brindisi, who owns a boutique. Maybe I can find a nice dress."

Bill just gave her a brief glance without saying anything.

The city traffic was still fairly heavy; it took them a while before they reached the Autobahn to the West where the little Fiat picked up speed. Bill offered to drive, but Ulrike declined.

"No need, I really like driving at night, she said. "Do you have a plan?"

"I want to look at the new place of his brother, also talk to him. It's likely that he knows where Stefano is hiding."

"But will he tell you where he is?" Ulrike replied. "After all, the police are looking for him as involved in a murder case. He'll protect his little brother, as I would."

"Of course, he won't. Still, what he will tell us can help us to get closer. For me the big question is: Are the Brindisis collaborating with the Mafia? What I saw at their restaurant didn't look like it."

"Maybe it's only Stefano who's working with the Mafia," Ulrike suggested.

"Why would he tolerate an attack on his own family?" Bill asked. "It doesn't add up."

For a while there was silence. Both of them were listening to the music on the radio and looking at the lights of the cars and trucks in front of them. When they passed Hannover Bill asked: "How far away are we from the town where they found the van? Is it close to the Autobahn?"

"Bielefeld? About an hour from here and close to this highway."

"In that case, let's find a hotel in Bielefeld and look at the parking garage tomorrow morning."

"Why? Did Kraft say anything?"

"No, I want to figure out why the assassins left the van at that place. There must be a reason."

In fact, it took more than an hour until they saw the sign for Bielefeld and left the Autobahn. They followed the road to Bielefeld. Within minutes they saw the sign of a hotel chain and decided to stay at the modest roadside hotel they found on the right side a minute later. The comfort level of the room was basic, but it didn't matter. Both of them were exhausted and wanted to sleep. Bill checked his email once more. There were no messages from New York, but there was a message from Kraft. They had been able to identify the owner of the van. The vehicle belonged to a small contractor in Düsseldorf. It had been reported as missing. The plates had been changed to mislead the police. Bill was too tired to think about the significance of this information. I'll do this tomorrow, he thought and fell asleep.

The following morning, they skipped breakfast and were back on the road by 8:00. This time Bill was the driver, while Ulrike looked at her smart phone and gave him directions. They parked in front of the central railway station, searching for the parking garage. It was not difficult to find it. There it was in plain view no more than five minutes from the station. Ulrike was cold and hungry. She longed for a cup of very hot black coffee.

"OK, there is the parking garage. Do we have to look for the spot where the van was parked?" she asked.

"No, what I observe from here confirms my hunch."

"Which is?"

"Later, first, let's find a place where we can get breakfast"

"Great Idea," Ulrike exclaimed getting back into the car. She pointed to a large older building. "How about the hotel over there. I bet they offer what we need right now."

"And what is that?" Bill asked.

"A really lavish breakfast to make up for last night."

"Agreed," Bill said after he got back into the car as well.

A waiter in formal dress assigned them a table and took their orders. All they needed to see was the rich breakfast buffet along the wall to make their decision. They generously filled their plates with as many things as they could find.

"This is splendid. Did you know this place?" Bill asked.

"No, but my experience has been that these older hotels tend to offer a good breakfast."

"I'll make a note of that," Bill replied, while he spooned a soft-boiled egg.

Ulrike's mood had improved a great deal after she finished her first cup of coffee. "So, why did you want to see the parking garage?"

"Not the garage per se, rather the distance from the railway station. I believe that the driver left the van in this garage because it is in easy walking distance from the railway. He was planning to continue his journey by boarding the next train going the west, to Düsseldorf for instance. Which means that at least one of them is familiar with the local topography."

"Not bad. Any proof?"

"Of course not, just a hunch. It also suggests that the operation was carefully planned."

Ulrike just nodded, looking at her laptop. She was searching for the address of the new Brindisi restaurant. She couldn't find it.

"Don't worry," Bill interjected. "Once we are there, we'll check with the tourist bureau or the local press."

When they saw the bill that the waiter had discreetly left at their table, Ulrike had second thoughts about her choice. But Bill just grinned and put the amount on his credit card. "We'll skip lunch, and everything will be fine."

Ulrike quickly decided to agree. Minutes later they were on the road again.

Finding a parking place in the old part of town in Düsseldorf turned out to be a challenge. It took Ulrike a quarter of an hour to find a spot that was in walking distance from the small hotel where they had a reservation. At the reception, Ulrike introduced herself as a reporter who was interested in the opening of the new restaurant of the

Brindisi family. The young woman who checked them in responded with a facial expression that told Ulrike that she had no clue. The clerk called for the director, who offered to help. He had heard of the new restaurant and was pleased to learn that the Berlin media took an interest in this, but he did not have details either. When Ulrike showed her impatience, he made a few calls. Finally, there was an answer. He connected Ulrike with the office of a local newspaper. The reporter seemed to be eager to talk to Ulrike.

"Are you calling about the opening of the new Italian restaurant?" Ulrike heard a male voice.

"Yes, I am. My paper follows the success story of the Brindisi family. They own a famous restaurant in Berlin-Mitte, at the Gendarmen Markt" Ulrike replied.

"I'm afraid there will be no opening in the near future."

"Why not? What's the matter?"

"There has been an accident. A fire badly damaged part of the building."

"My God, when did this happen?"

"Last night. We will cover the story."

"Just an accident?"

"Good question. We talked to the fire chief this morning. There were some open questions."

"Arson?"

"The fire chief hasn't ruled it out."

"Have you talked to the owner?"

"No, he wasn't available, I understand. After all, this was a huge blow for him. He planned to open next week."

After Ulrike got the address and thanked her colleague, she turned to Bill who stood next to her, watching her increasing excitement. The conversation in German had been too fast for him to get the details.

"Something went wrong?" Bill asked.

"That's an understatement," Ulrike said turning back to the clerk at the counter. "There was a fire at the new restaurant last night that did serious damage."

Ulrike asked the clerk for directions. The young woman showed her a map of Düsseldorf's inner city and marked the place. With the map in hand Ulrike motioned Bill to the elevator.

"Let's just check in and then we should have a look at the place before dark," she exclaimed. "Maybe we'll find the brother at the restaurant."

"You mean Stefano?"

"No, Roberto, the older brother."

In the room Bill studied the map. They were in walking distance from the restaurant. It took them no more than ten minutes to find the building, a large white house with a view of the Rhine. The large windows of the lower floor indicated where the restaurant was supposed to be. When they got closer they noticed dark streaks on the wall of the first floor. In front of the heavy wooden door they encountered a pile of burned materials. They stepped into the large room, which seemed to be empty. The traces of the fire were in evidence all over the room. Burned furniture, damaged curtains, soiled rugs. It was a depressing sight. It took them a while until they realized that they were not alone. In the far corner a man was sitting on a chair with his head bent down. They walked up to him and introduced themselves, but he seemed not to notice them.

"Are you Roberto Brindisi?" Ulrike asked.

"Who are you?" the man replied, looking at them for the first time.

"I am Ulrike Pfanner, a reporter from Berlin, and this is my colleague Bill McDonald from New York. I'm working on a story about successful Berlin families and learned that a member of the Brindisi family means to open a second place in Düsseldorf. Do you know Signor Brindisi?"

For the first time the man focused his attention on the visitors: "I am Roberto Brindisi. Yes, I meant to open my own restaurant here next week. But look at the mess. Look at the mess."

He stood up, opening his arms. His face was pale, his hair unkempt. For a moment he was lost in thought again, unaware of the presence of the visitors.

"Who did this?" Ulrike asked, holding his right arm, "Who did this?"

There was no immediate answer. Brindisi just stared at the damaged room. Finally, he responded: "It was an accidental fire."

"I don't believe this for a moment, Signor Brindisi," Bill interjected. "I have a different theory. A few days ago, I visited your father's restaurant in Berlin. There was also an "accident." A window was broken, because someone had thrown a large brick into the room. It wasn't an accident, and this isn't an accident either."

"Someone is after your family," Ulrike said in a low voice.

"It was an accident. Bad wiring, the fire chief told me," Brindisi insisted with a weak gesture that showed his own doubts.

Bill felt that this might be the moment to get the information from Roberto Brindisi that he needed. He faced him and said raising his voice: "I'm looking for your brother Stefano. He has been missing and I have to talk to him. I have been sent by my law firm to look for a missing file and I believe that he can help me."

Roberto Brindisi stared at Bill, who was not sure that he had comprehended what he had said.

"Stefano, yes, he is missing," Brindisi repeated, "what kind of file are you talking about?"

"It's connected to his company, KreuzbergChem," Bill explained.

"Ah, the start-up, yes, that's where all the trouble started. Stefano's ambition!"

"Tell us more about this," Ulrike urged him.

Brindisi asked them to follow him to a smaller room in the back, his office it seemed. There he invited them to sit down and apologized that he was unable to offer them anything.

"The water is still turned off," he muttered.

"Do you know where your brother is right now?" Ulrike wanted to know.

"No, no idea. He looked me up a couple of days ago."

This was the moment for Bill's question: "So, he came to you. What did he want?"

"He needed cash, he told me and asked me for a place where he could stay for a couple of days. I offered him this place, but he said no. Too noisy, he told me."

"Did he tell you why he had left Berlin where he really was needed? David Klein was very upset about this when we talked to him."

"I don't blame him," Brindisi whispered, "he's in a tough spot."

"Why is your brother hiding?" Bill insisted impatiently. "When we were looking for him at your parents' cottage we were attacked by two armed sinister figures."

"He didn't tell me," Brindisi replied. "When he stood at the door he just wanted cash. He told me that he needed a vacation from the pressure of the company after Herwig's death."

"Any idea where he might look for a quiet place?" Ulrike asked.

"Not really, once he mentioned Anna."

"Who is Anna?" Bill asked.

"Our cousin who owns a boutique in town. They used to be close."

"Do you realize that the police are looking for your brother?" Ulrike said in a low voice. "In connection with the death of Herwig Stollberg. Do you believe that he was somehow involved?"

Brindisi stared at her with an expression of horror. Then he replied: "Stefano involved in Herwig's death? Impossible. They were close friends and built the company together. Who is saying such nonsense? If anything, my brother was protecting Herwig."

"I believe you," Ulrike said, touching his arm lightly, "but hiding doesn't help him right now. He has to come forward. He should talk to us und explain himself."

Brindisi got up and was pacing back and forth. He was obviously agitated. Bill observed him from a distance for a while. Then he decided to try a different approach: "You mentioned that the trouble started with the company. What did you mean by that?"

"Did I say that?" Brindisi asked. "What I meant is that they needed more capital. My father gave him some money, but that was not enough. And Stollberg was financially not in a strong position. They weren't good at this. When they couldn't get the money from the bank they approached private investors. I don't know the details. Stefano talked to my father about this. Also, more recently there were problems with Herwig's finances. This worried my brother a great deal. I believe that he either loaned him money or arranged the access to a private lender. Connections in the Italian community. Don't ask me for details."

"How about David Klein? Did he know about this?" Bill insisted.

There was a moment of silence. Brindisi appeared to be distracted.

"No, Klein was not part of this. Klein joined the company more recently. In my opinion a good move, because he has a much better grasp of the financial aspect than my brother and Stollberg."

"I am wondering whether Stollberg's money problems had an impact on the company?" Bill suggested. "Was there talk about selling the company?"

This, Bill knew was a shot into the dark. It dawned on him at this moment that in Stefano Brindisi's mind the very existence of the start-up was possibly threatened by Stollberg's debts. And, if his brother's story was true, possibly it was Stefano Brindisi who had invited the dark money in order to help his friend. Did he also invite dark money into the company? Bill thought. How much does the older brother know about this threat? Spontaneously Bill decided to probe this topic by asking Roberto how much he knew about Stefano's arrangements. Was he familiar with the persons who financed Stollberg and possibly also the company? Brindisi's answer gave him less than he had hoped for. Roberto had not paid much attention to this, since he was preoccupied with his own project. He was planning to open his own restaurant, either in Köln or in Düsseldorf. What he remembered were meetings with individuals at his father's place. Mostly members of the Italian community. Friends of friends. They were considering giving money to Stefano and his friend because they knew his father and his grandfather.

"These friends seem to be less friendly now," Bill exclaimed. "They threaten your family, your father, you, and Stefano. What precisely do they want?"

"I don't understand what you are talking about," Roberto Brindisi replied, covering his face in his hands.

"You know quite well what I'm talking about, Signor Brindisi --- organized crime. They invested money, now they want control. Look at this place. This is a warning."

"I never took a dime from illegal sources," Brindisi objected. "Why would they threaten me?!"

"I believe you, Signor," Bill said. "It seems, however, that your brother and his friend took their money."

Bill realized that he was on thin ice. He had no factual evidence for his claim, but what he had learned would fit rather neatly into his story. He recalled what Ulrike had told him about Stollberg's gambling debts and the calls that his wife had received. All the known facts pointed to the same thing: The Mafia felt that they owned the Brindisi family. And they wanted something. Control the company? That might be the goal. And that's where Alerta entered the competition by making a deal with Stollberg, but a deal that didn't work out. Stefano's dark friends got wind of this and decided to strike. Bill's thoughts moved with great speed. It must have been Stefano who alerted them. But why is he running away from them now and remains in hiding?

He glanced at Ulrike who was trying to calm Roberto Brindisi down, moving him gently back to his chair. What were her thoughts? Does she understand the contradiction? At this moment he heard her voice:

"Signor Brindisi, how do you explain the evidence that led to a warrant for Stefano's arrest in Berlin?"

We are on the same page, Bill thought. This is my question as well. If he cooperated with the Mafia, sitting in the van that killed Stollberg, why is the Mafia after him?

"What evidence?" Brindisi asked, looking at Ulrike with an expression of confusion.

"The police found his fingerprints inside the van that was used to kill Stollberg," Bill told him.

"There must be a misunderstanding, some mistake," Brindisi said in a low voice. "Stefano would never kill Herwig, never!"

"Even if Stollberg planned to sell critical research results behind the back of his partners?" Ulrike wanted to know. "Remember Stollberg's debts? He needed money. He was desperate. Maybe your brother felt that he had to protect the company."

Roberto Brindisi did not reply. He just stared at the visitors.

"It would be wise to contact the police and tell them that somebody has sent you a negative message. You need protection." Bill suggested.

"The police cannot protect me. You have to deal with this situation directly," Roberto Brindisi said calmly and stood up. "This is all I can tell you. Now you have to excuse me. I have to deal with an emergency."

"Good luck," Ulrike said. Bill shook Brindisi's hand. Then they left.

In the meantime, the weather had changed. A light rain fell on their faces. Both of them felt exhausted and hungry.

"Let's get a bite somewhere in the neighborhood," Ulrike said. They moved back in the direction of their hotel until they noticed a pub at the next intersection. Ulrike grabbed Bill's arm and rushed to the entrance. The inside was quiet. There were a few customers at the bar. Most of the heavy wooden tables were empty.

"Try the local beer?" Bill suggested.

"Not now," Ulrike replied. I'm starved. I need solid food."

A bored waitress dropped menus and promised to return. They glanced at the menu. It was unappealing. When the waitress returned they ordered small local sausages for lack of a better choice. But when the food arrived they were pleasantly surprised.

"Quite tasty," Bill commented.

"Could be worse," Ulrike admitted.

"Do you think Roberto Brindisi told us the truth?" Ulrike asked.

"My sense is that he did," Bill replied, while he signaled to the waitress that he wanted a small beer. "Of course, he realizes that the fire at his new place wasn't an accident. He understood the message, but he doesn't want to involve the police. Just like the father. If Stefano is hiding in this area, it's much more likely that his cousin could find a secure place."

"You want to talk to her?"

Definitely, that's our next step."

"Will she talk?"

"Only if she trusts us."

"Good question, why should she? But she is our only chance."

Ulrike shrugged her shoulders. She got her smart phone out and searched for the address of the boutique.

"It must be close," she exclaimed, "part of the old town, see!"

She showed her phone to Bill, who needed a minute to make sense of the map.

The rain had stopped when they left the pub and the foot traffic in the narrow street had increased. They found themselves among small groups of tourists, moving from shop to shop. It took them a while to find the small road with the boutique. It was a surprisingly elegant store, offering merchandise that was well above the level of the average shop in the neighborhood. Ulrike glanced at the dresses in the windows. They were expensive.

"This is serious Italian fashion," she exclaimed. "Not the stuff tourists pick up on a trip."

For a while, they just observed the store from a distance. A young woman was talking to a customer. She looked too young to be Anna Brindisi. Ulrike was eager to enter the store, but Bill held her back.

"Wait," he whispered. "Look at the two young men standing across from the store, obviously keeping an eye on the two women inside. Let's wait and see what these guys are up to."

They moved further away from the store, seemingly interested in the shirts and hats of the store next door. One of the men got his smart phone out of his pocket and began to check his mail, the other one observed the large window of the store.

"I shouldn't be seen here," Bill said, "this is your turf, Ulrike. How will you introduce yourself?"

"KreuzbergChem will be my cover. I need to interview Stefano after talking to David Klein."

"I'll keep an eyes on these guys."

A minute later Ulrike stepped into the store, seemingly just browsing. Bill noticed that the sales girl was still busy with another customer. Finally, she turned to Ulrike. There was a brief exchange. Then the young woman walked to a curtain in the back. She motioned Ulrike to follow her. After a few seconds, she returned to the front, while Ulrike remained behind the curtain. Bill focused his attention on the second man who had been observing the store. He has noticed Ulrike's presence, Bill thought. Is she just another customer to him or does he recognize that something else is going on? Now, two middle-aged women entered the boutique, first browsing and then talking to the sales girl, who showed them more dresses. Ulrike was still behind the curtain. All of a sudden, the man with the smart phone started to talk and then left his position after a brief exchange with the other man. He walked toward Bill, who quickly tried on one of the hats to hide his face. Why was he leaving and where was he going? Bill changed his own position by entering another store from where he could easily observe the man and the store. He checked his watch. Almost ten minutes had passed since Ulrike had entered the boutique. The sales girl was still busy with the middle-aged women. Bill pretended to be interested in a beer glass with the logo of a local company. When he focused his eyes on the store again, he realized that Ulrike was moving to the exit. At the door she looked for Bill. When she realized that Bill was not in evidence she consulted the little map and then moved slowly in the direction of the hotel. Bill focused his attention on the young man. What will he do next? After a few seconds it became clear that he was following Ulrike. Bill got his phone out and typed a text message: "You are being followed by one of the men who observed the boutique. Try to get rid of him. Meet you later at the hotel." He saw that Ulrike looked at her phone. Then she nodded without turning around. She appeared to be walking aimlessly, changing directions, stopping in front of shops, entering stores, sitting on public benches. After a while, Bill realized that Ulrike was enjoying herself, forcing the young man into difficult situations where he had to run, duck, turn around and hide behind other people in order not to be recognized. At least half an hour had passed this way until she entered a large department store, giving her follower ample time to get closer. All of a sudden, she stepped into one of the elevators. There was no time for the young man to get into the same elevator. He rushed to the next staircase. Bill followed him at a distance. Now the man was clearly frustrated, yet uncertain what to do next. He got his phone out and made a call. Then he ran up to the second floor. Bill's phone rang. He heard Ulrike's voice: "Where is he?"

"He's moving to the second floor now," Bill replied.

"I'll leave the elevator on the third floor and use the escalator to go down. Keep me posted about his moves."

"Will do" was Bill's short answer. The man stood in front of the elevator when the door opened. He remained there. Then he turned around and walked to the staircase. Bill followed him from a distance. A Minute later, he heard Ulrike's voice again: "I'm on the escalator from the third floor to the second. Are we clear?"

"It looks that way. He's still on the way up. I'll meet you at the exit."

They left the department store together. Bill showed Ulrike a picture of the young man that he had taken inside the store.

On the way to the hotel Ulrike filled Bill in on her conversation with Anna Brindisi. As Bill had predicted, she also claimed not to know where her cousin was. He had asked her for cash as well. His explanation had been that he needed an "Auszeit" after the turbulence of the accident and the funeral. He had declined her invitation to stay with her for a couple of days, but he had accepted the keys for a space on the periphery of town where she keeps incoming merchandise.

"Did she mention the address?" Bill wanted to know.

"No, just the area," Ulrike replied, "and I thought it wasn't wise to ask."

"Of course not, but we have to find out. I think this may be the place where he is hiding. Does she know that she is being observed?"

"No, she believes that we must be mistaken."

"What about the fire at her cousin's new restaurant?"

"An accident. I tried to ask her questions about KreuzbergChem and take it from there. She claimed not to know much about the start-up. But she had always wondered about the financing. Smart woman with a good head for business, if you ask me."

"Did you mention the warrant?"

"I decided not to. It seemed to be counterproductive."

Bill just nodded. His mind was already working on the next step: finding the place where Stefano Brindisi was hiding.

CHAPTER 13

The phone rang at 11:05pm. It took Charlotte a while to reach the near-by extension, because she was in the bathroom brushing her teeth. She was not at all in the mood for a late phone call. It had been an exhausting day filled with many small and tedious tasks and meetings. The only really positive thing had been a long email from Bernd Moeller from Sidney. Typically, he was not inclined to share emotions on the internet. This message had been an exception. The words "I miss you very much" had lifted her spirits. Who would call her at this hour? Her friends knew that she retired early. When she pushed the button of her phone, she heard Werner Kraft's voice:

"Sorry to call you this late, but I thought you better know about this. Dorothea Stollberg called a few minutes ago. She has received threatening phone calls again, and there was someone at the door of her apartment. She is scared."

"Who took the call?" Charlotte asked with a firm voice.

"The local police station. The officer immediately informed me. She recalled that we had asked to be informed."

"Have they responded?"

"I don't think so."

"Ask the officer to send a team to her apartment immediately and let her know that we are on the way. Can you pick me up?"

Kraft assured her that he would be at her place within ten minutes. Charlotte noticed that he seemed not to mind the interruption. He's always ready to spring into action, she thought. It was good to have him around, especially in situations like this one. Actually, she was not totally surprised to hear from Dorothea Stollberg. The latest development of the Stollberg case suggested increased pressure on all those who had been close to him. This was not accidental. We may also hear from David Klein, she thought. What I don't really understand is the time aspect. Why is there this increase now? She realized that she did not really comprehend their ultimate goal. By focusing exclusively on the homicide, she had cut out the larger context. Maybe this had been a mistake. The case was not as clean as she had wished. Stollberg's life had been messy, so was his death, creating problems for his wife and his friends. Charlotte felt sorry for Dorothea Stollberg. She did not deserve to be hounded because her ex owed large amounts of money. Charlotte put on a warm coat and a cap. She locked her apartment and moved to the front of her apartment building, keeping her hands in the pockets of her coat. The night was colder than she had expected and she was shivering a little. Minutes later she saw the headlights of Kraft's little sports car and walked toward the glistening wet road. Kraft greeted her with his usual enthusiasm, inviting her to get into the very low vehicle.

"Let's go", was all that Charlotte replied, leaning back in the comfortable seat.

"A police car with two officers should be at her house already," Kraft told Charlotte.

"Good," Charlotte replied.

After this brief exchange they did not speak until they arrived at Dorothea Stollberg's place. A police car with blue lights stood in front of the building. One of the officers was checking the cars parked on both sides of the road. Kraft walked over to him, trying to find out whether there had been suspicious people. The officer told him that there was nothing out of the ordinary.

"What about the car with the two men Frau Stollberg reported?" Kraft wanted to know.

"Nothing unusual. They probably left immediately when they saw our police car."

Kraft followed Charlotte to the apartment where the other officer, a young woman, talked to Dorothea Stollberg, who looked upset and frightened.

After introducing herself and Kraft, Charlotte invited Dorothea Stollberg to tell her what had happened. She wanted to hear the details. It took Dorothea Stollberg a while to focus. She was clearly shaken by the incident. There had been a threatening phone call reminding her that she still owed the money. But then, half an hour later she noticed a car with two men in front of the building. Five minutes later there had been a knock at her apartment door. A male voice had demanded that she open the door. When she refused, he had tried to open the door by force. That was the moment when she had called the police.

"I'm glad you called the police," Charlotte said, "you should not stay in your apartment tonight. The intruder might come back. How did he get into the building in the first place?"

Dorothea Stollberg had no explanation. She sat on a chair in her living room looking at Charlotte with an air of relief that somebody had come. Charlotte asked Kraft to inspect the front door. His report was not encouraging. It would have been rather easy to force the door open. It appeared that the intruder's intention was primarily to frighten the victim.

"Do you have a friend where you can stay tonight?" Charlotte asked. It took Dorothea Stollberg a while until she responded: "I could stay with a colleague who lives in Dahlem."

Charlotte encouraged her to contact this person. Once she had found out that the victim had a safe place, she asked the uniformed police officers to take care of this task. But before Dorothea Stollberg left, Charlotte approached her with a question:

"This may not be a good time for an extended conversation, how much do you know about Stefano Brindisis and the finances of KreuzbergChem?"

"Stefano and Herwig were very close friends," Dorothea replied. "They first met at the university when they majored in Chemistry. But I don't know that much about the company and even less about the finances. In the beginning it was just Herwig and Brindisi. Klein came later."

"Where did they get the money?"

"I think most of it came from Stefano's family. Herwig had some money, but not that much. He had the ideas," Dorothea Stollberg replied in a low voice. "Later David Klein joined the company. I understand that he came with additional money. But they were always underfunded. At least, this is what my ex told me when I reminded him that I expected him to contribute to our family budget."

"We have to look at the company's financial records more thoroughly," Charlotte suggested to Kraft after Dorothea had left the apartment escorted by the uniformed officers.

"Money appears to be the critical issue in this case, not only Stollberg's gambling debts that haunt his wife, but also the company's financial situation. Where did they get their capital? I think this will be a topic at our next meeting. Maybe I will have to contact the LKA officers from Hesse whom I met in Frankfurt."

"What about Stefano Brindisi," Kraft interjected, "could he have family contacts that would extend to organized crime?"

Charlotte shrugged her shoulders: "Good question, Werner, we have to find him to find out. The parents will not talk unless it gets really bad. There is a link, but what sort of link is it?"

The meeting of the SOKO was set for 10:00 in the morning, giving all members time to get organized for their presentations. There was a surprise, however, without warning, Kriminalrat Sieverts, Charlotte's boss, showed up. Everybody in the room realized that suddenly the parameters of the investigation had changed. He took a seat and signaled to Charlotte that he would explain his unexpected presence later. Charlotte opened the discussion by informing the group of the official search for Stefano Brindisi. The search has been extended to West Germany after it became likely that Brindisi had been in the van that was found in Bielefeld. The LKA of North Rhine Westphalia had been informed. All police stations were on alert, but no result so far. At this point, Kraft mentioned in passing that internal sources suggested that the fugitive might be hiding in the Düsseldorf area.

"But there is no official confirmation," he continued.

Charlotte glanced at him with an expression of surprise. He returned her glance, indicating that he would fill her in later. Next, Hans Trommler, the specialist reported on the results of analysis of the fingerprints in the van. The fingerprint on the backdoor was identical with the print on the left front door. The man has been identified through the data system of Interpol. He was familiar to the Italian police but no recent address was available. According to Italian records, he was a member of the Costanzo family that was known to extend its activities to Austria and Germany.

"Can you be more precise?" Charlotte asked.

"Unfortunately, the information is incomplete, no recent activities. In Italy he was last seen in the Milano area in connection with money laundering. More than a soldier, but not a capo."

"We need more information about this guy who is clearly involved in the death of Stollberg," Charlotte interjected. "Did he come to Berlin with an order to kill Stollberg? And why would the person or persons who sent him be interested in eliminating Stollberg? According to a reliable source, Stollberg was on the way to a meeting where he would have sold valuable research results. There is only one problem with this theory. The file containing the information is missing."

"What kind of file are we talking about?" one of the officers wanted to know.

"Good question," Kraft interjected. "Our source cannot specify the nature of the file. One thing is clear, however, Stollberg didn't trust the internet. He used either paper or some kind of digital archive. We searched his body carefully. He didn't carry anything in his pockets or the small bag he had with him."

There was a longer discussion focusing on the potential buyers of the research results and the role of the Frankfurt detective in the case. As Charlotte pointed out, there might be more than one customer. There was no doubt about the interest of the pharma company Alerta, but there might be an Indian company as well.

"In addition, we have to assume that organized crime is interested as well," Charlotte pointed out.

At this point, the Kriminalrat, who had followed the debate without saying anything, interrupted the conversation: "There are two things that worry me: first the presence of organized crime and, second, the lack of a clear motive for the homicide. Listening to your discussion, I didn't get the sense that the case has been clearly defined. There is the reasonable suggestion that our case is linked to the homicide in Bad Homburg, but the exact nature of this link seems to be vague."

Charlotte had to control her impatience. His analysis only repeated her own conclusions. Why is he here? Why is he interfering with our investigation? she thought. I have to assure him that we are on the right track.

"Yes, the link between the Kellner case and the death of Stollberg is not yet clear, but that doesn't mean that we can't move forward," Charlotte exclaimed. "We will focus on the evidence left in the vehicle used for the killing. It points to the member of an Italian gang and Stefano Brindisi. Our top priority is Brindisi. Once we have him in custody, it will be easier to put the pieces together."

The Kriminalrat just nodded. He seemed to be satisfied with her response.

"There is one more significant development," Charlotte continued. "Last night we received a call from Dorothea Stollberg. She received abusive phone calls and found herself threatened in her apartment. Someone knocked at her door and tried to force the door open when she refused to open. For the time being, she is under police protection. As you recall, Stollberg owed a large amount of money. The lender, most likely a criminal organization, wants the money back."

"Do we assume that this organization is identical with the gang that arranged the death of her husband?" a member of the team asked.

"Indeed, this is a good question," Kraft interjected. "There are many loose ends."

"I believe that we are dealing with one organization," Charlotte replied calmly. "In my opinion it's a sideshow to the attack on Herwig Stollberg. He died because he planned to sell the results of his recent research to the highest bidder."

The discussion continued for a while. Among other things, there was a report on the financial situation of the Brindisi family. It turned out that they were doing well, much better than initially assumed. They had no problems getting the money from a local bank in Berlin for opening a second restaurant in Düsseldorf. Also, there was no evidence of any connection to organized crime.

"Very good," the Kriminalrat intervened. "But we can't stop there. All financial aspects of this case, broadly speaking, have to be checked rigorously. As long as we see it as an isolated homicide we will not understand the broader ramifications. It seems that the victim was no more than a small player who made a bad decision."

"Our best chance to explore these aspects is Stefano Brindisi's arrest," Charlotte replied. "Once he talks we will have a much better access to those who pull the strings."

Everybody in the room realized that Charlotte was defending her strategy of using a rather narrow focus, following concrete leads. There was immediate support from Werner Kraft:

"It is likely that we will arrest Brindisi within days. We know that he moved to Düsseldorf where he contacted his brother and a cousin. He is hiding in the Düsseldorf area."

Charlotte gave him a surprised smile. Where did he get this information? she thought.

"Let's hope that Brindisi doesn't slip away or, what would be worse, get hurt," the Kriminalrat suggested and got up, suggesting that he considered the meting closed. He turned to Charlotte with a smile.

"I walk you to your office. There are a few things that I want to discuss."

Charlotte returned the smile and collected her files. Together they walked to her office, followed by Kraft who was eager to explain his unexpected intervention. Although he had no reason to complain about the Kriminalrat, the man wasn't on his list of favorite persons, too distant and aloof, not his kind of police officer.

When they reached Charlotte's office, Sieverts carefully closed the door before he started the conversation: "I'm afraid there is some bad news, Charlotte. The brass is not happy with the results of your investigation. They want to see an arrest that demonstrates that we are on top of the situation. They are worried about talk about organized crime in connection with this case. They don't like the idea that gangs are getting a foothold in Berlin."

"But that's exactly what you think," Charlotte replied looking at him. "That speaks against an easy solution with a single killer."

The Kriminalrat agreed: "Yes, I don't share the expectations of the brass, but I have to keep their views in mind. There will be pressure to present results soon. They are nervous because there has been a complaint."

"Who has complained?" Charlotte asked. The tone of her voice showed that she was getting irritated.

"No name was mentioned, but given the list of your suspects, it was most likely David Klein telling his political friends that we was roughed up by the police."

"Nonsense," Charlotte cried, "he was treated like everybody else. After all, this is a homicide. He was not cooperative when he was asked for a meeting. Finally, we told him to come to us at a day and a time we set."

"The point is not correct procedure but political sensitivity," the Kriminalrat emphasized. "Our local economy needs young people like Klein. They shouldn't find the city a hostile environment."

"A murder investigation is not a question of diplomacy," Charlotte insisted. "My job is to nail a killer, and if Klein looks suspicious, we have to grill him. He's not above the law."

"Nobody is saying that, Charlotte, it's a matter of style. You have an excellent record, which I told the brass. But there is a limit to what they will tolerate."

"Am I being suspended?" Charlotte asked.

"No, not yet," the Kriminalrat replied in a soothing voice, "but they expect you to coordinate the investigations more closely with me. Keep me posted. I'll attend the meetings of the SOKO."

"Will you formally chair the meetings?" Charlotte asked.

"No, the investigation is in your hands, I'll just attend the meetings."

"Thanks, I appreciate the difference," Charlotte replied in a low voice.

The Kriminalrat just nodded and left the room.

A minute later there was a knock on the door. It was Kraft who was eager to share the news from Düsseldorf. When he saw Charlotte's face, he stopped at the door.

"Give me five minutes," Charlotte told him. "I have to make a call."

"Sure," Kraft replied. He immediately grasped that she just needed time to calm down. It must have been an unpleasant meeting, he thought. Why is this stiff bureaucrat messing with our investigation?

"I'll be back later," Kraft said with a big smile.

When he returned ten minutes later, Charlotte had regained her composure. She calmly invited Kraft to join her, eager to find out why he was certain that Brindisi was hiding in Düsseldorf. She had experienced a brief moment of intense anger and irritation. And she had realized again that she would never completely understand or appreciate the concern of the brass. She disliked the political aspect of police work. Her job was to uphold the law. It was about justice, not politics. She had believed that the Kriminalrat saw it the same way, this morning she had found out that he was closer to the brass than she had imagined. But was that true? After all, she was still in charge of her team. Possibly he had protected her. When she looked at Kraft's eager face, she was calm and in control.

"Sorry about the lack of coordination this morning," Kraft said, "I tried to reach you before the meeting, but first you were involved in a private conversation and then you were on the phone."

"No harm done," Charlotte replied. "How did you find out?"

"I got a message from Bill McDonald last night. He and Ulrike are actually in Düsseldorf. They met with the brother and a cousin. Both of them confirmed that Stefano had approached them, asking for cash but not for a place to stay."

"Did they realize that there is a warrant out for Stefano's arrest?"

"I don't think so, after all they are not the police. But there is another side that we have to keep in mind. Organized crime continues to put pressure on the family. There had been a fire in the new restaurant and two men were observing the boutique of the cousin. Bill sent me a picture of one of them. He followed Ulrike after she had talked to the cousin."

"Did McDonald inform you of his next step?" Charlotte wanted to know.

"No, he didn't, but I'm sure he means to find Stefano Brindisi. It makes sense. If Brindisi was in the van, he should know more about the missing file. After all, Bill is supposed to bring the missing file back."

"The missing file," Charlotte mused, "I'm no longer sure that it exists."

"What is our next step?" Kraft asked.

"I mean to talk to Dorothea Stollberg, if possible, this afternoon."

"How about the evidence of Mafia activity?"

"Definitely important, we have to figure out the link to the Brindisi family," Charlotte replied. "We may need help. It seems to be not just a local problem in Berlin. McDonald's message confirms this. I want to talk to the LKA officers in Wiesbaden again. Maybe they have a better explanation of the increasing activities. Now that we have at least identified the family, they may be able to crosscheck our information with their data."

"I'll send you the picture of the guy who followed Ulrike in Düsseldorf."

With this remark Kraft got up and left the room.

Charlotte decided to use the subway to visit Dorothea Stollberg. Kraft had suggested that he should drive her, but she had declined the offer. She wanted to downplay the official character of their meeting. Probably the woman was still in shock and would close up as soon as the conversation looked like a police interview. Of course, for Charlotte the purpose of the meeting was to get more information about Stollberg's connection to organized crime. When and how did it start? Had his wife been involved? She had never admitted that she had anything to do with her husband's financial transactions. But maybe she didn't tell the full story. Maybe there was an angle she had not mentioned in her interview with Ulrike Pfanner. An involvement would explain the threats. Their purpose would be to enforce compliance by terrorizing the victim. In any case, it was obvious that the gang was unwilling to write the loan off even after Stollberg's death. Somebody was expected to pay. For the first time, it occurred to Charlotte that the other person perceived as responsible for the loan could be Stollberg's close friend, that is Stefano Brindisi. Was he on the run for this reason? I have to find out. Maybe there is more than Ulrike learned.

It took Charlotte a while to reach the house of Dorothea Stollberg's colleague in Dahlem. She had to take the line number 3 and get off at Thielplatz. From there it took her another fifteen minutes of walking to the brick duplex located on a quiet street. When she rang the bell, there was no immediate answer, although she had announced her visit. She rang again. Now the door was opened with the chain in place. Charlotte announced herself and held her ID close to the door. Finally, Dorothea Stollberg opened the door and invited Charlotte to enter the house. Charlotte could see fear in her face. Last night's events were clearly still on her mind. I have to be very careful with my questions, Charlotte thought. Any pressure at this time will be counterproductive. She was glad that she had decided to come without Kraft.

"How are you?" Charlotte asked in a soft voice after they had moved to the living room.

"Better than last night," Dorothea Stollberg replied, moving her hands in a way that showed how delicate her state of mind still was.

"My friend and her husband are at work. That's why I was extra cautious when I answered the door," she continued. "I'm a bit jumpy after last night, as you will understand."

Charlotte assured her that she fully understood her cautious response and suggested that she stay with her colleague for at least a few days.

"I also recommend that you do not yet return to work where they can track you down and follow you to this place," Charlotte suggested. She realized that it would be very difficult to open a conversation about the causes of the threats. But she had to try. They talked for a while about future measures to protect Dorothea Stollberg. Finally, after the victim had calmed down, Charlotte returned to last nights' events.

"Do you understand the meaning of the threats? Did the man say anything that would give you a clue?"

For a while there was no response. Finally, Dorothea Stollberg exclaimed: "It's about money. They want the money back they loaned Herwig."

"But that's not your responsibility!"

"They insist it is. I am supposed to make monthly payments. I have refused. Herwig's gambling debts are not my problem."

"Who are these people? Do they have names? A company?"

"They never use a name. They just talk about a 'Chef' who is expecting me to cooperate by making monthly payments."

"Are there threats of violence?"

"More recently, the demands have become more urgent and suggestions of violence were part of it."

Dorothea Stollberg put her hands on her knees staring at her feet. Charlotte got up and walked to the kitchen where she looked for a glass. She filled it with water from the tab and returned to the living room.

"Please, take a sip of water," she encouraged the pale woman who was still sitting on her chair without moving. She held the glass with both hands, moving it slowly to her mouth. After taking a few sips, she glanced at Charlotte.

"Do you have any idea how your ex-husband got involved with these people.?"

"I don't know the details. But I'm fairly sure it was through his friend Stefano Brindisi. Initially, they needed money for their little company. Later he needed the money to cover his gambling debts. I warned him and pleaded with him. But he couldn't stop. It got worse and worse. Finally, I left him."

"The friends of Stefano, where did they meet them?"

"As far as I recall, at his father's place. The family owns a well-known restaurant."

Charlotte just nodded, urging the woman to tell her more.

"When they started out, five years ago, they got most of their capital from Stefano's father. Herwig put in some of his own money, but he didn't have a lot, and his family did not support the idea. Too risky for their taste."

"What about David Klein?"

"This happened all before Klein became a partner. Herwig was very happy, because the extra funds allowed them to get a bigger lab and hire more people. It was essential for the company's new project."

"How about you? Did you give them some of your own money?"

"Money? I was a young high school teacher with a small salary. My family doesn't have money. No, it was Herwig's idea, and he and Stefano turned it into a business project."

Dorothea Stollberg looked tired, she took another sip of water, still holding the glass with both hands. Charlotte gave her time to compose herself. After a long pause, she asked: "Did your ex-husband have any idea about the source of the capital he and Stefano Brindisi received from this friend of the family?"

"All he told me was that it was a private investor from Rome, a man with deep pockets who was willing to wait. I didn't care about the details. What am I supposed to do now? I don't feel safe in my own apartment anymore."

"No, you shouldn't go back," Charlotte replied in a calm voice. "I suspect that we are dealing with organized crime. I cannot exclude the possibility that they will actually use violence."

Charlotte promised to be back soon with a plan. In the meantime, she advised Dorothea Stolberg to keep a very low profile and to call the police immediately if there was any sign that she was followed. Then she did something that wasn't part of the official visit. She gave the young woman a hug.

"Take care," she said in a low voice.

"Thank you," Dorothea Stollberg whispered.

On her way back to the train station Charlotte changed her mind. She called Kraft and asked him to pick her up at Thiel Platz. He promised to be there in fifteen minutes.

"That would be a record, if you can do it in twenty minutes I'll be happy."

She continued to walk in the direction of the train station at a slower pace. It gave her time to think about the information she had just received. What she had learned was critical indeed. At the center of the case was money, venture capital, to be more precise. The Hesse LKA officers at the Frankfurt meeting had been right. She had to admit that. She had considered their theory as far-fetched and somewhat outlandish. Ulrike did not get the whole story when she talked to Dorothea Stollberg, only the part about the gambling debts, not the more fundamental aspect of funding KreuzbergChem. There had been dirty money from the very beginning, possibly without any awareness of the partners. And what about Klein? Did he know and failed to tell her when she talked to him? Her gut feeling was that he was not aware of this link. But she needed to talk to him again. Maybe Stefano Brindisi vouched for this private venture capitalist from Rome. Her specialist for financial issues would have to go over the company records once more. It was not a question of bad money threatening the company from the outside, it had been on the inside from the very beginning; through a friend of the family! Stefano Brindisi, Charlotte realized, was the central figure in this case. His arrest would be crucial. Charlotte was so deeply lost in her thoughts that she didn't notice Kraft's car pulling up next to her. Only when he honked, did she turn her face toward the road. As usual, he got out of the car and opened the door for her.

On the way to Headquarters Charlotte shared the new information with Kraft.

"So, we must be glad that there were threats to Dorothea Stollberg," he responded. "This motivated her to call the police. Otherwise, it might have taken us weeks to figure out the connection between KreuzbergChem and organized crime. I feel sorry for Stollberg's wife. She was dragged into this mess without realizing it."

"Most likely you are right," Charlotte replied. "She will need police protection for a while and shouldn't be in her apartment."

"Do you really think the men who threatened her will be back?"

"I'm afraid so," Charlotte replied. "She is expected to make payments."

"In that case, I think we should set up a trap," Kraft exclaimed.

"What do you mean?" Charlotte wanted to know.

"The victim officially returns to her apartment in a manner that is very public. But the person moving back to the apartment is a female police officer dressed as Dorothea Stollberg. We'll give them an opportunity to get into the apartment where we are waiting for them. The catch would be small fry but we can squeeze them for information."

Charlotte couldn't help smiling. This was a classic Werner Kraft project, but she had to admit that it might be a useful plan. They needed a trace that would lead them to Stefano Brindisi. And this was urgent. In the meantime, she would have another conversation with Stefano's father and David Klein. How much did they know about the Roman venture capital?

Back at her office, Charlotte tried to arrange a meeting with Brindisi senior but was told that he was not available. Supposedly, he had not yet recovered from a bad cold. After a fruitless exchange with his wife, Charlotte sent two members of her team to the Brindisis restaurant with a summons for the following morning. She was not in the mood to play games.

CHAPTER 14

When Bill opened his eyes, the room surrounding him looked unfamiliar. It took him a moment to orient himself. He heard strange noises from the bathroom. Dim light fell through the heavy curtains, but not enough to tell him whether it would be a sunny day or not. He stretched his left arm out to find Ulrike, but she wasn't there. She must be in the bathroom taking a shower, he thought. He turned his head and looked at the alarm clock on the nightstand. It was 7:30. He didn't feel like getting up. It hadn't been a restful night. He felt tired. What am I doing here? He had to remind himself that he was on a mission. He had to find Stefano Brindisi, a man who was involved in the death of Herwig Stollberg, his close friend and partner. I have to get up now, he told himself. This is urgent. We have to find him before the Mafia finds him. But maybe he is part of the arranged accident. But if this is the case, why is he running and hiding? He got up and walked to the window. When he opened the curtain, the light was so bright that he had to close his eyes. Still, it felt good to see the sun. He felt reassured. It would be a day when they would accomplish their task. What they had learned yesterday was promising. Brindisi was hiding in this area. Bill suspected that he was using his cousin's place, either an apartment or some other place. If the Mafia was observing the boutique, they would also watch Anna Brindisi's apartment or house. It must be another place. One possibility was a cottage or hunting cabin outside of town, another one some kind of storing facility where Anna kept her surplus. But how do we figure out the location, if there is such a place? Bill decided it was too early to follow up on this question. First, he needed a large cup of very strong coffee. He turned around and walked toward the bathroom where he found Ulrike in a robe, her hair still wet. She looked energetic and agile.

"Hurry up, Bill," she exclaimed, "I'm hungry. How was your night?"

"Could have been better," he muttered, "I need a cold shower and hot coffee."

"Go right ahead," Ulrike replied, inviting him to enter the bathroom, while she was moving back to the bedroom.

Half an hour later they were sitting at a small table in the crowded breakfast room, sampling the buffet and sipping black coffee.

"This is really great," Bill cried. "To be sure, the Germans haven't invented service, but the breakfast buffet is great. In the US you always have to pay extra and usually it's overpriced."

He had filled his plate with eggs, sausages and other goodies. His mood had improved considerably, as Ulrike noticed, while she was studying a map of the Düsseldorf area.

"Did you get anything out of Anna Brindisi with respect to Stefano's possible location?" Bill wanted to know.

"I tried to pressure her, but there was no useful response. Either she didn't know or she was evasive. We clearly need more information. How about her apartment?"

"Stefano would never stay there. He knows that the gang would look for him there."

"So, we are looking for a space that she owns or controls, but the other side is not aware of," Ulrike suggested, while she refilled her cup.

"Right, what could that be?"

"Wait a minute," Ulrike interjected, "When I talked to Anna Brindisi in the back room, I realized how small the boutique really was. There was barely enough space for all the merchandise. There must be a storage space somewhere else. Where could that be?"

"Let's find out," Bill insisted.

"How?"

"We pretend that we have to deliver merchandise and need the address," Bill replied. "Do you know the phone number of the store?"

"Wait, I took the business card along. It must be in my bag," Ulrike said, opening her handbag. It took her a while until she found the card. She handed it to Bill, who picked up his phone and typed in the number. He heard a youthful voice.

"The sales girl," Ulrike whispered.

Bill introduced himself as the English driver of a delivery van with a large package for the boutique.

"I'm not aware of any delivery," the girl answered.

"No, of course not. This is a special offer that you can look at and then decide. All I need at this point is an address. You must have a storage facility?"

"Yes, we do but I don't have the key."

'Never mind, I'll call you when I am there. Right now, I still need two hours before I reach Düsseldorf."

There was a moment of silence. Then the girl mentioned the name of the street and the area where he would find the storage facility. Bill thanked her profusely and assured her that he would be in touch to arrange the details.

Ulrike gave him a big smile. This was a promising start. She studied the map again and pointed to a spot where she had located the street Bill had mentioned. It was a place outside the city, close to the river.

"Let's give it a try," Ulrike exclaimed. Bill gave her just a nod. He was not yet done with his breakfast and returned to the buffet

"You can join me when you are done," Ulrike suggested and walked to the elevator.

Fifteen minutes later Bill was ready to leave the breakfast room, when the humming noise of his phone alerted him to an incoming message. He sat down and opened his phone. It was a brief message: "Increasing disagreement between the partners, Hinchcroft is in the minority. Majority wants to continue to do business with Alerta. Will keep you posted." The sender was the paralegal, his ally at the firm. She must have posted the message very late last night. Bill looked at the message twice before he put the phone away. The news was not reassuring. He had the feeling the ground under him was sinking. He could be called back any moment. He decided not to share this information with Ulrike, because it might undermine their efforts to find Stefano Brindisi. There was no strong reason to assume that Brindisi was in possession of the file, but he realized that he did not really care that much. His priorities had shifted. He wanted to find the murderer.

It took them half an hour to reach the street that the sales girl had mentioned. Without a GPS they would have missed it. It was a district filled with small somewhat run-down factories and grey storage buildings. There was hardly any traffic. The whole area looked deserted.

"What an unattractive place," Ulrike exclaimed. "Why would Anna Brindisi rent storage space in this unappealing neighborhood?" Ulrike asked.

"It's probably cheap," Bill replied. "The dresses don't mind the tristesse of the area."

"That's what you think, Bill McDonald," Ulrike protested. "I think it's inappropriate for a fashionable boutique to use this neighborhood for storage space."

Bill shrugged his shoulders and got out of the car. They were looking for the number 33, but there were no clear references. Finally, they found a grey building with the number 39. Ulrike parked the car and followed Bill who walked toward the end of the street, searching for house numbers on the buildings. After two hundred feet he stopped. He stood in front of a brick wall with a large door opening to a courtyard with cobblestones. He turned around, inviting Ulrike to catch up. Together they looked at the empty courtyard. At its far end, they saw an older brown brick building with narrow windows. It was impossible to overlook the Number 33.

"Here we are," Ulrike said in a low voice.

"Let's go," Bill responded, moving toward the large house that looked almost deserted. For a moment they stood in front of the wide entrance door, then they opened it and entered the hallway. They needed a moment to adjust their eyes to the rather dim light. To the right, they noticed a board with the names of the companies that had rented storage space in the building. It was Ulrike who first discovered the name of the boutique.

"Second floor," she exclaimed, moving to the large freight elevator.

Bill, who was right behind her, touched her arm and pointed to the staircase next to the elevator.

"Let's use the stairs," he suggested. "I don't like surprises."

Both of them turned to the rather narrow staircase. At the bottom they listened to the humming noise of a distant machine. There seemed to be no human traffic. Bill took the lead, moving up cautiously. The second floor was empty as well. The humming noise seemed to be stronger, but they were unable to locate the source. Ulrike made a gesture, indicating that they had to turn to the right. After walking about thirty feet, they found a door with the name of the boutique. Bill pressed the door handle, expecting the door to be locked. But to his surprise the door opened. The room in front of them was completely dark. Ulrike searched for a light and found a switch. The bright and harsh neon light fell on a small almost empty room with two doors in the back. Two old armchairs failed to offer any sense of comfort. Bill walked to the doors and opened them. The larger room to the right contained am old wooden table with smaller packages and several long boxes on top with dresses, jackets and pants, still in their original packages. Ulrike opened the left door. Because the curtains were drawn, the room was dark. She needed a moment to recognize the empty bed in the far-left corner. A blanket on top had been pulled up. There was an empty glass in front of the bed. Next to it Ulrike noticed an old newspaper.

"You have to come here," Ulrike cried. "I think I have found the place where Brindisi was hiding. But he's already gone."

She walked toward the bed and picked up the newspaper. It was a copy of the *Morgenspiegel* from the day before yesterday. She showed it to Bill who had joined her.

"This must be Brindisi," Bill said. "He was checking the Berlin news for his status. Either he is just out for a short time or he has left. I suspect it is the latter."

"But why is the door open?" Ulrike wanted to know.

"Good question, it makes no sense. Unless he is still around and just gone for breakfast."

He checked his watch. It was 10:45.

"Let's give him time," Bill suggested.

They returned to the front room and sat down in the armchairs. They had been waiting for half an hour when they heard the engine of a car. Then the engine stopped. Bill rushed to the window of the smaller room and looked at the courtyard below. A large black SUV had pulled up. Three men stepped out of the car and moved toward the front door. Bill ran to the front room.

"We have to get out of here in a hurry," he exclaimed. "Three men are approaching the front door. They don't look like the police, but I suspect that they are looking for Brindisi as well. And they will not appreciate our interference with their business."

"OK, let's get out before they find us," Ulrike replied. "At the other end of the hallway I saw some furniture. We can hide there."

They turned the light off and quickly left the apartment, hurrying to the other end of the hallway where they found some old desks and large cabinets. The loud noise of the freight elevator told them that the men were approaching. They crouched behind the furniture. The men were talking among themselves in Italian, but the distance was too large to understand what they were saying.

"Shall we stay here to observe what they are doing after they have searched the place?" Ulrike whispered.

"Not a smart move," Bill decided. "They might come down the hall, looking for Brindisi, once they are inside the apartment, we leave the building. If I had a gun, the situation would be different."

As soon as the men disappeared in the apartment, they rushed toward the staircase. They had almost reached the staircase, when one of the men stepped out of the apartment. There was no place to hide. Bill and Ulrike slowed down, walking calmly to the staircase, pretending not to notice the man at the other end of the hallway. He approached them, ready to interfere with their movements.

"Either we have to calm him down or eliminate him," Bill whispered, while he moved toward the man.

They met in front of the staircase. Ulrike gave him a friendly smile.

"Can we help you," she exclaimed. "I have not seen you before. You must be a new renter."

The man, heavy-built, in his thirties, did not immediately respond. His facial expression told them that he was ready to attack them any moment. He stared at them. Finally, he told them to get lost immediately, while he moved his right hand close to his left side. This was clearly more than a verbal threat. Bill decided that it was not wise to turn their backs to this man, while they were on the way to the ground floor. Bill stepped to the man's side and twisted his arm with force in such a way that he lost the gun, which fell to the ground. Before he fully realized what had happened, Ulrike picked it up and stepped back. At the same time, Bill moved forward and kicked him in the stomach. The man bent forward, making a hissing noise. Before he could return a blow, Ulrike handed the gun to Bill, who turned it on the man, motioning him to move to the staircase.

"Keep quiet and follow the staircase down," Bill ordered him in a low voice.

The man nodded, while he walked.

"Slowly," Bill cried. "Nobody will get hurt, if you do what I tell you."

They reached the bottom of the staircase. Bill noticed a door that looked like the entrance to the basement. He asked Ulrike to check it out, while he ordered the man to kneel down. When she came back, telling him that it was indeed the basement door, he asked her to tie the man's hands behind his back, using her scarf. Then he directed the man to stand and walk towards the basement door. He opened the door, turned on the light and motioned the man to walk down to the basement. Once the man was at the bottom, he turned the light off and closed the door.

"Let's get out of here before the other guys notice that their man is missing," Bill cried. "We have only a few minutes."

They ran to the front entrance and quickly crossed the empty courtyard. Within minutes they had reached Ulrike's Fiat and drove away. Bill was still holding the gun in his hand.

"Close call," Ulrike said. "Will they come after us?"

"Probably, once they have discovered their guy in the basement. We surely don't want to wait for them. There must have been a source that told them about Brindisi's hiding place. Fortunately for him, he left before they found him."

"You are sure that he left for good?"

"Not certain, but more likely. The newspaper was the only thing he left. No bag, no overcoat or other personal things. Maybe he was warned."

By whom?"

"Maybe his brother called him after the fire. Or the gang paid a visit to the cousin. He's on the run!"

"Agreed, but where is he going?" Ulrike wanted to know. "Do you have a clue?"

"I'm afraid we will have to go back to the storage building and look for clues."

"How promising is that?" Ulrike replied, giving Bill a skeptical look.

Bill just shrugged his shoulders, encouraging Ulrike to move faster.

Later they stopped at a nearby supermarket where they found a small coffee shop. It was time for a strategy session. The coffee left room for improvement, but at least it was hot. Bill looked at Ulrike whose face expressed disappointment and fatigue. We were so close, he thought. Brindisi must have found out that the Düsseldorf area was not safe for him after all, that the gang had figured out his movement. But what was his next step?

"Bill, you have to get rid of the gun," Ulrike said in a low voice.

There was a moment of silence. Bill took just a sip of his black coffee.

"I don't think so," he replied in a low voice. "After the open confrontation with the Mafia, we are no longer safe. We are a target now, and I think we need a gun for our defense."

Ulrike gave him a skeptical look, suggesting that she was not persuaded, but she knew that he would not change his mind. When it came to guns, their approach fundamentally differed. Carrying a gun struck him as completely normal.

"If Kraft finds out, he will arrest you," Ulrike told him.

"He won't find out, and he won't arrest me," Bill said calmly. "I know him well enough. He respects my position."

Ulrike just shrugged her shoulders. After a moment of silence, she said: "Do you really mean to go back?"

"I'm afraid so," he said. "We have to find clues about his movements."

"I don't like it."

"Neither do I, we have to wait until the men have concluded their search."

"Ok, I'll go over to the newspaper stand. Maybe there is more information about the search for Brindisi."

Ten minutes later Ulrike came back with a copy of the local paper. It took her a while to find the page with the information on crime. There was a small notice about the search for a certain Stefano B. for his involvement in a Berlin homicide. All police stations in the Federal Republic had been advised to look for him. So far, there had been no results. Bill took out his phone and sent a brief message to Kraft. Within minutes he received a reply: "We have checked train stations and hotels in and around Düsseldorf. He is still at large. His parents' place is under observation around the clock."

Bill showed Ulrike the message and suggested that they should pay the brother another visit. Maybe he had changed his mind about cooperating with the police and was willing to tell us more about Stefano. Ulrike folded the newspaper, focusing her eyes on the empty cup in front of her.

"Do you really believe that he'll have changed his attitude? Cooperation with the police exposes his entire family to pressure and violence by the gang."

"True enough," Bill replied, "but there is also a limit to what he is willing to accept. If he and his father accept a deal, it's a deal for life..."

"But we cannot offer him anything that would improve his situation," Ulrike said. "Not even Charlotte could, possibly the LKA Berlin or the BKA. Exposure by the media has not made a significant difference."

"Are you planning to write about this?"

"Definitely, the public of Berlin should find out what is going on."

"Glad to hear this," Bill interjected, "my own mission is more modest, if there is a mission left. The latest mail from my law firm is not encouraging. The partners are fighting among themselves and there is no clear information what Amos Hinchcroft has decided to do."

"Will he terminate the contract with Alerta if he finds out that the company has deceived the law firm about their arrangement with Stollberg?"

"I believe so, he is not an easy man but he has never tolerated shady deals."

"What does that mean for you?"

"If they break up and he leaves the firm, I might be without a job." Why?"

"Because I have been seen as his man. It was he who proposed to hire me."

"Have you thought about the consequences?" Ulrike wanted to know.

"Not a lot, to be frank. Right now, I'm focused on finding Brindisi and solving the Stollberg case."

"That makes you an unpaid assistant to the Berlin police."

"That's fine with me, at least for the time being. How about you?"

"I think there is an important story for me, in fact, two stories. The first one has to do with start-ups in Berlin. I would like to write about KreuzbergChem, its past and its future. Second, I mean to write about the presence of the organized crime in Berlin. The latter will be much more difficult. Lots of research. And I have to finish my book before I can get started."

Bill stood up, grabbed the cups and carried them to the counter. Then he followed Ulrike who was already on the way to her car.

It took them almost an hour to get back to the center of town. The traffic had been heavy, stop and go on one of the main highways. Ulrike parked her little Fiat hundred yards away from Roberto Brindisi's restaurant. The place looked better. The damaged furniture had been removed, and the windows had been cleaned. On the inside, the smell of burned wood and other materials was still in the air. Workers were busy removing torn drapes and damaged tables. They found Robert Brindisi in his office. He looked surprised when he saw them. There was no welcome.

"I'm glad to see that you are in the process of restoring your place. There is remarkable progress, Signor Brindisi," Ulrike said in an emphatic voice.

Roberto's response was less than enthusiastic: "What do you want? Why have you returned?"

"We almost found your brother. We got very close. Possibly we missed him only by and hour or so," Bill exclaimed.

"Really, tell me more," was the curt answer.

"It seems that he used your cousin's storage space for a couple of days. But he was gone when we arrived. Do you know where he went?"

Roberto Brindisis looked weary when he said: "No, I don't. He has not been in touch."

"That surprises me," Bill replied. "There is no doubt that he is on the run. The same people who have damaged your place are after him."

"How do you know?"

"We encountered them this morning. It wasn't a pleasant encounter,' Bill told him. "They are following him. Somehow, they must have figured out where he was hiding. They showed up at the storage space shortly after our arrival. And they carried guns."

"Really?"

"One of the men threatened us with a gun," Ulrike interjected. "It wasn't funny."

"Maybe you should go back to Berlin and leave us alone."

"We can't do that," Bill responded. "My firm expects me to talk to your brother about a file that he may have removed."

"How does that concern me?" the brother retorted.

"Not directly, but you have become part of the problem by sharing contacts. It's vital that we find your brother before they do. Believe me. Has he been in touch? Do you know anything about his location?"

Roberto Brindisis looked at the papers in front of him and seemed to ignore Bill and Ulrike. Finally, he said in a low voice. "Stefano tried to reach me last night, but I couldn't take the call because I was busy. When I called back there was no answer."

"Are you worried about your brother?" Ulrike asked.

"Of course, I am. But I don't know where he is."

"Have you been in touch with your cousin Anna?"

"No, right now I'm much too busy to worry about her."

"No attempt on her side to reach you?"

"Not today. She called me after the fire."

"Anything that would help us to find your brother?" Ulrike asked.

Roberto looked at her: "No, I have no idea where he may have moved. All his important connections are in Berlin. Would he go back?"

Bill realized that their visit would not yield results. It appeared that the brother did not know more than they did about Stefano's movements. He signaled Ulrike that it was time to leave. They wished Roberto well and returned to their car, which had been ticketed in the meantime. Ulrike's frustration expressed itself in foul language against the police. When Bill grinned, she threatened to leave him right here in Düsseldorf and return to Berlin immediately.

"Calm down," Bill urged her. "How much is it? I'll pay it out of my expense account and deal with my firm later."

Ulrike navigated the small car cautiously to the main road where she picked up speed.

"Back to the storage facility?" she asked turning to Bill who was studying the map.

"Yes, back to the storage space," he muttered folding the map.

When they got close to the building Ulrike parked the car under a large tree, more than two hundred yards away from the entrance. The street was not quite as empty as this morning. There was a crew of city workers busy fixing a part of the blacktop. A number of children were watching the workers.

"Shall we walk from here?" Ulrike asked. Bill shook his head. "Let us observe the entrance from here for a while and then drive by before we get out."

He took out binoculars focusing them on the entrance to the

courtyard. There was not a lot of traffic. A grey van, coming from the opposite side of the street, turned into the courtyard. A few minutes later black car left the yard, coming toward them. The driver was a middle-aged woman who was carrying on a phone conversation. After ten minutes they decided to drive by the courtyard slowly enough to see what was going on in front of the building. The van was standing in front of the main entrance, the backdoor wide open. An older Mercedes stood at the far end. Ulrike followed the street for half a mile; then she turned around and drove back to the entrance. She parked the car close to the exit of the courtyard. They left the car and walked slowly toward the building. On the inside, they checked the hallway, looking for the three men. The hall was empty. They were ready to move to the second floor when the basement door opened, an older man stepped out into the hallway with a large box under his left arm. When he noticed Ulrike and Bill, he approached them with a friendly smile.

"What can I do for you?" he asked.

Ulrike was the first one to understand the opportunity. She eagerly walked over to him.

"We are here to pick up a friend who may have stayed in one of the apartments for a night or two. It is the storage space of Anna Brindisi, the owner of a boutique. Where would we find the apartment?"

"I'm afraid you are coming too late," the man replied. "He was picked up very early this morning."

"Are you sure?" Ulrike replied. "We were asked to pick him up in the very late morning and take him out to lunch."

"I'm quite sure. I am the custodian of the building and was busy removing old boxes from the basement. I saw the young man around 7:30 this morning standing near the entrance, obviously waiting for someone. A few minutes later a white sportscar pulled up. The driver was a young woman. Clearly, they knew each other well because they embraced. Then he followed her to the car. They were gone in minutes."

"You are sure about the make of the car? Did you get the number of the plate?" Bill wanted to know.

"I am absolutely sure about the color, but not about the make of the car, something foreign and expensive, but I don't remember the plate. It started with two letters."

"What did the woman look like?" Ulrike interjected.

"I didn't have much time to get details. Fairly tall, blond, dressed in a light long overcoat."

"Did they go back into the building?" Bill asked.

"No, certainly not. They seemed to be in a hurry."

Ulrike thanked the custodian and added: "There must be a misunderstanding. We were supposed to pick him up for lunch. Very strange!"

The custodian just nodded and went back into the basement.

"That was our lucky break today," Ulrike exclaimed. "We missed him, but there is a trace. A lady in a light coat picked him up."

"In an expensive car," Bill cried. "Too bad the guy did not remember the plate number."

"Who can she be, this mysterious woman?" Ulrike exclaimed. "This is the first time we find out that she exists. Showing up in time to rescue him!"

Bill and Ulrike walked back to their car, both of them lost in their own thoughts for a while. It was Ulrike who resumed the conversation. She turned to Bill with the question: "What do you think? Do we have to rethink the case?"

"There is a new element, possibly an important new element," Bill replied, "but I believe there is no reason to completely rethink the case, at least not yet."

"A girl friend?" Ulrike suggested.

"That would be my guess," Bill said. "But a person that is not part of his Berlin environment. Nobody has mentioned her, neither his parents nor his brother. What about Dorothea Stollberg?"

"No, she mentioned Stefano as a close friend, but there was no mention of a girlfriend."

"For the time being," Bill said, "it doesn't matter that much. Important is that she shows up when she is needed. Someone he can count on."

They continued their conversation in the car, debating the next move. Brindisi had found a new hiding place but where? Without more information about the young woman their search had come to an end.

"Let's go back to Berlin," Bill suggested, "and figure out who this woman is and where she lives. Someone in Berlin must know her."

"How about contacting Roberto again? He might know her?" Ulrike suggested.

"We can try, but I don't believe that he is aware of her. It seems that Stefano is playing his cards very close to his chest."

"Let's do it anyway, while we are in the neighborhood," Ulrike suggested.

Bill agreed with a shrug and Ulrike started the engine.

When they entered Brindisi's restaurant again, he stood in the middle of the large room, giving orders to a group of cleaning women. His gaze was weary and distant.

"You seem to take pleasure in interrupting my work," he said.

"We apologize for taking more of your time," Ulrike responded. "We went back to your cousin's storage space. There we found out that your brother was picked up this morning by a young woman. She showed up in a white car. That might interest you."

"Are you sure? What woman?"

"Possibly Stefano's girl friend?" Bill suggested.

"They broke up two years ago," Roberto Brindisi said. "He had met her in Naples when he visited our relatives."

"Was she blond?" Ulrike asked.

"Positively not," Roberto replied.

"We are talking about a blonde," Ulrike explained.

"What am I supposed to say?" Roberto asked. "I have never seen this woman. Stefano has never mentioned her."

"For you the good news is that your brother is safe, at least for the time being," Bill exclaimed, "the bad news is that we cannot reach him."

"That may be bad news for you, but is it also bad news for him?" Roberto quipped. "You have to excuse me now, because I have to deal with a crisis."

He turned away and walked back to the cleaning women.

Five hours later Ulrike and Bill stood in front of her apartment building in Berlin. Their mood was calm, not elated, but not depressed either. The search for Stefano Brindisi had not been successful; this they had to admit. On the other hand, they had learned a lot.

"We'll figure out who this mysterious woman is," Ulrike insisted.

"But not now! How about pizza?" Bill suggested.

"No, not tonight," Ulrike replied. "Let's go to the Indian place two blocks away. I haven't been there for a while. You will like it."

Bill, who was hungry, was agreeable. As they unloaded the car, Ulrike' phone indicated a message. It was her brother Volker. He was planning to come to her apartment later. The expression on Bill's face told Ulrike that he was not excited about the news.

"What can I do?" she said. "He's my brother."

"So, let's go to my place then after dinner," Bill replied.

Ulrike all of a sudden dropped her bag and gave Bill a hug.

CHAPTER 15

When Charlotte returned from a meeting with Kriminalrat Sieverts midmorning, Werner Kraft was waiting for her. She knew the purpose of his presence. He was eager to prepare the trap for the gang members at Dorothea Stollberg's apartment. She realized that she was reluctant to support this venture, although she understood the potential gain. They might get access to critical information about the structure and the strategy of the gang that was using its power to terrorize individuals. But there was always the possibility that the encounter resulted in a violent death. She invited Kraft to explain the details of the operation, which he did with enthusiasm. A police officer dressed up as Dorothea Stollberg would be delivered to her apartment by a police car. Several police officers would surround her and bring her to her apartment. The same police officers would leave the building a few minutes later, giving the impression that the potential victim would be alone. In reality, members of a special unit would be waiting inside the apartment for any attempt to attack the woman. The element of surprise should make it very unlikely that the intruders would have time to resist. It's a simple plan and should work, Charlotte thought, if the gang falls for it. There was no reason to stop the plan. Still, Charlotte was uncomfortable with the idea.

"When do you plan to carry this out?" Charlotte asked.

"Either tomorrow night or the day after tomorrow," Kraft replied. "I need time to put together a special team. This I cannot do without green light from you. Do you need the consent of the Kriminalrat for this operation?"

Charlotte shook her head. "The operation is close enough to the Stollberg case to be under my supervision. Still, I would keep him posted. Things have become a bit tight and nervous. What we need is a clear result that demonstrates to the public that we are capable of finding the murderer."

"If successful, this operation will show that we are capable of protecting the victim of a vicious and violent threat" Kraft exclaimed.

"Good, let's do it," Charlotte said. She knew that her assistant would put all of his energy into this operation. The more immediate task was another conversation with Brindisi senior. later this morning. Charlotte had invited the Kriminalrat to participate. If he was concerned about the political side of her case, he should be there, she thought. But she was not sure what kind of politics he had in mind. She had mentioned his criticism in one of her emails to Bernd Moeller, who had advised her to steer a neutral course, away from party politics. She became aware again how much she missed him and how much she depended on his advice. Why did I immediately decide not to go to Australia when he invited her, she thought on her way to the special room where the meeting with Brindisi would take place. Maybe it would have been great to meet his daughter in Sidney. She had seen her on pictures that Bernd had sent though his smart phone, a friendly face with her father's brown eyes.

To her surprise, Kriminalrat Sieverts was already waiting in the meeting room, accompanied by his assistant, a young woman with long flowing hair and sharply dressed. She hardly acknowledged Charlotte, while the Kriminalrat motioned Charlotte to sit next to him. Brindisi was not yet present. When Charlotte tried to tell the Kriminalrat more about the background of the case and the link between the Stollberg case and the Brindisi family, she found out that he was well informed. He must have studied the file, she mused. Finally, the older Brindisi entered the room. He was accompanied by his wife, who looked even smaller today than the last time, and a middle-aged man with a briefcase. Brindisi walked slowly, as if he needed physical support. He looked almost ten years older than the last time. His hair had turned almost white. It took Charlotte a while to overcome her shock and open the conversation.

"Thank you, Signor Brindisi, for coming to this meeting," she said, trying to be as cheerful as possible. After introducing the Kriminalrat and his assistant, she encouraged Brindisi to tell him more about the so-called accident at his restaurant. Brindisi seemed to have difficulties focusing on the question, his eyes moving back and forth between Charlotte and the Kriminalrat, as if he wanted to determine who was conducting the interview. His reply was a repetition of what he had told them before. It had been an accident. Nobody got hurt, the damage was taken care of. At his restaurant it was business as usual.

Charlotte gave him a faint smile, while she said: "Signor Brindisi, you have told us this story before. It doesn't persuade me. A large brick is not thrown accidentally through the big window of your restaurant. This was done deliberately to threaten you. Someone was sending a message and we want to know who this person or organization was."

Brindisi just shook his head and stared at the table I front of him.

"You must realize that you are in danger," Charlotte continued. "They will be back and the violence will increase unless you decide to trust me and let the police investigate the threat."

Brindisi sat motionless at the table. All of a sudden, his wife interjected: "You cannot protect us. We have to deal with the situation our own way."

"But it apparently does not work, Signora Brindisi," Charlotte replied. "You must realize that your son's place in Düsseldorf has been damaged as well. There was a fire that Roberto declared to be accidental. Come on, you don't believe this and we don't either."

This was the moment when the Kriminalrat entered the discussion: "Please keep in mind that not only you and Roberto are exposed but also your son Stefano. He is in hiding, because he is afraid of the Mafia. If they get to him first, it is unlikely that you will ever see him again."

"Why do you pressure us? Why can't you just leave us alone? We can take care of ourselves," Brindisi exclaimed, lifting his hands from the table.

"You are mistaken," the Kriminalrat interjected. "You and your family are actually in an almost desperate situation. The only way out is cooperation with us."

Brindisi did not reply. Instead, he looked at his lawyer, who was sitting next to him.

"My client has reason to be cautious," the lawyer said. "Cooperation with the police exposes him to retaliation. As the owner of a well-known restaurant in Berlin he is very visible, part of the public sphere, frequently mentioned by the media. He has to keep the police at a distance."

"In normal times we don't mind the distance," Charlotte replied. "But these are not normal circumstances. Several members of the Brindisi family are facings serious and violent threats. I would not exclude the possibility that the organization means to eliminate Stefano because he was involved in the death of Herwig Stollberg"

"No, he was not," Signora Brindisi protested. "This is a lie. They were close friends. Stefano would never harm Herwig"

"There is proof that Stefano was inside the van that killed Stollberg," the Kriminalrat insisted. "He was not the driver, but he sat next to him."

"He didn't kill his friend," Brindisi protested.

"Why don't you help us then to clear his name?!" Charlotte exclaimed. "Maybe he was not part of the murder, but you have not shown us that he was not involved. He has to come to us."

"We don't know where he is," Brindisi replied, "He has not been in touch."

"You are worried, right?" Charlotte asked in a low voice.

"Yes, we are," Signora Brindisi said. Her voice was hardly audible.

"You can help him and yourself, if you can explain to us why there is this threat to your lives."

There was a long moment of silence. Then, the lawyer addressed the police officers: "Let me talk to my clients. Maybe we can reach a compromise."

The Kriminalrat nodded and got up, signaling to Charlotte to get up as well.

"Give me five minutes," the lawyer suggested.

The police officers left the room. It took more than five minutes, but fifteen minutes later they resumed the interview.

"My clients are ready to cooperate, if you promise full police protection."

"We will do our utmost," the Kriminalrat replied."

"What can you tell us about the funding of KreuzbergChem, your son's start-up?" Charlotte asked. "Where did he and Stollberg get the initial capital?"

"Most of the money they received from me," Brindisi replied. "Stollberg and his family did not have a lot of money."

"Was there an additional source?" Charlotte wanted to know.

"I'm not sure," Brindisi said. "But it is possible that Stefano also accepted funds from an old friend of my father. He was a regular visitor. They used to meet at my restaurant."

"They used to?" Charlotte interjected.

"He died a few years ago. In Rome. My father misses him."

"Can you tell us more about this man?" the Kriminalrat said.

"He and my father used to be close when they were young. But then my dad moved to Berlin. For years they didn't see much of each other. Then he showed up in Berlin. My father, who was already retired, was delighted. They talked about the old days, which were supposedly always better. That's all I know."

"Was he a business man?" Charlotte asked.

"You would have to ask my father. There is only one problem. He is 92 and his memory is not what it used to be."

"I believe the family owned a shipping company," his wife mentioned, "But I'm not sure."

"Would Stefano have accepted money from him for his start-up?" Charlotte asked.

"He was considered a close friend of the family. Why not?" Brindisi replied.

"This may be the source of your problem," Charlotte exclaimed. "There may be a connection to organized crime."

"I don't follow," Brindisi replied. "My dad's friend a Mafioso?! Not likely!"

"We will have to look very closely at the financial aspect of your son's company."

"Have you noticed recent changes in your son's behavior?"

"Of course, he was devastated by Herwig's death. They were close," the wife interjected.

"But that is no reason to go into hiding. He is afraid of something or someone. Who is after him?"

"I have come to the same conclusion as you," said the lawyer addressing the police officers.

"I suspect that Stefano is hiding because there was some deal with a private venture capitalist who is using very unusual means."

The Brindisis stared at the lawyer. It was obvious that they had not expected this move.

"What do you think happened?" the Kriminalrat asked turning to the lawyer.

"My hunch is that the Mafia at one point succeeded in penetrating the friend's business and wants to make sure their investment is profitable. There must have been a crisis. The exact nature of this crisis, however, I don't understand. I have discussed this question with Signor Brindisi, but he doesn't understand the sudden threats either. The only thing he and his wife noticed was that Stefano, who has his own apartment in the family building, seemed to be depressed."

"Depressed about what?" Charlotte asked. "Personal or professional issues?"

The lawyer hesitated, thereby encouraging the Brindisis to answer this question. They looked at each other. There was another moment of silence. Then Signor Brindisi exclaimed: "It had to do with his friend and partner Herwig Stollberg, I'm sure of that, but Stefano refused to talk about this. He seemed to be frustrated and angry. There were phone calls he didn't like.

"Any visits?" Charlotte asked.

"There was a meeting with Herwig at Stefano's apartment," Signora Brindisi mentioned. "After it, when he joined us at the restaurant, Stefano seemed to be very upset. But he refused to talk about it." She repeated the sentence in Italian to underline its importance.

Charlotte noticed that the couple began to look very frail and suggested a break. Coffee was ordered. The Brindisis had time to talk to their lawyer, while Charlotte and the Kriminalrat left the room.

They walked to Charlotte's office. Where they picked up a cup of coffee from the machine.

"Can you make sense of the statements?" the Kriminalrat wanted to know.

"Yes, what they have told us confirms our theory," Charlotte replied. "The crisis they talked about was Stollberg's plan to sell his latest research to an outside company, a huge threat to KreuzbergChem. It seems that Stefano got wind of the plan and wanted to prevent the deal."

"OK," the Kriminalrat interjected, "that makes sense. But how did young Brindisi figure out what his friend was up to?"

"I have no factual answer," Charlotte said. "My hunch is that Stollberg had borrowed money from the same source that funded the company, namely the Roman friend, in short, organized crime."

"I don't see the connection," the Kriminalrat said.

"It was a familiar strategy," Charlotte replied. "They loaned Stollberg the money, when he couldn't pay back, they pressured him and made a claim for a larger share of the company. When Stollberg refused and looked for another buyer, they got in touch with Stefano. He was expected to intervene."

"Any factual proof for this theory?"

"No, not yet," Charlotte had to admit. "But all the factual evidence we have gathered so far supports my theory. It also explains why Stefano Brindisi is on the run."

"You tell me", the Kriminalrat insisted.

"Stefano Brindisi collaborated with the gang up to a point, but then he refused. Stollberg was eliminated because he crossed the gang, now they are after Stefano. Either he will comply or share the fate of his friend."

At this moment a uniformed police officer knocked at the door and told them that Brindisi was ready to continue the interview.

The Kriminalrat said: "I am very pleased that you decided to cooperate with us. It will allow us to go after the people who have threatened you. What can you tell me about the recent threats?"

Brindisi looked at his hands before he responded. His voice was hesitant: "There have been several calls demanding that we persuade Stefano to come home and negotiate the contract with the capo of the family."

"They were calls in German?" Charlotte interjected.

"No, the caller spoke Italian with a Naples accent," Brindisi replied.

"Did he have a name for the capo?" the Kriminalrat asked.

"No, I was expected to know who he is." Brindisi said in a low voice.

"Do you?" Charlotte asked.

"Actually, I don't. The caller reminded me to think of my father's friend, but he didn't say that the friend was the boss."

"Could he be the boss?" Charlotte wanted to know.

"It never occurred to me that he could be linked to organized crime," Brindisi emphasized.

"We will not give in, no matter what," Signora Brindisi interjected. "And we will advise Stefano not to negotiate any contract with this gang."

"Do you know where your son is actually hiding?" the Kriminalrat asked.

"I have no idea and neither does my husband," Signora Brindisi said. "But I'm worried. Please help us."

"Of course, we will take measures. Your building will be protected by policemen. They have been there for a while,' the Kriminalrat assured her.

"Any guess where he might have turned for help?" Charlotte asked.

"Possibly he contacted his brother in Düsseldorf, who plans to open his own restaurant. Roberto told me that he had been threatened as well, but he didn't mention Stefano," Signora Brindisi replied.

After another half hour the interview was coming to an end. Both Brindisi looked exhausted. They left the room with the promise to keep Charlotte informed if Stefano would try to contact them. The Kriminalrat once more underscored that their son had only the choice between the Mafia and the police. It was the lawyer who assured them that there would be complete cooperation.

The time was 11:00. This was the first moment that Charlotte had a chance to check her phone. Most of the messages could wait, however there was a message from Ulrike that called for an urgent reply. It was not even clear from where it was sent. Charlotte noticed that the Kriminalrat and his assistant were still waiting. She quickly decided to offer a summary of the interview by late afternoon. Sieverts seemed to be satisfied, overlooking the remarks of his assistant who had taken notes and wanted to insert herself into the discussion. "Good work," the Kriminalrat said before he and his assistant left the room. Charlotte felt that she needed a break. The result of the interview had been far-reaching. It had confirmed her suspicion that some of KreuzbergChem's capital was linked to organized crime. She would have to talk to David Klein again, as much as he would resent it. A Mafia family was planning the take-over, and Stollberg got in the way when he, desperate for money, contacted buyers for his research. How did they find out? Was it Stefano Brindisi who told them? And who were they? She realized that she didn't fully understand the Italian background of her case. She might have to get in touch with the two detectives of the Hesse LKA. But right now, she had to return Ulrike's call.

"What's up?" Charlotte asked when Ulrike accepted the call.

"Thanks for calling back," Ulrike replied. "We are back from our trip to Düsseldorf. We didn't find Stefano Brindisis, but we were close."

"I want to know more about the details," Charlotte responded. "Can you join me for lunch?"

"Only if it's close to my office. I have to catch up because I missed almost two days," Ulrike said.

They agreed to meet at an Indian restaurant in the neighborhood of the *Morgenspiegel*.

"Give me half an hour and I will meet your there," Charlotte exclaimed.

Fortunately, the place was not crowded, they found a quiet corner for their conversation. They ordered from the short lunch menu. Then

Charlotte asked Ulrike to give her a full and detailed account of the trip to Düsseldorf. As she expected, it became a colorful narrative with many exciting moments. In a way, Ulrike was already working on the big story she was planning. For Charlotte, on the other hand, the importance of the report consisted of the factual information that could be checked and compared with this morning's interview. It became very clear that the grip of the gang included other members of the Brindisi family as well. And most important of all, they were still tracking Stefano Brindisi. And there was no doubt that they were prepared to use violent means. Ulrike's description of the encounter with the three men at the warehouse made that very clear. She also realized that Ulrike was somewhat hazy when it came to the details of the encounter, but there was no doubt that it had been dangerous, possibly more dangerous than Ulrike understood.

"We decided to return to Berlin when it became obvious that Brindisi got away before we or the gang could reach him," Ulrike exclaimed. "The mysterious lady with the foreign sportscar. But I'm determined not to let it go. The public deserves to learn more about this story."

"What story?" Charlotte asked, looking at Ulrike's excited face.

"The infiltration of regular companies, start-ups like KreuzbergChem, by organized crime. This is much bigger than a murder case."

"A wake-up call?"

"Exactly," Ulrike replied.

"Do you have the facts? Have you done the research to make the case?" Charlotte asked.

"No, I don't, Charlotte, you know that as well as I do. What I have in mind is different. I am thinking of a more personal intervention, an opinion piece."

"Will they let you do this in your paper, Ulrike?"

There was a moment of silence.

"Good question. I really don't know. Lately, things have not been especially good for me. My boss and I don't see eye to eye on a lot of things. She expects me to be more circumspect, more measured. Which is not my style."

Charlotte had to smile. She couldn't even imagine a cautious and measured Ulrike Pfanner. Was I like her when I was her age? Charlotte thought. Yes, I was as motivated and ambitious, but not like the young woman in front of me. I have always seen myself as part of a larger whole. Ulrike's nervous energy was alien to her. Charlotte listened to Ulrike's determined voice:

"If I don't get the space, I'll negotiate with another paper in Berlin. My old employer would do it under an alias. I don't care about the byline."

"In the meantime, tell me more about the lady with a white sportscar," Charlotte suggested.

"The way the janitor talked about her was rather vague: tall. Blond, dark glasses, long coat," Ulrike replied. "How much can you do with that?"

"Depends on the make of the car and the license plate," Charlotte suggested. "In any case, my hunch is that we are dealing with a personal rather than a professional relationship. She picked him up to move him to a safer hiding place. Tell me more about the three men whom you encountered at the warehouse."

"All three in their twenties or early thirties, speaking Italian among themselves. We were lucky that we had to deal only with one of them when we tried to leave the building. Bill took care of him before he could pull his gun."

"Yes, Bill. How is he doing by the way?"

"Frankly, not great. There seems to be trouble at his law firm because of Alerta. The partners disagree about the ethical standards in their relationship with their client. If the partners split up, Bill might be without a job. For the time being, he has decided to focus on finding Stefano Brindisi."

There is an unexpected ally, Charlotte thought. She realized that she should be upset about the interference of a foreign private detective in her own case, but she wasn't. On the contrary, she felt good about Bill's decision to get involved. Why have I changed my mind? There was something about him that she agreed with. His strong belief in the importance of the law despite his unconventional methods? She had acknowledged but never emphasized his presence at the periphery of her case to her own boss. And Sieverts had not asked questions. What did he think?

"I'll get in touch with our Düsseldorf colleagues to interview the janitor. Maybe he will recall more details when he is prodded," Charlotte said, looking straight at Ulrike. There had been something vague about her account of the encounter with the gang member. What about the gun, he was about to pull? And what happened to him after Bill overpowered him? She isn't telling me the full story. I will have to ask Bill about this at our next meeting, she decided.

Ulrike just nodded. She had finished her lamb dish, which turned out to be rather mediocre.

Then she said: "Of course, you must by now realize that the Stollberg homicide is only the tip of the iceberg. Also, we must acknowledge that the murder of the Frankfurt detective is part of the pattern. What we experience is the deep corruption of our public life. Law is becoming meaningless, if organized crime can set up business as they please. Something has to be done."

"For instance, bringing the killers to justice," Charlotte replied in a low voice.

"Yes, that is necessary but not enough," Ulrike insisted. "There has to be a public conversation about business and business ethics. Take the case of Alerta. They were willing, even eager to buy Stollberg's research results, knowing well that Stollberg's offer was shady. Later when they find out that they lost the deal to the competition, they hire a private detective to recover a missing file that they never owned. Where is the line between legitimate business and criminal outfits in the pharma industry?"

"You know that I don't have the answer to your question, Ulrike," Charlotte replied, while she asked the waiter for the bill. When Ulrike began looking for her purse, she insisted on inviting her. "Lunch is on me; you provided the information."

Ulrike shrugged her shoulders with a casual "Thanks."

Half an hour later Charlotte stepped into her office at headquarters. A glance at her desk told her that there would be little time to reflect on the results of this morning's interview and the conversation with Ulrike. A large pile of mail and files filled the desk. She had to work through this pile as efficiently as possible or it would get worse. This was the part of her job she liked least. In fact, she was ready to admit that she disliked the bureaucratic aspect of her position, although she had been taught that it was the backbone of steady police work. It took her most of the afternoon to clear her desk. Finally, she found time to communicate with the Düsseldorf police and arrange a short meeting with the financial expert of her SOKO. He had the reputation of being slow but very thorough. If the books of KreuzbergChem were cooked, he would uncover the deceit. To her surprise, she learned that the company's financial statements were incomplete. He had seen only the more recent statements, going back two years.

"How come?" Charlotte asked him.

"It appears that David Klein, when he joined the company two years ago, introduced a new and more efficient system. The older files were not readily available," said the officer. "I didn't find anything unusual, so I did not dig deeper. There seemed to be no need."

"We were wrong," Charlotte exclaimed. "We have to dig deeper and include the early years. What I learned this morning, strongly suggests that parts of the initial capital came from unusual sources."

"Can you be more specific?" the officer replied.

"Organized crime, funds came from the Mafia," Charlotte said.

"Are you sure? We are in Berlin, not in Palermo," he replied.

"It appears that Palermo is closer to Berlin than we imagined," Charlotte emphasized. "You have to go back and ask for the older files as well. This cannot wait. I need the results fast, understood?!"

The officer, who realized that Charlotte was determined, promised to act immediately.

"If they don't make the books available, we will come with a court order," Charlotte said.

"We'll knock at their door tomorrow morning," the officer replied, while he gathered his papers and prepared to leave.

Before Charlotte had time to think about the outcome of the meeting, her phone rang. It was Werner Kraft, who needed a signature for the special operation. She invited him to join her in ten minutes. All she needed was a few minutes to tell the secretary what to do with the files on her desk.

Kraft was eager to report about his preparations. He assured Charlotte that all aspects had been taken care of. A small special team had been selected, including a female officer who would be the substitute for Dorothea Stollberg. The operation would begin tomorrow afternoon, giving the intruder the opportunity to make their move later that evening. All Charlotte had to do, was to sign off.

"Will they go for it?" Charlotte asked. "How important is Dorothea Stollberg for them?"

"Important enough to observe the building, as we found out," Kraft exclaimed. "There must be more than just the monthly payments she is expected to make."

"What could it be?"

"The missing file? Maybe they believe she knows more about this."

"Interesting idea, but very unlikely."

"Their search is as intense as Alerta's effort and that of the organization that killed Walter Kellner in Bad Homburg. There is a fierce and violent competition to get the hands on this file, it seems. By the way, I have been in touch with Bill McDonald. He and the journalist tracked Stefano Brindisi in Düsseldorf. They almost caught up with him. They found his hiding place, but they came too late."

"I know, I had lunch with Ulrike Pfanner. A mystery lady showed up to move him." Charlotte said. "I have asked for assistance from our Düsseldorf colleagues."

"Any results from the Brindisi interview this morning?" Kraft wanted to know.

"Much more than we expected. Brindisi and his wife decided to cooperate and seek police protection. They confirmed what we had suspected. They have been threatened by the Mafia. At the center is Stefano and the dubious funding of his start-up company. We will have to look much more closely at their books. Maybe David Klein knows more than he told us. There will be another interview.:

"How will the Kriminalrat respond?"

Charlotte laughed: "This time he will be on our side. He attended the interview this morning."

"Then it will be he who has to deal with the pressure from the top. Klein appears to have influential friends in town," Kraft said.

Charlotte just shrugged her shoulders, indicating with a gesture that she was ready to go home. Kraft decided to ignore the hint because there was something else on his mind. He had additional information about the van. It belonged to a rental company that had reported it as stolen before the attack on Stollberg in Berlin. Someone had pretended to be a mechanic, who was supposed to check the vehicle before it was rented again. He drove the van off the lot and disappeared.

"Where did this happen?" Charlotte asked.

"In Cologne," Kraft replied. "There is a description of the thief, but it is not very helpful. He sounded like a local guy. Shall I follow up?"

"By all means," Charlotte suggested. She was tired and ready to leave. It had been a long day. Even the report for Sieverts had to wait.

Charlotte declined Kraft's offer to take her home in his car. She needed to be by herself without the pressure to keep up a conversation. A headache was beginning to form above her eyes. On the way to the subway she changed her mind and hailed a cab that delivered her at her apartment building twenty minutes later. When she stepped into her apartment, she had the sense of a surrounding that was not quite her own. Everything was a bit too dainty for her taste, too sweet and feminine. The mere thought of bringing her police gun to this place seemed to be inappropriate. It was a furnished apartment that she had rented when she decided to leave her partner and move out. She had made small adjustments by displaying some of her own things, but this had only increased the contrast between what she had found when she rented the place and what she wanted. I really have to get my own place, she thought when she walked into the living room. The only piece of furniture she had brought along from her old apartment was a large and very comfortable armchair. It overwhelmed the rest of the furniture. This cannot go on like this for ever. I have to look for a new apartment. But then Charlotte decided not to follow this line of thought, because it immediately raised bigger questions about her future, especially about her relationship with Bernd Moeller. Would he consider to move from Hamburg to Berlin and would they look together for a larger apartment? Did she really want that? This was not the time to approach these issues. What she needed now was a simple meal and rest in her armchair. She found two messages on her phone. One was from an old friend of hers, a psychiatrist, who had been a big help when she was struggling to get out of an old but increasingly stale relationship. More recently, they had seen less of each other, which had to do with Bernd's increasing presence in Berlin and the fact that the friend had advised Charlotte against getting closer to Bernd. The second message was from Bernd. He just wanted to hear Charlotte's voice. She tried to call him back, but there was no answer. Still, this was a good moment. He will be back in the not too disrant future, Charlotte thought.

CHAPTER 16

Bill was pacing up and down in his room at the Brandenburger Hof. There had been a completely unexpected message from his father, informing him that his old friend Amos Hinchcroft was seriously considering leaving his law firm because of the dubious actions of Alerta's top management. He had suggested a clean break with the pharma company, but his partners had resisted the move because of financial considerations. His father had warned him of the possible consequences and invited him to come home to Chicago, if Hinchcroft actually left the firm and Bill's position could be in jeopardy. He was surprised to find out that his father cared enough about his career to contact him, which was very rare. He had to admit to himself that he was moved, but then there was almost immediately the sense that this invitation was also another opportunity for his father to suggest a decisive career change. He knew that he had been a disappointment to his family when he dropped out of law school and moved to a profession that especially his father considered inferior to his own. In Chicago, he would face the family again, not only his father but also his older brother, by now a successful lawyer in Chicago. He already knew the advice: Give law school another try. There was still time. Did he really want this? Could he see himself focusing on estate law or becoming a trial lawyer? He didn't want to think about this. Not now, while things were not moving well in Berlin either. After their return from Düsseldorf, Ulrike had become increasingly frustrated with her own situation. The fact that they had not found Stefano Brindisi had not helped. It seemed that for Ulrike there had been the expectation of a story that would make a difference in a complicated murder case. She became irritable because she felt that there was not enough support for her work at her newspaper. Bill had decided to retreat to his hotel room, where he meant to figure out the next step. Was there a chance to track Stefano Brindisi down? There was not enough information to track him down. A blond lady and an expensive foreign car were not enough clues. Possibly, the tools of the police might get him closer, but he couldn't count on their help. Kraft had not responded to his last message. He felt cut off. He had also tried to call the young detective in Bad Homburg to find out whether the interrogation of the arrested suspect had resulted in new information. But he was told that she was not available. Would this whole mission turn out to be a failure? Only a few days ago he had been confident that he would solve the case, even though he didn't really understand Stefano's role in Stollberg's death. He was still convinced that there was a connection between the two homicides, although he couldn't figure out how they fit together. Why was the Frankfurt detective killed? If he had worked for an Indian company interested in Stollberg's research, who was aware of this interest and was determined to disrupt the deal? Was it possible that Alerta, after realizing that they had lost the deal, ordered the hit to get their hands on the missing file? That would be a very strong reason for Amos Hinchcroft to cut the ties to the pharma company, if he had knowledge of the link. But Alerta's Frankfurt office seemed to be unaware of plans to use violence. But would that be an argument against it? I have no factual knowledge, he thought. Only one thing was apparent: there had been fierce competition for the research results. And most likely there still was. And if this is the case, there might also be more action in Frankfurt. Maybe I have to go back to Frankfurt, Bill thought.

The ring tone of his smart phone interrupted his thoughts. It was Werner Kraft, who claimed that he had been looking for him.

"I thought you were staying with Ulrike," he said.

"Yes, I was, but then decided to move back to the Brandenburger Hof,"

"Trouble?"

Bill hesitated a second before he responded: "No, we each needed a bit more space. What's up?"

"Special operation at Dorothea Stollberg's apartment."

"Is she in some kind of danger?" Bill asked.

"She was, but is no longer," Kraft replied.

"So, why the operation?"

"Join us and find out."

This is the exactly the break I need right now, Bill thought. I need action. He asked for the address and told Kraft that he would be there as soon as he could. He picked up his coat and left the room. While he was in the elevator, he checked the map app on his phone for directions. When he stepped out of the hotel, he noticed a cab approaching the curb delivering a hotel guest. Two minutes later he was on the way to Dorothea Stollberg's apartment. Once the taxi got closer, he directed the driver to drop him off three hundred feet away from the building. For a moment he stood at the curb looking around. It was a quiet street lined with mature trees, well-kept apartment buildings on both sides. It must have been raining, since the pavement was still wet. Bill took out his phone and contacted Werner Kraft.

"Where exactly do I find you? Bill asked.

"Move in the direction of her building and look for an unmarked older black Mercedes, about fifty meters away from her entrance on the same side. Close to an intersection."

"OK, give me a minute," Bill replied.

He moved to the other side of the street from where he could observe the parked cars more easily. It took him no more than a minute to spot the black Mercedes with Kraft behind the wheel. Bill crossed the street again and opened the car's right front door. After he had settled into the seat, he greeted Kraft and asked him to fill him in. Kraft explained the situation while keeping an eye on the apartment building.

"You're setting a trap," Bill said. "Do you really think that they will go for it?"

"There's no telling, but we think it might well happen."

"Why?"

"For some reason that we don't fully understand they are after

Dorothea Stollberg. Maybe they assume that she knows more about her ex-husband's research." Kraft replied.

"Ah, the missing file," Bill interjected, "I don't think so. She was never part of this."

"It doesn't matter, as long as they believe it," Kraft said.

"And you are sure that they are keeping an eye on her movements?" Bill asked.

"Most likely. We have spotted persons here who do not quite belong to this neighborhood," Kraft answered, checking his watch. "In a few minutes the police car with our female officer dressed as Dorothea Stollberg should arrive."

They waited in silence for another twenty minutes, both of them observing the traffic on the street. There were a number of pedestrians, some of them with their dogs. Otherwise, it was rather quiet. Close to the intersection Bill noticed a van with two workmen who unloaded materials. The sign on the side of the van indicated that they were part of a plumbing company. All of a sudden, two police cars approached from the opposite side and stopped in front of Dorothea Stollberg's building. A police officer in uniform opened the right rear door of the car assisting a woman in a long dark overcoat, her head covered by a scarf. Another police officer stepped out of the car and moved close to the woman as well. The two officers accompanied her to the entrance of the building. A few minutes later, the officers returned to the car and drove away. A minute later the second police car left as well.

"All right," Kraft whispered, "the trap is set. Let's see what happens."

He grabbed a small microphone: "The police cars just left. Everything in place?"

There was an immediate response: "The special team is in place and ready, but we don't expect anything to happen before dark."

Kraft and Bill continued to watch the entrance for another hour without detecting any suspicious movements. A group of children ran after a ball. Sometimes a bicyclist passed their car. The utility van was still parked at the intersection with two men setting up a small work bench on the side walk. Bill asked Kraft for his binoculars and focused them on the two men. They seemed to be involved in putting together a new heating system. He tried to make out the license plate, but it was too dirty to read the number. Then his attention was drawn to a young couple who walked hand in hand on the side walk. In front of the entrance they stopped and embraced. Without success, Bill tried to see their faces. He gave the binoculars to Kraft, pointing to the couple. Kraft focused them on the couple.

"I don't like this," he exclaimed. This is not normal."

"No lovers in Berlin?" Bill responded.

In the middle of the street at this time of the day?" Kraft said, grabbing the microphone.

"There is a young couple standing in front of the entrance. This could be significant."

"Yes, we can see them from the window and will keep an eye on them," the voice responded. "Let me know if they try to enter the building."

"Will do," Kraft replied. Bill turned on the radio looking for a music station. After a while he found a jazz station that suited him. Kraft gave him a look and nodded.

An hour had passed when Bill checked his watch. He was no longer convinced that anybody would attempt to get to Dorothea Stollberg. This could be a waste of time and money. He turned to Kraft. "Werner, are you sure this operation makes sense?"

"There can be no certainty, but it's worth pursuing. The crucial point is interrogating them. As long as we have not arrested Stefano Brindisi, this may be our best way of getting on the inside of the gang."

It started to rain again. Rain drops ran down the windshield. After a while, the view became a bit blurry. The street was now almost empty. Bill didn't see the workers next to the utility van anymore. They must have moved inside. Also, the young couple had disappeared. All of a sudden, a postal delivery truck pulled up. For a while it just double parked in front of the building. Then two men got out of the truck carrying a number of large packages to the entrance.

"How about this?" Bill asked.

"Why, a postal truck, nothing unusual there!" Kraft exclaimed.

"With two delivery workers?" Bill asked softly.

"No, never, this is odd indeed," Kraft exclaimed, grabbing the microphone.

"Attention, there may be a phony postal delivery, watch out."

The answer came promptly: "We got it."

Meanwhile Bill observed the two men moving toward the entrance. Now they stood in front of the entrance and would ring a bell. But they didn't. They used a key to open the door. No doubt, this was it, a brazen attack in the middle of the afternoon.

"This is an attack," Bill shouted. "They used a key to open the door."

"OK, we are ready."

At the same time, Kraft noticed the utility van moving towards the postal truck, taking up a position in front of it. The two men stepped out and opened the backdoor.

"What's going on?" Kraft exclaimed.

It took Bill a second to understand: "They are part of the same team to kidnap Dorothea Stollberg. But we can block them before they escape.

"Any noise in front of the apartment? Anyone ringing the bell?" Kraft asked.

"Nothing stirring," the voice replied. A second later he whispered: "Someone is trying to open the front door with a key. We are ready."

Kraft kept the microphone open. For a few seconds everything was quiet. Then there were gunshots and screams. More gunshots and the noise of bodies in motion. Somebody was yelling something in Italian. Then a powerful voice shouted: "Police, get on your knees with your hands up." The answer was a curse in Italian. For a moment there was silence. Then another male voice could be heard. "All right, we are in control. Both intruders have been arrested. One of them is wounded, possibly critical. I'm calling an ambulance."

Bill had kept his eyes on the two men behind the utility van. They appeared to be tense and restless. One of them talked into his smartphone. All of a sudden, he gestured to the other man and quickly moved to the front of the van. Bill realized that they were about to leave the scene. They must have learned that the intruders had failed.

"Werner, quickly move our car in front of the van," he shouted. "They mean to run."

Kraft just nodded and started the engine. Within seconds the Mercedes moved forward and blocked the van. One of the men tried to steer the van around the Mercedes and failed. The other one pulled a gun and started shooting at Bill and Werner Kraft in the car. The bullets hit the front window and missed Bill by a few inches, only because Kraft had pulled him down. The man with the gun turned around and ran away. Kraft got out of the car and pulled his gun. He fired twice. The man screamed but continued to run. Suddenly another car came up from behind. It stopped close to the running man, who flung himself into the open door. Within seconds the car was gone. Kraft turned around and walked back slowly to the van where Bill had pulled the second man out of his van and knocked him down with force.

Bill and Kraft looked at each other, both of them still coping with the speed with which the attack had developed in the last five minutes. Standing in front of the van with the overpowered man at his feet, it dawned on Bill that he had been lucky. Without Kraft's fast move he might be dead. Looking at Kraft, who gave him a grin, he realized how much more violent the special operation had become than they had anticipated. The attack was carefully prepared and came earlier and faster than expected. Obviously, kidnapping Dorothea Stollberg had become a very high priority. Bill searched the man for weapons before he asked Kraft to put on handcuffs. Within minutes, police sirens could be heard, several police cars with blue lights filled the street. Officers blocked off the crime scene pushing back curious bystanders and keeping a path open for an ambulance that pulled up in front of the apartment building. At the same time, several heavily armed police officers stepped out of the building, cautiously moving the arrested intruder to one of the waiting police cars. The officer in charge approached Kraft, who was already on the phone to inform Charlotte Herberg of the successful outcome of the special operation.

"We were lucky," the officer said. "Without your call they might have caught us by surprise. They were prepared to use guns when they pushed the door open and opened fire as soon as they realized that they faced police. The smart thing for them would have been to retreat as quickly as possible and flee. Instead, they decided to fight, which forced us to use force. One of them took a bullet. I'm afraid the injury is critical. Let's hope he will survive. He is still in the apartment, under surveillance of course. I'll write a detailed report for the Hauptkommissarin."

"As you can see," Kraft replied, "the confrontation extended to the street. There were two guys in a utility van across the street, who had been there to observe the building. It appears that their van was supposed to transport the kidnapped woman. By the way, any clue why Dorothea Stollberg was so important for them?"

"Not really, you will have to interrogate the prisoners," The officer replied, ready to collect his men and lead them to the special truck that was waiting further down the street. He agreed to take the second prisoner with him, who was clearly still in shock.

Charlotte had been busy reviewing an older case when Kraft's call reached her that the special operation had been a success. He gave her a brief summary, promising a more detailed report when he was back at headquarters.

"Any casualties?" she asked.

"Fortunately, the answer is no. But it was close. We almost lost Bill McDonald," Kraft replied.

"Tell me later," she said.

Charlotte realized that now she had to play her cards right. In the last couple of days, public pressure had increased to demonstrate progress in the Stollberg case. The Kriminalrat had called twice to learn whether there were significant developments. Of course, the hope had been that the arrest of Stefano Brindisi would be the longed-for breakthrough, but he had completely disappeared. There was no use of his credit card. He had left his smartphone in Berlin, which meant that they couldn't track his movements. The attempt to identify the young woman who had picked him up in Düsseldorf had failed, since a second interview of the janitor at the warehouse did not result in more significant information. The man had been unable to give a precise description of the car, not to mention the license plate. It was a dead end. The most promising lead had been a tip from the LKA Hesse about the driver of the van that killed Stollberg. He had been sighted in Frankfurt, possibly in connection with the Kellner homicide. The two detectives had offered their help, suggesting that they might even come to Berlin to compare notes. Maybe this is the time to encourage such a move, Charlotte thought. Then she decided that it was too early to invite them. First, she had to look at the prisoners. Kraft's story had been too thin to draw any conclusions. The one thing she knew, however, she had to inform Kriminalrat Sieverts immediately. If possible at all, he had to be present at the interrogation. Unfortunately, it was not Sieverts but his assistant who picked up the phone. She promised to leave a message for her boss, but Charlotte was not certain at all that this would actually happen. Possibly, she had to walk up to his office at the right time to get his attention when she needed it.

Half an hour later, Kraft showed up at her office, telling her that the two arrested gang members were being fingerprinted and processed downstairs. The third prisoner, still in critical condition, had been moved by ambulance to the hospital Charité where he was being prepared for an operation. Charlotte shook Kraft's hand and congratulated him for his successful operation. Then she invited him to give her a full report, which he was eager to do. The collaboration with the special units had been perfect and it was good to have Bill McDonald around, who turned out to be quite useful at a critical moment. Three of the criminals were apprehended, only one of them escaped. Charlotte insisted on getting the details, which helped her to reconstruct the plan of the gang. The fact that they could send a car to pick up one of their men when he was fleeing demonstrated how carefully the whole operation had been planned.

"Do you have any idea why Dorothea Stollberg is so important for the gang?" Charlotte asked.

Kraft shook his head: "I have asked myself the same question. No, I don't. They could have done this right after Stollberg's death when it was much easier."

"Maybe at that time they still believed to get what they wanted from other persons. Let's put pressure on the prisoners when we interrogate them" Charlotte suggested.

At this moment, Charlotte's phone rang. An officer reported that one of the prisoners was ready for interrogation. He was a German national by the name of Detlev Hoberg, a plumber from Potsdam. Charlotte informed the officer that she would come to the interrogation room in a few minutes.

"How about the other prisoner?" she asked.

"An Italian national who refuses to speak German. He asks for a lawyer in Italian as far as we can make out," the officer replied.

"A difficult Italian guy and a German national, a plumber from Potsdam," she said, looking at Kraft, "does that make sense?"

Kraft shrugged his shoulders and got up. Together, they walked to the elevator to meet the prisoner in the interrogation room.

The middle-aged man with greying hair and glasses sat at the table with his hands folded. He was clearly uncomfortable and tense. He was wearing dark-blue work clothes.

Charlotte looked at the folder in front of her with the information gathered by the team preparing the interrogation. The man was a trained plumber, who owned his own small firm. No priors, but some problem with taxes. There was also a note that he had occasionally employed undocumented Polish workers. This man is vulnerable, Charlotte thought. She decided to give him a chance to make a full statement before she used more pressure.

"Herr Hoberg," she opened the interrogation, "you must realize by now that you are in serious trouble."

The prisoner remained silent.

"Refusing to answer doesn't improve your situation, Herr Hoberg," Werner Kraft interjected. "You were part of a kidnapping operation, which could get you as much as 20 years in prison. If you help us, on the other hand, the judge may be more lenient."

Hoberg stared first at Kraft and then at Charlotte. It was not clear whether he had understood what they had said. Charlotte therefore repeated Kraft's statement in a low voice.

"I didn't have a choice," the man finally whispered. "I owed them a favor and they told me that the whole thing would be legal. The point was to keep the woman safe. She was threatened by a violent ex-lover. I was told that they needed my van to move the woman."

"Who are they?" Charlotte wanted to know.

Hoberg seemed to be confused by the question.

"Are you talking about friends?" Kraft asked.

"Well, sort of, more acquaintances. They did me a big favor a year ago. I really owed them," Hoberg insisted, lifting up his hands to underscore the truth of his statement.

"Do these friends have names?" Charlotte inquired.

"One of them is called Fredo. His German is pretty good. This was important because I don't understand Italian. He explained the situation and how I could be of help. There would be nothing illegal. That's what he said."

"I'm afraid he lied to you, Herr Hoberg," Charlotte responded. "In reality, you became involved in a kidnapping. We will help you to explain your situation to the prosecution, if you give us a full and truthful account of the story in writing. We'll give you time to write everything down, including the names and the dates. Who, for instance, was the man in your van who escaped. He almost killed police officers before he disappeared."

The man nodded. He is beginning the grasp his situation, Charlotte thought.

"What was the big favor your friends did for you?" Kraft wanted to know. "Why couldn't you just say no?"

"Problems with some Polish workers. They harassed me because the thought I owed them backpay. Once they talked to them, the workers let it go."

"Just by talking!?"

"I didn't ask for details. The Poles just shut up."

"That was convenient, and you saved money!"

There was a moment of silence.

All of a sudden, the door opened and a police officer approached the table. He put a brief note on the table and left without a word. Charlotte glanced at the text. It appeared to concern the second prisoner. She was about to set it aside when she looked at it more carefully. There it was. <Fingerprints of second prisoner matches the fingerprints in the van that killed Stollberg>. This can't be true, Charlotte felt. A match, the killer apprehended by accident. She stood up and showed Kraft the note, who stared at it.

"This can't be true," he said in a low voice.

"I will check this out, while you conclude this interrogation."

Charlotte gave Kraft a nod before she left the room.

When Charlotte arrived at the processing room downstairs, the first person she encountered was Kriminalrat Sieverts. He came up to her with a big smile.

"If this information turns out to be true, today will be our lucky day, the break that we have been waiting for. An officer led them to the desk where the images of the fingerprints were on display. There could be little doubt, there was a match.

"Where is the prisoner now?" Charlotte asked the attending officer.

"He is being kept in one of our interrogation rooms under guard," the officer replied. "So far, he has refused to answer any question. He pretends not to understand German."

"This will not help him once he finds out what we know about his identity," interjected the Kriminalrat. "Let's go."

When he and Charlotte entered the interrogation room, the prisoner sat at the table with his eyes closed. Although he must have noticed the presence of the police officers, he did not change his position or open his eyes.

"Signor Esposito," Charlotte said after taking a seat on the opposite side of the table, "do you want to make a statement to explain your attempt to kidnap Dorothea Stollberg. This might be a good time for you make a confession before we come to a prior incident in which you played an even more negative role."

There was no answer. The prisoner just opened his eyes, staring at Charlotte with an expression of hostility.

Charlotte exchanged a brief glance with Sieverts before she resumed the interrogation.

"We have proof that you killed Herwig Stollberg and will charge you with murder. This is your chance to cooperate, which might help you to find a more lenient court. I can only advise you to make use of this opportunity right now before the prosecutor takes over and formalizes the charges."

"You have no proof, you are just making empty threats," the prisoner replied in heavily accented German. "I not talk to you without my lawyer."

"You are mistaken, we do have the proof. When you cleaned the van, you did a bad job. You left evidence that ties you to the killing of Stollberg. Hard evidence! You will not walk away. Your best chance is full cooperation with us. There may have been reasons that you did what you did, which you want to share with us. We are eager to hear your side of the story, but you have to tell us the story first. How did it happen?"

The defiant stare of the prisoner had given way to a more concerned look. Her words, Charlotte noticed, had made an impression on the man, but she realized that he was not yet ready to confess. There had to be another harder hit to undermine his self-confidence.

"There is not only material evidence, Signor Esposito, there are witnesses as well. You chose a busy morning hour for your violent act. They will testify that you were the man behind the wheel, not to mention the second man on the inside of the van."

The last remark appeared to upset the prisoner. He showed anger by making a fist, thrusting it toward Charlotte's face. The police officer, who stood behind him, was ready to control him, but Charlotte signaled that she didn't feel threatened.

"You lying," the prisoner exclaimed. "You have no witnesses, there is no second man who can testify. You have nothing."

"Wrong, we have eye witnesses and your word now that you were in the van, at the wheel."

"Bitch, I never admitted being in the van."

"You did implicitly by denying that the second man in the van could testify."

There was no reply. The prisoner closed his eyes, folding his hands on the table, indicating that he would no longer talk.

This was the moment when the Kriminalrat joined the conversation: "Signor, you had your chance, you have refused to cooperate. We will just keep you until you are ready to cooperate."

"I want lawyer," the prisoner replied.

"You will get a lawyer, who will advise you to cooperate," Sieverts said before he got up, indicating that the interrogation was closed.

Outside the room, on the way to his office, he asked Charlotte to accompany him.

"How strong is our case?" he asked Charlotte, when they were sitting around a small table in his office.

"The strongest piece of evidence are the fingerprints. We could call two or three eye witnesses. But I'm not sure how much would stand under cross examination," Charlotte replied.

"It would be difficult to prove intention, which means that he would get away with manslaughter," the Kriminalrat suggested.

"If we had captured Stefano Brindisi, that would completely change the situation," Charlotte said.

"There are only two small problems," Sieverts replied. "First, we have to find him, and, second, we have to persuade him to testify."

"I am sure, we will eventually apprehend him," Charlotte exclaimed. "But I am not certain about his role in this."

"How close are we?" Sieverts inquired.

Charlotte shrugged her shoulders. There had been no strong leads since he had been sighted in Düsseldorf. The Kriminalrat made a gesture, indicating that he understood her problem. Charlotte was already on her way to the door when he said:

"By the way, I mean to be in touch with our LKA colleagues from Hesse. I hope they will come to Berlin to assist us. They have a different angle. That should be helpful. Maybe they can persuade him to cooperate."

"Very good, sir. I'll let my unit know."

She wasn't sure whether she liked this turn at this moment. She preferred to keep things tight and clear. Still, she realized that this case was unusual in more than one way. It reminded her of the fight against the network of the Russian Mafia two years ago. Somehow, there were no final victories.

In the other interrogation room Werner Kraft was just rapping up his questioning of the first prisoner. There was not a wealth of fresh information, but there were a number of new insights. It appeared that the gang was still in the process of establishing themselves in Berlin. Once, the plumber had been summoned for a meeting to an office in Berlin-Köpenick. It was a small shipping company with a few trucks. All the men were native Italians with varying degrees of competence in German. Occasionally, he had been asked to make errands or stow boxes at his place. These services were considered favors he owed. One thing had become clear: Hoberg was never privy to their plans and projects. He was a mere tool. Looking at this case, it was hard to say how strong their local network actually was.

Charlotte and Kraft returned to her office where Charlotte quickly checked her email messages. Sitting at her desk, she turned to Kraft:

"Did you get more information about the second guy in the van, the one who escaped?"

"Only his first name and the plumber's feeling that he was more important than other members he had met, but not as important as the guy who was captured in the apartment."

"Which one of the two, the injured one?"

"No, the other one, the guy you just interrogated."

"How high in the hierarchy?"

"According to Hoberg, sort of a lieutenant. But then, you have to keep in mind that he doesn't have a clear understanding of the organization."

"By the way, what happened to McDonald after the arrest?" Charlotte asked.

"He went back to his hotel. I'm having dinner with him tonight," Kraft replied, while he was picking up his folder.

"Enjoy your dinner and say hallo. He should stay in touch."

Kraft was tempted to invite her, but he decided against it. He would be out of line. Their relationship was strictly 'dienstlich,' i.e. an office relationship

CHAPTER 17

Charlotte had already left her office to join a lecture about new guidelines, when there was a call from the desk downstairs that two detectives from LKA Hesse wanted to see her. There was some confusion among the staff how to respond. Fortunately, Werner Kraft was just entering the door and took over. He met the detectives at the entrance and guided them to Charlotte's office.

"Coffee?" he asked. "By all means," said the older officer. "We got up at 5:30 to catch the early flight to be here by 9:00. As soon as we learned that you arrested the man who killed Stollberg, we had to rethink our priorities. We need to interview him before he talks to his lawyer and refuses to cooperate."

"By the way," the younger officer said, "were you present when the man was apprehended?"

"I certainly was," Kraft replied. "It was a complete surprise. We set a trap because we suspected that they planned to kidnap Dorothea Stollberg. They fell for it and we were able to arrest three of them. One got away."

The officers expressed their strong approval of the operation, asking Kraft to share the details, which he did with pride. To his surprise, they were particularly interested in the German plumber, whose van they had used, and the postal truck.

"Any information, how and where they got the postal truck?" the older officer wanted to know.

Kraft had to admit that the investigation had just started. "We still have to check out the origin of the postal truck. It looks genuine."

After Kraft had asked the secretary to prepare a fresh pot of coffee, he turned his attention back to the LKA officers: "It may be already too late. He has refused to cooperate until he has seen his lawyer."

"It will be a lawyer from the family, who will make sure that he doesn't talk," the older detective said.

"We have enough material evidence to convict him," Kraft responded.

"Enough for a murder verdict?" the other detective asked.

"Definitely enough for a hit and run, that is manslaughter," Kraft replied.

"We are not interested in the details of this case," the second detective interjected. "We are here to learn more about the organization of this gang. Where and how they operate? Who is in charge and how much have they penetrated Germany?"

"My sense is that they either have a foothold in Berlin or are in the process of building it," Kraft said. "What we have seen recently, strongly suggests a more permanent presence."

"Which doesn't surprise us," replied the older officer, who was keeping his eyes on the coffee machine, which was producing strange noises. "We have observed a similar development in Frankfurt and Cologne. The local police don't understand the symptoms."

"If we can persuade this guy that his best chance is cooperation, we might be able to fill in our gaps, which are still pretty big."

Kraft explained to them that he was not authorized to take them to the prisoner but offered them the report that was put together after the last cross-examination. The LKA officers were eager to read this document. They moved with their coffee to a small table where they studied the report, taking notes while they were talking among themselves.

When Charlotte returned half an hour later from her meeting, the two officers were still studying the report. Noticing her, they got up and introduced themselves, explaining why they had come from their headquarters to Berlin. Charlotte invited them to join her at her desk where she tried to explain the sudden turn of events.

"No need to fill us in," the older officer said, "your assistant has already given us a detailed account of yesterday's events. Congratulations. That was a real coup."

Charlotte just smiled, trying to figure out what motivated these men to get on the next plane to interview a suspect. They don't look quite like regular police, she thought. Not the kind she was used to working with. But she couldn't put her finger on the difference. It was partly the manner of their dress, the white shirts and ties. But there was more. There was an element of distance, coldness, although they were very polite and friendly. They asked for permission to interrogate the prisoner in the context of the Kellner murder in Bad Homburg. Not so much the murder per se, as they explained, but the criminal network behind the case.

"I have already checked with my boss," Charlotte said. "He approves the interrogation under the condition that one of our men is in the room and you will share the results with us after the meeting."

"He is known to be a cautious man," the younger officer said. "Of course, we agree to these conditions. Goes without saying. Will you accompany us?"

"I'm afraid not, unfortunately, I am not free, but Werner Kraft, my assistant, will guide you to the prisoner and stay with you. I'll see you again later this morning, possibly Kriminalrat Sieverts will join us."

With a gesture of her hand she invited Kraft to take over.

Two hours had passed when the LKA officers and Werner Kraft returned to Charlotte's office. She looked at them, to find out whether the interrogation had been successful. But she could not read their faces. Only when Kraft gave her a nod, she realized that the interrogation must have been worthwhile. The older detective, who spoke with a noticeable accent of the Frankfurt region, thanked her for the opportunity.

"So, did Esposito talk?" Charlotte opened the conversation.

"Yes and no," the younger detective replied, "he refused to talk about yesterday's operation and the killing of Stollberg. He claimed that the accusations were unjust and unfair. But that's not why we came in the first place. We are much more interested in the Frankfurt context, the killing of Walter Kellner, the disappearance and later killing of his presumed murderer, in short, the Frankfurt network. Once we talked with him in Italian, things became easier. He became less cautious, giving away a little piece here and another little piece there."

"You spoke Italian? You have my respect, gentlemen," Charlotte exclaimed.

"We made accusations that he could easily refute. By doing so, he gave things away, which allowed us to follow up and press the point. We could show him dated pictures of him in Frankfurt where he can be seen with known members of the local crime scene. Never the big shots, usually petty criminals and middlemen of the drug scene and sex trafficking."

"Do you believe that he was in some way involved in the murder of Kellner?" Charlotte asked.

"Possible, but by no means certain," interjected the younger officer. "You need the big picture to understand the individual pieces. At the center we have Stollberg's research, something that must be a true breakthrough in diabetes research, highly valuable. For that reason, stiff competition. Not only the Americans but also the Indians. In the meantime, we have talked to the man who represented the Indian company. He claims that his company made a legitimate offer to Stollberg, a better deal than Alerta. But they never got the file. They assumed that Kellner brought it back from Berlin and was killed because he had it at his home."

"That cannot be true," Charlotte said, "since Kellner never received the file from Stollberg."

"Correct, but the Indians did not know this," the older officer replied. "Neither did the two hired killers, by the way. Presumably, they were also searching for the file."

"How does Esposito fit into this picture?" Kraft asked.

"This was what we were trying to find out," the older officer replied with a faint smile.

"Did you?" Kraft asked.

The older officer looked at him with a friendly grin. Then he said: "He didn't tell us, but what he told us, narrowed it down. There is another player in the competition. Most likely another criminal gang. We now believe that they organized the hit on Kellner because they assumed that he had the file."

Who are they?" Charlotte asked.

"We are not sure. We thought that Esposito might know, but it seems that he didn't know either. But it is possible that he was involved in the killing of the hit man."

"What leads you to that conclusion?" Charlotte asked, expressing her doubt with a gesture.

"He wanted to find out who the competition was," the older officer said in a low voice. "He showed up in Frankfurt, talking to a lot of people, inquiring about the Kellner murder. Then, the body of the hit man is found in the Main. And importantly, he had been tortured before he was killed. Someone tried to get information out of him."

"Maybe the time has come to put more pressure on Esposito," Charlotte suggested.

"That may be difficult, because he is probably more afraid of his own organization than the German police," exclaimed the younger detective. "You would have to find his vulnerable spots. One of them would be the fear that his own people will eliminate him. The other one would be the expectation that the organization ordering the murder of Kellner is seeking revenge. You want to let him go and spread the word in Frankfurt that he is back in town?"

"You know that we can't do that," Charlotte replied. "He is a murder suspect. Once we have arrested Brindisi, we will also be able to prove it."

"But you can suggest it and see what his response will be," the older officer declared.

Charlotte just shook her head, indicating that she was unwilling to consider this path.

"You have to keep in mind that these extreme activities, the murders, extortions, and kidnappings, are ultimately no more than the noise around an important financial process," he continued. "Organized crime has discovered that investing in start-ups is a smart and profitable way to launder dirty money. KreuzbergChem is only one company that we follow. Once the dirty money is on the inside, it's much harder to prove its criminal origin."

"OK, I understand that," Charlotte asserted, "tell me then: What is the role of our prisoner in this context?"

The younger officer chuckled: "He's a small fish. Someone who carries out orders, lower rank. Talking to the second prisoner, the German plumber, was really helpful, precisely because he doesn't understand the organization he was dealing with. They are clearly in the process of establishing themselves in Berlin. The actions against the Brindisi restaurant is part of it, but only part of it. To confront this process, you need more than a SOKO."

"You may be right," Charlotte replied, "but my SOKO has to solve a homicide. We got lucky when they tried to kidnap Dorothea Stollberg. And I'm confident that I can get a conviction of Esposito once we have arrested Stefano Brindisi, the second man in the van.

"You think it was Brindisi in the van who ordered the murder of his partner" the older officer asked, looking straight at Charlotte.

"Frankly, I'm uncertain," Charlotte said. "If that were the case, why would they be after him?"

"Are they?"

"Yes, they are. We have reliable sources."

Willing to share?"

"Yes, McDonald, the young American detective and a journalist from Berlin."

"Ah, McDonald. How is he doing? Is he still around?"

"Yes, he is. I had dinner with him last night," Kraft interjected.

"Very good," the younger officer declared. "We hope to talk to him before we return to Frankfurt. Where can we find him?"

"At the hotel Brandenburger Hof," Kraft replied.

Charlotte just nodded. The conversation continued for a while. Charlotte followed the exchange with mixed feelings. While she appreciated the deep knowledge of the LKA officers from Hesse, she was frustrated at the same time, since the background information did not help her to solve her case. What they call the noise, is the center of my job, she thought. It seemed that Kraft felt the same way.

He was sitting in his chair with his arms crossed, very attentive with a quizzical expression on his face. Finally, the older officer got up thanking his Berlin colleagues for their support.

"The interrogation of the two prisoners was very valuable for us, possibly more than you can imagine. Our picture of the organization is more precise now than before."

They politely declined the invitation to have lunch with the Berlin colleagues and left.

"This is a very different kind of police work than we do," Charlotte exclaimed.

"You can say that," Kraft asserted, walking to the coffee machine for a refill.

"More analysis than action, not my thing" he added with a frustrated look because the machine was empty.

"Let's go to lunch," Charlotte declared, moving to the door. Kraft followed her after giving the machine a final but unsuccessful punch.

Bill sat at the small desk in his room at the Brandenburger Hof, bent over his laptop. He stared at the e-mail from the paralegal, his ally at the law firm. He had found it in the morning. The message was not encouraging. It confirmed that the partners could not agree on their relationship with Alerta. It seemed that Hinchcroft had given his partners an ultimatum. Either they would cut all ties or he would leave the firm, which would be a real blow, since he had more important clients than the rest. The message described the mood as depressed. Everybody in the firm realized that Amos was very angry. People were standing in corners whispering. They were all worried about job security. The message ended with the sentence "I am polishing my resumé!" I'll be confronted with a decision in the very near future, Bill thought. My position here in Berlin is becoming a joke. Does anybody in New York care what I am doing here? Is there any interest left in the missing file? The ground under his feet was shaking. Bill realized that his father meant well. He offered him an elegant exit. He would talk to his old friend Amos and they would arrive at an agreement. But was he ready to accept this exit? Do I really want to go back to law school? Bill's thoughts returned to his days at Cornell, not very happy days, trying to do what the family expected. Of course, things would be different now. He was five years older and had seen more of the world. But, if he was honest with himself, he had to admit that he could not really see himself as a lawyer. What am I supposed to do with my life? Security work was good for now but in the long run? For the first time, he wished Ulrike were here in the room with him. It would be good to have someone with whom he could discuss his situation. But Ulrike faced her own crisis, although she didn't talk about it. She was not happy in her new position at the *Morgenspiegel*, although it was a big improvement over her previous job. But now she had to deal with a boss whom she didn't like and who did not like her, it seemed. She doesn't like regular hours, he thought, just as much as I hate regular hours. My God, we are made for each other.

He was still lost in his thoughts when the telephone rang. It was the front desk of the hotel, telling him that two gentlemen wanted to see him. They had introduced themselves as his friends from Bad Homburg. Bill needed a moment to grasp the message. Bad Homburg? Then he realized that the men must be the LKA officers. This was an unexpected turn. It revived his spirits. He told the clerk that he would meet them in the lobby. Stepping out of the elevator, Bill noticed the officers standing close to the reception desk, both of them checking their smart phones. When they saw him, they greeted him like an old friend.

"Hallo, Mr. McDonald, good to see you again," the younger officer exclaimed. "We just learned that you are still in town and decided to make a stop at your place. Will you join us for lunch before we catch the afternoon flight to Frankfurt?"

"My pleasure," Bill replied. "I had no idea you were in town."

"Is the hotel's restaurant any good?" the other officer asked.

"Actually, quite decent, and the place is usually pretty quiet at this time of the day. No tourists."

"Excellent, then let's just stay here."

They found a quiet table close to one of the windows. While they were waiting for a waitress, Bill tried to figure out why the officers were seeking his company. Their faces did not tell him much about their thoughts. They made just small talk in English until the waitress arrived, not even trying to find out how good his German was. The waitress was the young woman who had served him the first night. She recognized Bill and gave him a big smile, which elicited an immediate comment from the older officer: "Ah, you have already made friends at this place. Good move, there can always be moments when it pays off."

Bill just smiled back, turning his attention to the menu. Once the orders were out of the way, it was time for business. They wanted to hear more about his role in the special operation.

"I was lucky to survive," Bill said in a low voice. "A bullet almost hit me. If Werner Kraft had not pulled me down, I might be dead."

"He mentioned your help with arresting the second guy in the van, but he didn't talk about this aspect," the younger officer said. He encouraged Bill to give them a more detailed account of the events in front of the apartment building. He wanted to get a description of the second man who shot at him and then got away.

"Can you describe him?" the older officer asked.

"In more general terms, I can, but not the face. Medium height, about 170 pounds, a guy in his forties, dark hair."

"Would you recognize him in a line-up?"

"Frankly, I'm not sure. Why?"

"Our guess is that he was the man in charge. They acted very fast to pull him out," the younger officer said.

"More important than the guys in the building?" Bill asked.

"We think so," the older officer replied. "Esposito is crucial for the murder case, but he is not close to the top. We are more interested in the plan to kidnap Dorothea Stollberg. What's your take?"

This was the question Bill had asked himself. What motivated the gang's sudden keen interest in Stollberg's ex. Did they expect him to know more? All I can offer is a hunch, he thought.

"I have no factual knowledge, gentlemen, all I can offer is a guess," Bill asserted. "They are looking for the missing file and think that she might know more about this."

"Do you think she does?" the older officer wanted to know.

Bill shook his head. The younger officer nodded. "Holzweg," he said in German.

Bill stared at him: "What do you mean? A wooden path?"

"No, a dead end," the other officer interjected.

Now it was Bill's turn to ask a question: "Do you believe that there is a missing file? The more I have searched the less certain I have become that it really exists."

The older officer chuckled. "I can see that," he said. "Given your experience with Alerta, you have no reason to trust their statements. By the way, have you followed the news from Boston?"

Boston?"

"Alerta's headquarters"

"Not very recently"

"The senior vice president for research was replaced. Changes in Frankfurt as well. The Frankfurt office was suddenly closed. The young deputy director whom you met is probably on the job market. When we came to interview her, she was already gone. But we believe there is a file with the results of Stollberg's research."

"What makes you so sure""

There was a moment of silence. Then the older officer said: "We know that Stollberg had serious financial problems. He needed cash. We also know that he contacted several pharma companies. Finally, he worked out a deal with the Indians. They asked Kellner to close the deal in Berlin where Stollberg would deliver. He was on the way, but never reached his goal. He had the information stored somewhere in some form."

"But the Berlin police have searched the body carefully. Nothing."

"The information can be hidden someplace else. All he had to transmit was a key or a code."

"If it's just an orally transmitted code, you will never find it."

"The Mafia and their unknown competition appear to believe that they can do it. Just look at their actions! Maybe Stefano Brindisi is looking as well. For him and his partner this is a question of survival."

"What do you mean by that?" Bill asked.

"The company lost its leading chemist and the second man is

on the run. If the third partner cannot turn things around soon, the company will go belly up," the younger officer declared. "We are sure Charlotte Herberg and her team are keeping an eye on this situation."

"What you are saying is that KreuzbergChem still owns the rights, which are worth a lot of money." Bill said.

"Correct," the officer replied. "Our estimate is 30 to 50 million Dollars. A small but decisive piece of research, a modification of the older formula that allows the transition from animal experiments to the use for humans. This is what we hear in the science community."

"Are you looking for the file?" Bill asked in a low voice.

"No, not our job," the older officer asserted. "That's where you come in."

Bill looked at the LKA men, who were calmly eating their lunch. Were they seriously recommending that he continue the search, which he had more or less abandoned? After a moment of silence, he asked: "Are you serious?"

"We are," the older officer replied in a matter of fact voice, without returning the gaze.

"Of course, your client would not benefit because there never was a legally binding contract," the younger officer added.

"I'm not sure at all whether my firm is still pursuing the search "Bill said. "I haven't heard from them for days. An unsettling situation."

"I can imagine," the older officer said looking at his watch. "We have to get to the airport to catch our flight." He gestured to the waitress and asked for the check. Within in minutes, they were gone. Bill slowly finished his meal and ordered coffee. By now the room was almost empty. The young waitress, who served him, was clearly in the mood for a chat.

"How is your business in Berlin progressing?"

Bill returned her smile: "Could be better, but coming along."

"Glad to hear it," she replied. "What happened in the case of the accident in which you got involved?"

"It turned out to be a homicide," Bill said casually, looking at her.

The young woman appeared to be disturbed and uncertain how to respond.

"That's terrible," she whispered and moved away after picking up his credit card.

Indeed, he thought, while picking up his phone. He tried to reach Ulrike, but she didn't answer the call. I'll go to her apartment later this afternoon, he decided. The more immediate task was finding a good response to his father's email. He was not ready to give up, especially after the conversation with the officers of the LKA Hesse. I have to keep things open for a few days, he thought. The struggle at his law firm would be decided in the very near future.

Ulrike was dismayed when she found her brother Volker in her apartment. He was the last person she wanted to see now. She needed time for herself to focus on the opinion piece she was planning to write under a different name after her boss had made it clear that there would be no place for this article in the *Morgenspiegel*. In her opinion, Ulrike was simply mistaken assuming that organized crime was a serious problem in Berlin. She had suggested to Ulrike to forget her former days writing for the Boulevard press. This is not Chicago, she had argued. Maybe not, but things were changing. The open European borders also made it easier for gangs to expand their territory. And the German police were slow in their response to the changes.

Volker was sitting at the kitchen table in front of a plate with warmed-up rice and vegetables. He glanced at his sister, trying to figure out what her mood might be. Within seconds he realized that he was not welcome.

"Hello sis," he exclaimed. "Great to see you. I was just in the neighborhood after seeing a friend and decided to see you and Bill. How is the Stollberg case developing? By the way, your refrigerator is almost empty. You have to do some shopping. I couldn't find a single piece of meat."

"Bill isn't here. He went back to his hotel," Ulrike declared, giving her voice an edge. "If you want to see him, you'll find him at the Brandenburger Hof."

Volker ignored the unfriendly welcome, to which he was used.

"A lover's quarrel?" he exclaimed. "I'm sorry to hear that. By the way, there is still enough rice in the fridge for a meal. Join me."

"I'm not hungry, Volker, I'm busy. I came home because I need a quiet place to write a piece."

"Without Bill? Did you have a falling out? I wouldn't like that at all, because I want to consult with him. I need his advice."

"Why don't you visit him at his place and leave me alone?" Ulrike realized that he was teasing her, but she was not in the mood to play his game. She needed time to focus on the piece she had promised to finish by late today. But she also knew that Volker could be a pest, trying to get her attention for his problems. Therefore, she decided to coax him gently.

"Do you think Bill can help you?" she asked.

"I'm undecided between the security field and police work," he replied. "I think his advice will help me, since he has followed a career in security and seems to like it."

"You may also consider attending university," Ulrike interjected. The moment she said it, she regretted her response. He would surely remind her of her own mixed record. Instead, he seemed to be open to her suggestion.

"Yes, I will, but you know that I'm not a book person. Sitting in libraries is not my thing."

"OK, nobody will force you," Ulrike declared. "Maybe police work will suit you better. I could ask a friend of mine to talk to you."

"Who is he?" Volker wanted to know.

"He is a she, a Hauptkommissarin by the name of Charlotte Herberg."

"OK, I'll keep that in mind. But before I meet with her, I want to talk to Bill."

"Great idea, Volker, shall I call him to tell him that you are on the way?"

"Can you do that for me? That would be great."

Ulrike picked up her phone and tried Bill's number, praying that he would answer the call. Then she heard Bill's voice, which immediately improved her mood. She explained that she needed a big favor because of her brother. Bill offered to come to her apartment where he could talk to Volker.

"No Bill, that won't work," she explained. "The two of you need a separate space. He should come to your place. This will be much more convenient for you."

"Ulrike, what's going on?" Bill replied. "I want to see you."

"Not right now, Bill. I have to write an article I promised. I have a deadline."

Bill's mood did not improve.

"OK, I understand, I'll talk to your brother. But there is a condition. We'll have dinner together at your place."

There was a moment of silence. Then he heard her voice again.

"All right, a late dinner at 8:00pm."

"Agreed. Send him over. I'll be in my room at the Brandenburger Hof. See you later."

Volker had followed the conversation and got up immediately when he realized that he had a date with Bill.

"Thanks sis, you are an angel, I owe you," he exclaimed.

"Yes, you do, and I will remind you," Ulrike asserted.

Within minutes he was gone. Ulrike walked to her small desk in the living room where she had her notes for the article. She looked at her watch. She had six hours to write the piece. That should be enough time, she thought.

It was almost 8:00pm when Ulrike heard the bell and pushed the button opening the door to the main entrance of her building. A minute later, Bill knocked at her front door.

"You really mean 8:00pm, don't you," she greeted him.

"I'm really hungry, I had nothing to eat since lunch with the LKA guys," he replied.

"What LKA guys?" Ulrike asked with a curious face.

"Remember, they interviewed me in Bad Homburg when I got caught up in the Kellner murder. They came to Berlin when they heard about yesterday's arrest of three gang members, among them the driver of the van that killed Stollberg."

"That's big news. Why do I find this out only now?!" Ulrike exclaimed.

"Because so far there has been no press conference. Don't ask me why. Charlotte didn't call you?"

"No, not a word. You will have to fill me in. This will change my story."

"I'd love to, but only after I have some solid food in my stomach. Here or at a restaurant?"

"My refrigerator is empty. Volker invaded the place and finished what was left."

"Yes, he must be a burden," Bill said in a teasing tone, knowing that Ulrike cared more about him than she was willing to acknowledge.

"How did the meeting work out?"

"You better ask him. What could I really tell him about my line of work in Germany. The police would certainly be a more regular career."

"I hope you told him that."

"That would have been a big mistake. He has to come to that conclusion by himself, Ulrike. It felt strange to advise someone about the advantages of security work at the very time when I'm faced with a real crisis. Two years ago, when we first met, I would have been a lot more enthusiastic."

"Restaurant or ordering food?" Ulrike, who wanted to change the topic, asked.

"How about pizza?"

"Good, let's do that," Ulrike declared, picking up her phone. "This way you can tell me more about the arrests. That has to go into my essay. I'll have to make revisions."

"Were you done?"

"I have a good second draft. I thought the rest would be just a matter of polishing, but now it will take more work."

For some unknown reasons, it took a good half hour until the delivery man rang the bell. To make things worse, the pizza was almost cold and had to be reheated. Ulrike had to deal with Bill's

growing impatience, which she did by inviting him to give her a full
and detailed account of the special operation.

"I'm really surprised they included you," Ulrike said, pouring Bill
a glass of Spanish red wine. "Somehow you have become part of the
family."

"I was more on the periphery of the real action, which happened in
Dorothea Stollberg's apartment. Together with Werner I was watching
the entrance of the building."

Bill explained the plan and the succession of events.

"But all of a sudden, the periphery became part of the action,"
Ulrike exclaimed after Bill told her about the van and the mail truck.

"I can't believe this," Ulrike cried, "this sounds more like Chicago
than Berlin. They really got their hands on a mail truck?"

Bill just nodded, taking small sips of the wine, which he found a
bit too heavy without food. Once the pizza was hot again, the special
operation was forgotten for a while. Ulrike watched with surprise how
fast the medium size pizza with three toppings disappeared. Both of
them had needed food more urgently than they realized. Holding his
refilled glass in his hands, Bill finished his story, including the shootout in front of the building. It had been a great success for the special
unit and indirectly for Charlotte Herberg and Kraft as well.

"And they really could confirm the identity of the van driver?"
Ulrike asked.

"That is what Kraft told me when we had dinner last night. The
fingerprints matched."

"I'm so glad that I can work this material into my article," Ulrike
exclaimed.

"Will you mention the specific events? That would expose me and
get me into trouble."

"No, not at all, just a stronger general description of our situation.
This is an opinion piece."

"With your by-line?"

"No, a pseudonym I have used before."

"What is it?"

"You'll find out tomorrow. Let's get to work. My deadline is 10pm. We have barely an hour."

Bill looked at the text, which was rather short, maybe 800 words. The sentences were short and simple. Bill was surprised that he could follow the German text without too much trouble. Here and there he had to look up words. He mentioned this to Ulrike, who was sitting at her laptop, working on the article.

"This isn't a piece for an elite paper, it's better than *BILD Zeitung*, but not *Morgenspiegel*."

She added sentences, which forced her to shorten other parts, since she had a total limit.

It was almost 10:00 pm when she had finished the revisions. She looked very excited and happy.

"Get it out of the house and then we can celebrate," Bill cried.

A minute later the job was done and Bill was holding her in his arms.

CHAPTER 18

The mayor's assistant called at ten minutes past 9:00, asking for the commissioner of police. There could be no doubt about the urgency of the call. The mayor wanted answers about an opinion piece in one of the local newspapers. An unknown journalist claimed that organized crime was becoming a real threat to the city -- with the police standing by, more or less clueless about the increasing danger. The mayor wanted to see his commissioner within an hour at his office. The assistant tried to be as polite as possible, but there was no way to hide that the mayor was furious. Once the bad news reached the commissioner of police, it spread within minutes. It became obvious that the commissioner was looking for someone who could be blamed, if the mayor was asking for a culprit. There were hardly any specific references in the article. Instead, the author pointed to a general lack of vigilance. Criminal organizations found it too easy to invest their money in legitimate companies, especially small start-ups. The reference to start-ups was at least a clue. It could be a reference to KreuzbergChem and the Stollberg case. At 10:30 Kriminalrat Sieverts found himself in the office suite of the commissioner of police. He was told to wait until the Commissioner was back from his meeting with the mayor. The atmosphere was tense, conversations were carried on in low voices. Sieverts noticed that the colleagues avoided eye contact. Something really bad must have happened, Sieverts thought, and I have been selected to take the blame. When he asked the assistant why he had been summoned, the young man claimed not to know the reason, obviously a lie. The man wants to distance himself as much from the problem and me as far as possible, Sieverts thought. There will be trouble.

It turned out to be worse than he had expected. The commissioner of police was in a very bad mood when he returned from his meeting with the mayor. Within minutes, it had become clear that the mayor had decided to shift the blame to the police, if the media would pick this up and start investigating the crime scene of the capital. The commissioner had tried to downplay the significance of the article, arguing that there was no evidence for the claims. But the mayor had not listened to his assessment because he was preoccupied with the potential political fall-out. The opposition would use the critique in their attack on the mayor. Knowing the importance of public opinion for his work, the commissioner cultivated contacts in the local media. But nobody had warned him. He would have to have a discussion with his assistant and the press officer. This was a serious threat to his reputation and he could not, as he realized during the conversation, count on the support of the mayor. In his car, on the way back to his office, he had already decided that he had to shift the blame to a lower level. First, the author of the article had to be found and then the leak had to be stopped. When he returned to his office, his assistant was already waiting for him, his face showing anxious attention and a faint smile. A thunderstorm was about to come down and he was ready to show his superior where the culprit could be found.

"How could this happen?" the commissioner roared. "It is your job, Meyer, to prevent this kind of media attention and keep me informed. Who wrote this piece?"

"We will find out. It will take a day or two, sir, to find out." The assistant replied. There is an indirect reference in the piece to an open case, the Stollberg murder. Stollberg was a partner in a start-up. The case was covered by the media, but there was no excessive attention on the part of the local press."

"Who's in charge?" the chief asked, his voice still showing anger and frustration.

This was the moment the assistant had been waiting for. Now he could shift the blame.

"The SOKO is led by Hauptkommissarin Charlotte Herberg, who is under the oversight of Kriminalrat Sieverts. I have summoned him and he is waiting next door," the assistant exclaimed.

"Very good, Meyer, show him in," the chief of police responded. "Let's hear what he has to say for himself."

When Sieverts entered the room, he saw the police chief behind an over-sized desk. There was no invitation to sit down. He immediately realized that this would be a highly unpleasant conversation. The assistant gave him no more than a nod and left the room.

"Sieverts, I have asked you to come to my office because we have a very unpleasant problem and I was told that you can help me to find a solution."

"I certainly hope so," Sieverts replied, looking at the chief's expression of frustration. He is looking for a scapegoat, Sieverts thought, while trying to figure out why he was summoned.

"We are confronted with an unfriendly article in one of the local newspapers, claiming that the police is not paying enough attention to the growing influence of organized crime in Berlin. Do you know the reporter, Sieverts, who wrote this piece?"

"No sir, I don't," Sieverts replied, keeping his voice controlled.

"There must be a leak, and I will find out who is spreading bad rumors about us, Sieverts," the chief continued. "I understand that you are supervising the officer who is in charge of the Stollberg homicide."

"Yes, sir, that is correct," Sieverts asserted. "A very reliable officer is in charge."

"Tell me, is there any connection to organized crime in this case?"

"Yes, there appears to be. The more recent report I have received suggests the involvement of the Mafia, although it is not yet clear exactly how and why the Mafia was interested in Stollberg. Possibly, Sir, it was their hit."

"Who is the officer in charge?"

"Hauptkommissarin Herberg, an experienced detective."

"Did she talk to the media, Sieverts?""

"That is most unlikely, Sir."

"I need a full report by tomorrow morning. It should mention all members of the SOKO. I will get to the bottom of this, Sieverts. This will not be tolerated. The mayor is very upset. I just had a long conversation with him."

This was the first clue Sieverts received. There was trouble at the top. The commissioner had been summoned and got a down-dressing. Now it's my turn, he thought. His facial expression remained completely controlled. The report would be his chance to shift the blame to Charlotte Herberg. But that would not happen, he decided at that moment. We'll use the article to our advantage.

A few minutes later he found himself dismissed, the assistant wishing him a great day, while the staff pretended not to notice him at all. When he had returned to his office, Sieverts' first impulse was to call Charlotte Herberg to arrange a meeting. But then he changed his mind. He decided to study her reports before he would approach her.

Ulrike woke up with a headache. Three glasses of the heavy red wine had not been good for her. During the exciting writing process last night, she had forgotten that two glasses were her max. Why can't I learn this, she asked herself when she stumbled to the bathroom to find a pain killer. This is going to be a miserable morning, she thought. Usually things got a little bit better after breakfast, but even that was not guaranteed. She was definitely not in the mood to carry on any conversation and was really glad that Bill was still asleep. He looked very peaceful and relaxed, while she was preparing herself for a strenuous day at the office. I have to wear my warrior outfit today, she thought, while she was taking her shower. She had left the office yesterday early to work on her essay, without telling her boss. But what could she do. If she had asked, the answer would have been negative. She had to take the risk. Now the article was published. She would try to get a copy of the paper on her way to the office. She knew that the article was a risk, it was meant to provoke a public reaction, to begin a public conversation about organized crime in the city. The next elections were getting closer, which meant that the mayor and his allies would be more attentive and more vulnerable. And she had been glad that Bill had joined her last night. His support had felt good.

She was sitting in the kitchen, holding a cup of hot black coffee in her hands, when Bill stirred. A few minutes later he showed up in the kitchen, turning to the coffee machine.

"Any coffee left?" he asked in a hoarse voice, not yet quite ready to make conversation.

Ulrike just smiled shaking her head. "You have to start your own, poor man. How was your night?"

"I'm not complaining," he declared. "The hostess has been very kind."

"The hostess has to leave in five minutes," Ulrike replied softly. "Wish me luck at the office."

"I certainly do," he responded with a faint grin. "In return, wish me well with the news from New York."

"Any messages?"

"I haven't checked yet. Let me have my coffee first."

For a while, he worked with the coffee machine, while Ulrike collected her things and prepared to leave.

Ulrike was already gone when the fresh coffee was ready and Bill poured himself a cup. Only after he had finished his cup, he returned to the bedroom and looked for his phone. He glanced at the messages. At first glance, there seemed to be nothing significant. But then he went back a bit further. And there it was: an email from the paralegal of his firm. <Amos abandoned us in anger. You are on your own. Expect to hear from the partners later today. Mood here very low.> Although he had been warned, the mail was still a shock. Clearly, his days in Berlin were numbered. If he was lucky, he would be recalled and reassigned, but more likely the partners would end his contract. It can be a matter of hours or of days, he thought. What is my next step? I should think of a flight. But I'm not ready to return to New York. For one thing, I haven't completed my assignment, not to mention my personal life, which appears to be upended again. I have to go back to my hotel now to get my stuff, he thought. Very soon there will be no account anymore. He decided to postpone the call to Ulrike for a while. Would she take him in for a few days? After last night, he counted on her good will.

When Ulrike arrived at the *Morgenspiegel*, she was relieved to find out that her supervisor was out of town to cover a meeting on economic policy in Brussels. There would be no questions about her possible connection to the article on organized crime. There was hardly enough time for her to catch up on her email, until she had to leave again to cover a trial. It involved a bank robbery that had received a lot of media attention six months ago. When she returned, it was late morning. On her desk she found a message with a phone number and the request to call back. She recognized the handwriting and asked the colleague who had taken the call about its purpose. The caller had mentioned the name Herwig Stollberg. She had assumed that Ulrike would understand the context and the relevance. Ulrike tried to get more information, but there was very little. The caller had been a younger woman, most likely in her thirties, soft-spoken, from somewhere in North Germany, clearly educated. It did not sound like a crank call. Ulrike looked at the number; it was clearly not a land line. She decided to call back. The phone rang six times before there was an answer. She heard a female voice: "Yes?"

"My name is Ulrike Pfanner," she said. "I'm returning your call. You mentioned Herwig Stollberg. What can you tell me about Herwig Stollberg?"

"Not more than you already know," the voice replied. "But I can tell you things about Stefano Brindisi that you don't know."

This was an unexpected turn. Ulrike got very excited.

"Stefano Brindisi, you said," she replied, raising her voice just a bit. "Who are you? And what do you know about him?"

There was a moment of silence. Then Ulrike heard the voice again: "You are speaking to his lawyer and I know where he is staying right now."

"Will you tell me?"

"That depends. Stefano is accused of being involved in the Stollberg homicide. He did not kill his friend. He is ready to give an interview. Would you be interested in doing that interview? We know that you covered the case for the *Morgenspiegel*."

There was another moment of silence. This time it was Ulrike who needed time to think. Is this for real? she thought. A voice tells me that she is the lawyer of a fugitive who offers me an interview, although or because he is accused of killing his close friend. Was this a joke or a trap? This could be the breakthrough she and Bill had been looking for. There was no time for reflection she realized. She decided to accept the offer.

"OK, I am ready to do the interview. Where can I meet him?"

"Thank you. We thought that we could count on you. You will have to travel, but not use your car, which can be traced. Once you are at the place, I will give you directions."

"Who are you afraid of?"

"Obviously, we have to avoid the police. After all, there is a warrant out for his arrest. But our real concern are his Italian friends, who turned out to be organized criminals."

"Who are you? You have to give me at least your name."

"Definitely not right now, you could either contact the police or be traced by the Mafia. Can you be ready this afternoon around 2pm?"

"That doesn't give me a lot of time, but I think I can do it."

"Call me back when you are ready."

The voice was gone. For a moment Ulrike stared at the telephone without moving. Then she took her private phone out and left a message for Bill: <Meet me at my apartment at 13 hours, very urgent.> A few minutes later she found his answer: <will meet you at apartment. Could this include travel?> Her answer consisted of one word: <Yes>

When Bill arrived at Ulrike's apartment shortly after 1:00pm, he found her busy collecting her gear. He looked at her preparations without understanding the purpose and asked her to fill him in. Initially, her response seemed to be somewhat incoherent, until he grasped the basic facts, the call and the invitation to interview Stefano Brindisi at an unknown location where he stayed under the protection of his lawyer.

"An interview with Brindisi? Really?" Bill exclaimed.

"Yes, I can't quite believe it myself."

"Do you have a name? Who could she be? Have you thought of the young woman who picked him up in Düsseldorf?"

"Yes, that occurred to me as well. Expensive foreign car. Somewhere in Northern Germany, I guess."

"Why North Germany?"

"Her accent. Probably a large town—Hannover, Hamburg, Bremen."

"No name, you say. She appears to be very cautious," Bill suggested.

"Mostly, because of the folks we ran into in Düsseldorf. Remember?"

"I do. This means that we have to be extremely cautious as well. They know you. They may even keep an eye on you here in Berlin. Your travel plans have to be fool proof."

"What do you mean by <we>?" Ulrike interjected.

"We are in this together, remember?"

Ulrike just shrugged her shoulders: "I can handle this!"

"But it's not the smart way. I want to be sure that you make it back with the interview. You have to slip out of town without being noticed. You need a disguise; a change of coats and a wig are the minimum. Your smart phone has to stay home. I have a little flip phone along that I bought a couple of days ago."

"Bill, come on, aren't you pushing it!" Ulrike exclaimed. "It's just an interview."

"Remember, an interview with a man for whom there is a warrant and for whom the Mafia is looking. I will shadow you to make sure that nobody follows you. Is there a place where you can change your outfit on the way to the railway station?"

"How about my office?"

"Is there a second entrance?"

"Sure"

"Good, let's do it."

An hour later, a young brunette in a long dark coat and sunglasses left the building of the *Morgenspiegel* though the back entrance. Over her left shoulder she carried a small travel bag, while her right hand carried a briefcase. At the corner she hailed a taxi that took her to the central station. Without stopping at the ticket booth, she moved straight to the platform area where she opened a small flip phone and made a call. The call lasted only a minute. Then she turned to the board looking for the next express train to Hamburg. Bill, who had been waiting in the area for a while, followed her at a distance. He observed the young woman boarding the waiting train. Once he was sure that nobody had followed her, he also boarded the train, but chose the next car. Inside the car he walked in the direction of her car.

Bill wanted to be sure that nobody had tracked Ulrike on her way to the train. He chose a seat from where he could see Ulrike, who had chosen a window seat in the center of the half-empty car. He wore his normal travel outfit: black jeans, a heavy shirt, and a brown leather jacket. His baseball cap made it difficult to see the upper part of his face. A middle-aged woman took the seat next to Ulrike. A few minutes later a man in his thirties occupied the seat in the row behind her. When he took his coat off and was searching for a hook, his glance focused on Ulrike. Then he sat down and took his smart phone out, making a brief call. Bill tried to follow the conversation, but the distance was too large for him to understand more than individual words. He decided that he had to keep an eye on this passenger. He wanted Ulrike to know that he was close. Once the train was moving, he got up and passed Ulrike's row. He walked slowly to the end of the car, seemingly looking for a better seat. Then he returned to his old seat without openly glancing in Ulrike's direction. A brief nod told him that she had noticed him. Within minutes the train picked up speed. A little bit later there was an announcement that the dining car was open and ready to receive guests. Ulrike decided to make use of this opportunity and walked past Bill in the direction of the dining car. When she passed him, she dropped a little note informing him that she would receive further instructions after she had arrived at Hamburg Central Station. What would happen next? Would the young man get up? Bill noticed that he tried to make eye contact with Ulrike, but when he realized that she discouraged him, he turned his attention back to his laptop. Ten minutes later Bill got up and followed Ulrike. He found her in the dining car, which was almost empty. The waiter, clearly bored, stood close to the entrance. Bill found a small table from where he had a good view of Ulrike, who had ordered a large cup of coffee. She was busy with the latest edition of the *Morgenspiegel*, pretending not to notice Bill. Nothing out of the ordinary, Bill thought. We must have succeeded to slip out of town without calling attention to ourselves. Of course, the danger could be at the other end. They had no more than the voice of a woman assuring Ulrike that she was Stefano Brindisi's lawyer. This could be a trap. Ulrike, however, seemed to be confident that the caller was genuine and that she would meet with Stefano Brindisi for an interview. After placing his order, Bill opened his laptop to check his mail. Still, no official word from his firm. But he found a short message from his mother, urging him to take his father's advice and come back to Chicago. He shook his head. They will have to wait for a while until my business here is finished, one way or the other, he thought. If we actually meet with Stefano Brindisi later today, there might be a chance that he knows more about the missing file. The train would arrive in Hamburg around 4:00pm. How much time would they need to get to the place where Brindisi was hiding? He remembered from his last visit two years ago that it was a big city. It could take them easily an hour to find the place. He wished he had a real map, but there had not been enough time to buy a map before he boarded the train. All he could do now was to study the map he found on Google. The affluent suburban areas appeared to be in the west in the neighborhood of the Elbe and in the north close to a small river called Alster. He got so involved in studying the map that he almost overlooked Ulrike asking for the check and leaving her table. When she passed him, she dropped a small note <At the station I will call the lawyer again to get directions. Call me to get the location and the address.> Bill glanced at the note, giving her a quick nod. He stayed for another five minutes. Nobody had tried to follow Ulrike.

The train was late because it had to stop for almost ten minutes close to the central station. Ulrike remained in her seat, while most of the passengers were already moving toward the exit, among them the young man in the row behind Ulrike. The middle-aged woman, however, as Bill noticed, also remained in her seat, seemingly undisturbed by the general commotion. He decided to keep an eye on her. Finally, the train began moving again, pulling slowly into the station. Bill followed Ulrike who walked along the crowded platform until she reached an escalator taking her to the central hall, where she was looking for a quiet corner. Bill, who had followed her, saw her opening her small flip phone and making a call. Where was the middle-aged woman? Was there anybody interested in Ulrike? He couldn't detect any suspicious persons. When he saw that Ulrike finished her call, he called her, using his own flip phone.

"What's up?" he asked softly.

"She gave me directions. I have to use the subway line number one northbound and get off at Fuhlsbüttel. There I will have to call her again," Ulrike replied.

"Do you know this area? Have you ever been there?" Bill asked.

"No, I haven't, too far removed from the offices of the media. We have to find the entrance to line one. This should be easy."

"OK, I'll follow you. Make sure that you see me before you enter the subway train. So far, we seem to be in good shape."

It took Ulrike a while to negotiate her way from the busy central hall to the entrance of the subway. Finally, she reached the platform where she looked for a ticket machine. She decided to buy a day pass in order to gain maximum flexibility. Standing in front of the machine, she noticed Bill passing her. A minute later, when the north-bound train was arriving, she saw Bill purchasing a ticket. She waited a few seconds before she boarded the train, just enough time for Bill to get his ticket. For a brief moment, they stood close to each other, then she found a seat in the middle of the crowded car, while Bill remained close to the door from where he could watch the people in Ulrike's surroundings. It wasn't easy, since the time of their arrival in the city coincided with the local rush hour. Especially when they reached the stop Jungfernstieg, the car became crowded. Then, at the next stop something unexpected happened. The young man from the express train entered the car. He stood close to Bill, trying to find space for his luggage. Bill was completely flabbergasted. How could this happen? He had been absolutely sure that nobody had followed Ulrike. Now this. He must have missed a move. There must have been more than one person tracking Ulrike. This was alarming news, he had to warn her without giving away their connection. The young man seemed to be out of breath. Did he seek to move close to Ulrike? He appeared to be completely preoccupied with his own situation. Not once did he look in her direction. But maybe he is part of a team and somebody else is watching her right now? Briefly Bill considered calling her but then decided against it. At this moment it couldn't be done without calling attention to himself. The young man stayed close to the door. At the next stop Bill had a chance to move away, while remaining close enough to observe the young man. How close were they to Fuhlsbüttel? He looked at the map posted close to the door and realized that it would take a while before they reached their own stop. Suddenly the situation changed; the train emerged from the tunnel. Bright light came in from the windows. The next stop was a crowded exchange with another line. For a moment the car was almost empty, before new passengers filled it again. Suddenly, Bill realized that the young man was gone. Had he been replaced? He took his phone out and dialed Ulrike's number. He observed her taking out her phone and opening it.

"Ulrike, you have to be careful, it's possible that you are being followed. The young man who sat behind you in the express train showed up in this subway car. He just vanished again. There may be more than one person shadowing you. When we come to our stop, stay on the platform for a while and let me check out the neighborhood before you call your contact."

"OK, will do."

The train needed another 15 minutes to reach Fuhlsbüttel. When they got out of the train, they felt fresh air surrounding them. The platform was almost empty. While Bill was moving toward a broad staircase leading to the exit, Ulrike found a bench where she sat down. She closed her eyes for a moment, enjoying the fresh breeze. When Bill reached the street level of the station, he found himself surrounded by a suburban landscape. In front of him were a number of red busses, picking up passengers coming from the train. There was an apartment building with shops on the other side of the street, and to the left he saw the mature trees of a small park. It was a busy space and it took him a moment to assess the situation. He was looking for the young man and the middle-aged woman. They were not in evidence. He slowly walked toward the busses, pretending to stand in line. From here he could observe the entrance of the station. Was there anybody just hanging around? Two women with shopping baskets stood in front of the entrance, involved in a lively conversation. Were they possibly here to track Ulrike? But they seemed to be completely absorbed in their conversation. After observing the scene for five minutes, he called Ulrike and asked her to proceed.

"Time to move," Bill declared. "Have you already talked to the lawyer?"

"Yes, I just called her. I'm supposed to go to a small nearby park and wait on a bench close to the playground for further directions."

"Good, I have seen the park already. It's very close. I let you go first and wait until I'm sure that nobody follows you."

A minute later Bill saw Ulrike. Once she had recognized the park to the left on the other side of the street, she walked in that direction. She moved slowly, giving Bill time to observe the space in front of the station. She avoided eye contact when she passed him and crossed the street. He left his position so that he could see her approaching the park and then disappearing behind the tall trees. Bill chose to cross the street closer to the busses. In front of the apartment building he turned left until he realized that there was another street turning to the right. Now the park was in front of him, on the other side of the street. He walked through the shade of the tall beech trees until he reached a large well-kept lawn. To the right he recognized the playground Ulrike had mentioned. He noticed Ulrike on one of the benches where she watched a small number of children playing in the sandbox. Bill remained motionless for several minutes. What would happen next? Suddenly, a younger woman in a light raincoat approached Ulrike's bench and sat down next to her. She seemed to ignore Ulrike, exclusively focused on her newspaper. After a few minutes, she got up and left the playground, moving to the far end of the park. Then she vanished between the large trees. There must be another entrance, Bill thought. He turned his gaze back to Ulrike, who was still sitting on her bench, seemingly busy with a newspaper. Then she got up and moved slowly in the direction of the woman. Bill got his phone out and tried to reach her.

"What's up," he asked.

"I have been asked by a young woman in a light raincoat to go to Farnstraße 25 where I'm supposed to meet with Stefano Brindisi. I have to use the other exit and then turn right. Farnstraße is the first intersection on the right. Anything unusual?"

"No, everything looks normal. Give me a chance to check this out before you arrive. I'll see you in front of the building."

Bill rushed to the left until he reached a lane with trees that formed an arch. He followed the lane to the end where he found the second exit. Now he turned to the right, following a street lined with single older houses with large front yards. Within a minute, he found the intersection and turned into Farnstraße, a quiet residential street. Here the houses were much older, villas built around 1900, but well preserved. They were surrounded by large yards with old majestic birch and oak trees. They seemed to touch the equally large trees that lined the street. Bill was astonished how quiet it was. He looked for the house numbers. The odd numbers were on his right side. Number 25 turned out to be a freshly painted white villa with high rather narrow windows and a balcony on the second floor. There was a metal gate with two names. Bill continued to walk in the same direction for a while. Then he turned around. The street was empty. He saw Ulrike approaching the villa. He gave her a nod, which she returned. Then she opened the gate and walked up to the building. The front door opened and Ulrike disappeared in the building. Bill moved back to the intersection and turned left. Then his phone rang.

"Bill, it's me. I am standing next to the lawyer and will meet with Stefano Brindisi in a minute. I'll stay in touch," Ulrike said.

"Good, I'm rather hungry and will look for a place in the neighborhood where I can get a bite to eat. Keep me posted."

The woman led Ulrike to the back of the house where she opened a wide sliding door. Ulrike stepped into a large living room, the floor covered by oriental rugs. In the far end she saw a person in a heavy armchair. It took her a moment to recognize Stefano Brindisi. He looked pale and tired. Then she heard his soft voice:

"I'm glad you found the time to visit me."

"My pleasure, Signor Brindisi," Ulrike replied. "I'm very curious to get your version of the events."

"You will, but first, let me introduce Birgit Hansen, my lawyer and a close and trusted friend. In fact, it was she who encouraged me to get in touch with you. She persuaded me that I could not hide for the rest of my life but had to deal with the events in Berlin that led to the death of my friend Herwig Stollberg."

"You realize of course that there is a warrant out for you," Ulrike interjected.

"Of course, I am, which is disturbing enough, but it's not my real problem,"

So, what is the real problem?"

"Friends who turned out not to be very friendly."

"How come?"

"We counted on their support, but they expect to control us, the future of the company."

"But why are you hiding?"

"Because they are violent. They might even kill me."

"There is time for all this later," Birgit Hansen declared. "But first, let me find out how you managed to get to our house. Are you certain that you were not followed?"

"I believe, we managed to slip out of town without being tracked. There was a brief moment though when we were no longer sure"

"What. do you mean by we?" Brindisi asked, his voice expressing concern.

"I took precautions by asking a friend, a private detective, to shadow me. A young man, who was sitting in the row behind be in the express train, showed suddenly up in the subway train. A few stops later he vanished. We have no explanation. An odd coincidence."

Stefano Brindisi appeared to be concerned: "Did you bring your smart phone?" he asked.

"No, I left it in Berlin and have a small flip phone instead that can't be traced."

"But what about the young man?" Brindisi asked.

"Where did he show up?" Birgit Hansen wanted to know.

"I think it was Stephansplatz," Ulrike replied.

"There is a possible explanation," Birgit suggested. "You got off the train at Central Station, but locals who mean to use the line one most likely get off at Dammtor and walk to Stephansplatz. It's easier."

"I'm glad to hear this," Ulrike said. "A coincidence then?"

"More likely. Where is your detective friend now?" Birgit asked.

"He's looking for a place where he can get something to eat."

"You trust him?" Brindisis interjected.

"Completely," Ulrike asserted. She opened her briefcase and began to take out her equipment. In the meantime, Birgit Hansen disappeared in the kitchen, apparently looking for cups and small plates. Then Ulrike heard the noise of a coffee machine. She sat down in an armchair next to Brindisi, putting her gear on a small side table. All of a sudden, she felt tired. She was looking forward to the coffee. I need fresh energy to get this right, she thought. Where do I start? The more he talks about the background, the better, since we know the facts.

Minutes later, the hostess came back with three cups of coffee, a larger plate with cookies and smaller plates, which she placed on side tables. Ulrike grasped her cup and took a sip. It was a wonderful aroma, which revived her spirits. This was a good omen. She thanked Birgit for the warm reception and inquired: "How did Stefano get to your house?"

"I picked him up in Dusseldorf where he was hiding in a warehouse where his cousin Anna rents space. I understand, the police showed up a few hours after we left, not to mention a few guys, who had broken into the rooms where Anna keeps her extras."

"Why is he not talking to the police, if he is threatened by old friends?" Ulrike asked in a soft voice.

"He better tells you his story himself, there are good reasons."

Ulrike turned her attention to Stefano Brindisi.

"I'm ready to talk," he exclaimed.

CHAPTER 19

Ulrike pushed the button of her audio equipment before she asked the first question:

"Stefano Brindisi, the police are looking for you, because you are implicated in the death of Herwig Stollberg. Did you kill him?"

"No, I certainly did not," Brindisi replied, raising his voice.

"You have to explain this statement, because your fingerprints were found in the van that pushed Stollberg to the ground."

"That may be the case, but I was not behind the wheel. I was just a passenger."

"The police will argue that it was you who gave the order to kill Stollberg. The driver is in custody and denies any responsibility for Stollberg's death. What do you have to say in response?"

At this point, Brigit Hansen, who was sitting next to Brindisi, shook her head.

"This exchange will not get us to the crucial question. Stefano, you will have to talk about the purpose of your presence in the van and the purpose of the trip."

"Well, on that morning, I noticed that Herwig, who had come to the lab early, was getting ready to leave. He was wearing his helmet. When I tried to approach him, he told me that he had no time. He looked very nervous and tight. All he said was <I have to go>."

"Was there a particular reason that you wanted to talk to him?" Ulrike asked.

"I suspected that he was about to do something stupid and harmful to our company."

"Can you elaborate?"

"I was afraid that he had decided to sell our latest research results on the black market, since he needed money. I knew that he owed a lot of money. By selling our research he could wipe out his debts."

"Did you know why he owed so much money?"

"Herwig was a heavy gambler, and like all gamblers he always believed that he could get his losses back by taking higher risks. Of course, he just incurred higher losses and borrowed more money. Finally, it must have been so much and the pressure from his creditors increased so much that he became desperate, looking for a radical solution of his problem."

"How did you find out? Did he confide in you?" Ulrike interjected.

"No, I wish he had. He might still be alive. I heard about his debts from his creditors, who were anxious to get their money back."

"Who were these persons?"

"They were friends of my grandfather. But not exactly, they were friends of friends of my grandfather. Herwig had met them through me when we needed more capital for our company. They gave us money to increase our capital, and they also loaned money to Herwig, as I found out later. When he couldn't pay back, they applied pressure and threatened him."

"Did he tell you that?"

"He just talked about people who threatened him and his wife. Only later, I realized who they were. They contacted me, because they got worried that their share of the company would be in jeopardy."

"I'm confused, Signor Brindisi," Ulrike declared. "Who was the target of the threats? Stollberg or you?"

"It might be better, Stefano, if you started at the beginning. Then things would become more transparent," Birgit Hansen interjected.

"OK, when we started our company and needed capital, it was primarily my father and my grandfather, who provided the money. Herwig and I had ideas but no money. Additional funds came from an old friend of my grandfather, who had built a small trucking company in Munich. When he retired and sold the company, he put some of his money into our start-up. This was all in the family and we didn't think much about this. We were first and foremost chemists, not investors."

"When and how did the friends of the friends, you mentioned, get involved?"

"About two years later when we needed more capital to expand our lab. They were ready to invest money they made in the trucking business, they told us."

"Did you realize at that time that you were dealing with organized crime?"

There was a moment of silence, then Brindisi said in a low voice:

"No, it never occurred to us. It seemed to be money from the extended family."

"But later you found out?"

"Much later. When Herwig got financially into trouble and was looking for a way out, things changed. First, they cut him off, then, they threatened him. They came to me when he began looking for buyers for his recent research. They must have found out somehow. In any case, now they approached me and warned me. I had to do something to stop this dangerous sell-out of the company's intellectual assets."

"How did you feel about this?"

"I was very upset. I felt personally betrayed. We had been close friends. And it was a real danger for the company. The results of our new research were commercially valuable and crucial for the future of the company. You must understand this. What Herwig had decided to do was a disastrous move."

"Which had to be stopped," Ulrike interjected.

"Slow down a bit and let Stefano explain," Birgit Hansen asserted.

"OK, explain," Ulrike exclaimed.

"When I approached Herwig, he denied that he was planning to sell his work. On that morning, there had been a phone call for Herwig. I couldn't follow the conversation, all I understood was the name of a hotel that was mentioned."

"Brandenburger Hof?"

"Yes, minutes later Herwig left. Ten minutes later, a guy by the name Esposito showed up to warn me again about Herwig's plans. I mentioned what had happened and he urged me to get into his van to follow Herwig. The plan was to stop him before he reached the hotel and persuade him not to sell."

"And you believed that?"

"Yes, I did. I was anxious to stop Herwig from making a bad mistake."

"But there was no conversation?"

"No, it never came to that. We caught up with him very close to the hotel. He was in front of us at an intersection. We had to wait. Then the traffic light changed to green. Herwig was crossing the intersection when Esposito suddenly accelerated and made a right turn. The van hit him with full force. I screamed, but Esposito didn't stop. He did the opposite, he drove as fast as he could. I was horrified. I yelled stop, stop, but he paid no attention. He shouted at me – in Italian. He told me that Herwig deserved his fate. He was a traitor, who was on the way to a meeting where he would have sold the property of the family. Then he said in German <schlechter Mann> bad man."

Brindisi's voice was barely audible. Birgit Hansen was holding his hand, while he closed his eyes. Ulrike remained silent. This had been an execution, she thought. Stefano Brindisi had to witness the execution of his friend. He had even become implicated in the death of his friend. Worse, he might be found guilty of collaborating in a murder plot. It was his word against that of Esposito, who might claim that Stefano Brindisi had ordered the killing. Ulrike looked at Birgit, who was still holding Brindisi's hand. Then, she heard her soft voice.

"You can see how desperate Stefano's situation is. For the police he is involved in a homicide, possibly considered the instigator, who wanted to protect the company, for the Mafia he is a traitor and a liability. They are looking for the missing file and believe that Stefano knows where it is hidden."

"What about this?" Ulrike asked. "Does he know anything?"

Birgit Hansen shook her head.

"I don't have a clue," Brindisi exclaimed. "What does the police know?"

"As far as I know," Ulrike said, "the file is still missing."

There was another moment of silence. The room had become dark. Ulrike noticed the larger trees outside the window turning into a massive dark wall enclosing the old house.

"What can you tell me about the content of the missing file?" Ulrike exclaimed. "What exactly did Stollberg mean to sell? How important was it?"

"Critical," Brindisi replied. "The life of our company depends on it. We changed course about two years ago and entered diabetes research. It's a very competitive field where the stakes are high. We were clearly outsiders, but we were lucky. Herwig solved a problem that the rest of the field has not figured out. We were ahead of the rest. All we needed was another six months or so to come out with a new medication."

"Can't you simply take over?" Ulrike asked.

"I wish it were that easy. In the last three months or so, Herwig was pursuing an angle without sharing the results with me. It didn't appear important. Now, I realize that it was intentional. He was already planning to sell this piece to solve his financial problems."

"And you can't somehow reconstruct his work from his notes and lab tests?" Ulrike inquired.

"I was looking for them. There was nothing left. He must have stored them in special files."

"What are you planning to do now?" Ulrike asked, focusing her gaze on Birgit Hansen.

"Stefano will have to turn himself in and trust that there will be a fair trial. He cannot be a fugitive forever.," the lawyer replied in a low voice.

"Will you take over his defense?" Ulrike asked.

"Certainly not for the trial," Birgit Hansen declared. "I'm an estate lawyer with no experience in criminal law. But even if I were, this would be a bad decision. I'm too close to Stefano to be effective."

"How long have you known each other?" Ulrike asked.

"We met half a year ago in Berlin," Birgit Hansen said. "Actually, quite accidentally at the opera. It was an outstanding performance of "La Traviata" at Deutsche Oper. I had to meet with a corporate client in Berlin and had a free evening. Stefano, who sat next to me, turned out to be an excellent guide. He is a real fan and much more knowledgeable than I. We shared a very pleasant evening. Later he visited me in Hamburg where I showed him around."

There was something in her voice telling Ulrike that there was a much stronger commitment than her cautious remarks suggested. She would not have gone to Düsseldorf to pick up a casual acquaintance. There must have been more after the conversation about "La Traviata," Ulrike thought. Would she ever pick up a guy at the opera? This was an impossible thought. She remembered the day about two years ago when she first met Bill at a police station where he tried to explain to a baffled police officer in halting German that he was looking for a missing person. Police stations, courthouses, that was her territory. It had been an almost comical encounter. She had translated Bill's awkward statements to an officer who showed hardly any interest in responding to Bill's problems. No doubt, she had immediately found the young stranger attractive but there had also been a potentially interesting news story. What has happened to us? I was really glad to see him again and realized that I had missed him, more than I was willing to admit to myself. But do we have a future? Very soon he'll go back to New York, and then what? I can't see myself in a lasting relationship with Bill. Why is that? Ulrike decided quickly not to follow this thought. This was not the time. I have to do an interview that will catch the attention of the public. She could see the headline <Who really killed Herwig Stollberg?>. She glanced at her watch. It was getting late and they had a train to catch. Where was Bill and what was he doing? Ulrike looked at Stefano Brindisi in his armchair, he looked exhausted and depressed. It was Birgit Hansen who resumed the conversation:

"When do you think your interview will be published?"

"I wish I could give you a date," Ulrike replied. "But first there is the meeting of the editors where decisions are made. If it were my decision, the story would be out tomorrow morning."

"I would like to see some public support before Stefano turns himself in. It's going to be difficult enough in any case."

Ulrike just nodded, while she was collecting her equipment. She was about to call Bill when Birgit Hansen, who had left the room for a moment, came back with the offer of a small meal. Ulrike looked at her watch again and politely declined. If they could catch the 8:00 train back to Berlin, she would be able to write the story, at least there would be a draft that she could polish later and then submit tomorrow.

Bill accepted her call with a brief "Hallo" that sounded strange, since he must be aware that she had to be the caller.

"Where are you now?" Ulrike asked in a soft voice.

There was a strange answer. Bill insisted that he could not talk to her right now.

"I'm done. Can you pick me up?"

There was no answer. Ulrike had a strong sense of an unreal conversation, but couldn't express why. Then she made small talk with Birgit Hansen about the house, which had been in the family for three generations.

After Bill had observed Ulrike disappear in the villa, he had slowly walked back to the subway station. Looking at the large red-brick apartment building he discovered a small pub. When he entered, it took him a moment to orient himself. In front of him he faced a counter with a number of stools, most of them empty. To the left there were a group of dark wooden tables. He picked a stool at the bar, putting his things on the counter in front of him. From somewhere music filled the room, some German pop that sounded slightly familiar. Nobody seemed to pay attention to him. To his left, two older men were involved in a conversation about their favorite soccer teams. One of them expressed concerns about the chances of the HSV, a local team, to stay in the first league, while the other one brushed this off as fear mongering, asserting the durable quality of the players.

"They'll come back, today's loss is only a temporary setback," the other one exclaimed.

"Wishful thinking," the first one replied, "they will be kicked out of the first league."

"No way," the other one cried.

"Want to bet?!"

Bill tried to tune the conversation out and focus on his own business. He took his laptop out and checked his mail. There were a couple of messages from home, mostly friends and acquaintances, nothing urgent and no news from the firm, which was good news. Finally, the bar keeper showed up, seemingly in a bad mood, asking for his order. Bill ordered a beer and asked for the menu. A brief look convinced him that this was not a good place for refined food. Still, he was hungry. So, he ordered two sausages with mustard and bread. The barkeeper filled his glass. Then he walked to the kitchen to place the order. At least the local beer is good, Bill thought after he had taken the first gulp. It had a certain bitterness that he liked. Five minutes later, the bar keeper came with the sausages on a large plate with two pieces of dark bread and plenty of mustard. Bill was pleasantly surprised. These were really big sausages that took care of his hunger. Even the bread tasted better than he had expected. In the meantime, the bar keeper had turned on the large television mounted on the wall behind him. On the screen Bill recognized a soccer match. An Italian team played a Spanish team. Still, the guests in the pub, mostly men, took a serious interest in the game, which Bill found odd, because no German team was involved. He couldn't even recognize the identity of the teams. He had to ask the bar keeper, who explained to him that the match was part of the European league.

"And your guests are interested in this match?" Bill asked.

"Sure," the bar keeper replied. "Real Madrid and Turin. They are very famous teams. Everybody knows them."

Bill just nodded, turning his attention back to his laptop. He looked once more at his notes, in particular at the early ones when he still believed in the claim of Alerta. The investigation had come a long way since then. Also, his relationship with the police had significantly changed. He was now clearly on much better terms with Charlotte Herberg, not to mention Werner Kraft. On the other hand, his relationship with his own firm had clearly deteriorated to the point of estrangement. Now, he expected to be notified officially that his employment was terminated. The more he thought about this turn of events the more he realized that he was less upset than he had expected. Clearly, he was irritated about the conflict between Amos Hinchcliff and the rest of the partners whose ethical standards obviously left room for improvement, but he also felt that this change might be good for him. He had to rethink his career. This moment reminded him of another situation when he had been sitting in the Chanticleer, a bar in Ithaca, NY, contemplating his faltering career as a student of law at Cornell. Then, he had come to realize that the law was not his thing, yet quitting would be a major disappointment to his parents, especially to his father. Now, he was expected to give the law another try, but was he really interested? For a brief moment, he looked at the tv screen. The camera was focusing on the goal keeper, who was preparing himself for a penalty kick, bent forward and moving nervously from the left to the right. Then, the focus shifted to the player of the other team, who was about to kick. Next, the camera followed the ball, which landed inside the goal. Bill heard the excited cries of the guests: "Tor."

"That was an excellent kick," a familiar voice declared.

Bill turned around and recognized Werner Kraft standing next to him.

"May I join you?" Kraft asked, sitting down on the stool next to Bill.

"By all means," Bill replied trying to hide his total surprise. "What brings you to this part of Hamburg?"

"I can ask you the same question," Kraft asserted.

"Yes, you can," Bill said. "I'm on business, how about you?"

"Same thing. Business. Orders from higher up. We were told to follow you when it became clear that you were on a train to Hamburg."

"How did you find out? Are you spying on me, Werner? That's not done among friends."

"Believe me, Bill, I didn't spy on you. This was done by someone else."

"Charlotte Herberg?"

"Certainly not. We don't even have the technology. But someone knows how to do it and has tracked you. Someone figured out that you and your reporter friend would lead us to Brindisi. The hunch was correct. You walked from the subway station to the park and then to Farnstraße. After that you turned around and ended up in this pub. My guess is that Ulrike is meeting with Brindisi."

Bill just shrugged his shoulders. How did I miss this? Bill thought. Nobody followed us to the station in Berlin. There were no really suspicious moves on the train. How did they track me?

"Bill, we are taking it from here," Kraft said in a soft voice. "We have been ordered to bring him in with the assistance from the local police."

Bill remained silent. This was not the way it was supposed to end, at least not in his mind. Can I warn Ulrike? he thought. But that would just delay the inevitable by an hour or two. They knew the street where Brindisi was hiding.

"What's the next move?" Bill asked.

"You and I will walk to the house. Then our Hamburg colleagues will knock on the door and apprehend the fugitive.

"OK, give me a minute. I have to use the restroom. Then we walk together."

"Fine, Bill, but no tricks. I'll come with you."

In the restroom Bill tried to shut the door of the stall so that he could call Ulrike, but Kraft kept him from locking the door.

"No tricks, Bill, I said."

Minutes later they returned to the main room where Bill paid with his credit card, while Kraft made a call, giving instructions to someone. When they stepped into the open air, Bill noticed that it had become completely dark. The air was moist. They slowly walked back to Farnstraße. They had just reached the little park, when Bill's flip phone was ringing. Bill tried to ignore the call. But Kraft remined him: "You want to answer that call, it may be important."

Bill opened the phone and pressed the accept button. He heard Ulrike's voice

"No, I'm sorry I cannot meet you tonight," without waiting for her to speak, he said, "But tomorrow we can get together. I'll call you back."

"A Berlin acquaintance," he continued, turning to Kraft, who just smiled.

When they arrived at the other exit, they turned right until they reached the intersection with Farnstraße. Here a large dark van blocked the road.

"What's this?" Bill asked.

"Being prepared," Kraft replied.

"Isn't that a bit of an overkill? A special unit!" Bill suggested. "We are dealing with a single person, a chemist"

"Our colleagues want to be absolutely sure, I guess."

Bill shrugged his shoulders. He realized that he had lost control.

"Why don't you tell me the number," Kraft suggested in a low voice.

"What number?" Bill asked.

"Come on, don't play dumb, Bill, the number of the house."

"Why should I do that? You worked behind my back."

"You know that we had to. He is a suspect in a murder case."

"OK, I'll give you the number, but there are two conditions."

"What are they?"

"First, you keep Ulrike completely out of this, and, second, you postpone the arrest until tomorrow morning."

"I can agree to the first," Kraft replied. "The second one is not my call. I have to be in touch with the special team. You have to give me five minutes."

"If they say no, they have to go from house to house," Bill said. "That's not good for their reputation, is it?"

Kraft walked over to the van and knocked at the back door. The door opened and he entered the van. Five minutes later he returned.

"They agree to your condition, as long as you promise not to get in touch with Brindisi or his host. The house will be under tight surveillance during the night. By the way, this agreement includes Ulrike. We expect her to go along. Can you promise that, Bill?"

There was a moment of silence. Then, Bill just nodded. "The house number is 25."

"Thank you," Kraft said in a low voice. "As I said before, we'll take it from here."

Bill turned away. It was time to find Ulrike, who must have left the house by now. She should have met him at this end of Farnstraße, but she didn't show up. Bill walked in the direction of the subway station. When he was out of reach of Kraft, he took out his phone and tried to reach Ulrike.

Ulrike stared at the little flip phone. What had happened right now? She wanted Bill to pick her up, while she was walking back to the subway station. Instead, he didn't allow her to speak and said something that didn't make sense. Something is definitely wrong, she thought. He must have been in a situation where he couldn't reveal that he was in contact with me. When she had reached the gate, she looked around. The street, now completely dark and appeared to be empty. The only thing she noticed was a dog barking in the distance. She waited for a moment. Then she decided to turn right and find another way back to the station. She realized that her sense of the street pattern was weak and she might get lost. But walking towards Bill was likely the wrong move, possibly a trap. After about 800 feet the street ended, she had to turn either right or left. She tried to form a mental map of the area. Turning left, would get her farther away from the train stop. So, she decided to turn right. Now, she was on a broader street with street lamps and more foot traffic. Here and there a car passed her. After walking for a few minutes, she came to another intersection. Should she continue walking straight or turn to the right? Why was there no sign telling her how to reach the subway? Ulrike felt uncomfortable. This was not her town. In Berlin this sense of being lost would not happen to her. She realized that her reaction was quite irrational; there were many parts of Berlin where she was equally unfamiliar with the topography. But she couldn't shake this threatening sense of being in a strange space. For a moment she was standing motionless. Then, she saw a young woman, who was walking her dog, approaching her. She turned to the woman.

"Excuse me, can you help me? I'm trying to get to the subway station. Where do I turn?" She asked.

There was no immediate answer. Instead, the dog, a large German shepherd, started to bark at Ulrike. The young woman was pulling the dog back, trying to calm the animal down. Only then she turned to Ulrike

"You have to turn right here. You are actually not far away from the station, no more than five minutes."

Ulrike thanked the young woman and turned right. She had barely walked hundred feet when her phone was ringing. It was Bill.

"Where are you?" he asked, his voice expressing concern. "I expected you to look for me on the way back to the subway station."

"Are you OK, Bill? Your response to my last call was so strange that I decided to find another way back to the station. Let's meet there. I should be there in a few minutes."

"Yes. I'm fine, but things have really changed," Bill replied.

"What do you mean by changed?" Ulrike asked.

"I'll fill you in after we meet."

The young woman had been right. It took Ulrike no more than five minutes to reach the station. She saw Bill close to the entrance and walked toward him.

"I'm really glad to see you here," she exclaimed.

"Same here," he said in low voice.

When they heard a train approaching the stop, the rushed down the stairs and barely managed to catch the last car. Bill checked his watch. It was a quarter past seven.

"If we are lucky, we can catch the 8:00 express train," he declared.

"So, what's the big change you mentioned?" Ulrike wanted to know.

"Did you get your interview?"

"Yes, I did. It's going to be a really exciting story. But what's the change you mentioned."

"The police will arrest Brindisi tomorrow morning," Bill said as casually as he could.

"Arrest? How is that possible? Who told your that?"

"Werner Kraft, when all of a sudden he stood next to me in the pub."

Ulrike stared at him in disbelief. For her this information made no sense.

"You were sure that we were not followed, Bill."

"Yes, I was. As it turns out, I was wrong. They tracked me and you."

"Who are they?"

"The police, Werner Kraft got the order to follow us. We would lead them to Brindisi."

"How did they achieve that? Was it Kraft?"

"No, Kraft just got the orders from Charlotte Herberg."

"They played you, Bill."

"That seems to be the case, but I don't know who it was and how they did it. Still, you got your interview?"

"I did. He's innocent. They will arrest an innocent man. It's an incredible story. On the advice of his lawyer, he is planning to turn himself in after the publication of my story."

"This will be no longer his voluntary choice. The police have already surrounded the house. All I could do, was to postpone the arrest to give him a peaceful night."

"We should warn Birgit Hansen," Ulrike exclaimed.

"What do you gain? He can't run away," Bill argued. "The best thing you can do for him is to get back to Berlin to publish the interview."

"The material needs editing," Ulrike replied.

"Can we do this on the train?" Bill asked.

"At least, we can get started."

The following morning at 9:00 Charlotte Herberg checked her messages and found what she was looking for, a message from Werner Kraft informing her that Stefano Brindisi had been arrested at 8:30 and would be transported to Berlin later the same day. She would be able to interrogate him in the afternoon. <I will take care of the local arrangements and make sure that we have a safe vehicle. The Hamburg colleagues have been very cooperative. Be prepared that his is lawyer, Brigit Hansen, in whose house he was hiding, insists on being present during the interrogation. She claims that he is innocent.> This is good news, Charlotte thought. His arrest will bring us much closer to solving the Stollberg case, which had turned into something much larger than a homicide. in a long meeting with Kriminalrat Sieverts yesterday afternoon she learned that the stakes were much higher for both of them. A newspaper article had stressed the growing presence of organized crime in Berlin. The commissioner was furious because he suspected a leak and blamed her and her SOKO, as she had learned from Sieverts. Of course, she immediately guessed the identity of the unknown author. It must have been Ulrike Pfanner. It was a topic she felt strongly about. Ulrike could be very useful, but she also could be a real pain. In Charlotte's mind, Ulrike had an overly strong opinion of the public's right to know. Some of the references in the article pointed to the Stollberg case. Now there would be a chance to examine the deeper financial involvement of a criminal organization, something they had only suspected. As she had found out in the conversation with Sieverts, she could rely on him. He would not throw her under the bus to save his own skin in a confrontation with the commissioner. This was actually more than she had expected and changed her feelings about her boss. The sense of distance she had always felt, had become much more comfortable, it had become a friendly distance.

Charlotte decided to call a meeting of the SOKO at 10:00 to go over the evidence and prepare for the interrogation of Stefano Brindisi. Also, she let Esposito know that Brindisi had been arrested and would testify. She gave him a last chance to cooperate. His lawyer immediately responded with a sharp rebuke, informing her of his client's innocence. It was becoming quite clear that there would be two conflicting stories about the death of Herwig Stollberg. Following procedures was the only way moving forward. Then, she received a surprising email. The officers of the LKA Hesse informed her that they were planning to come back to Berlin when Stefano Brindisi had been moved from Hamburg to Berlin. They requested to be part of the interrogation. How did they already know? Charlotte realized that it would be difficult to deny the request, because possibly it was their preliminary work that had led to the arrest. Did they place the tracking device? In yesterday's conversation Sieverts had instructed her to use the information, she felt uneasy about the method. There was an element of betrayal in using Bill McDonald, and she noticed that Werner Kraft felt the same way when she ordered him to go to Hamburg with a small team and carry out Brindisi's arrest. His face expressed reluctance. "Do we have to do this?" he had asked in a low voice. She had simply referred to Sieverts and repeated his orders. That decided it. This was police work. After all, there was not only the material evidence but also a strong motive for Brindisi to kill his friend, who was on the way to sell the company's valuable research. This was more important than ties of friendship between Kraft and McDonald. We follow procedure, Kriminalrat Sieverts had stated. For both of us the outcome will be decisive, Charlotte thought. How deeply was the Mafia involved in this crime?

CHAPTER 20

Slowly and cautiously Bill opened his eyes. There was an unpleasant noise coming from the outside. It took him a moment to recognize the source. It was the sputtering sound of a motorbike that someone tried to start without success. Bill closed his eyes again, hoping that the noise would go away, which was not the case. He opened his eyes again and looked around. Where was he? He slowly moved his left hand until it reached Ulrike's arm. He listened to her soft breathing. Then he checked his watch on the nightstand. It was 6:30 in the morning. Through the curtains he could see the early sunlight. He turned around and decided to remain in bed to recover from a turbulent day. Had it been a successful day? Definitely, from Ulrike's point of view. She got the interview and wrote an article that should make a big difference in the public perception of the Stollberg case. For him the outcome had been mixed. The meeting with Kraft in Hamburg had left a sour taste in his mouth. It bothered him more than he was ready to admit. There was the sense of betrayal. Werner was not supposed to shadow him and use him to find Stefano Brindisi. Of course, there was the counter argument that he should have informed Kraft and Herberg of Brindisi's hiding place as soon as he found out. He had also violated the rules by not sharing information. Why? He had done that because of Ulrike. But when he looked at the situation in Fuhlsbüttel more soberly, what bothered him most was the fact that he had been used. Someone had indeed played him. Although he realized that the outcome had been good for all parties, he felt diminished. It was his professional pride that got in the way. He was not eager to see Werner

Kraft, not to mention Charlotte Herberg, who gave the orders. But according to Kraft, she was not behind the successful tracking. Who did this? On the way back to Berlin, he and Ulrike had discussed the problem. They were unable to come up with a persuasive answer. Had someone put a cookie on his laptop? But his computer was well protected. Finally, they had just given up, since otherwise the endeavor yesterday had been successful. I'm glad that this mission will come to an end very soon, he thought. But was that really true? His relationship with Ulrike had never been better. What would happen to them once his firm terminated him, as he expected. Did he have other options than returning to New York City or perhaps Chicago? In either case, he would lose Ulrike. This was a very unpleasant thought, which he immediately pushed to the background. Instead, with his left arm he reached over and very gently touched her arm. Finally, the noise from the motorbike stopped. What, if I just stay in Berlin for a while? Who will miss me? I can tell my parents that I'm considering the law. That would give me time to carefully look at my options. What he wanted to avoid more than anything else was a repeat of his last departure two years ago when he found himself all by himself at the airport, while Ulrike was on an urgent assignment.

Bill decided to take his shower before Ulrike would stir. When he looked at his face in the mirror, he noticed that he needed a shave. He checked for a razor and shaving cream in vain. This was one more reason to get back to Brandenburger Hof. For me it's time to pack my things and move out before they charge my personal account. When he was already dressed and busy with the coffee machine in the kitchen, he heard Ulrike moving to the bathroom. He tried to set up breakfast as best as he could. There were at least eggs in the refrigerator, which encouraged him to look for a pan and work on scrambled eggs. Also, he discovered sliced bread that could be toasted and remnants of jam. It looked almost like a regular breakfast, he told himself, while setting the table. From the bedroom, he heard Ulrike's voice. It must be a phone call, but he couldn't figure out to whom she was speaking. When she finally appeared in the kitchen, finding breakfast ready, she was all smiles. Bill offered her a cup of fresh coffee, which was graciously received. Ulrike was in a good mood.

"I just talked to Charlotte," Ulrike opened the conversation. "They expect the arrest to occur very soon. His transport to Berlin has been arranged. There will be a press conference this afternoon, which I will cover, of course."

"I thought, this might have been Birgit Hansen," Bill exclaimed. "There will be an unpleasant surprise at her house very soon, I suppose."

"I'm sorry about that," Ulrike replied, sitting down at the kitchen table, "but the arrest doesn't change the basic situation. Brindisi can explain his presence in the van. My article will redirect the attention of the public."

"Let's hope so," Bill interjected, pouring himself a cup of coffee. "I wouldn't be surprised if Birgit Hansen will reach out to you after the arrest. After all, this was not her plan."

"She will have to focus immediately on the defense strategy," Ulrike declared. "I know the local scene and could recommend a good lawyer to her."

"What about his own family? Won't they want to be consulted?" Bill asked.

"I'm sure they care," Ulrike replied. "But in this situation advice from another lawyer might be the most important move. My sense is that Stefano Brindisi is in good hands with Birgit Hansen."

"What makes you think so?" Bill asked.

"Observing them yesterday in her home," Ulrike said in a soft voice. "I think she is in it all the way."

"Lucky man"

"Lucky man indeed."

For a while they were just busy with their breakfast. Bill went back to the stove and prepared scrambled eggs, while Ulrike focused on making toast. Finally, Bill resumed the conversation.

"At what time is the meeting of the editors?"

"At 9:00, and I should check my mail before that."

"I have to get back to the hotel, to get a fresh shirt and a shave among other things, but there may be other stuff as well. Can you give me a lift?"

"In that case, we are already in a hurry," Ulrike declared. "Can you be ready in ten minutes?"

"No problem, all I've to do is finish my toast and grab my gear,"

Of course, it took them twenty minutes before they climbed into her little Fiat. It was a sunny morning and both were confident that things would take a positive turn. When they arrived at Brandenburger Hof, Ulrike promised to be in touch after the meeting. Inside the building, Bill walked straight to the elevator until he heard the voice of the clerk at the reception calling him.

"Mr. McDonald, there's a letter here for you. Looks important."

Bill walked over to receive the large brown envelope. It took him no more than a few seconds to recognize the sender. It was his law firm. There was no rush to open it, he thought, because there could be little doubt about the content. In his room, he placed the letter on the small desk together with his laptop. He took his leather coat off and threw it on his unused bed. Then, he noticed something strange. The way he had thrown the jacket exposed the underside of the left lapel. There he saw the head of a small pin. He was positive that he had not put a pin there. He picked the jacket up to investigate the lapel. He removed the short pin and studied the head. This was no ordinary pin, he realized. This was a tracking device that someone had placed there, certainly after he arrived in Berlin. When was it placed there and who did it? Kraft had denied to be connected with this and Bill was inclined to believe him. But who had succeeded? It had to be someone who was familiar with his mission in Berlin and was also aware of his connection with Ulrike. Charlotte Herberg came to mind. He carefully placed the pin on the desk next to the envelope. He had to think about this. But first, he decided to open the letter. He glanced at the page. There it was.

<Dear Mr. McDonald, in view of necessary changes at our firm, we regret to inform you that your services are no longer needed. Accordingly, your appointment at our firm has been terminated. We herewith ask you to submit your expenses, for which you will be duly reimbursed, as long as we

find them reasonable and adequately documented. Files and other documents you have discovered and retained in connection with your mission should be delivered to this firm without further notice. Also, you will find enclosed a check, covering three months of your annual salary. This will allow you to find a new position without undue pressure. With our best wishes, Sincerely, Andrew Taylor for the partners.>

Indeed, there was a check enclosed. He also noticed that his old mentor Amos Hinchcroft had received a copy, which meant that by now also his father would be informed. This was also a clean break with Hinchcroft, because their former partner, had hired Bill. They had decided to remain close to Alerta despite their client's ethical violations. This is fine with me, Bill thought. Actually, it comes at a good time. I'm ready to open a new page. But he found it much harder to fill this page with a concrete picture. Bill turned away from the table and began collecting his things. Ten minutes later, he walked with his briefcase and traveling bag to the elevator, ready to check out. When he arrived at the reception, the clerk who had checked him in was on duty again.

"You are leaving us, sir?" he asked.

"Yes, please prepare the bill and make sure that all items are clearly marked and properly dated."

"Expense account, sir, I understand. Sorry to see you leave," the clerk said.

While Bill was waiting for the final bill, he took his phone out and tried to reach Ulrike. There was no answer. She must be in the meeting, he thought. He left a brief text message. He was still waiting for the bill, when his phone was ringing. It was Werner Kraft who informed him of a press conference this afternoon that he might want to attend.

"Herberg is going to inform the media that Brindisi has been arrested," Kraft exclaimed.

"I know that already. Why should I listen to the announcement? Remember, Werner, I was there."

"You are still angry, Bill. We need to talk. I didn't choose the method. I followed orders."

"Is that all you have to say for yourself? Werner!"

"See you this afternoon, Bill," Kraft replied. Then his voice was gone.

Because she had to find a parking space for her car, Ulrike arrived late. She barely found a seat close to the wall in the large meeting room of the *Morgenspiegel*. The editor-in-chief, a man in his early sixties, had already begun with a brief summary of the important issues of the day. One of them was the upcoming election and the perennial budget deficit of the city. He also mentioned a growing sense of vulnerability among the citizens of the metropolis, which showed itself in the greater presence of radical movements on both sides of the political spectrum. Ulrike was pleasantly surprised by this view. It seemed to her like a perspective that would include her reporting on the city's tougher crime scene. She had worked on her piece on Stefano Brindisi and the role of organized crime until the early morning hours when she was finally satisfied with the result and had submitted her article as an attachment to her email to the editor-in-chief and the section chief, her boss. Turning the interview into an article about the role of organized crime in Berlin had not been an easy task, because she had to preserve the exciting crime story and at the same time develop a more general argument. When she was done, she was confident that there would be a prominent place for the piece in the next days' edition of the newspaper. Finding and interviewing the presumed murderer of Herwig Stollberg was an extraordinary story. It was bolder and more exciting than what her colleagues had to offer. Once the editor-in-chief finished his overview, he asked the section chiefs to present their issues and materials. The first point on the agenda would be the title page. Ulrike's article was mentioned once or twice in the discussion. But despite the provocative title "Who really killed Herwig Stollberg?", there was not enough support. It was moved to the local news section. Then something unexpected happened. Her boss expressed doubts about the usefulness of the entire article.

"I'm not sure this article, in its present form, is the right thing for our paper," she interjected, raising her voice, while looking at the editor-in-chief. "There is a certain sensationalism that may be good for the *Berliner Morgenpost* but not for us, at least not in my opinion. There is some useful information that should be published in our local section. But it should be rewritten and substantially shortened. I'm glad to assist with that."

There was complete silence in the room. All present realized what had happened. The wings of a promising young reporter were being clipped. This reporter had been a favorite of the editor-in-chief. What would he do next? He just shrugged his shoulders.

"If you are willing to spend your time on this, Annegret, go ahead," he said returning her gaze with indifference. "We certainly do not support sensationalism, do we?"

Ulrike had followed this exchange in horror. She had hoped for a spirited defense by the editor-in-chief. But he had treated the whole thing as an internal difference of opinion between a reporter and a section chief. He had treated the criticism of her boss as petty, but he had withdrawn his support for her work in public. This was a major blow at a moment when she had expected to succeed. Her heart was beating fast and her face had become pale. She had the sense that the colleagues next to her were seeking greater physical distance. Now, she had to pay the price for seeking the limelight, for her obvious ambition. She was shown her place in the hierarchy. Her article would be edited to such an extent that it would become unrecognizable. She felt like leaving the room, but she realized that this move would seal her fate at the *Morgenspiegel*. She had to sit through the meeting, keep a straight face, and later ask the section chief for advice. I have to be on my knees and eat dirt, Ulrike thought.

When the meeting was over, she tried to get the attention of the editor-in-chief, but he avoided looking in her direction and left the room accompanied by the editor of the business section. Ulrike rushed down the hall to avoid any interaction and ran down the staircase to the level of her office. She was close to tears and furious at the same time. It had been a carefully planned public humiliation. She was too upset to think clearly. Where was Bill when he was needed? Then she remembered that most likely he would be informed that he had been fired. Outside, the sun was shining, but this was not a good day. Everything had looked so promising. I must calm down. We have lost a battle, but we must ultimately win the war. What's my next move? There will be a report about Brindisi's role in the Stollberg case on page 10 of tomorrow's edition. It will be toned down to such an extent that the readers won't get the story's relevance. Maybe that was the point. For the first time, it dawned on her that there might be more involved than the jealousy of an older colleague. Could it be that the *Morgenspiegel* did not want to push her line of argument? Is the mayor's office influencing the editor-in-chief? Or the owner of the paper? Am I becoming paranoid? What is my next move? I will have to contact Birgit Hansen and prepare her for the latest development. This would be another blow after the unsuspected presence of the police and Brindisi's arrest early this morning. She must be even more upset than I am. And I have to find out what happened to Bill. She noticed that he had called, but there was only a brief message that he was leaving the hotel with his stuff.

Ulrike took her coat and left the office. She needed a walk to clear her head without running into colleagues. Outside the building, she walked in the direction of a small coffee shop where she could find a quiet corner to make her calls. Although it was fairly crowded, she discovered a quiet isolated table. She ordered a double espresso, before she got her phone out. Birgit Hansen responded to her call almost immediately.

"I hoped you would be in touch," she said in a low voice. "Things didn't quite turn out the way we planned."

"No, they didn't," Ulrike replied. "Where are you right now?"

"In an express train to Berlin, where I will arrive in an hour to be present when the police will start Stefano's interrogation. He was very upset when the police knocked at our door this morning. How could this happen?"

There was a moment of silence. Ulrike tried to find words.

"We are still trying to figure this out," Ulrike replied, not mentioning Bill's role.

"What about the story in your paper?"

"This is why I'm calling. There will be a story in tomorrow's edition," Ulrike said, "but it will not be the story I wrote and submitted. I ran into rather fierce resistance this morning at the meeting."

"Why?"

"I haven't quite figured that out either," Ulrike replied. "Sorry, it has been a setback."

"I really counted on your story for shaping the public perception of Stefano's case. We have to find another way. Can we meet late this morning, before the expected press conference, which I mean to attend?"

"I can pick you up at the train station."

"Great, my train arrives at 11:45. Meet me on the platform. My car is at the end of the train."

"I'll be there."

Ulrike was surprised how calm Birgit Hansen's reaction had been. First, she had to deal with the unexpected arrest and now with the failure of a plan she had worked out to protect Brindisi. She checked her watch. She had half an hour to get to Central Station, enough time to catch up with Bill.

Kriminalrat Sieverts had set the press conference for 14:00 hours. It was supposed to be brief, informing the public of the arrest of the second suspect in the Stollberg homicide case. He meant to be present but he put Charlotte as the leading investigator in charge. In the morning Charlotte had gathered her special team to go over the available evidence and rehearsed the strategy for the interrogation of the suspect. As Charlotte had emphasized in the meeting, they knew that Brindisi had not been at the wheel. If he was responsible for the death of his friend, he could have been guilty only by giving the order to the driver. In fact, Charlotte anticipated that Esposito and his lawyer would argue that he was merely doing what he was told. And, on the other hand, Brindisi's defense would probably try to show that he was merely a passenger who had no prior knowledge of the driver's plan. There was evidence for both scenarios. What spoke in favor of Brindisi's involvement was his possible, even likely awareness of Stollberg's severe financial problems, which motivated him to offer the results of his recent research on the black market. Brindisi acted in order to protect his company, that is, his own interests. Esposito, on the other hand, would have acted as a member of the gang that had loaned large sums of money to Stollberg and was determined to protect its interests. But why kill him? However, there was also the possibility of a financial involvement in KreuzbergChem. The interview with Brindisi's parents at least suggested this possibility. After almost two hours of intense discussion, it had become clear that the available evidence was not conclusive. Maybe, both sides were finally in agreement that Stollberg had to be eliminated. But if this were the case, the gang should have left Brindisis in peace, which was not the case. Especially McDonald's reports undercut this assumption. The gang, including Esposito, were after Brindisi, although the reason was not yet clear.

Kriminalrat Sieverts had hoped for a small press conference – a few local papers and radio stations would show up, and the whole thing would be over after fifteen minutes. When Charlotte entered the room, she immediately realized that their expectation had been wrong. There was a larger group of reporters, including well-known reporters from national newspapers and TV stations. Something had changed. These journalists would not show up for a local homicide case, unless the victim was famous. Charlotte looked at Sieverts for an explanation, but he appeared to be as clueless as she was. He just shrugged his shoulders. Only Werner Kraft, who had delivered Brindisi late this morning, was smiling. In the audience, Charlotte recognized familiar faces, among them Ulrike and the two officers of the LKA Hesse. In one of the corners, she also discovered Bill McDonald, whose face was stern. Why was he here? Would he ask questions about the background of their search? She was not planning to go into details. As far as she was concerned, all the public had a right to know at this point was that a suspect in the Stollberg case had finally been apprehended. Accordingly, she made a brief statement and then allowed a few questions. Within minutes it became clear that it was difficult to limit the number of questions. There were simple factual questions concerning the circumstances of Brindisi's arrest, which Charlotte handled without going into the minute elements. But the line of questioning, particularly form the national newspapers, indicated that they perceived the Stollberg case as part of a larger problem, namely the spread of organized crime in Germany. The focus shifted from the victim to the company of the victim. This shift became especially clear in the question posed by the reporter representing DER SPIEGEL, the famous German political magazine. "Can you elaborate on the connection between Stefano Brindisi, a co-owner of KreuzbergChem, and Bruno Esposito, a known member of a Mafia family?" Charlotte was still looking for an appropriate answer, when she heard Sieverts' voice: "This is the kind of question, sir, that we will have to answer, but not today. The purpose of this meeting is to inform you of the arrest of Stefano Brindisi. We will certainly keep you posted. Thank you for your interest."

The meeting was adjourned. Charlotte looked at Sieverts, who gave her a brief nod, telling her this way that the ball was back in her court. She could proceed to begin with the interrogation later this afternoon. She was about to move over to Kraft to find out where she would find the prisoner, when a tall slender woman in her thirties stood in front of her. "Frau Hauptkommissarin, I want to introduce myself," she said in a soft voice. "I am Birgit Hansen, Stefano Brindisi's lawyer. I understand that you mean to interrogate him later this afternoon. There will be no interrogation without my presence. I want you to understand this."

Charlotte looked into her dark gray eyes and instantly caught her determination. This woman will be a fierce opponent, she thought.

"We will follow procedure, Frau Hansen," she replied in a voice that left no doubt about her own determination. "As usual, you will have to present your credentials to be admitted."

There was a faint smile on Birgit Hansen's face, before she turned around and left.

"What did she want?" Kraft, who had observed the encounter, asked when he approached Charlotte to report on the latest development.

"She introduced herself as Brindisi's lawyer," Charlotte exclaimed.

"She will not yield an inch," Kraft said, "very polite but firm in her decisions, as we found out when we arrested Brindisi."

"Personal interest?"

"Definitely personal," Kraft asserted.

When the initial interrogation began two hours later, Charlotte was prepared to be interrupted and blocked by Birgit Hansen every step of the way. She expected a strategy of delay, where the police have to prove every factual detail, where every argument will be immediately questioned with the assumption that the police are acting in bad faith. Given the available evidence, in particular Brindisi's fingerprints inside the van, this strategy made sense. The defense would persistently raise doubts, thereby undermining the argument. After a few questions, however, it became apparent that Birgit Hansen had decided on a very different strategy. She offered her client's cooperation with the police, under the condition that he would be immediately released from jail and would be available for questioning at agreed upon times.

"My client is physically and psychologically exhausted. He should not be jailed for a crime that he didn't commit. We offer full cooperation with the law and believe that this cooperation is the only way to solve this case," Hansen asserted, facing Charlotte and Kraft at the other side of the table.

Charlotte could not completely hide her surprise, glancing to the side, she noticed an expression of surprise on Kraft's face as well. There was a moment of silence. Hansen made no attempt to break it. She was waiting for Charlotte's response.

"I am truly pleased to hear that your client has decided to cooperate with us, in order to solve the crime," Charlotte declared, raising her voice slightly, while keeping her eyes focused on the lawyer. "However, I 'm not in a position to grant the release from Untersuchungshaft (detention awaiting trial). Only a judge can do that, as you must be aware of."

"Yes, I'm aware of that, of course," Hansen replied, "So, I formally ask for the release of my client on the basis of his mental and physical condition and his readiness to fully cooperate with the police."

She handed a prepared statement to Charlotte, who glanced at it.

"Let me explain our approach, Hauptkommissarin," Hansen continued. "We believe that the Stollberg case can be solved only in the context of a broader inquiry into the history of my client's relationship with Herwig Stollberg and the history of their company, KreuzbergChem. He has become part of the case, but he is innocent of Stollberg's death. He is prepared to submit a full statement, which would serve as the basis of our future conversations."

As Charlotte immediately realized, this was a bold move. Birgit Hansen must be very certain that she can prove her client's innocence, Charlotte thought. And it would be a bold move for us as well. She was not sure at all how Sieverts would react, not to mention his superiors, for whom this case had become a political liability.

"I'll immediately forward your motion to Kriminalrat Sieverts, who will prepare the opinion for the judge. In any case, there will be no decision today, which means that Herr Brindisi will stay in our custody at least until tomorrow."

Since Birgit Hansen agreed to these conditions, the meeting was over before it had seriously begun. The two Hesse LKA officers, who had observed the meeting through a window from the outside, expressed their deep disappointment. For them, this was a lost opportunity to assess the economic context of the case. Charlotte promised to keep them posted by sharing Brindisi's statement. It became clear in their brief conversation, that in principle they welcomed this development, which would more fully expose the economic aspect of the case.

For Charlotte, the unexpected brevity of the meeting had one advantage: she would be at home much earlier than expected. When she opened the door of her apartment, its stillness came over her. Here she would be alone again until the next human contact at her office. She took her coat off and walked into the living room. There she sat down in her big armchair, putting her legs up and closing her eyes. This was the first really quiet moment of the day. She didn't even feel like turning on the TV for the evening news. There would be more of the same: the budget crisis, the upcoming elections, disagreements about car emission standards. For a moment, she wanted to be free of these worries, think of a vacation with Bernd later this year when he was back from Australia. Lately, his emails had been shorter and more sporadic, which she had initially hardly noticed, because she herself was preoccupied with the Stollberg case, which had the tendency to change and broaden exactly when she felt that she was getting closer to a conclusion. The long conversation with Sieverts the other day about the concerns of the commissioner had left her worried, since it was turning a criminal investigation into a political case with uncontrollable ramifications. Sieverts had opened her eyes to the political aspects of the case but also assured her that he would fully back her in her examinations of the facts, where ever they would lead her. That was reassuring. Still, in this situation she missed Bernd even more. His presence and advice would have been welcome. He knew her world in a way that her former partner, an architect, had never known and appreciated. She must have fallen asleep. A phone was ringing. It took her a few seconds to realize that it was her own phone. When she picked it up, she heard a familiar deep voice:

"Hallo, Lotte, I was about to give up. I thought you were out."

"Bernd, it's you. No, I must have fallen asleep in my chair. I have been home for an hour already because the interrogation was postponed." Charlotte replied.

"It's good to hear your voice. I tried yesterday, but there was no answer."

"Where are you right now?"

"Back at my daughter's house. We had been traveling for a few days. She wanted to show me the countryside."

"And? How was it?"

Interesting"

"Meaning what?"

"Also, rather strange, outside my idea of nature."

"Ready to come home?"

"No doubt about that"

"You are being missed."

"I'm glad to hear that. Any particular reason?"

"The Stollberg case is becoming more difficult."

"Why? No arrests?"

"The opposite, two arrests and good material evidence, but external complications. Political concerns higher up. An upset commissioner and a concerned mayor, who faces an election."

"What is the mayor worried about?"

"A recent article in a local newspaper, suggesting that organized crime is penetrating Berlin."

"How does this relate to your case?"

"There is a possible connection between the death of Stollberg and the activities of a local gang. References to my case showed up in the article."

"Who's the author? You know him?"

"Published under a pseudonym. Most likely Ulrike Pfanner. All of a sudden, my case gets lots of attention. This afternoon at the press conference, the room was full of journalists sent by national papers, who would never attend a local press conference. My case has become a political football, Bernd, I don't like it."

"I understand, not a pleasant turn, but I'm afraid, Lotte, you have to run with it now."

"What do you mean by <run with it>?"

"Accept the political implication and proceed extra carefully. Stay close to the facts. Do you know who will take over Brindisi's defense?"

"I met her this afternoon, a woman by the name of Birgit Hansen, from your hometown. Do you by any chance know her?"

"Never heard her name. Did you get a sense of her strategy?"

"She advised her client to fully cooperate with us, on the condition that we don't keep him jailed. I expected the opposite, a fight about every detail to undermine our case, which is pretty solid."

"She may realize that and therefore hopes to persuade you of his innocence by putting her cards on the table, or she plans to create a public drama by stressing the political side of the case."

"Yesterday she arranged an interview with Ulrike at her house in Hamburg. Fortunately, we were informed of this in advance and could arrest him later."

"This sounds like a mystery to me. How did this happen?"

"We got a tip from the LKA Berlin. It appears that they had an eye on Ulrike Pfanner. I wasn't privy to the details. In any case, we'll continue the interrogation tomorrow. Brindisi is supposed to submit a full statement of all pertinent facts."

"Good luck, dear. Be ready for a public drama in the media. I hope you can trust Pfanner. Try to reach me when you are done, OK?" Bernd Moeller said softly.

"Thanks, and take care."

Charlotte put the receiver down and took a deep breath. She felt much better. The fatigue was gone. Now she noticed that she was hungry and went to her kitchen. She found part of a meatloaf in the refrigerator that would suffice as a meal. She heated it up and finished it at her kitchen table with a glass of her favorite Chianti.

CHAPTER 21

After the brief press conference had ended, Birgit Hansen was looking for Ulrike, who was standing in a corner engaged in a conversation with a young man, probably the American private detective. She wanted to arrange a meeting with the journalist before she focused her attention on the upcoming interrogation. Still, she hesitated to approach Ulrike, since she realized from the way they were standing next to each other that she would interrupt a private conversation. Fortunately, Ulrike noticed her and with a gesture invited her to come closer.

"Ms. Hansen, I would like to introduce Bill McDonald, a private Detective from New York. You didn't have a chance to meet him last night in Hamburg. We have been working together on the Stollberg case," Ulrike exclaimed.

"Pleased to meet you," Birgit Hansen replied. "Why is an American detective interested in the Stollberg case?"

"There is no short answer to this question," Bill replied in German, choosing his words carefully.

"No, indeed, this is not the time and place to delve into this aspect of the case," Ulrike declared. "I suggest that we meet tonight after the interrogation and compare notes. Then Bill can explain his interest in the case."

"How about 8:00 tonight at my hotel, the Albrechtshof?" Hansen suggested.

They agreed to meet there for drinks in the bar. After this brief conversation, Birgit Hansen moved to the front of the room, where she approached Charlotte, while Bill and Ulrike left the room together.

Within a minute Bill noticed that Ulrike's mood had completely changed. From looking at her, he couldn't figure out whether she was depressed or just very angry. He took her hand, trying to see her face.

"What's wrong?" he asked in a low voice.

"Not now, Bill," she replied. "It hasn't been a good day."

"No, it hasn't been a good day at all," Bill confirmed, holding her hand tightly. "But we are in this together. Aren't we?"

Ulrike turned around, looking into his eyes. Then she gave him a faint smile.

"You have been fired?" she asked.

"Yes, they fired me," Bill said. "I received the official letter this morning when I got back to the Brandenburger Hof."

"My article will not be in tomorrow's edition," Ulrike said in a very low voice.

"How come?"

"My boss blocked it."

"The editor-in-chief?"

No, the section chief, but he didn't come to my aid. In fact, he did nothing."

Ulrike's voice expressed anger and disappointment.

"Let's go home and talk about it before we meet Birgit Hansen. I mean, if I can stay with you for a few days. Remember, my official mission is over. I'm on my own and homeless."

Ulrike just nodded, pressing Bill's hand.

"Let's go home," she confirmed.

Albrechtshof was an older hotel located in the vicinity of the railway station Friedrichstraße in the old center of Berlin. It took Ulrike five minutes to find a parking place for her little Fiat. There was mostly foot traffic in the narrow street, couples and groups trying to find a table in one of the many smaller and larger restaurants. Bill who had not been in this part of town was intrigued by the names of these places. One of them was called "Ständige Vertretung," another one "Kartoffelkeller."

"What is a ständige Vertretung?" Bill wanted to know.

"It was the name of the West German embassy before the fall of the wall, when the two Germanys did not fully recognize each other but of course needed to negotiate agreements."

"Weird," Bill declared.

"No longer our problem, Bill," Ulrike exclaimed.

From their parking space, close to the river, they walked to the hotel, a building from the turn of the century with high but narrow windows. They found the bar in the back of the building, where they discovered Birgit Hansen sitting at a small table with a glass of white wine in front of her.

She appeared to be in a good mood. At Least, she was all smiles when she saw Ulrike and Bill.

"Please join me," she exclaimed, while she was signaling to the bar keeper that his services were needed. "What can I order for you?"

They settled on white wine and a Bourbon. Once the orders were out of the way, Ulrike was eager to hear more about the first interrogation.

"Actually, it went the way it was planned," Birgit Hansen explained. "The meeting was brief and succinct. I could see the surprise on the face of the police."

"How come?" Ulrike asked.

"They expected confrontation. Instead, I offered full cooperation if they release Stefano, who is not in good shape, as you know."

"Will they accept this deal?" Bill asked.

"At least they accepted my motion," Birgit Hansen replied.

"What about the defense attorney?" Ulrike asked.

"I have made a couple of calls," Hansen said. "So far I haven't settled on a specific person."

"Let me mention a name," Ulrike exclaimed. "I have seen him in action several times. He is fabulous. Committed, sharp, aggressive if need be. His name is Rudolf Wendt."

"Can he handle the political side of a criminal case, which will be central to Stefano's defense."

"No doubt, that's where he shines. Give him a call," Ulrike exclaimed.

Hansen nodded and made a note on her smart phone.

"I have to prepare the ground for the defense very carefully, because most likely it will be a situation where the driver will argue that he was ordered by Stefano to run Stollberg down."

"Maybe, Bill can help you with this," Ulrike interjected. "He was sent to retrieve a lost file that Stollberg supposedly had with him when he was on his way to the meeting with the middleman."

"Yes, indeed, what happened to the file? Stefano mentioned it several times," Hansen asked.

"I was sent by my law firm to find the lost file," Bill replied. "In the version I was given, Stollberg had sold his research to Alerta, an American pharma company, and died in an accident before he could deliver the goods."

"What do you mean by <this version>?" Hansen asked, looking at Bill with a curious expression.

"As it turned out, Stollberg never sold his research to Alerta," Bill said. "Instead, he accepted a better offer from an Indian company. A German middleman was supposed to receive the file at the Brandenburger Hof. But the meeting never occurred and the file has been missing ever since."

"What about this middleman, have you talked to him?" Hansen insisted.

"No, unfortunately, before I could meet him he was killed at his house in Bad Homburg."

"My god, who did that? The Mafia?"

"No, more likely another party that was and still is interested in the research," Bill asserted.

Birgit Hansen's facial expression changed from surprise to shock. Her eyes were widening.

"My God," she exclaimed, "this is horrible. So, there have been two murders because of the file."

"In fact, so far there have been three, because the hitman, who killed Kellner, the Frankfurt contact, was found dead in the Main river a few days later. You have to keep that in mind when you look for the file."

"Do we have a choice? Stefano reminded me that access to Herwig's recent research is critical for the company. He is convinced that it cannot survive without it."

"Have you been in touch with David Klein, the third partner," Ulrike asked.

"Not yet, but I'm meaning to look him up to get his input," Hansen said. "While Stefano was hiding, I avoided contact, since I suspected that the police would keep his phone under surveillance. We were never sure whom to fear more, the police or the gang."

"In my opinion, the gang is the more serious threat," Bill exclaimed. "I regret that our visit did lead to Stefano's arrest, but this is much better than being in the hands of the gang."

"How did the police manage to follow you to my house?" Hansen asked, looking at both of them. Ulrike shrugged her shoulders, while avoiding eye contact. It was Bill, who gave the answer: "After the press conference, I had a brief chat with two officers of the LKA Hesse, with whom I have been friendly. I showed them a little pin that I had found on my leather coat, clearly a surveillance device. They think it was placed there by their Berlin LKA colleagues to keep an eye on me and Ulrike. In their eyes we are meddling with the search for organized crime in Berlin."

"Do you believe them?" Hansen asked softly.

"Frankly, I'm not sure. There is another possible version. It was they who put the pin under the lapel when we had lunch at the Brandenburger Hof."

Why?"

"They are just as curious about the rise of organized crime in Berlin. That's why they follow the Stollberg case. As they explained to me, their primary interest is the economy of organized crime."

"If they did it, that wouldn't be a pleasant discovery," Hansen added.

Bill just shook his head. He was still struggling with the discovery. Ulrike, who noticed his reluctance, turned to Birgit Hansen, trying to change the topic.

"For a successful defense, you will need public opinion on your side. Have you given thought to that?"

"It has been on my mind all the time," Hansen replied. "It was the reason I contacted you after learning about your opinion piece. Too bad that your article was blocked. Maybe we can use the material in a different format."

"Looking at this from an American perspective," Bill interjected, "I would make use of the social media. You have a live interview. That's hot stuff. How about a podcast?"

"Of course," Hansen said in a low voice, "I thought of that route. But I'm also afraid of it, because it's almost impossible to control. It could also turn against Stefano."

There was a moment of silence. Birgit Hansen glanced at Ulrike with a question in her eyes.

"Do you have a choice at this point?" Ulrike asked.

Birgit Hansen shrugged her shoulders, while taking a sip from her glass.

"I still own the interview, since my paper didn't accept my story," Ulrike asserted. "we could turn it into a podcast."

"That would be useful," Hansen exclaimed.

"I have listened to it several times," Bill interjected. "it has the potential for grabbing the public."

"Let's do it," Ulrike declared, raising her voice. "Let's give Stefano Brindisi a voice. Cheers."

She raised her glass. Bill and Birgit Hansen did the same.

The continuation of the interrogation on the following morning was set for 10:00am. Charlotte gave herself an hour for preparing her questions and arrived at her office by 9:00. Before she had a chance to look at her notes, she was asked to come to Kriminalrat Sievert's office. There the atmosphere was as frosty as usual. She was asked to wait, and the young assistant made sure to ignore her presence as much as possible. When Sieverts stepped out of his office to invite her, Charlotte noticed his worried face. He was his distant polite self again. What he had to share did not brighten Charlotte's mood. The Stollberg case had become <Chefsache,> there would be no move and no decision without checking back with the hierarchy. The commissioner insisted on being informed all the time and having the final say.

"How are we supposed to do our work under these conditions? They don't trust us?" Charlotte asked.

"It seems that way."

"What's the purpose?"

"They want the case to get as little media attention as possible. Remember, the mayor is up for reelection."

"That's terrible and unacceptable. We are dealing with a homicide."

"We are also dealing with an election and the approval rating of our mayor. By the way, the commissioner will send his assistant to be present during the interrogations."

"Lucky us," was all Charlotte was able to say.

Thirty minutes later she entered the interrogation room. She looked at Birgit Hansen and her client at the other side of the table. On her side, she found Kraft and the commissioner's assistant, giving her a brief nod. The lawyer was clearly poised to respond, while Brindisi looked unfocused and exhausted. Again, the meeting was very brief, since Hansen only presented her client's written statement, which covered several pages. Charlotte promised to read it and resume the meeting in the afternoon with questions. For her, the next steps were clear. She immediately shared a copy with the commissioner's assistant, sent a copy to Sievert's office and created several copies for the meeting of her SOKO, where they would discuss the details. The basic claim was that Brindisi was innocent. He had been concerned about Stollberg's decision to sell his research to a third party and had accepted Esposito's urgent invitation to track Stollberg, because he wanted to talk to him before the meeting with the middleman at the hotel. But why was Esposito, a member of a gang, there in the first place? Here things became murky. According to Brindisi, they had loaned money to Stollberg and somehow gained a stake in the company. They meant to block the sale at all cost, including murder. This was clearly a highly unusual narrative, but it was confirmed by statements of Brindisi's parents in an earlier interview. KreuzbergChem, it seemed, had also served as a means to launder money. This was exactly what the mayor's office was afraid of. For the defense, on the other hand, this was the crucial point: Brindisi was the victim of criminal pressure. He was hunted by the gang because he was supposed to have knowledge of the missing file. It took the group the rest of the morning to dissect the document and prepare the line of questioning Charlotte would pursue in the afternoon. At a later point, she would confront Esposito with Brindisi's version of the events. Would he change his story?

Charlotte realized that there was another urgent task. The revelation that KreuzbergChem had been used by organized crime to launder dirty money called for further investigation. Sieverts had ordered her to secure all financial records of the company, going back to its beginning. It was early afternoon when she and her team knocked on the company's door in Kreuzberg. She asked the secretary, who opened the door, to speak to David Klein. It took a few minutes until Klein showed up and invited her to come in. He seemed not to be surprised at all by her unannounced visit. Charlotte was not quite sure how to read his polite expression that treated her team's presence as a minor inconvenience:

"Please come in, Hauptkommissarin," Klein exclaimed. "You and your team have been expected."

"I'm glad to hear that." Charlotte declared. "I hope I can count on your full cooperation."

"We do everything to please the police," he said. "Even the more absurd things. I understand that Stefano has been arrested and our company is suspected of being part of organized crime."

Charlotte glanced at him, trying to read his face. What was the point of his weird answers? He clearly knew more than she had disseminated at the press conference. She decided to ignore his strange manner and come to the point:

"I have a court order to ask for your entire financial records."

"Go ahead," Klein asserted, raising his voice, "our bookkeeper will show you where they are. This is absurd. Do you seriously assume that Stefano Brindisi and Herwig Stollberg were Mafiosi, using their small start-up to put dirty money to work?!"

"Herr Klein, what Brindisi told us, sounds different. But yes, there seems to be a connection with organized crime. That's why we are here."

"Yes, you are not the first one to tell me. This morning Frau Pfanner, the reporter of the *Morgenspiegel*, showed up with questions that I couldn't answer. When I joined the company two years ago because they urgently needed a chemical engineer, I realized two things. First, the company needed more capital and, second, the bookkeeping was in bad shape. That had not been done in a professional manner. I persuaded the partners to take care of this problem by hiring an accounting firm to do our books."

"Had you any idea?" Charlotte probed.

"I was told that the initial capital had been raised by the family, mostly by the Brindisi family. It's absurd to assume that Stefano was connected to organized crime. Completely absurd."

"Do you think, he is responsible for the death of Stollberg?" Charlotte asked.

There was a moment of silence. Klein was staring at her.

"Is this the latest theory?" he replied, his voice showing irritation and anger.

Charlotte remained silent.

"This is equally absurd. They were close friends. There were personal problems on Herwig's side. As far as I could see, Stefano tried to help him."

"You had any idea of the nature of these problems?" Charlotte asked.

"No, I didn't. I had little to do with their private lives," Klein replied in a low voice. "Let me tell you something. The past weeks have been hell. First, we lost our chief chemist, then his close collaborator disappears and we are told that there is a warrant out on him. Meanwhile, I'm struggling to keep the company alive. If Brindisi doesn't come back in the very near future, our survival is going to be in jeopardy."

"I'm sorry to hear that," Charlotte replied. "However, it doesn't change my orders. And I have to ask you to stay in town. It's likely that we will have more questions."

Abruptly, David Klein turned around and disappeared in one of the rooms in the back. In the meantime, members of her team had collected numerous boxes containing the company's financial records. Charlotte had anticipated that this visit would not be a pleasant task. It had turned out to be worse. She had to fight a sense of futility. We have to get the facts straight, she thought. Otherwise, there will be no firm ground for a lasting solution.

On the way back to headquarters, Charlotte received a call from the Kriminalrat's office informing her that Esposito requested an urgent meeting. When she entered the interrogation room together with Werner Kraft half an hour later, she found him and his lawyer already at the table. Esposito looked nervous and distracted, as if he hardly noticed her arrival. It was the lawyer who greeted and addressed her, expressing his gratitude for her timely response to his client's request.

"My client wants to make a statement," the lawyer declared. "After carefully considering his memory, he has concluded that he was mistaken when he said that Stefano Brindisi ordered him to kill Stollberg."

Charlotte remained silent, looking first at the lawyer and then at Bruno Esposito, who avoided eye contact. This was a completely unexpected turn.

"Signor Esposito, you have to explain this change of mind to me," Charlotte exclaimed.

"I was confused when I first spoke," Esposito replied with a strong Italian accent. "Not Signor Brindisi, he was showing me the way. I lost control of the van when I had to make a sharp right turn."

Charlotte leaned back, glancing first at the speaker and then at his lawyer. This sounded highly improbable. It is a much weaker position than the prior statement. Why is his lawyer counseling him to do this? Charlotte wondered.

"Why on earth did you lose control?" Charlotte insisted. "You are an experienced professional driver."

"I drove too fast because I was in a hurry," Esposito replied.

"Come on, you have to do better, if you expect me to believe you."

Esposito just shook his head. Charlotte turned to his lawyer:

"Signor, I need more than this story. Your client has to show us that he is serious in his cooperation."

"I understand, but this is all he told me," the lawyer replied in a low voice.

When it became obvious that neither the lawyer nor his client could be persuaded to add to the initial statement, Charlotte closed the meeting. Together with Kraft she walked back to her office.

"That was a very strange meeting," Kraft exclaimed. "His statement didn't help his defense. Declaring that he just lost control of the vehicle, will not help him at the trial."

"No, you are right. It won't help him," said Charlotte, while pushing the button of the elevator. "I'm surprised that his lawyer advised him to do this."

"Brindisi was the perfect scapegoat for Esposito's former narrative, because Brindisi had a strong motive."

When they arrived at her office, Charlotte stood for a moment motionless at the center of the room with her eyes closed. Kraft, who had followed her, remained close to the door, waiting for a sign.

"What?" he finally asked.

"There is something wrong with his story," Charlotte declared. "It's not his narrative, it's the lawyer's narrative. Esposito showed no enthusiasm at all, in fact, he looked distracted. We will of course have doubts. The material evidence does not support his claim. There was no attempt to stop the van. But now there is relief for Brindisi. That's the point, Werner."

"How come? I don't follow," Kraft said.

"In this version Esposito is the fall guy," Charlotte exclaimed. "Change of plan. They don't want Brindisi in prison. They want him out, working for his company", working for their investment."

"You lost me. Who is 'they'?" Kraft asked.

"The Mafia, of course, as Brindisi explained," Charlotte asserted. Looking at the financial records has absolute priority. We have to find out if there is dirty money, And I will have to contact Sieverts. This is not good news for the mayor. He will be frustrated and become even more difficult.

When Charlotte finally came home, it was 7:00pm. It had been a difficult and stressful day. A glance at her refrigerator convinced her that there was not enough left for a decent warm meal and she was too tired to think of cooking. She put on her overcoat again and walked over to a small Greek restaurant around the corner where she was known as a regular customer. The young owner greeted her personally when she entered the restaurant and guided her to her table. Without waiting for an order, he came back with a glass of Charlotte's favorite Greek wine, which he carefully placed in front of her. Noticing that she looked exhausted, he just expressed his pleasure to see her again and left her with the menu. Charlotte was grateful for his discretion. This sense of being welcome was the reason why she liked to come here all by herself after a busy day. She could count on a good meal and the feeling of having a second home. There would be the opportunity for casual social contact without any pressure. The young owner had taken over a year ago when his father decided to retire. He had completely redone the menu, eliminating many of the heavy Greek dishes and replacing them with smaller and more refined dishes that appealed to his new customers. Like Charlotte, they were younger and more sophisticated. While Charlotte studied the menu, she was looking around. She recognized a number of familiar faces, regulars like herself. Close to the window she recognized a retired couple from next door. He had been working for an insurance company, she had been an elementary school teacher. When he recognized Charlotte at her table, he raised his beer glass to welcome her. After her stressful day, the gesture felt good. Charlotte didn't feel like talking. She just needed distance from the pressure. The commissioner's assistant had been as unpleasant and difficult as expected. At one point, he had even tried to influence the interrogation. He had discouraged all questions that would touch on the financial aspect, especially the presence of unaccounted money in the company. As a result, there had been a sharp exchange between him and Kriminalrat Sieverts, who had reminded him that he was no more than an observer. Sieverts had shielded her, possibly damaging his own career. There had not even been an opportunity to thank him. Before continuing Brindisi's interrogation later in the afternoon, she had briefly talked with the expert for financial corruption in her team, who had looked at the records of KreuzbergChem. He had confirmed disturbing irregularities in the early phase of the company, but was unwilling to define them as criminal. "It looks like dirty money, but we need more time to prove it," had been his verdict. In the interrogation, she had pushed Brindisi to explain his relationship to Esposito, his own presence in the van, and the supposed need to talk to Brindisi. Brindisi had emphasized his close relationship to Herwig Stollberg and his awareness of Stollberg's financial problems. After almost two hours of questions, there was no clear evidence that Brindisi had influenced Esposito to kill Stollberg. But on the other hand, as Sieverts had pointed out, there was also no clear evidence that he had not been involved in the death of his friend. By admitting that he wanted to prevent the sale of Stollberg's research, he also admitted to a strong motive for eliminating the person who was betraying the company. The financial aspect was at the heart of this case, as much as the mayor and his advisers disliked it. The fact that Esposito had retracted the earlier claim that Brindisi had ordered him to kill Stollberg, changed the balance in favor of Brindisi, yet not strongly enough to dismiss the case against him. I'm still uncertain, Charlotte thought. Looking at the available facts; Esposito's new narrative makes sense, but in her mind, there was still the possibility of another interpretation of these facts. What dawned on her, however, was the likely presence of organized crime in this case. The recent attempt to kidnap Dorothea Stollberg definitely demonstrated the presence and the power of the gang. I have tried too hard to separate the Stollberg murder from the criminal activities surrounding it, Charlotte thought. I wanted to have a clean case when there never was a clean case.

She was still lost in her thoughts when the owner of the restaurant served her the first course of her meal. It was a wonderful hors d'oevre consisting of sautéed mushrooms and small pieces of lamb. It was a delicate dish that she had enjoyed before when she had been here with Bernd Moeller, who had come to love the intimacy of this place. The dish immediately reminded her of him. She wished he could be here. It would be calming. What she remembered most of the lengthy meeting were the lawyer's eyes, the intense gray eyes of Birgit Hansen.

They had followed her every move. It had given the exchange a very personal character, although not a single personal word had been uttered. Neither Sieverts nor Kraft seemed to notice. Their eyes were fixated on Stefano Brindisi, who was speaking haltingly, with many interruptions and pauses. There had been moments when he seemed to be unable to cope with the numerous questions and interjections. More than once, Birgit Hansen had interrupted the process, rejecting a question or insisting on rephrasing. Although clearly inexperienced as a defense lawyer, she had been surprisingly successful in shaping the interrogation. The intensity of her performance had been extraordinary. Charlotte could still feel the emotional energy, while she was eating her dinner. Especially the fact that her motion to release Brindisi had been denied by the court had embittered Hansen. The court had argued that Brindisi might use the opportunity to influence potential witnesses, an argument Charlotte had found less than persuasive. Charlotte would have been much more concerned about the gang's possible violent interference. She had tried to convey this indirectly to Birgit Hansen, but she was not sure at all if she had understood Charlotte's assessment of the situation. The jail was an unpleasant but safe place for Brindisi.

Suddenly, her train of thought was interrupted by the ring of her smart phone. It was a message from Ulrike, asking for information about the interrogation. She just put the phone aside. Right now, she was not in the mood to respond to the media. She had the feeling that Ulrike was up to something big, a story about the Stollberg case that would catch the attention of the broad public. It would do what she resisted most, it would politicize her case. Ulrike had arranged a meeting with Brindisi in Hamburg and at the press conference she had noticed Ulrike and Birgit Hansen standing together. After that, she had expected a lead article in her paper. Instead, there had been only a brief piece in the local news. And the article did not sound like Ulrike at all. It read more like a communique of the commissioner's office. Of course, the irony of the situation was that Ulrike's activities had finally led to Brindisi's arrest.

Birgit Hansen was back at her hotel room when she received Ulrike's message, asking for details of the interrogation. She had to hold back her tears. From her point of view, it had not gone well. They had delayed her motion to release Stefano. They had not understood that he needed help now, that he needed to be in touch with a psychiatrist to get him over the trauma of watching in horror the violent death of his closest friend. Their response had been that of distant officials concerned with the fears of the public. As she had to admit to herself, she had failed to convince the two police officers in charge of Stefano's innocence. Occasionally during the exchange, she had believed that at least the woman, the Hauptkommissarin, understood Stefano's situation, but, as it turned out, she could not overcome her doubts. She was incapable of overcoming her professional suspicions. Yes, there was a strong motive for Brindisi, but there were different interpretations possible as well. Some of her questions suggested that she was trying to grasp a different narrative, but then she always fell back into the search for the murderer and once she did that, Stefano could not be excluded. There was almost no empathy. She and her colleagues were just doing their duty. She had come to realize the limits of her own power. Stefano needed a professional criminal lawyer. She would arrange a meeting with Rudolf Wendt tomorrow morning. I can't muster the necessary distance from Stefano to do a successful defense, she thought. I can do that with my own clients when we make decisions about estate law, cases that can be as personal and wrenching as this case. The idea of meeting the same police officers again was more than she could bear at this moment. She stood up and walked back and forth in her room. She realized that she needed food but didn't feel like eating. The idea of going down to the restaurant was immediately rejected. After pacing for a good ten minutes, she decided to order dinner. She looked at the menu she found on a side table. The selection was limited, but that didn't matter. She just had to eat something to keep her strength up. Finally, she called the kitchen and ordered a pea soup with a piece of bread. Only then did she answer Ulrike Pfanner's message: 'Right now, I'm too exhausted to give you a full account, hope to meet you tomorrow. Will be in touch.'

After Birgit Hansen had finished her ham and pea soup, which was surprisingly good, she felt better. She felt calmer. Maybe she had expected too much. She still had plenty of resources to influence the case. She meant to contact Stefano's parents, who were probably completely unaware of her existence. Their relationship was too new and undecided to include the parents. There were no parents on her side, anyway. They had died early, leaving her with her older brother in the hands of a grandmother. Most of her relatives lived in Kiel and Flensburg or on the other side of the Danish border. How would she introduce herself? As Stefano's lawyer or as his girlfriend? I'm officially defending your son, since I'm his girlfriend. Would that persuade his parents? Also, she had to see David Klein, the third partner. Maybe he had information and insights that would strengthen Stefano's case. She had to convince the police that Stefano had been in the van because he was concerned for the well-being of his friend, not because he was greedy. If Klein could testify, that would be helpful.

Birgit Hansen decided to lie down for a while. It was a surprisingly soft bed that almost enclosed her. On another day, this would not have pleased her, but right now it was exactly what the needed. The moment she closed her eyes, she fell asleep. When she opened her eyes again and looked around, it was 11:00pm. The nervous anxiety of the early evening was gone. She could more clearly see the path to Stefano's freedom. She got up and moved to the desk. Before I go to bed I have to make a list of all the things I have to take care of tomorrow, she thought. She took her laptop out of her travel bag. But before she created a list, she checked her email. There was a very recent message from Bill McDonald requesting additional information about the missing file. How much did Stefano Brindisi know about it? <Are we chasing a phantom?> he wrote. Then he requested a meeting. She would respond to this request tomorrow. Finally, there was a brief message from her brother, who was concerned, since he had not heard from her. She immediately answered, telling him that she was fine, right now on business in Berlin. Details had to wait until tomorrow. All she could do now was the list.

CHAPTER 22

It was 8:00 in the morning when Birgit Hansen was looking for a table in the crowded breakfast room. She was ready to turn around when one of the waiters found a small table for her close to one of the windows. She ordered coffee, a fruit cup, and a croissant and asked for a newspaper. A few minutes later she had the *Frankfurter Allgemeine Zeitung* in her hands, glancing at the headlines. Much of the news struck her as a rehash of yesterday's news, but then she noticed an opinion piece that caught her attention. The commentator focused on the growing infiltration of local start-ups by organized crime. The author pointed to a silent take-over that German law enforcement had studiously neglected, according to the motto: If we don't see it, it isn't there. There were no specific references. The author, whose name Birgit Hansen recognized as a regular contributor to the business section, proposed a special unit at the highest level to look into this matter. Was this a coincidence? A leading national newspaper doesn't devote an essay on the front page to this question out of the blue. She recalled the crowded room at the press conference following Stefano's arrest. Something was happening. She went to the newspaper rack and searched for the *Süddeutsche Zeitung*. There she found an article on business and crime on the second page. She postponed reading it, since her breakfast had arrived. The first cup of the strong coffee lifted her completely into the day, reminding her of all the things she had put on her list. But after finishing her breakfast, she decided to return briefly to the article and at least get the main points. There was a similar concern for the erosion of lawful business by the influx of dubious capital. She was about to leave when she noticed Ulrike standing at the entrance of the breakfast room. Hansen waved her hand, inviting the reporter to join her.

"What a pleasant surprise," she exclaimed." I was meaning to call you. No need for that anymore. What brings you to this place early in the morning?"

Before she answered, Ulrike gestured to the waiter, asking him for a cup and filled it with what was left in Hansen's pot of coffee.

"I happened to be in the neighborhood and decided to look you up to figure out what the next steps would be."

Hansen realized that Ulrike's claim was a stretch, but accepted the ruse to find out what the real purpose of the surprise meeting was.

"Later you will be preoccupied with finding a suitable place for Stefano and getting him settled in," Ulrike said in a low voice.

"What do you mean by finding a suitable place?" Hansen asked.

"So, you haven't heard yet", Ulrike cried. "Your motion has been granted. He will be released later this morning. Congratulations. I'm very happy for both of you."

There was a moment of silence. Birgit Hansen was unable to respond, because she was completely overwhelmed by the news.

"Thank you. How did you find out?" she asked.

"I've got my sources. The official announcement will come at 10:00 am. I mean to be there and follow up. Shall we meet at police headquarters and take it from there?"

Hansen readily agreed. Before she ended the conversation, she wanted to share some good news with Ulrike: "Have you already looked at the newspapers?"

"Nope, I was too busy with my story. Anything important?"

"You may have lost a battle at your paper," Hansen exclaimed, "but you seem to be winning the war. Both the FAZ and the SZ published articles on the infiltration of smaller start-up companies by criminal organizations. This will help Stefano's defense."

"I certainly hope so, that's great news," Ulrike replied. "Also, the podcast is beginning to be noticed. Believe me, we will push the mayor and his allies to acknowledge a serious problem. It's just a matter of time."

"What about your own paper?" Hansen asked casually.

"You can forget it," Ulrike declared, raising her voice. "I'm not sure I want to stay there much longer. Lately, it has become rather disagreeable. I have received feelers from other papers, but nothing firm so far. So, I stay put and do my work."

"Have you ever considered leaving Berlin?" Hansen wanted to know.

Actually, this was the first time that this question came up, and Ulrike was completely lost for an answer. Berlin had been the only place where she could see herself, after she had left the small town in Brandenburg where she had been born and raised. She looked at the elegantly dressed young lawyer, trying to figure out what her question meant. But there was no clear answer in Hansen's facial expression. Still, it was apparent that Birgit Hansen could easily see herself outside of Berlin. There was an ever so light expression that she considered herself only a guest in this town.

"Can you recommend a good private clinic where Stefano can get the rest and treatment he urgently needs," Hansen asked.

Ulrike mentioned a couple of places, trying to describe their special character and location. But in the end, Hansen decided to leave the decision open until she had spoken to Stefano Brindisi, who was a Berliner and might have his own preferences. But with Ulrike's help she managed to arrange a meeting with Rudolf Wendt for the same afternoon. Once she explained the nature of the case, she could feel that the lawyer was interested. This was the kind of case that had made him famous in Berlin. By the time she had completed the arrangement, it was time to get to police headquarters where the conditions of Brindisi's release would be decided.

Charlotte was already in an early meeting with her special team when the official communication of Stefano Brindisi's impending release reached her. The interrogation would be indefinitely suspended until his recovery. He would be transferred to a hospital or clinic for medical care with the order not to leave town. An ankle bracelet would be attached to monitor his movements. The transfer, set for 10:00 was to happen in the presence of his lawyer and the police officer in charge of the ongoing investigation. Charlotte's first reaction was irritation, but then she realized the advantage of this outcome. It would give her more time to examine the financial records of KreuzbergChem, which would be crucial for the assessment of the case. If they could prove substantial or even significant money laundering in the early days of the company, Brindisi's narrative had to be taken seriously. At this point, the early records looked chaotic and suspicious, but there was no definite proof of dirty money. The specialist on her team had just reminded her that they would have to examine the bank accounts of the Brindisi family to determine the origin of the start-up's initial capital. He had asked for a week to do a thorough job. Also, he reminded her of questioning other family members, especially the parents, about the background of the family friends, who had supposedly generously contributed. Most likely, the second prisoner, Bruno Esposito, would have little to contribute, since he was too low in the gang's hierarchy. The latest move of his lawyer had clearly shown that he was considered as expendable. He would take the fall for Stollberg's death, go to prison for manslaughter and be modestly rewarded after his release. The family would take care of him for keeping his mouth shut. Could he be persuaded to break his silence and what would he know? These were unanswered questions at the end of the meeting, which had to be adjourned early so that Charlotte could be present at the release.

Birgit Hansen and Ulrike arrived early at police headquarters and were shown to the room where the release would take place. It was a dark and somewhat neglected office with old desks and chairs. Ulrike noticed how uncomfortable Birgit Hansen was in this environment. She is used to the elegance of corporate offices rather than this shabby dusty space, Ulrike thought. She observed Hansen taking out a facial tissue and cleaning the chair before she sat down. A few minutes later Charlotte and Werner Kraft entered the room, moving to a table where they spread the documents needed for the release. Charlotte briefly acknowledged the presence of the lawyer and Ulrike with a

<good morning> and a nod. There was no conversation until Brindisi was brought in by two guards. Charlotte told the guards to take the cuffs off and then invited the prisoner to take a seat. His face showed no expression. The formal release took no more than ten minutes. Charlotte read the conditions and reminded Brindisi of the severe consequences of breaking the rules. Finally, he and Birgit Hansen as his lawyer had to sign the form. The guards retreated and Charlotte, followed by her assistant, left the room as well. It was only then that Brindisi seemed to come alive. He got up and turned around where his eyes met those of Birgit Hansen. She was in tears. They were embracing until Ulrike reminded them to get out of this unpleasant room as soon as possible. Then she quickly took a picture.

"This might come in handy at a later stage of the procedure," she exclaimed. At the same time, she realized that her presence at the meeting had not improved her relationship with Charlotte. She had taken sides in this case by first interviewing the accused and later publishing the podcast. She had noticed that Charlotte had avoided eye contact during the meeting. I will have to mend fences, Ulrike thought, while she was closing the door after Brindisis and Hansen had left. All of a sudden, she felt very tired. She couldn't see a clear path for herself. The situation at her newspaper was getting increasingly difficult and unpleasant. She remembered the enthusiasm with which she had started two years ago. Now, there was nothing left. She was uncertain whether she could go on.

After getting several messages, Bill finally agreed to a meeting with Kraft after that morning. The official reason was a conversation about the status of the Stollberg case, but of course, both of them knew that the real reason was the unresolved tension. They had to get over the awkward encounter at the pub in Fuhlsbüttel. Each of them had reasons to be uncomfortable: Kraft for tracking a friend, Bill for not sharing important information. When they actually met at a coffee shop near police headquarters, they chose to avoid the difficult subject. Instead, they discussed the importance of the file. Bill reminded Kraft of his mission for Alerta. He was supposed to find a valuable file. There had been three deaths, but nobody had actually seen the file. Neither the police of Bad Homburg nor the LKA Hesse.

"We have gone over Stollberg's things more than once," Kraft declared. "There is no file."

"Let's do it again," Bill suggested.

Kraft shook his head but agreed to search once more. Together, they went to the special room where material evidence was kept. As Kraft had predicted, the search did not reveal the missing file. There were papers in the briefcase, but they clearly did not contain the information they were looking for. Bill was disappointed, although he should have known better.

"What about the bike?" he asked.

Where could you hide a small object like a flash drive on a bike? The saddle was the obvious place, Bill figured. He and Kraft carefully scrutinized the bike. They even took the saddle off the frame. But there was nothing. Either the file was really a phantom or Stollberg must have hidden it some other place. Where could that be?

"Maybe our mistake has been to assume that he had the file with him that morning," Kraft suggested, looking at Bill.

"But he needed access to it at the meeting planned with Kellner," Bill replied. "No money without the file."

"What if the file was deposited in a bank safe?" Kraft said.

"Yes, I have thought of that as well," Bill exclaimed. "But in that case, there would have been a key in a pocket or attached to a part of the bike. There is a further drawback. Kellner would have been forced to access a safe at a bank, creating attention. Not a good thing in a deal like this."

"Good point, Kraft acknowledged.

They had reached a dead end and Bill took his leave. It was on his way back to Ulrike's apartment when all of a sudden, he had an idea. Maybe the file was already at the hotel before Stollberg left his office. Maybe, all he wanted was to receive the cash from the middle man. If that was the case, he must have entrusted the file with somebody at the hotel or hidden it somewhere inside the building, but easy to reach during the final negotiations. Bill decided to go back to Brandenburger

Hof. It took him no more than twenty minutes to reach the hotel. The reception area was empty. He had to ring the bell at the desk to get the attention of a clerk.

"Oh, Mr. McDonald," the young man cried, "Glad to see you again. Are you planning to come back?"

"No, But I have a question for you," Bill replied. "Do you recall the day before the accident in which Herr Stollberg was killed.?"

"Of course, I do, I'll never forget it, although I didn't see it with my own eyes. What about it."

"Do you remember Stollberg? Did you ever meet him?"

"Yes, I do, I saw him the day before when he was here to make the reservation for his friend. I don't recall the man's name."

"Kellner?"

"Yes, that' right, Walter Kellner, for one night."

"Was there anything out of the ordinary when he made the reservation?"

"No, not that I can recall anything extraordinary"

"He just came, made the reservation, and left?"

"No, wait, at the end he asked where he could find the restroom."

"And you told him?"

"Of course, he used the restroom and left."

"Thanks, that may be helpful."

Bill walked over to the corner where he found the door to the men's room. Once on the inside, he locked the door and looked around. Where can you hide a small object for a day without the danger of someone accidentally finding it? There were two places, either the washstand or the water-tank of the toilette. He checked the washstand first, going down to his knees, inspecting the underside. There was nothing. Then he stepped on the seat of the toilet and looked into the water-tank. He was about to give up when he doublechecked the wooden rim with his hand. Yes, there was a small object. It was taped to the inside. Carefully, he loosened the tape and recovered the object. It was a small metal box. His heart was beating faster. Slowly, Bill opened the box. There it was: a flash drive. He put it back into the box and put the box into the pocket of his leather jacket. He stepped down and looked into the mirror. He saw his own pale face, breathing heavily. He needed time to grasp what had happened. He had found the file! It had been there all the time. Of course, the content had to be checked. Did the drive really contain the information Stollberg meant to sell? Only Brindisi or perhaps Klein could verify that. I have to look calm, Bill thought. He washed his hands, left the restroom, and headed for the door. He heard the voice of the clerk wishing him a good day and his own voice returning the wishes. Outside, he hailed a cab and directed the driver to take him to Ulrike's apartment.

When Bill tried to open the apartment door with his key, he noticed that it was not locked. Still, the place seemed to be empty. He walked into the kitchen where he still found the plates and cups of their common breakfast on the kitchen table, but not Ulrike. He returned to the hallway, calling out her name. But there was no answer. Slightly frustrated, he stepped into the living room, which turned out to be empty as well. Finally, he walked over to the bedroom. When he opened the door, he saw Ulrike in front of her small computer desk, completely immersed in a writing project.

"Hey, what's going on?" Bill asked in a low voice, approaching her from behind. "Aren't you needed at the office?"

It took Ulrike a moment to realize his presence. She turned around, still hesitant in her focus on Bill.

"Oh, it's you Bill, I'm composing a letter to the editor-in-chief," she replied. "I can't simply go on as if nothing had happened. He has to make up his mind."

Bill stepped closer and looked at the text on the screen. What he read, he found disquieting.

"You should not send this mail," He declared, but keeping his voice low. "If you send it, it will be the end of your career at the *Morgenspiegel*. He will have no choice."

"I was publicly humiliated and he did nothing," Ulrike exclaimed. "This whole appointment has been a mistake. I was better off as a free-lancer where I was my own boss. Bill, I'm not good in a hierarchy."

"Still, this is the wrong moment. You are still upset and angry.

Give it more time," Bill replied. "There is news that may well change your mood."

Now Ulrike turned around, facing him. There was an inexplicable grin on his face. Why is he smiling when he had been sacked the day before? she thought.

"Remember the missing file?" he asked softly.

"Of course, what about it?"

"I think, I found it."

"Really? Where?"

"At the hotel, in the restroom."

There was a moment of silence. Ulrike's facial expression signaled disbelief. Bill took the small metal box out of his pocket, putting it on the small desk. Ulrike stared at the object, without moving.

"So, it really exists,"

"Yea, it's a flash drive. I'll get my laptop to check it out."

Bill walked back to the living room to fetch his computer. When he attached the flash drive to his laptop, he recognized a document on his screen. There was Stollberg's name and a file number, but the text made no sense. It was encrypted.

"We need the code," Ulrike whispered. "Do you have the code?"

"No, we will need help. But let's copy the document first and take it from there."

"What are you planning to do with the file?" Ulrike asked, looking at Bill. "You are no longer employed by your law firm."

"Right, I was a free agent when I discovered the file. I'll discuss this with Klein and Brindisi when we meet them."

"That will be tomorrow morning," Ulrike exclaimed. "I promised Birgit Hansen to visit them at the clinic."

"Good. I'll be there. In the meantime, please stop the message to your editor-in-chief, OK? You don't want to ruin your career."

It was late afternoon when Birgit Hansen returned to the Grunewald Clinic where she had left Brindisi in the care of the medical staff, after arranging a medical examination and a light lunch. The doctor had confirmed that he needed rest more than anything. To her surprise, she found a guard outside Stefano's room. There was concern, she was told, that his life could be threatened. The police were worried that the gang that had hunted him would renew their efforts when they learned of his release. For the first time, Hansen felt grateful to the woman in charge of the case. There was possibly an element of empathy with Brindisi, even though he was still a suspect. Having received a sedative, Brindisi was asleep when she entered his room. She sat down next to his bed, gazing at his pale face. There was still so much to do, but she had reason to be satisfied with the developments of the last two days. The transition from the horror of the arrest and the subsequent imprisonment to the peaceful environment of the clinic had been much better than she had expected last night. Now, there was hope. If there would be a trial, there was a good chance that Stefano's innocence would be established. She counted on Ulrike's undiminished support to enlighten the public about Stefano's terrible dilemma. Without her help, she might not have been successful in persuading Rudolf Wendt to take Stefano's case because of prior commitments. It was Ulrike who had explained the broader social ramifications of the case to the lawyer. Hansen had been impressed by the force of her engagement, although she faced problems at her newspaper. Still, Hansen could not overlook Ulrike's interest in this: She wanted to get a story out of this. There is no denying: We are using each other. It's a temporary alliance. Ulrike had promised to be back tomorrow morning together with her American friend. His role was not yet quite clear to Hansen. She understood that he was sent to look for Stollberg's file, but why an American law firm would take an interest, remained unclear. On a note that the nurse had given her she saw two names and telephone numbers. David Klein had called to find out how Stefano was doing. And there had been a call from the Brindisi family, requesting to see their son. For this I'm not prepared, Hansen thought. I want to talk to Stefano first, before I meet them tomorrow. All of a sudden, she realized for the first time how deeply she had become involved in Stefano Brindisi's life. What had been a budding romantic relationship two weeks ago, had turned into an existential bond where his life depended on her decisions and actions. Did she realize this when he called her from Düsseldorf, seeking help? Of course, she was a lawyer and had known the possible implications, but she had not anticipated the fundamental change of their relationship. His life was in her hands. And I have accepted this development, I'm glad of it, she thought. Now, that she had a moment of rest, Birgit Hansen noticed how fatigued she was. The continued stress had exhausted her. She needed rest as well. She checked her watch. It was 5:00pm. She was about to get up to find a more comfortable place when Stefano Brindisi opened his eyes. With his left hand he reached out for her. She took his hand, pressing it firmly.

"How are you feeling? "she asked softly.

"Actually, much better. It's not over, but we have been given time to recover and prepare for the trial."

"Let's not think of the trial now, Stefano," she exclaimed. "I'm just grateful to see you at a secure and comfortable place. Tomorrow we can begin planning."

The following morning, the doctor decided that Stefano Brindisi needed at least another day of complete rest. He was allowed to see friends, but the visits were expected to be brief and not upsetting. Birgit Hansen realized that this would be difficult, since both David Klein's visit and the reunion with his parents in the afternoon might well become stressful and overwhelming. It was obvious that Brindisi was happy to see David Klein, who arrived at 10:00. Klein had to control himself not to show his shock about his partner's looks. He looked frail and worn-out, as much as he tried to focus the conversation on the present situation of their company. Klein realized that he would overburden his partner by sharing the actual problems with him. He just urged him to get as much rest as possible to recover. Once he would be back, they would figure out how to overcome the present crisis. The police investigation and the upcoming trial was never mentioned in their conversation. This came up only later when Klein, after taking his leave from his partner, talked to Birgit Hansen on his way back to his car.

"Will there be a trial?" he asked.

"Quite possibly there will be a trial. I will do my best to prevent it though. There is only circumstantial evidence of Stefano's involvement. I have hired a good defense lawyer, who will argue in favor of a dismissal."

"Let me know when I can help. The idea that Stefano ordered Herwig's killing is preposterous. I'm ready to testify."

"Thank you, Herr Klein," she replied. "That's good to know. How about the company?"

"Not too good," Klein replied in a low voice. "In fact, the situation is desperate. We are running out of cash very soon. I need Stefano back to oversee ongoing research projects."

"What about the missing file?" Hansen inquired.

"To get it back will be critical," Klein exclaimed. "What do you know about this?"

"Only what Stefano told me," Hansen replied. "It has not been recovered. But it seems that it never reached the middle man at the Brandenburger Hof."

"So, the deal was not closed? The information is still ours?"

"It looks that way," Hansen said. "How much is it worth on the market?"

"We would have to study the details," Klein replied. "At least 20, possibly 50 million, enough to save the company."

"That would be a welcome change of your and Stefano's situation," Hansen responded.

Klein took his leave with the promise to be back tomorrow. Birgit Hansen was about to return to the building, when she recognized Ulrike and Bill stepping out of a small Fiat. She walked towards them, greeting them with a smile.

"You just missed David Klein, Stefano's partner," Hansen exclaimed.

"Too bad," Ulrike cried, "because there is interesting news."

"What is it?" Hansen wanted to know.

"Actually, it's Bill's news," Ulrike replied.

"The missing file is no longer missing," Bill said slowly in German.

Birgit Hansen just stared at him until he repeated the information.

"My God, I just talked with Klein about the file, which he considers critical for the survival of the company. Let's go inside and share the news with Stefano. This will be an enormous relief for him."

Indeed, Brindisi's face expressed excitement when he learned that the missing file had been recovered. He insisted on finding out the details of the recovery, getting quite agitated. Soon, Birgit Hansen had to remind him to calm down. The sudden change of the fundamental situation with all its financial and legal implications took time to process.

"What is the legal situation?" Ulrike wanted to know. "Who owns the information?"

"Good question," Hansen replied. "I will have to look into this. Most likely, the information is the property of KreuzbergChem, since the deal was not closed. No money was paid to Stollberg. In addition, he had no right to sell the research results behind the back of his partners. The deal would have been illegal. And finally, there is the question of the finder's fee, which is a percentage of the commercial value."

There was a moment of silence in the room. Then, it was Ulrike who first responded.

"Are we talking about serious money here? Bill just lost his job and could use a bit of cash."

"Definitely," Hansen declared. "Once the property has been returned to KreuzbergChem and has been sold on the market, there will be a very significant finder's fee. You wouldn't need a job for a long time."

"Great," Ulrike cried. "Bill did you hear this? Your worries are over."

"Not so fast," Hansen interjected. "If the police considers the file evidence in the murder case, the whole process can be on ice for a while."

"You are the lawyer, Birgit," Ulrike exclaimed. You have to find the argument why this should not happen. It might destroy the company."

"Only a court can decide that," Hansen declared.

Brindisi was pacing up and down in the room, talking to himself without any regard for the presence of his visitors. Birgit Hansen signaled to Bill and Ulrike that it was time to leave.

"I'll be in touch," she said before she turned her attention to Brindisi and led him back to his armchair. Bill and Ulrike left in silence.

A day had passed. Charlotte had been out for a walk. She needed fresh air after a rough day in the office. When she was opening her apartment door, her phone was ringing. At this time of the day, she didn't expect a call and let it ring until she heard a familiar voice. It was Bernd Moeller, leaving a message. She rushed to the living room and picked up the phone, just a second before he finished his message.

"Bernd, sorry, I didn't expect your call. I'm just back from a walk. Had to clear my head after a day with plenty of stress.," she said.

"Good to hear your voice," he replied, "the reason for my call is mostly to let you know that I'm home."

"That's a huge surprise, Bernd, I expected you only next week. What happened?"

"I decided to cut my stay short," Moeller said in a low voice, "the common ground with my son-in-law was very limited. The only common interest we had was soccer. Otherwise, I didn't want to talk to him, and he wanted to talk to me even less. Things were becoming tense, and my daughter was stressed out by mediating. So, I decided to book an earlier flight."

"That's great news, I mean that you are home, not the trouble with your son-in-law. But I'm grateful to him for bringing you home early."

"How are things in Berlin?"

"Confusing, the Stollberg case ought to be clear and well defined after the arrest of the two suspects. But it's not, far from it. Brindisi has been released and interrogations have been suspended. The mayor's office tries very hard to keep the case out of the news because of the Mafia connection. It's not even clear if there will be a trial for Brindisi.

"Why not?"

"He has found a clever lawyer who is good at influencing the media."

"Charlotte, relax, you have done your part."

"You know that I don't relax until a case is really solved."

"I know that, but it doesn't help you," Bernd Moeller said softly. "Life is messy and crime is no exception. You need a bit of distance. How about visiting me?! I really want to see you."

There was a moment of silence.

"OK, I'll check my calendar and see what I can do."

"I'm counting on your visit, Lotte," Moeller exclaimed before he hang up.

Charlotte sat down in her armchair, closing her eyes. This call had come at the right moment. It changed her mood. She would visit Bernd in Hamburg and step out of her role for a few days. The case could wait. Eventually, it would be resolved, one way or the other.

Another day had passed. Bill and Ulrike had celebrated the recovery of the missing file with a dinner at a small Italian restaurant in the neighborhood. Bill had even ordered a bottle of extra dry champagne. But both were restless. Ulrike avoided the office as much as she could without an open confrontation with her boss, who pretended not to see Ulrike when she worked in her office. Eventually, Ulrike would have to talk to the editor-in-chief, but she was uncertain how her complaints would be received. He made no effort to get in touch with her or to explain himself. When Ulrike looked at Bill, she noticed how much he was preoccupied with his own decisions. There was the pressure coming from his family to go back to law school and the wish of his mother to see her son back home. What would be the alternative? Could he stay in Berlin? That would be great, she thought. But as a foreigner he can't work here. And she knew that Bill would not just want to hang around, even if he had the money to do so. Maybe he could build up his own security company in Berlin? But she realized that right now this was not a realistic plan. What they needed today was time out. Getting away from the pressure. Fresh air, different people, not Berlin. Then it hit her. Scotland, the place where his family came from and her favorite country. She immediately went on line. There were so many opportunities. Places she remembered fondly and wanted to show him. She was getting excited.

"Bill, can you join me for a moment?"

"What's up? I'm in the middle of an online exchange," he called.

"Drop it and come here."

A minute late Bill stood next to her, looking at pictures of Edinburgh Castle on the screen of her laptop.

"Let's go there," she cried.

"Where?"

"Edinburgh"

"When?"

"Now, let's get out of Berlin."

He looked at her excited smiling face, which he could not resist. He leaned down and kissed her.

"OK, we deserve a break. Let's go to Scotland."

Within minutes Ulrike had booked a flight and a hotel for the next day. The next day, early in the morning Bill and Ulrike were checking in their luggage at Berlin's Tegel Airport and moving to the gate of Lufthansa flight 463 to Edinburgh. Ulrike was too restless to sit down in the lounge. She paced up and down, while Bill was checking his email.

"Don't check your messages now, Bill," Ulrike exclaimed. "We want to get away from all that stuff."

"It's OK, Ulrike, calm down," he replied in a low voice. "I'm ready. Come, sit next to me and tell me about Scotland."

Ulrike took the seat next to him and leaned against his shoulder with her eyes closed. This is my first really happy moment in days, she thought. She would talk to him later.

Minutes later their flight was called. They got up and slowly walked to the exit holding hands.

The End

Printed in the United States
By Bookmasters